THE BLACK CARNIVAL

THE BLACK CARNIVAL

HARLEQUIN GRIM

The Black Carnival
by Harlequin Grim
Published by Quill & Crow Publishing House

This book is a work of fiction. All incidents, dialogue, and characters, except for some well-known historical and public figures, are either products of the author's imagination or used in a fictitious manner. Any resemblance to actual persons, living or dead, or actual events is purely coincidental.

Copyright © 2025 by Harlequin Grim

All rights reserved. Published in the United States by Quill & Crow Publishing House, Ohio. No portion of this book may be reproduced in any form without permission from the publisher, except as permitted by U.S. copyright law.

Printed in the United States of America

Cover/Interior Design © 2025 by Astrid Tobrand

Cover Formatting by Fay Lane

Interior Typesetting by Cassandra Thompson

Edited by Lisa Morris, Mathew L Reyes

ISBN: 978-1-958228-88-3

ISBN: 978-1-958228-87-6 (ebook)

Publisher's Website: www.quillandcrowpublishinghouse.com

For Astrid and my brothers

PUBLISHER'S NOTE

Although a fiction story with fantastical elements, *The Black Carnival* draws upon history, including dialect and slang, to help create an immersive reading experience. For your convenience, please find a glossary of terms located at the back of the book (Index A).

Please also note that this book contains depictions of graphic violence toward women and children. Please consult Index B located at the back of the book for a list of potential triggers.

PROLOGUE
JUNE 1, 1886

The streets of Whitechapel smoldered with the discontent of humanity searching for its soul, lost in the dogged smoke and fog-fouled air. Under the glow of gas lamps, dreams themselves were trampled to the rhythm of rolling carriages, horse trots, and the hurried steps of indifferent citizens melting into one another's shadows.

Few people knew this cold indifference as well as the young girl with a crutch, a fake limp, and a bandage over a perfectly healthy eye. The way her pleas plucked heartstrings put a violinist's concerto to shame. Her limp looked as convincing as any amputee's.

Today, she worked the crowds with more fervor and even less shame.

Just that afternoon, a troupe of performers had passed through her street to advertise their circus. Their striped garments smelled of campfires, rosin, and the winds of faraway cities she'd never seen. Something in their eyes had asked her if she knew how to cull starlight, if she'd ever wanted to taste flight from a trapeze, to feel her veins rush with the expectation of a thousand audience members.

A part of her even dared to believe she could.

It was not the first time she'd been cast under this spell. Each year, the foreboding tents crept up beyond the city limits, and every year, her curiosity had grown. Without fail, the streets became abuzz with rumors of gangsters, undercity dealings, and occult activity. This would be the week, she told herself, that she'd muster the courage to go.

This time, there was a different air about one of the performers in particular. It wasn't just his darkly striped garments, his smudged, black greasepaint, or the subtle grin when he caught her staring. The coin he flicked into her hand was warm with knowing. He saw through her act but tipped her anyway—this she felt was certain. Just as she felt that his fate, too, had once been jerked around over a handful of farthings.

After the performers left, she examined the heralds they'd plastered over a nearby wall. The words explaining the acts were illegible to her. But the illustrations said it all. She stared at hand-balancers on a stack of chairs, unicyclists teetering on wires, and jugglers laughing beneath a cascade of five blades.

There was, of course, one symbol she understood. The admission price.

It would take two nights of begging to afford a ticket, she reckoned.

A passerby paused to scoff at one of the fliers, tearing it off the wall before tossing it into the street.

The young girl stooped to pick it up. All she deciphered was an illustration of a tent housed by a talking board's planchette, its edges rimmed with smoke and skulls.

Dusk was burning its last. But it wasn't the growing chill that caused a shudder to roll through her.

She tossed the handbill into a nearby brazier. Fiery tendrils lapped the paper's edges, liberating the wrinkles in its tattered body. The words caught, turning to ash as they swirled into the air:

THE BLACK CARNIVAL — IVORY'S SPIRIT ASYLUM — SPEAK TO THE DEAD

I

LESTER
APRIL 20, 1886

Lester Black's cloak undulated as the circus grew around her, a black heart pulsing at the center of it all. Winter ebbed from England's shores, but twilight still brought with it bitter winds.

Though her body might've been tired after decades of show business, her soul burned like the lanterns around her. Her heart drummed with the rhythm of the Romani music that threaded through the carnival air—a feverish tune of neglected duties and the cursing of death. Even more than the performers practicing all about the grounds, the workmen enjoyed it, hammering, hoisting, and hollering away to it.

The tents rose by the dozens, stretching up in skeletal frames of various sizes. Some slender and tall, others wide, their canvas flesh wrapped in stripes or triangular markings. These misfit cathedrals were not like their competitors. They were decorated in dark, earthy tones—grays, blacks, tea-stained cream, deep violet, and burgundy. The ominous combination of black and crimson was loudest amongst the combinations. Wrought iron gates and lampposts dug into the earth, as though the circus itself was sinking its teeth into Cardiff's outskirts.

It never failed to amaze her how quickly the small town would appear. This was a place where fantasies went to perish. Not to rot, but to be resurrected into reality.

Construction had taken nearly a week. All the while, heralds and handbills plastered every street and alley of Cardiff. They promised the spectacular—sparing no indulgence—with genuine displays of witchcraft, and even a menagerie home to infernal creatures, tamed by individuals not far better. One of Lester's favorite rumors claimed the circus was haunted, pursued by persistent phantoms, sprouting up wherever their caravans settled.

Much like the rumors, all about the grounds clung a faint but putrid aroma. Yet, between roasted honeyed nuts, kettle corn, eel pies, and sheep's trotters, it was impossible to trace. The fresh grass the circus claimed quickly became trampled, worn, and cut by the hundreds of boots hurrying about. Natural pathways between the tents revealed themselves, the veins of something greater than its parts, doing little to simplify the seemingly infinite array of spectacles.

Before the guests arrived, rehearsing and training performers littered the grounds with the sounds of soft grunts. Balance artists teetered on highwires, unicycles, and rola bolas. Juggling props bobbed and spun blithely in the air—balls, clubs, rings, knives, and torches. On the ground, contortionists tied their bodies in knots beside the acrobats taking flight from springing heels and hands. Their respective expertise in select disciplines formed natural cliques, revealing quirks in their personalities. Where the jugglers seemed more prone to introversion, their aerialist peers were oftentimes more charismatic and loud.

Their gazes contained bursts of euphoria, steeled concentration, and a curious, silver gleam. Halos of light shone softly from strung lights and lanterns whose flames seemed not to burn at all but rather breathe, a gleaming web between every tent. It was prettiest when it rained, Lester thought.

Unlike other circuses, the impossibilities on display from the artists were juxtaposed by the earthy tones of their costumes. Particularly bright colors were difficult to find, while whites, blacks, and grays dominated between crimson or burgundy accents. But even the deepest of blacks seemed to catch a glimmer, if only from those lanterns blessing them all.

It felt as though the days of construction had raced by in a minute's time. The jump. That's what they called it.

Twilight and dawn had chased each other across the horizon and now careened to a halt. Save for the now plodding melody of its musicians, the circus was eerily quiet, holding its breath. Soon, the guests would arrive.

The tinkling of a jester's cap drawing nearer interrupted Lester's musing.

Wearing it was a short clown dressed in a patched waistcoat and a collared shirt tucked into gray and black striped trousers. His lean, watchful face was decorated with sharp, black points running beneath his downturned, hazel eyes, betraying a youthfulness robbed of its naivety. His chestnut-copper hair stuck out every which way in wavy locks.

When she didn't acknowledge him, he tapped her shoulder with a wooden juggling club. A bell on his cap chimed again.

"Are we ready?" she asked. Her silver-streaked, black hair swayed in the salty wind.

The clown nodded.

She waved him away, and he set off toward the entrance gates. A line of locals had formed, stretching nearly to the city. Some peered over the shoulders of others, the carnival lights aglow in their eyes.

"So we begin," Lester murmured softly, "as we have begun a hundred times before—from darkness to bring the people stars."

2

ATHERTON

APRIL 21, 1886

He knew he was getting closer because of the stench. Excrement, sodden flesh, blood, bile, and even a heavy pinch of despair all commingled to create that smell which isn't ever one single smell: human rot. Some might balk at the idea that despair had a scent, but for Atherton Graves, it was as recognizable as sea spray or fresh bread.

Atherton had been torn from the womb only to be cradled in a house of death. Conceived, birthed, and reared in his father's mortuary, death wasn't so much an old friend but a family member, a business partner, and he its humble servant.

New Sarum's backwoods were steeped in evening gloom. The warmth of spring was forgotten in the night, now crisp and chill. Twilight peeked through thousands of boughs as the wood's peaceful sounds rippled through the air. The rhythmic creaking of a rusted lantern was Atherton's only company.

Armed with a shovel and an iron stomach, he broke off the trail. Smoke billowed out from his sixth cigarette that evening, and given the rank stench currently guiding him, he reckoned he might have six more.

The lantern found them before his eyes did.

With a sheen of moisture, they all but glowed in the gaslight. A pair of feet—bare, gnarled toes caked with dirt—swayed at eye level. The closer he got, the louder the groaning sounded from the branch supporting the hanged man.

"Clark's boy found him. A ghoul. Some vagrant, by all rights," his father had told him over lunch. "Just get him in the earth before tomorrow. Remind the city what we're good for."

Atherton took a few drags before setting down his lantern and taking off his cap. "You know, I was having a perfectly pleasant afternoon before you showed up," he said, jabbing his finger into the corpse's foot. "Not that you asked, mind you. Who runs off and hangs himself in the middle of nowhere? You've got some nerve."

The stranger's distended, black tongue didn't retort, which was a blessing, as the undertaker's conversations with the dead were growing more discourteous by the body.

Climbing the tree to cut down the noose failed to rekindle any warm childhood memories. Instead of running about the school yard, Atherton had played hide-and-seek with his younger sister, where an empty embalming table or coffin was a preferred hiding spot. Strange echoes whispered in his ears when no crushes dared. Instead of playmates, he had bodies needing his care.

There were always bodies.

Atherton murmured an apology before cutting him down. Crouching over the decedent, he peered at the deathly visage. The ghoul looked only a few years older than he. Lifting up the ghoul's shirt and coat, he found the edges of his ribs protruding from gray flesh.

"Hungry, eh?"

He laid the ghoul upright against a tree trunk, his limp neck and bloodshot eyes making him appear rather disappointed as his final resting place was dug in front of him. Not that anyone would be overjoyed to witness it.

As Atherton worked, he spun stories about his new friend, and the task went by quicker for it. Having finished digging, Atherton leapt out of the shallow pit and rewarded himself with another cigarette. Perhaps it was loneliness, or a touch of madness from socializing too often with the dead, or an act of peacekeeping for what he was about to do—either way, Atherton popped one of his Woodbine cigarettes between the ghoul's blackened, cracked lips.

"You really must forgive me," he said. "Old habits and all that. But do try and understand—not a coin's being passed around for the likes of you. And that grave was a bugger to dig."

It was nothing personal, going through cold pockets. And the prospects for these particular trousers were slim. At best, a nice matchbook. A sixpence, if luck was on his side. With his fingers creeping through the body's clothes like spiders, an uncanny feeling bubbled up in his stomach.

Death always turned people into objects—strangers and mangled bodies, especially so. But no matter how grotesque or unfamiliar the corpse, the longer Atherton spent with them, the more that waxy barrier melted away—the more he felt watched. Heard.

He learned the hard way about catching feelings. A simple job could turn cumbersome. And once that sympathy found a place to burrow, it sank in its fangs. Each pocket was an exchange of secrets—every article and pilfered object a confession. A broken timepiece. A worn photograph. A sheaf of pages from a Bible.

He created a neat pile of the ghoul's belongings by the lantern. With nothing else left to do, Atherton took hold of the ghoul's noose and looked over the body for a final moment. He never did like that term —*ghoul*. They were no more inhuman than some poor soul with consumption.

"A damned shame you've found yourself here," he said. "At the crossroads of nowhere, only to fall headlong into Hell."

The undertaker slipped his fingers between the rope and the damp flesh of the man's neck, loosening the noose until he could remove it. When he lifted the body by its lapels, he felt something else.

He let the corpse slump back, searching with renewed interest. Something small was tucked away in a clever inner pocket. He lifted his lantern and brought it close to what now lay in his palm, smeared with cold blood —two pieces of paper. Small. Identical in shape and size, rectangular with ribbed, sturdy edges.

The two tickets were black with white lettering and scarlet accents. Before he could make out the faded print, his lantern hissed and guttered, leaving them enveloped in the forest's thick gloom. Pocketing the tickets, Atherton felt about until his hands found the corpse once more. Having dragged it into the shallow grave, he took up his shovel and began burying a nameless past.

It was no trouble working in the dark. After all, he had done this more times than he cared to count.

❧ 3 ❦

BOO

APRIL 23, 1886

A clown dressed in monochrome stripes and laced, leather leggings accepted tickets from a pair of guests, his hands flourishing as they erupted in a flash of fire. His exuberance was made eerie by his still expression and large, curious eyes decorated with red and black greasepaint. Some got the impression that Boo was a puppet, a golem of some kind, stuffed with cotton and whatever mischievous magic winds the heart of a mime.

The women looked between his hands and the ashy remnants that floated away in winking embers. With a deep bow, he ushered the two ladies through the entrance gates and, arm in arm, they ventured into the circus, discussing whether the trick was sleight of hand or some concealed contraption.

Having consulted a clock plucked from his waistcoat, the clown eased the wide, double gates shut before opening the far smaller exit.

It was the Black Carnival's final evening in Cardiff. Behind the clouds and their wraithlike glow, a sea of stars pulsed. Beneath that glittering silence was the booming heart of the circus—the fluttering lights and garrulous crowds, the roar of ringmasters over trance-like accordion melodies bleeding through bursts of muffled applause—a seemingly unmanageable cacophony humming along in orchestrated chaos. In the distance were the gloomy outlines of Cardiff's docks and the bobbing silhouettes of ships, their masts bony protrusions nestled in foggy, sable waters.

The clown had precisely thirteen minutes before he was needed elsewhere. With a swift turn of his heels, he disappeared among nearly a thousand guests exploring the grounds.

He strode by sideshow entertainers working pitches, past steaming food stands, beneath the draconic exhalations of fire breathers, and between the legs of stilt walkers. Shadows cast by acrobats, contortionists, and jugglers danced over the throngs, who moved with uncanny precision as they balanced upon high wires strung between tents. He was another painted face among hundreds.

Walking through the circus was not unlike wandering into a cornfield except for every stalk there was a performer, and for every dead end, another exhibit bound to tempt a coin or two—another show to turn hours into minutes. But the clown understood this dizzying maze better than he knew himself.

To slip through the backstage of the aerialists' tent for a quicker path or cartwheel atop a tightrope to avoid the crowds required no more conscious thought than his own heartbeat. Though the circus may have traveled the world, seldom did he leave its grounds—thus the entire world might as well have been the circus, and the circus his world.

The clown's striped top was accented by a charcoal, ruffled collar. The patterns stopped at his plain, once jet-black waistcoat. Then there was that hideous, oversized patchwork mess of a fool's cap he couldn't be caught without, bouncing with three diamond-shaped bells. Leather belts, harnesses, and straps decorated his body, each for a different prop. Clubs hung from his thighs, juggling balls nestled in a pouch at his hip, and knives crossed at his back, with six red rings hanging beneath. These spoke nothing of his proficiency in aerial acrobatics. He was not merely another performer—he was a walking array of acts.

For all his talents, he lacked a name. A proper one, at least. When Lester had plucked him from Bethlehem Asylum and brought him to the circus over a decade ago, the others quickly noted the permanent unease on his face, as though he'd just been startled.

So "Boo" it was.

Boo moved to the northernmost edge of the circus, just beyond its gates, where the delighted shrieks were drowned by the chatter of wetland toads. There were no guests here, no performers, no signs nor arrows to guide a full purse down a path of liberation. Still, he glanced about to be sure he hadn't been followed.

A single, solitary tent fluttering with gaslight stood tucked away in an otherwise unlit corner. It emanated a steady clinking—precise, steel tools being carefully used—and the mutterings of a crew working within. Shrouding the place was an unmistakable odor of moldy meat and soured milk, worsened rather than masked by harsh chemicals.

Boo made his way toward a burning brazier behind the tent. The shadow of a towering, brawny man with pallid skin was cast on the trampled grass. He peered at a ledger, his pencil like a matchstick between his fingers.

"Evenin', Boo," he said. His milky eyes caught the fire's glint as he scrupulously examined a list of goods received and shipped out.

"Thomas," the clown replied.

Thomas opened his cigarette case and plucked out one for each of them.

"It's sweet at first. Molasses. Biscuits and licorice." He sighed after lighting Boo's. "Then chestnut, maybe oak. It 'as layers, like a secret. Or a sausage roll. I pinched it off a shipping vessel a few days ago. It's Virginian."

There wasn't a cigarette strong enough to mask Thomas's mortifying breath, and not much else besides the flavor of putrefied flesh could get him to wax poetic. His ghoulism gave him an unfortunate appetite for rotten meat of any sort—human flesh being the most satisfying.

Boo eagerly inhaled the smoke through his nostrils. They'd found privacy behind makeshift walls created by dozens of crates stacked atop one another as Thomas checked the contents in each, scratching at his ledger every now and then.

Nearly twice as wide and tall as Boo, Tommy was built like the carnival's strongmen. The Scottish giant wore a long, gray coat, its collar brushing his clean-shaven jawbones, over gray-and-black striped trousers. Suspenders clung to his bare chest. His white hair—another effect of his malady—was combed messily over his shaved sides. Before Lester Black had recruited him from London's betting rings, Thomas's nimble fingers and propensity for brawls made him an excellent *gonoph*, a thief of varied talents that leeched off London's high society.

Boo went to sit on his customary chair, only to find it occupied by a large mass covered by a tarp.

"Oh, that?" Thomas pulled away the tarp, unveiling the slack features of a dead man. He was a little over middle-aged, with a spectacularly long line of snot solidifying from his nose. His eyes were uneven and staring. "Somebody found the old bloke in the mirror house. All alone, he was. Imagine that—some real posh-like couple comes around the corner and sees this dead'un's ugly mug leering from twelve sides. Do you reckon he scared 'imself to death?"

"It *is* advertised on our heralds that our grounds are not for the faint of heart. Tsk, tsk."

"Well. His heart was faint. At least we're living up to our reputation," Thomas said, snatching up the man's top hat and fitting it to his own head.

Boo went through the man's clothes and found a spare shilling, the coin no sooner vanishing into his waistcoat.

"Folks who found him think we reported him to the bobbies. But judging by the state of 'im, no one's going to come looking. He's worth much more to us like this, at any rate. Kayne will throw a parade."

Boo stood up and covered the corpse again. "What do you think he'll fetch at the medical college?"

"If I were a betting man—and I am—I'd say four pound."

"Five, at least. He's still warm."

"If we can get 'im there before daybreak, that is. And that task will fall on yours truly." The ghoul sighed.

Boo's lips curled into a smirk. "You willing to wager on that?"

"One pound."

Boo and Thomas each spat into their hands and shook.

"It looks as though we'll be discussing coin soon enough. Best not spoil it," Thomas said.

Boo recognized the jostling of a carriage in the distance and took off his cap to hear better. Doing so unleashed a sweaty, oily nest of copper locks sticking out every which way.

Then came the *woahs* from a driver just outside their wall of crates. The carriage arrived with the aroma of cigars and the mutterings of its two passengers.

"That'd be the men of the hour," Thomas said.

"Late," Boo noted.

"I 'ave adjusted my expectations. I suggest you do the same."

Before Boo could grumble any further, two gentlemen turned the corner in matching gray suits. Silver crosses studded the toes of their boots. The two brothers could be told apart by the elder's moustache, his dead eye, and the younger's insistence upon sounding more educated than he was.

"There's my favorite biter!" Arthur, the older sibling, exclaimed with outstretched arms. The movement was purely symbolic, as he'd sooner throw his arms around the Devil himself.

"Just *ghoul* or the standard *cretin* will suffice, thank you," Thomas said. "Shall we?"

"A'right, a'right, I meant nothin' by it," Arthur scoffed. "All business, then? That's fine by me, Mr. Barker. That's a fine hat, if you don't mind me saying. We was in a hurry, anyhow. Wasn't I just sayin' that, Henry?" Taking off his own bowler, Arthur twirled it between his hands to show just how hurried he was.

"That is verifiable, that is," Henry said. "You all right, clown? He looks a trifle more forlorn this evening."

"No more talkative than our last meeting, though." Arthur grinned. "You a'right?"

Henry pressed closer to Boo. "It's no wonder a woman like Lester prefers men like you. Nice 'n quiet-like. Do what you're told. No questions asked, is it?"

Henry was close enough now that Boo could see the flecks of amber in his brown eyes, the scars on his nose—crooked beyond repair. The clown took a deep drag, saying nothing over the gently sizzling tobacco.

"Boo is here for assurance, gentlemen—nothing more," Thomas explained. "You'd 'ave better luck getting a cat to crow."

"Yeah, that's right, eh? The clown isn't too...mendacious, is he?" Henry looked at the others with a smirk, met only by confusion.

"Loquacious," Boo murmured.

"What was that?" Arthur asked.

"My colleague 'ere seems to think your brother meant to say *loquacious*," Thomas translated.

Henry advanced on Boo. "You painted runt. How about you correct my speaking after I've finished recapitulating your insides."

"Rearranging?" Boo corrected.

Taking hold of the clown's lapels, Henry stammered, "You bloody mute. Who're you to correct *my* English?"

Boo glared back with stiffening indifference.

"For fuck's sake. I ought to 'ave brought a ruler. 'Cause I didn't realize we'd gathered to measure our cocks. Where's your man? Where's Mason?" Thomas asked.

Relinquishing Boo, Henry said, "Mason's on hiatus."

"Oh, Henry," his brother groaned. "No, he ain't! You oughta stop usin' words you ain't knowing the meaning for. Mason's not on hiatus. He's off on business elsewhere. New something? What was it called?"

"New Sarum," Henry said.

A curious spark crackled in Boo's heart. They'd be making the leap to that city after Cardiff. The circus had never been there before.

Arthur snapped his fingers. "That's it! So we'll be checkin' your numbers ourselves this time around."

Handing over his clipboard, Thomas hooked his thumbs into his suspenders and stepped aside. They settled into an uncomfortable silence broken only by the opening and closing of crate lids, the popping fire, and Arthur's guttural mutterings as he went about the stimulating task that Thomas had performed three times already that evening.

"Who's the cold one?" Henry asked with a nod toward the corpse. "Your supper?"

"I don't eat rubbish," Thomas replied. "Somebody could serve you up on a gold platter and I wouldn't be tempted."

"You'd do better to watch your tone around a Disciple. I've killed for less."

"Killing? Oh, that's the cardinal act, is it?" Thomas leaned in with a hand on the boy's shoulder, speaking low. "Where I come from—the family, it's sometimes called—I spilt the blood that'd gone 'n built that world. You're just living in it, kid."

"If you think you can—"

Arthur interjected. "Oi, oi, pipe down, baby brother. A dead bloke's not our problem. What *is* our problem is that you and your crew of the fashionably undead are behind, Mr. Barker." Shoving the clipboard into Thomas's chest, he continued. "Your numbers are square. But that's just the problem, innit? The numbers. Look at this lot! You 'aven't sold nearly half of what we've tasked you with."

"It was far easier when we were selling your stiffs, aye," Thomas replied, reaching into a crate and fishing up an expensive piece of china from the straw bedding. "There's not always a market for oriental teacups on this side of the Thames. Stolen ones, leastways. You want us to make your contraband disappear? We'll need more bleedin' time. Will that suffice, *Mr.* Fletcher?" In all his wisdom, Thomas flipped open his steel case and offered a cigarette to Arthur.

When Arthur took the cigarette, Boo thought for a moment that his circus and the Disciples might finally see eye to eye.

For a moment.

"We don't want your fuckin' smokes," Henry said. "We want the coin promised for goods provided, and in a timely manner!" In a single blow, he slapped both the cigarettes and the case from their hands.

They landed in the brazier's burning coals.

Though neither of the brothers knew the ghoul as well as Boo did, they seemed to sense that Thomas was stifling a particular breed of wrath.

"If you have half a mind, brother, you'll get back in the coach," Arthur said.

"Mason won't be satisfied with excuses, not from the likes of him!"

Arthur grabbed his younger brother as though reining in a disobedient pup and landed a firm smack to the back of his head. "Coach, now!" he shouted.

Henry's face flushed red. He strangled his cap, huffing petulantly. Beneath the scars and the tailored suit, Boo saw the Whitechapel youth that learned how to pickpocket before being taught his letters. Giving the dead man a kick, Henry skulked off into the carriage, slamming the door shut.

Rubbing his stubble, Arthur said, "I apologize for 'im. I do. He's still young, eh? But listen, he's not wrong. Dealin' with us, that's one thing. But Mason is another matter. He'd 'ave your head for this shit."

Thomas folded his arms. "The facts remain. We fence your goods as quick as we may. But this? All of this shit? We're only men mitherin' 'neath the boot of time, just like anybody else."

"No, Thomas. You're a bloody circus. You sell the impossible. You've the Devil in your corner, to boot, and the Disciples don't do mercies or confessions. Next time we meet, you'd do well to have replaced all this with the hard coin obliged to us. If you can't, well, you bloody well know what 'appens then." Putting on his bowler, Arthur patted the wall of crates as he turned in the direction of the carriage, saying, "We know where you'll be. You've three weeks, Thomas."

The light from the brazier fluttered across Thomas's stony expression. Crumbling, the coals spewed sparks and settled deeper. His steel case was blackened, the prized Virginian tobacco ashes among the coals.

Boo listened to the Disciples' carriage rolling away. He wiped the sweat that had bloomed on his forehead, smearing his makeup in the process. "You a'right?" he asked.

"If it weren't for Lester's sake, and of every soul owed to this place, I'd have stripped the flesh from those wee bampots and made 'em hand deliver it to Mason fuckin' Cross."

"The night is young."

Thomas took off his coat with a snort and bent over the corpse. "Come on, lend a hand. Let's give Kayne a reason to smile. One, two..."

4

ATHERTON
APRIL 28, 1886

"...three."

Atherton slid his arms out from beneath Alice, laying the child's delicate body upon the embalming table. After placing a head block beneath her neck, he smoothed out the girl's black hair. The deep color was intensified by her ivory skin, the azure of her veins, and her pale eyes growing foggier by the minute.

He draped a spare towel over the only mirror in the preparation room. This part of his home often felt particularly crowded.

As he was gathering implements to set the child's features, the door to the back room swung open. His father strode through, steaming cups of Earl Grey in each hand.

Allan leaned against another embalming table, the back of his trousers brushing the bare arm of elderly Mrs. Merrick, scheduled for viewing in just thirty minutes. He sipped his black tea, setting his son's beside an instrument used to wire jaws shut. The steam from the mug reminded Atherton that he hadn't had a cigarette in at least an hour, which he fixed promptly.

Through the tiny windows in the dead room, he watched another spring afternoon pass over New Sarum. He could hear children playing at the edge of the market—children who weren't frigid and stiffened with *rigor mortis*.

Allan removed his spectacles and rubbed his eyes. "Must you do that in here?"

"I'm working, aren't I?"

"Sometimes, I suppose... Well, I wonder if you are becoming rather relaxed in the preparation room."

"This is our home. My bedroom is a hallway away from where I pump people full of embalming fluids. My personal and professional habits are damned to intersect."

"Fair enough." Allan spread out his hands in a sign of surrender. "She's the third child this month, that one."

"I know."

"Does it not bother you?"

"Of course it bothers me." Atherton pinched his face as if the very thought was a nuisance, only to pinch it further after taking a sip of tea.

Bitter. Far too bitter.

"Because you don't seem bothered."

"Fine. It doesn't bother me. You're right. But you also over-steeped the tea—again."

"I admit I became distracted. And you've become detached. Cold. Unfeeling."

"Goodness, I wonder why." Tilting open Alice's jaw, Atherton cleaned out the inside of her mouth with a piece of cotton. "That's what you wanted, anyway. It's scarlet fever, isn't it?"

"No, not what I wanted. In fact—"

Atherton groaned and wiped his forehead in exasperation. The action left behind a smear of blood that had dried on his forearm earlier that day.

"Another time then," Allan conceded. "Right. The scarlet fever. There have been no signs of illness, no conceivable source. Whatever it may be, it is some fierce stroke of misfortune. Your sister is terrified of it. She thinks she's next. You'd do well not to discuss this with her."

"I will not make it a point to show Delma, but I will not hide the truth from her, either. You paid me no such courtesy when I was her age. You've had me digging graves and hoisting the dead since I was seven."

Finding the towel his son had placed over the mirror, Allan pulled it off. "Have we not discussed this nonsense?"

Concentrating on scraping food from Alice's molars, Atherton murmured, "It helps me focus. Grandfather always said you'd see spirits in the reflection."

"You know who sees spirits? Those who wish to. It drove your grandfather mad, these superstitions. And yet here I am, my sensibilities perfectly unshaken by the very same profession. I would not have you share his fate, rambling like some Bedlam patient about phantasmic visitations and their secrets."

"And what about their secrets?"

Atherton spotted the edge of a metallic object in the back of Alice's throat. It was the size of a coin, shining with saliva, and lodged so deep he nearly missed it. Pulling it free, he set it upon the embalming table and toweled off his hands. A few of the sharp points were tipped with blood.

Allan donned his spectacles. "What is this?"

"A trinket of some kind. A pendant? The cause of her untimely demise, most likely."

"It wasn't fever, then. Alice choked."

"But what child wears a symbol like this? A six-pointed star bound in a circle? Are you familiar with it?"

Taking the pendant in hand, Allan rubbed his thumb over it and held it up. It drank in the overcast light coming from the window. He scoffed. "Familiar is a queer word for those people. God knows they like to keep their secrets. If Alice's parents were Gehennics, it's no mystery then—they aren't the type to keep a careful eye on their children." With a disdainful shake of his head, he set the pendant down. "A heap of lost souls, if you ask me. Look where it got them."

"Gehennics," Atherton repeated, his voice distant from his body. "Mum said they were just vindictive Catholics taking the piss out of God."

Allan coughed up a chuckle. "Yes, well. People of the Morning Star. Keepers of the black faith. Friends of the Devil. Witches, in short. As the story goes, a little church popped up in London in the mid-1600s, where people like Alice's parents, I suppose, congregated. Went to pray and sing hymns, just like any good Christian. Except, they weren't praying to God and his archangels—rather, their counterparts in Hell. Gehenna."

"What compelled them?" Atherton asked.

Allan rubbed at his already pristine spectacles with a handkerchief plucked from his pocket and shrugged. "Behold. The mantle humans bear." He gestured to Alice. "Some people don't like the world God gave them. You almost can't blame them."

Thoughtlessly, Atherton found himself tucking a stray lock of hair behind Alice's ear. Images of her playing outside with the other children seeped into his eyes. He gnawed on his lower lip.

"There was a great fire in London in 1666," Allan continued. "Nearly turned the whole city to ash. But guess what was spared, eh? That little church. Between that and the fact that they offer asylum to ghouls and the like, they've had quite the following since then. Who knows—maybe the Devil looks out for his own after all."

"If that's true, he didn't think to spare her," Atherton said.

Allan sighed. "Then the Devil and God have that in common. They have a habit of disappointing their followers. But!" Allan clapped his hands together. "More importantly, however she came upon the pendant is immaterial. What we have just discovered does not leave this room, do you understand? Save for your mother, of course. It would assuage Delma's fears, too. But should Alice's parents ever become privy to this, it would destroy them, even more than her death already has. Such a tragedy, the loss of a healthy child, for naught but an accident. An oversight. No."

"But, Father—"

"We confirm their suspicions. Trust me in this. It was scarlet fever, just as you said. Yes. Nothing more."

"Surely you can't expect me to—"

"The horrors of some truths spoil the virtue of honesty. Now, get a change of clothes. Wash up. Our monthly deposit is due. We wouldn't want to try Mr. Cross's patience, now would we?"

"What about Alice? Mason expects you this time around. He asked to have words with *you*."

"I'm afraid it will have to be you once again, my child. Alice isn't going anywhere. Consider it a promotion! Meeting with the Disciples is integral to our operation. Ugh, not that look, Athie. The Merricks have requested me for their grandmother's viewing, specifically. You remember how they were with their grandfather."

"It's not my fault he started purging like a fountain during the viewing! And are you mad? Promotion, my arse! This farce of their 'taxing' us under the false pretense of protection is infuriating. It's extortion. They're mobsters. Thieves. Bloody mutchers and prigs, all of them."

"And I call paying them *keeping my family safe*. As far as I'm concerned, you getting to shout obscenities at me with your vocal cords intact is proof of purchase. Besides, Mason's always taken a shine to you."

Atherton knew there was no use quarreling with his father, precisely because they'd had the same argument countless times before. That didn't change how good it felt, shouting and slamming surgical implements around. "I despise Mason," he said much quieter, "and he knows that."

"Then you have a splendid opportunity, don't you? Letting bygones be bygones. Water beneath the bridge and all that." Producing an envelope from inside his suit, Allan tucked it into Atherton's waistcoat and patted it. "Give Mason my regards."

Standing by the entrance of the White Horse pub, Atherton was beginning to regret wishing away his chores at the mortuary. For all the tedium the dead demanded, he far preferred it to the living's unpredictability.

The bustling marketplace teemed with familiar faces. Customers he'd come to know only in their grief. At best, their recognition of him was tolerant. Like a tax or lawman, Graves Mortuary Services was considered a necessary expenditure. At worst, the Graves family was thought to bear both curse and plague, and to swindle you on the price of a coffin while they spread it. A family walking in the Devil's shadow by doing the Lord's work.

He spotted the Merricks' coach clattering through the throng, and caught Mrs. Merrick's attention with a wave, receiving only an uncertain look from behind her black veil in return.

Atherton pushed through the heavy doors of the White Horse and was met with a few dispirited nods from folks already drunk before noon. Smoky fumes of spilled ale and stale tobacco engulfed him.

Over the steady hum of conversation, Atherton called, "Mollie, Mollie!"

The barkeep ignored him, lingering with her regulars before begrudgingly making her way over. "You aren't my only customer, Mr. Graves. You do know that, yes?"

"I am not your customer at all. Not today, leastways," he said as he outstretched the envelope his father gave him. "Here is Mason's payment."

"He's in the private lounge. You can give it to 'im yourself."

Summoning his most charming smile, which came across as plainly arrogant, he asked, "Would you be so kind as to deliver it to him? A favor. Just this once, Mollie."

"A favor, is that it? And what am I to tell 'im when he asks why you haven't delivered it ya'self? Hm?" Mollie's Scottish lilt became more pronounced the more annoyed she became, the lively curls in her red hair bobbing as she tilted her head. "I have other customers to tend to. Eh, Athie? Paying folk, mind you."

"Wait, wait, wait. Business! Tell him I had other pressing business. The business that is earning him coin! Yes, that's good. Tell him that."

"An emergency burial? Is that it?"

"Well..." He searched Mollie's brown eyes.

There was an intense, despairing silence.

"Please, I implore you," he continued. "Most beautiful and luscious Mollie, whose graces are a blessing to the philistines who stumble their way in here, I would be most honored if you took it to him. He'll hardly notice, I assure you." He took her hand and began to wrap her fingers around the envelope.

"God bless you, Athie," she said, pulling away. "For all your black moods, you 'ave a heart full of hope. Sadly, asking a barkeep to stand in the path of Mason Cross for you is too tall an order."

"Damn you, Mollie."

The crack of wood slapping wood shunted all conversation. Quiet enough for Atherton to hear his own nervous heart.

The whole pub turned to watch Mason Cross emerge from the back room's double doors, beaming a sharpened smile. Just shy of two yards tall, London's notorious crime baron didn't have to tower over anyone to make them feel small. The fine threads of his suit failed to hide the musculature of his back and arms, outlining their imposing curves. Evidently, his tailor was just barely keeping up with his training regimen.

"Well, if it isn't Atherton Graves. The boy born with a shovel in hand," Mason said, approaching closer. "Why don't we get you sorted?"

Guiding Atherton into a private booth with a firm hand on his shoulder, Mason asked, "I trust your father 'ad other business, then?" His gravely voice carried the eloquence of careful thought honed by decades of violence. Were it not for the sheer terror it inspired, it might have been endearing. "Not that it matters, see, s'long as I've one of the Graves in my company." He winked.

Mollie returned with two glasses and the specific bottle of gin requested by the simple calling of her name, and left just as quickly.

Once the doors were closed, the undertaker cleared his throat and said, "A viewing."

"Eh?" Mason poured himself enough to impair a small family.

"My father had to attend a viewing. The, ah, the Merricks." Watching Mason pour himself a more modest quantity, Atherton couldn't help but notice a few drops on the lacquered table.

Blood.

"Well, that's convenient, innit?"

"What is, sir?"

"No, no, *sir*. We're business associates. You understand that, don't you? So you won't *sir* me like you're some groveling li'l beggar child with a fake limp. It's disrespectful. To both of us, mind you. Now. Your father knows when we agreed on our next meetin'. So what d'ya make of that? Go on, he ain't 'ere. I won't tell 'im."

"Perhaps he scheduled the viewing knowing he'd have to send me in his stead?"

"You said it, not me. All's I'm saying is it's interesting." Smirking, he folded his hands across his chest.

Atherton could feel him drinking in his expression.

Amber and black stripes ran down Mason's waistcoat. His bronze hair was pulled back, curling in unruly locks at his neck. The scars on his stubbled, angular jaws and crooked nose spoke of fighting rings and threats that didn't prove empty. Atherton failed to count the scars on the mobster's hands.

"Wouldn't you agree?" Mason finally asked, giving one of those looks with his mossy eyes that could dissuade a bull from charging.

"Certainly." It was a shame—the gin was excellent, fouled by the dread bubbling in Atherton's throat. He withdrew the envelope brimming with banknotes, coins, and receipts from his suit and handed it over.

Mason counted every sixpence and note against the sale slips. The minutes passed with few remarks. All the while, Atherton reflected on the times he'd repeated this ritual or watched his father endure it when he was too young to understand. It wasn't the first time, either, that he began to fantasize about ending the humiliation. He had tended to the care of countless corpses—he called it an art. But he had never made one himself.

"So what is it then, Athie?"

He took a deep drag of a cigarette—his third since he entered the booth. "What is what?"

"Fear or trust? Your father knowingly sending you 'ere in 'is place, I mean. Our families 'ave known each other for some time, now. We've been doing this dance for years, eh? You n' I 'ave had our chats when I've come around your parlor, but...this *is* special, this. Our l'il connection. So what d'you reckon?"

"Trust. Mine and your father reached an understanding long before we met."

"But you don't. Trust, that is. You're no snakesman, Atherton, but you ain't gulpy, neither," Mason smiled—the gleam of a gambler with a loaded card. "So long as we're being honest, my trust in you is falterin' right about now."

Atherton tossed back the rest of his drink, a white flame slithering down his insides. It failed to scald his throat like the next words he dragged from it.

THE BLACK CARNIVAL

"I do trust you."

Mason scoffed. "It's strange, innit? While we try so vainly to utter intricate deceits. Little flams. Our bodies tell the truth. An unsteady gaze. A stutter. A drummin' knee. Back when 'the Disciples' was just a name whispered in Whitechapel's alleys, it was tells like them which decided whether I lived or died. My ability to read 'em. D'you know what I'm readin' now? Your 'ands. They're shaking." Mason reached into his inner breast pocket and pulled out a straight razor. "'*A righteous man 'ateth lying: but a wicked man is loathsome and cometh to shame.*' Proverbs."

"Surely you would not punish me for failing to admit I am shaken by your demeanor. You see the absurdity in that, don't you?"

Unfolding the blade, Mason chuckled again. "Right you are. That would be absurd. No, your fear—of which I am certain, mind you—ain't my concern. There's been an oversight in your earnin's this month. 'Ave a look yourself."

Taking the receipt handed to him, Atherton looked over the services charged.

He recognized the name.

The Crowleys had lost their twin boys at the beginning of the month. They had been Alice's age, and their deaths just as mysterious and sudden. He didn't just remember their faces—he could see them. Feel them. Smell them. Hear them.

"I'm afraid I don't understand. This is the standard fee we render for such services," he explained. "Coffin, burial, embalmings. It's all here. See?"

Mason didn't bother looking where his finger pointed. "Notice the two 'embalmings' but only the one 'coffin.' The one 'burial.' It's strange, innit? Two pieces of this transaction are missing, Atherton. Two. One coffin and one burial. There should be *two*, one for each chavy. Where've they run off to? Did the dead dig 'emselves up and demand business elsewhere?"

"The Crowleys requested specifically to have their children interred in the same coffin. They were buried simultaneously and, therefore, required one plot. The children were laid in such a way as to fit them into one coffin. I arranged them myself."

"How so?"

"Head to feet. Like this," Atherton said, laying his arms on top of each other to demonstrate. "I remember remarking it was rather like a jigsaw."

Mason snorted. "I've always liked that about you. That black humor. You don't 'ide your calluses. That's why you're so bloody unnerving. Nevertheless, it was an odd request, was it not?"

"The bereaved often make requests one cannot always anticipate. As New Sarum's only funeral parlor, we do everything to accommodate such requests, no matter how odd."

"Well, that is a relief," Mason said.

Atherton let out a breath. "It is?"

"'Course. I see it clear now. You weren't tryin' to mizzle from us. Takin' a cut of our cut, as it were. Far be it from me to tell you how to run your business, but I do, 'owever, know the smell of a lost opportunity. 'Coz this 'ere is a bloody travesty. Two burials. Two coffins. Two plots for the price of one. That *does* interfere with my cut, see. That's not just the Graves Mortuary Services' loss. It's the Disciples' loss."

"But the children were scarcely five years old. A single, grown man would be more trouble to bury." His cigarette was cold in his trembling fingers. "And their mother. Their mother, she was—"

"Put your 'and on the table," Mason said.

"What will you—"

"*Put* it on the table. Do not make me ask again. I'll even be kind. I'll let you pick which."

Having seen many times what would happen if he continued to protest, Atherton laid his left hand upon the table. The straight razor caught the light of the chandelier above them. Its blade was a sheet of gilded flame.

Before he could ready himself, Mason slid it in, slicing into the tight flesh of his knuckle, drawing it to the nail. Atherton's other hand gripped the table, paling as the blade sank into each finger, cutting steady lines in each.

After the work was done, as his blood seeped into the tabletop and pattered into his lap, Mason said, "I will gift you this implement of singular craftsmanship so that each day, as you rise to greet the morning 'n shave that darling chin of yours, you remember it's the Disciples who 'ave your best interests in mind."

Tucking the razor into Atherton's breast pocket, Mason gave him a pat. "Until next time, Atherton."

※

The roar of the pub had been replaced with the chatter of the Butler House orphanage. Tiny hands on an untuned piano played offbeat melodies while the six other orphans dirtied their elbows and knees in the yard. At the dining table, Atherton watched his blood drip and swirl into a washbowl's darkening water while Lilian Butler wound fresh gauze over his fingers.

"It was humiliating," he continued to lament.

"There is no shame in being victimized by a power you have no control over. If that were the case, we'd all be creatures of great indignity," she replied. Though she had finished wrapping his cuts, their hands lingered together.

This alone was enough to intensify the throbbing in his fingers, propelled by the rampant beating in his chest. Given the excuse to be this close to Lilian, Atherton almost felt some gratitude to the man who'd nearly maimed him. His infatuation bloomed the day he'd been called to collect her late husband some seasons ago. She possessed a quiet assuredness, a stillness, perhaps from all those years she had on him. Maybe she, too, dwelt in a world of brief joys shadowed by melancholy. He heard it in her laugh whenever he indulged her morbid fascination with his work stories, saw it in her gaze, how it scrutinized him with a curiosity that almost felt eerie, as though they spoke with a veil between them. He liked the sharp angle in the bridge of her nose, the pronounced overbite on her full lips, and how her small frame had deceived him at first, as her spirit was anything but meek.

"And what is indignity if not being forced to endure suffering that affords nothing? To forfeit myself to this brute? I would do unspeakable things to see that his shadow never darkened this city again. Sometimes at night, it is all I can think of, but it doesn't leave by morning. It haunts me."

Lilian leaned in. Her eyes were nearly pitch black, with only the faintest difference between her pupils and irises. It was only noticeable when standing close enough to smell the weeds that had rubbed off on her gray dress from playing with the children. The bergamot on her breath. The lavender soaked into her black curls from bathing the night before. All of this visibly stunned Atherton, so much so that Lilian grinned sheepishly and pulled away. "And what of those other shadows that haunt you?" she asked. "The ones you've spoken of before?"

"Shadows, yes," he replied distantly. The heat running through his veins was replaced with a dreadful chill, and for a moment, he felt alone in the orphanage. The playful cries of the children outside became a distant world, fading to the coldness seeping into his flesh. It made him forget about his dealings with Mason, about Lilian's face filling with concern.

"I am afraid I'd rather not revisit that subject," he finally said as the sounds of a bustling orphanage returned.

"Even in the company of a loyal confidant?"

Atherton artfully dodged the question. "I owe you an apology. Here I am seeking medical assistance on a Sunday afternoon, only to burden you with troubles that should be mine alone."

"The time of day is immaterial. I never was one for hymns and Bibles. And what else would friends be for if not the shouldering of weights we cannot bear on our own? You have always been a welcome sight in our home, Atherton. After my husband's passing, I thought the world lonesome and cruel. You reminded me of who I was before him. That is a kindness I can only hope to repay."

"Friends," Atherton repeated with a forced grin. That word. He would let Mason butcher his other hand if that meant getting her to consider another. Given that she was recently widowed and nearly a decade his senior, he hesitated to shower her with declarations of his abject affections, especially since he did not know how they'd be received. "May I admit something?"

"Certainly."

"There are few I could turn to. Friends, that is. And my father doesn't see the Disciples as I do. He's determined to accept them as a permanent fixture in our lives. He sees no alternative to paying them a percentage of our profits or suffering their intimidation. Their abuse."

"You do not share this sentiment?"

"No. I..." Perhaps it was the loss of blood or the intense fluctuation of emotions, but Atherton saw something peculiar when he glanced at the open door of the house.

It was Alice. Standing in its frame.

She was as real as the other children, yet as pale as when he transferred her body to the hearse that very morning. Her colorless lips were slack. Her mouth moved, long before he heard its words.

> *Have you been to the water*
> *Have you been 'round the market*
> *We'd a-looked and drained the Thames*
> *But our bones ached, our little old legs*
> *Ran red looking for Minnie Pegs*

Not knowing how to tell Lilian that he was currently seeing a child who, at this moment, was lying cold on his embalming table, he placed a cigarette between his lips and stood up to leave. "My apologies. I would be remiss to overstay my welcome. I fear I already have."

"Don't be absurd. You're white as a sheet and can barely stand. Stay for supper. You know how the children adore you."

Alice's gown fluttered in the early spring breeze. She moved, striding into the house, and disappeared up the long staircase to the second floor.

Lilian struck a match and raised the flame to his cigarette. "Wanting to untangle your business from the Disciples may as well be like cheating the Devil out of a signed contract," she said. "But I tell you what, Atherton Graves, if ever there was a man to do it, he may just be the one I'm looking at."

The rhythmless notes from the music room ceased, followed by the hammering of small feet on wood flooring.

Atherton jumped, but it was only Lola.

One of the orphan's eyes had a lazy slant toward the side of her head, made up by the other's sharp, questioning gaze. Bulbous, hazel, and piercing. Her bottom set of teeth jutted out so as to give the impression of an angler fish. Atherton couldn't help but grin as the child looked up at him.

Lola snatched up his hand and swung it. "Will Mr. Graves join us for supper?"

Combing through the child's wild hair with her fingers, Lilian gave her guest a smirk that made his insides perform backflips. "Well?"

"I will," Atherton decided. "But not to enjoy your company. This one exudes a sense of class that is utterly lacking from the woman who runs this house. Isn't that right, Lola?" Setting down his cigarette, Atherton jumped to his feet and picked the child up with him. He raised her over his head and swung her about until she burst into a fit of giggles. The pair fled the kitchen laughing, with Lola spreading her arms out wide, telling all the world, "I'm flying!"

5

LESTER
MAY 6, 1886

The tents multiplied by the day, blossoming like striped flowers in the verdant tones of New Sarum's countryside. The flags were streaks of scarlet waving in wild currents at their peaks, a burst of blood in the morning fog that gave way to a gray fleet of clouds swarming the afternoon sky.

But it wasn't just the fields being overrun.

Already, the city teemed with performers and workers from the Black Carnival. By day, the streets grew more crowded and boisterous. By night, crime spiked, business boomed, and pubs became a frenzy of socialization between the locals and the travelers.

Their heralds, posters, and fliers arrived a week before the caravan. As per Lester's orders, not a single brick was left bare. Their promises were instant conversation pieces—a menagerie of outlandish beasts, flying trapeze artists and renowned jugglers, and even a spiritualist who could summon the late relatives of guests. With the circus still under construction, the streets became busking stages for more sideshow displays like strongmen, fire-breathing, and sword swallowing.

From a third story window of Frederick Griffin's home, Lester watched Boo and a troupe of jugglers walk into the courtyard below for a midday performance. She clicked open her watch. Several minutes late.

Behind her, Mr. Griffin's oily moustache was twitching steadily. He was delivering some rehearsed pleasantries—nothing she cared to hear. Despite his position as the city's mayor, there was little about him that suggested he had much of a spine. His most striking detail was a horrendously severe center part in his curly, golden hair.

Thomas had accompanied Lester to the meeting. The ghoul was nestled in an armchair, his face buried in a newspaper, releasing a steady trail of cigarette smoke.

"Why, Mrs. Black, you have—"

"*Ms.* Black. I never married."

"My apologies, Ms. Black. You've hardly touched your tea."

"Coffee."

"Excuse me?"

"I prefer coffee. I employ several expats from America, and I've become partial to their particular taste for Colombian beans. Not that I expect you to have any—I was simply being forthright."

Stiffening, Frederick took a seat at his desk. "I see. Well then, perhaps I should join you in being forthright."

"I am not here for the tea, evidently."

Frederick choked on his surprise, his teacup and plate clattering together. "Very well. Are you at all familiar with the rumors regarding your traveling company?"

Lester sat in silence as she considered the question, one she had heard posed and twisted in more ways than the limbs of her best contortionist. Beneath her wide-brimmed hat, she eyed him with a placid grin. A scarlet ascot wrapped the high collars of her button-down shirt, and her striped suit was, like the circus tents, impossible to ignore. Wavy, black locks streaked with silver bordered her face, while her gray eyes, unwavering and sharklike, hid behind tinted glasses.

A grandfather clock ticked away with painful clarity.

"That is a loaded question," Lester said. "Do you mean the sacrificial rites or our alleged ties to the crime lord Logan Cross and his gang of Disciples? This is often a point of confusion, as we have also been accused of child abduction, cannibalism, and prostitution. Baseless, of course. However, I won't deny that the last one, at least, has some credibility. But who can control an aerialist on her fourth gin in London anyway?"

"Nadya did it for a bet," Thomas added from the back. "With, oh, who was it? Chief inspector so-and-so? A bobbie. Abberline, wasn't it? That's how the rumor started, anyhow."

"Ah, well, there you have it. Nadya fucked Chief Inspector Abberline of Scotland Yard. For a bet. Thank you, Tommy. As you can see, Mayor, we have our rumors, but not without reputation."

Frederick cleared his throat. "It remains a matter of principle. This is

Christian land. When the sun sets, it casts the shadow of our cathedral over the city. People travel to see it. It is well known that a coven operates as the management of your circus. Do you see the conflict?"

"*My* coven, that is," Lester replied. "But I fail to see the issue. Please understand that this meeting is more of a social courtesy. The legal consequences of our setting up outside your gates pale in comparison to the benefit we offer your people. I also find it terribly garish when a sleepy city like yours sends its only constables to shut down an organization of our magnitude. Several of our strongmen practice the art of bending steel, mind you. A few bones wouldn't prove much trouble."

Flashing a smile dripping with loathing, Frederick continued. "Nevertheless, your organization is Gehennic in nature. Governed by witches, no less."

"The Gehennic Church is a relative of the Catholics and Protestants. Always has been. What's that saying? 'The Devil keeps God in business?' Like it or not, we share the same blood."

"And yet I remain skeptical of the effect your circus's presence will have on my citizens."

Lester took off her riding spectacles and stood. "Why don't you join me by the window? I think you will find the only citizen here who needs convincing is you. Whether you like it or not, Mayor, your city has already warmed up to us."

A sizable crowd had gathered in the courtyard below. Boo and three other jugglers were passing clubs with the precision of a ballet, so numerous they were impossible to count as they twirled past one another. A child in the crowd, waiting for Lester's signal, whistled as soon as she waved back.

"Hep!" Boo called.

Boo and the others sent a final flash of clubs hurtling into the air, thrown high enough that the jugglers had time to pirouette twice. When the clubs came tumbling down, their handles produced punctuating knocks of wood against wood as each snapped into their palms.

The quiet marketplace of New Sarum was overcome by a sound it likely seldom heard—applause. Thunderous, booming applause with approving whistles and the giddy shrieks of children.

Lester turned to the mayor, his astonishment breaking through a thin veneer of indifference. "So you see? Your people are hungry for entertainment, Mayor Griffin. My people are just hungry. They need work. Countless cities before yours have hosted us. The only wound your people will have to nurse is the bleak sadness they will feel after we've left. Should you openly endorse it and allow our shows to go unimpeded by the authorities, we would be interested in offering you two percent of the profits for the duration of our stay. Nearly two weeks in total."

Frederick's whiskers fluttered. "Two-and-a-half percent, and you have New Sarum's blessing."

Lester's eyebrows shot up in feigned surprise as she picked up her handbag. "Well, well, Mr. Griffin," she grinned. "Quite the negotiator, are we? Two-and-a-half it is. Tommy?"

Thomas set his reading material down and got to his feet, ducking to avoid the chandelier. The giant withdrew a contract from his coat and set it on the mayor's desk. Frederick snatched it up, bristling with a mixture of fascination and annoyance that he himself was having difficulty understanding. "It already says here two-and-a-half percent," he stammered. "We amended your initial offer."

"And?"

"That would mean you'd already anticipated my counteroffer!"

"Oi! Talk's cheap, but time is money," Thomas said. "You'll be paid just for sittin' on your cotton arse. What's to debate?"

"That's quite enough, Tommy."

"I've been meaning to ask about him. Does he have authorization to be here?" Frederick wagged a finger in the ghoul's direction, cheeks flush with anger. "Don't think I hadn't noticed his eyes and hair. I knew what he was the moment he walked in here. Surely I don't have to tell you that ghouls require permits to work in city limits."

Thomas pulled out his identification card and flashed it. "I have my rights. By the seal of Queen bloody Victoria."

Frederick turned to Lester and said with an air of suspicion, "New Sarum cannot risk an outbreak of ghoulism, Ms. Black. I don't want to see his *kind* about my streets so long as you are here."

"I don't appreciate you speaking of my associate in the third person while he is standing within striking distance of you. Do you appreciate it, Tommy?"

"No. The living do not stir my appetites, Mr. Griffin."

Frederick traded scornful looks with each of them.

Lester offered her most innocent smile and tapped her nail on the form. It appeared the mayor was not accustomed to being browbeaten by a towering ghoul and a witch in his own office. Of course, Lester would never permit Thomas to use violence to get their way—that wouldn't do well for their reputation—but the implication never hurt anyone. Like many others who'd pressed the tip of a fountain pen to a Black Carnival contract, as Frederick scratched his signature upon the line, bristling at Lester once he'd finished, she understood that, to him, this may as well have been a deal with the Devil.

And there could be no mistake. As Lester folded the contract and slipped it into her suit pocket, it did rather feel like collecting a soul.

6

IVORY
MAY 7, 1886

Beyond the outskirts of the circus grounds stood a man looking down upon the corpse of an adolescent girl. A sea of reeds reeling and lurching in the wind enclosed them. Beetles, flies, and maggots feasted in feverish abundance, such that parts of her fidgeted and throbbed. Few people, having come across this sight on their morning walk, would count themselves lucky. Then again, few people were in the business of collecting ghosts.

Ivory Todd was one of those few people.

Locks of peppered black hair billowed about his clean-shaven cheekbones in the blustering gales. They revealed his hawkish nose and a single, protruding incisor, which had a habit of hooking over his bottom lip whenever he pursed. He was dressed in simple trousers, a working shirt, and suspenders. Deep mauve rings perpetually hung beneath his inquisitive, pale blue eyes. He often stood with a slight slouch to one side, as he was then, with his right hand folded over the gnarled and chipped prosthesis attached to the base of his left forearm.

Ivory's prosthesis was no mere hunk of wood fashioned into the vague shape of a half-closed fist. Rather, it was like an illustrator's model hand, with each finger fully articulated and posable. It was a hand fond of reaching into death's pocket.

Kneeling beside the twisted carcass, Ivory brushed aside the girl's hair, matted with mud. The hand creaked, simultaneously limp and stiff where its hinges had rusted over. He got to his feet with a tired groan.

Constables Welsh and Bishop were standing by, cobalt caps in hand.

"And you found her when, exactly, sir?" Bishop asked. He had a notepad and pencil in hand, but had written nothing besides *Avary Tod.*

"Just before I called upon you, gentlemen. I admit I took some time to dress myself and enjoy a morning cup. The dead are nothing if not patient, after all. I'm afraid I was half-awake when I discovered the child, it being rather early." Ivory spoke with confidence. After all, he fancied himself an entertainer practiced in wrapping half-truths in convincing hyperbole, its smoothness bitten with the rasp of long nights spent barking those deceptions over rowdy crowds.

"It's 'alf-past noon, sir," Welsh said.

Ivory struggled against the wind to light a cigarette, gripping it between his teeth as he said, "Business predisposes me to late nights and late mornings. It's my morning now. That's when I found her, and that's what I would like on record."

The constables shared a glance at the sharp temper that burst through that thin mask of jubilance. Bishop composed himself with a bit more decorum than his partner, whose uniform was wrinkled and stained with a splash of cream. In a city where the majority of crimes were ones that Mason Cross paid them to ignore, Ivory supposed the constables had little else to do but drink tea and eat scones all day.

"And what business would that be, sir?" Welsh asked.

"Spiritualism. Precious few are active in the din of day. They like the quiet, ghosts. The dark. They want to be seen. To be heard. Isn't that what any of us wants?"

The constables looked grateful to be interrupted by the sight of the carriage of *Graves Mortuary Services*, pulled along by a single black horse that stopped outside the wall of reeds. The young driver, dressed in a well-fitted suit, hollered, "You'll have to forgive me, constables! I came as soon as I received word."

"Nothing to be forgiven, Atherton!" Bishop called back.

Having pulled on the reins, the man named Atherton hopped off, thrusting his coat onto the driver's seat and rolling up his sleeves.

"Excuse me," Ivory interjected. "Who is this?"

"This is our undertaker," Bishop said. "Our man of all things stiff and cold. Atherton, this 'ere is the gentleman who found her. A spiritualist for the circus, if I 'ave it right. Ivory Todd."

"'Man' is a bit of a stretch, isn't it? Meaning no offense. The boy's hardly a hair on his chest." Ivory gestured toward the young undertaker.

"A naked chest, maybe, but Athie here's tough as old boots, isn't he?

I've seen 'im hoist twelve stone in dead weight all on 'is own. He's been burying the dead with his father 'fore he scarcely knew how to speak. That's the truth, innit, Athie?" Welsh said.

"It is, but I'm afraid my associate here enjoys exaggeration. A single man with a bedsheet could usher an army into the earth, let alone twelve stone. I'm not without my tricks, after all. Atherton Graves, sir, of *Graves Mortuary Services*. A pleasure. Well, not in these circumstances, of course."

"No," Ivory agreed, though he was grinning from ear to ear. "No, of course not. All the same."

Ivory extended his prosthetic hand with a wink, enjoying the surprise on Atherton's face as he took in the leather belts strapping it to his forearm, secured to a brace looped over his neck and shoulder. The boy tried to feign indifference, giving the wooden hand a firm shake.

"What do you think, Atherton? Do you recognize 'er?" Welsh asked.

Crouching, the undertaker inspected the child's remains. Though bone peeked through her sloughing jaw, and her skin had turned a darker green than the fields she was rotting in, he recognized her instantly. "Begging Betty," he said.

"Come again?" Ivory asked.

"This 'ere's a child beggar, Mr. Todd," Bishop explained. "Folks thought she came all the way from Southwark, few years ago. People fed 'er. Stables housed 'er. The streets adopted 'er. She was New Sarum's cobblestone child. Beggin' Betty, as Athie said. The Butler Orphanage even took 'er in, but she didn't take to it much. Learnin' her letters n' all. Was back out surviving on people's good graces by the month's end."

"You don't suspect murder, then?" Ivory asked.

Shaking his head, Welsh said, "We 'ad already made up our minds once we saw her. She was starved. Likely caught a chill, wandered out 'ere to die... We was just waiting on another opinion. Atherton 'ere knows the streets as well as us, having picked up one relative or another of most everyone."

"We'll leave 'er in your capable hands, Atherton," Bishop said, tucking his cap upon his head. "Give your father my regards. A pleasure, Mr. Todd, and welcome to New Sarum."

Left alone, the two death workers stood in the foul aroma that meant to each of them—more than gore and tragedy—enterprise. A vengeful wind with considerable bite whipped about their clothes and hair. The circus grounds were far behind Ivory, one of its largest tents being raised. An odd warmth bubbled in the spiritualist's chest as he took in the young man's quiet but strong posture. A sense of familiarity. Trust? Obligation?

"How does it feel to be so young, yet carrying such a burden? The weight of a whole city's dead," Ivory said, drawing closer. "To be healthy but always near death? To be unversed in the touch of a lover, yet keenly aware of how flesh turns to stone? That the expression of a corpse can tell you everything you need to know about their last moments?"

The boy's jovial grin twisted into a suspicious scowl, as though Ivory's words had stirred a demon within him. "What would you know about me?" he asked.

His response delighted Ivory—such disdain could only mean he'd already plucked on a sensitive vein, though he did well to conceal his satisfaction with a shrug. "Am I wrong?"

"My father warned me about people like you—talking boards, scrying orbs, fabricated photographs, cold reading. Parlor tricks, all of it. You take advantage of people whose grief renders them vulnerable so you can turn coin. The same people we help, you manipulate."

"Such a description befits your business just as well, I'm afraid. Deep down, you understand that, more than coffins, graves, or talking boards, what people like us sell is *closure*. Catharsis. And what tricks are there to spin here, Mr. Graves?" Ivory gestured at the corpse. "You have no connection to this...Bessy."

"Betty."

"If you cared so much, you wouldn't have been making small talk when you saw her."

"With all due respect, a sideshow entertainer would know nothing of the calluses I bear after a short lifetime of this work. Work that I must be tending to." Atherton moved to the back of his hearse and pulled out a folded bed sheet. Grasping its edges, the wind unfurled it like a wild sail over the body. Ivory was charmed, watching such youthful hands handle something so grim. It was like looking at himself in a mirror twenty years before.

"From one who walks in the valley of death to another," Ivory said, "you would do well to make friends of those who share your blight."

Atherton draped Betty with the sheet and then pushed her onto her side. Her limbs, stiff with rigor, crunched with every movement. Ivory was no stranger to decay. He knelt beside the young undertaker and supported Betty's lower half so Atherton could tuck the fabric fully beneath her. As they worked, her softened skin rubbed into their wrists like soil.

Ivory pretended not to notice how Atherton's gaze lingered upon him with suspicion. Perhaps the boy expected him to groan or turn green. Of course, Ivory did none of this and only attended to the task with quiet reverence.

"I have no fear of disease, Mr. Todd," Atherton said while they worked. "Though I may not be a man of faith, I am not without optimism. You have my gratitude for your assistance." Having centered the body on the sheet, Atherton started to bring the ends together.

Ivory held his tongue as he helped Atherton tie three knots in the sheet—one at the head, the second at her chest, and a third at her feet. This would make it easier to carry her. The colors of her decomposition painted the white cloth, her blood brightest among the earthy tones.

"Done this before, have you?" Atherton asked, once they'd finished.

Ivory dabbed a bit of blood on his prosthetic with a handkerchief. "Oh, just following your lead, is all," he replied coolly. "But that is not the blight I speak of, Mr. Graves. They cling to you, like sailors to the driftwood of a shipwreck. Lost souls clutching to one who feels them. The ghosts of those you carry. Even as we speak, another thread of hundreds before her is being tied to you."

Atherton took up a knot in each hand and hoisted Betty up. "What is this, more American spiritualist quackery?" he asked with a contemptuous laugh. Before he could embark on the undertaking, his foot slipped in the wet earth, and the body fell with a moist smack to the ground before he nearly joined her, were it not for Ivory steadying him with a firm hand.

It was odd. Ivory had thrown fists for less, but watching Atherton squirm under the scrutiny of somebody who saw his naked soul only made him pity the boy. Wordlessly, Ivory took up one of the knots to help. The girl was lighter than he anticipated, but her rot and mud made it a messy haul.

Once they'd gotten her onto the hearse, Atherton mumbled his thanks. Ivory waved it off, though he grimaced to see his fresh trousers now colored with old blood.

"I think I see you clearer now," Ivory pressed further. "You are so mired in terror that you refuse to see what you've become. What *they've* made you. To accept it would usher you into a realm of solitude you haven't yet the courage to face."

"I haven't the faintest notion what you're on about," Atherton said, though he looked like he was fighting back tears.

"So be it," Ivory conceded with a sigh. "What will you do with her?"

"Bury her beside those who took pity on her. Beneath the soft earth of the city that treated her as its own," he grunted, dragging her back further into the hearse. "That is as good a fate as any could hope for."

"And what of payment?"

"A service tax from the city. Scraps. Given she is a beggar, we'll be grateful for even that. And after the damned...well," Atherton cleared his throat. "Who's asking?"

"I am. I'll give you five pounds for her," Ivory dared.

"I beg your pardon?" Atherton stumbled back.

"Five pounds if you leave her to me and say not a word of it to anyone, especially your father. I will take care of the rest. That's five pounds that you won't have to share with the Disciples, and an afternoon's work taken off your hands. How's that for a bargain?"

Atherton slammed the hearse doors shut. "You're mad. You're mad, and you're sick, and you need help, more than I. How would you know about my dealings with the bloody Disciples?"

Ivory laughed and reached into his pocket for a business card. He extended it. Just like the circus's tickets, it was pitch black with scarlet and white lettering. It read IVORY TODD - SPIRITUALIST - THE BLACK CARNIVAL.

"The naivety of your youth shows itself, Mr. Graves. To be fair, I wasn't sure it would. You think your troubles are yours alone. I knew the moment I saw your left hand." Ivory nodded at Atherton's scars. "You're not the only one who's paid a price for the malice of Mason Cross." He raised his wooden hand and clicked his tongue. "I understand that you are suspicious of what I might do with Betty. Understand that, under the care of my wife and me, the remains of this poor girl will do far more than feed the worms."

Atherton reached out to take the card.

Just when Ivory felt the boy's fingers pinch and pull, he gripped it hard, locking him there. "You aren't alone in this," he said. Only when he saw that sink in did he let go, the relenting force causing Atherton to catch himself on his heels. His gray eyes brimmed with confusion and misplaced loathing.

"First, you ask me questions whose answers you have no right to," Atherton huffed. "Then you attempt to buy off a stiff. And for what purpose? An anatomist has no use for a body this far decayed. What did you have in mind? Popping bits of her into pickling jars for a freak show?"

Ivory was amused. "That was the fourth time you insulted me since we met, so long as we're counting. But, no. I assure you, it would be nothing of the sort. We'd both be long in the ground ourselves before you guessed correctly."

"I'm keener than most give me credit for."

"That I don't doubt. Which is how I know you won't be sharing our conversation."

Atherton sighed. "Now, why would that be, Mr. Todd?"

Ivory stepped closer and dropped his voice to a murmur, as though it were a secret even Betty shouldn't hear. "Because in your heart of hearts, you know we exist in the same world. A world of restless pasts, of shades who whisper in our ears and caress our bones. And though you lack conviction for God, you've tasted the Devil on your tongue. Held his hand, felt his shadow in the brightest of days. Even in the most crowded spaces, you feel alone. And alone, well," Ivory scoffed, "truly alone, that is something you never are—in the worst of ways. Our work with the dead is a plague, Atherton Graves, and there is no cure. That alone binds us."

Ivory watched his words crawl over Atherton like a brood of freshly hatched spiders. Already they were burrowing, itching into crevices where they would lie, dormant, ready to reemerge long after that conversation ended. Ivory knew this with as much certainty as he knew why the young undertaker's eyes wandered to something behind him—something more unsettling than a stranger unearthing parts of his soul that he himself didn't understand.

He sensed her, too.

Atherton's voice came hollow. Small. Missing that indignation which so easily slipped between his teeth moments before. "I fear I have work of great import to tend to. I suspect you do as well. The circus opens tomorrow evening, does it not?"

"Indeed, it does. You ought to stop by. Perhaps you can see some of those parlor tricks you're so fond of."

Athreton just scoffed, turning to leave.

If the boy wasn't an uncanny incarnation of Ivory's younger self, down to the brooding willfulness, Ivory might've let it go. After all, he had enough responsibilities. But he knew just how ruinous this gift could be, and just how doomed Atherton was the longer he tried to convince himself it wasn't real.

Even then, he stood with a head bowed, prepared to make himself forget. Then he remembered how the muzzle of his own revolver had felt cold against his temple, how it promised eternal reprieve. The millimeter of pressure that he somehow resisted in his own finger, the oblivion that nearly sprayed through his skull, and all the torments he no longer regretted having survived since then. He was around Atherton's age when it all became too much.

Ivory gripped Atherton's arm and squeezed hard. "Indulge me once more, then never again, if you must. You stand on strong principles, Mr. Graves. Integrity. Stoicism. Reverence. I only hope you see that, at this moment, they do not serve you. You say you are a man without faith. You haven't prayed in some time, then. But when was the last time you asked questions? About the work you do, about the kind of person that makes you. The things only you see. The words only you hear. If you ever need help asking those questions, you know where to find me."

The stinging winds coerced a single tear from Atherton's eye. "Good day, Mr. Todd."

7

ATHERTON
MAY 8, 1886

An empty bottle of laudanum lay beside the glass of whisky on Atherton's nightstand. Even with the opium, faces crowded his dreams, and murmurs of the dead lingered in his ears. Like wine, their madness matured, self-cannibalizing and rotting.

He'd seen Betty and Alice in the shadows. They crept into his room, bringing with them the fresh soil that he'd packed around their coffins. It was only after he managed to fall asleep that they moved to lie beside him, to watch him writhe in his dreams.

But it was morning now.

Atherton stood and drank in the crisp air from his window. His mother's garden was just below. He breathed in amaryllis and roses, strong enough to mask the smell of their dead room down the hall. At his dressing table was his washbowl. Mason's straight razor, his own timepiece, and Ivory's business card lay beside it. Looking over the card, Atherton thought about what he might do with five pounds. He thought about what the spiritualist had said, about what an American conman from a traveling circus could do with a corpse halfway rotted to Hell. Atherton splashed his face with cold water and dragged a razor across his stubble. Looking in the mirror, he didn't see greed in his gray eyes, but curiosity.

It was midmorning by the time he left for the circus, the smell of freshly cut grass permeating the circus grounds. Birdsong and the buzz of insect wings overlapped with workers talking over breakfast. A gentle breeze wafted the tails of Atherton's black necktie.

He didn't get far. The entrance gates were bolted. An aroma of buttered potatoes, sizzling pork, and lobster made his stomach growl against the only thing he'd had that morning—tea and tobacco. Ever since the circus arrived, New Sarum's butcher shops and bakeries were selling out of their staples before noon.

A clown in a monstrous fool's cap caught him standing there. He held three juggling clubs in one hand; in the other, a single, half-eaten sausage dangled from a fork. His monochrome makeup gave him an odd, if not intimidating, expression. It was faded from the night before, or perhaps applied hastily that same morning, as suggested by the smears on his fingertips. Black tights and a plain, white shirt outlined his toned frame, one of his suspenders hanging free.

The two stared at each other for some time, rather like a pair of critters who hadn't expected the sudden collision.

Realizing the clown had lost interest and was headed elsewhere, Atherton stammered, "I-I'm here to see one of your performers. Your spiritualist, I believe."

The clown stopped. Oil ran down his chin after taking a large bite. "The gates open at sunset," was all he said.

"No, you misunderstand. I'm here on business. Ivory Todd—he expressly invited me. We met yesterday. Here." Atherton produced the card and held it out.

The clown remained silent. He drew forward to inspect the card through the gates, making Atherton feel like he was goading a squirrel with a nut.

The clown's dark eyes lingered on the fresh scars on his left hand, only to settle on his face, studying him as he finished his sausage. Atherton never thought it possible to feel insecure staring down someone in full clown makeup.

Just as he was about to retreat, the clown unlatched the gate and swung it far enough to let Atherton in before locking it again. Atherton stood a head shorter than the clown, whose body was toned by what Atherton assumed was his training as an aerialist and acrobat.

"I'll take you to him," the clown said, tapping him on the back with a club. "This way."

"It is remarkable work you've done here," Atherton said, observing the dozens of tents. The varied heights and widths and careful placement made it feel rather like stepping into a small town with its own alleys and squares. Tightropes and trapeze nets were strung up like webbing. Lantern posts and food stands solidified the odd sense of permanency. "What has it been? Three days?"

"In circus, nothing is impossible," the clown replied. "Ours in particular caters to taboo tastes. Somebody of your nature, for example. Ideal. After dark, this place gleams like the night sky. You would hardly recognize it. And the music—the music will break your heart. After the aerialists make it beat out of your chest, that is." Although a nomadic performer in patched clothing, the clown spoke as if he grew up in a library, his accent marred by a rasp like a thin layer of dust. But there was no mistaking his pride when he said, "It's been my home for a decade."

"That's charming and all, but how would you know my nature? I don't even know your name."

"Boo," the clown said simply. "If Ivory has any business with you, that means you are an undertaker or a resurrectionist. Am I wrong?"

"No," Atherton admitted. "It's the former."

"The smell gave you away." Boo winked.

Atherton stole a moment to sniff his lapel and underarm. "Consequences of the trade."

"How is it, burying the dead?"

"I was born into it. Sometimes it feels as though I know it too well. Then again, I suppose most everyone bears the weight of burdens they never asked for. How did you find yourself here?"

Boo hummed. "I was adopted into it. Before that, I was another orphan of Whitechapel. Lester Black, our proprietor, took me in herself. Pulled me from a place blacker still."

"What place is blacker than the alleys of Whitechapel?"

The clown declined to answer. "We're nearly there," was all he said.

Walking between the tents quieted Atherton. It was one thing—seeing them from a distance. Standing beneath them, they were cathedrals of canvas and stripes. Though each had a scarlet flag, some flagstaffs were punctuated with symbols he didn't recognize. Here and there, entertainers behind tent flaps were practicing routines.

They arrived in a kind of courtyard, with tents and several food stands making up the outer ring. The tent closest to them was smaller in comparison only to the big top, reserved for finales and simultaneous acts. Atherton had to crane his neck just to see the signage. Painted in bold, scarlet print rimmed with gold, it read, *The Flying Maffickers*.

"This one is my favorite."

Atherton spotted the aerialists through the flaps. Trapezes, silks, and steel hoops hung from rigging high above, the performers contorting around the apparatuses. Climbing, inverting, and dropping with control. Atherton heard a catcher on a trapeze shout, *"Hep!"* signaling a flyer to leap off the board on the opposite side. The flyer swung from the trapeze once, and at the apex of her next, let go of the bar, hurtling in the air.

Boo stepped in front of the flaps and cleared his throat. "Wouldn't want to ruin the show," he said. "Perhaps this evening, should you return. It's the best bull you'll ever spend. You may even catch me in one of the acts."

Atherton neglected to inform Boo that he had, in fact, a pair of tickets, thanks to a certain deceased and nameless body in his backwoods. "Certainly," he replied.

The clown pointed across the courtyard. Calluses decorated every finger. "Ivory's tent is that one over there."

A quarter of the size of the aerialist's tent, it was just large enough to fit an intimate stage and four dozen seats. *The Spirit Asylum*, as it was called, was bordered by two tall lamp posts with lanterns. Banners hung beneath them, one with an anatomically correct human body, and the other an illustration of a skeleton holding up its own skin.

Unlike the Flying Maffickers, the Spirit Asylum had a sigil at the top of its flagstaff.

Reaching into his waistcoat pocket, Atherton examined the pendant pulled from Alice's throat and compared it. He turned back and began hastily, "Do you know what this…" only to find that Boo had disappeared inside, the flaps to his tent tied shut from within.

Atherton walked through the empty courtyard. Though he was distracted by the sights, as he neared the tent, the entrance lanterns sputtered to life with a quiet gust. But the sound was lost to a breeze, and the confused train of thoughts whistling through his mind.

8

ATHERTON
MAY 9, 1886

Atherton found solace in a ritual he often performed before entering the homes of cases he knew would mark him indelibly. Suicides. Double murders. Bodies that had been left unattended for months. He massaged his hands, closed his eyes, and steadied himself with a few deep breaths.

That's when he heard an odd melody croaking through a phonograph. It filled the Spirit Asylum, as lively as it was twirling with sadness, and coaxed him through the tent flaps. A Romani tune composed mostly of string instruments, the song was looping as Ivory tinkered with pieces of a machine. Its parts were spread across his desk at the center of the stage, a meticulous disorder. Sporting a pair of goggles with loupes and magnifiers, Ivory didn't so much as glance in his direction.

Atherton ventured to break him from the trance. "Mr. Todd?"

Ivory jumped, replacing his goggles with spectacles. As soon as he saw who it was, his incisors gleamed. "Well, if it isn't Mr. Graves. What a pleasure. Bold of you to traipse in here in the dead of night. No less fitting, of course, given your intentions."

"Dead of night?" The undertaker checked his pocket watch. "It's half past ten, sir. In the morning, that is."

Ivory peered through the haze of tobacco smoke and incense, glimpsing the thin ray of light piercing between the tent flaps. "So it is. No matter."

"A long night, then?"

"Unending, apparently. And with a fully booked show this evening. Joyous!" Ivory slammed his fist against the table. Cranks and cogs jumped in unison, and a piece of newspaper with a small pile of black licorice fell to the ground.

"My apologies, sir."

"Save it. The constables aren't around. Dispense with the niceties. But you deserve a degree of decorum, don't you? Coming to test the boundaries of your virtue, and here I am, raving. The price of passion, as it were," he said as he gestured to his table, "a thousand lifetimes wouldn't suffice. Goodness." Ivory polished off a shot of gin before switching off the phonograph.

"May I ask what this contraption is?"

"Should it ever function properly, I believe I will call it a ticket dispenser."

Struggling to find the use in replacing a man with a complex machine for a simple task, Atherton nodded with feigned enthusiasm. "Fascinating. I had no idea a spiritualist had use for engineering."

"Who in their right mind is only one thing, after all? I'm afraid after many years of parading around for audiences, I've become unfulfilled by the gasps and guffaws of the rubes. But you are not here to listen to the woes of an old hack. How did you get in here, this time of day?"

"A clown with a rather large, uhm, cap," Atherton made ambiguous shapes with his hand above his head, "I'm afraid I've already forgotten his name."

"Boo?" Ivory clarified, his face scrunching up as if it left a bad taste in his mouth.

"Yes. He let me in. Rather welcoming, isn't he? Thank you." The undertaker took a piece of licorice that was offered and bit into the soft confection. Spiced molasses and anise coated his tongue.

Ivory snorted. "Welcoming, right. It's good that you have some humor about it. Most don't take kindly to his eccentricity. Boo isn't his real name, mind you. I wouldn't be surprised if he's forgotten whatever preceded it. He hardly talks to the rest of us, let alone a stranger. And he's been here longer than I have, if you can believe that."

"Perhaps I caught him in a good mood. He was in no short supply of words."

"Pocket it. This small talk is unnerving me, and you're here on business."

Atherton opened his cigarette case and plucked one out. Ivory struck a match and lit it for him.

Sitting at the edge of the stage, he looked as though choosing his next words would cost him the rest of his strength. "If I recall correctly, five pounds was my offer. As you likely know, it's a fortune for a case that far gone. Still, for the sake of the men who will do the hauling, we pay less for messier cases. Or indeed, charge more if we are assisting in disposal—well, you don't need to know that." Ivory took a deep drag and waved away the remark with the smoke. "Call it a service fee. You understand. Luckily, I've taken a shine to you. So, four pound is my final offer, on account of you saying some things in awful taste yesterday."

"For which I apologize. But I will consider your offer. That is, if you accept my terms."

Ivory's piercing inquisitiveness returned, as he had displayed when they first met.

"And what would that be, Mr. Graves?"

"I wish to know what it is you intend to do with her remains."

Ivory chuckled. "Most boys your age, you put four pounds in their pocket, they go skipping right along to the whorehouse quicker than a jackrabbit."

"Betty died in my city. Was buried in my cemetery. Was lowered into the earth by my hands. That makes her my responsibility."

"*Betty* is gone. Hell, she's damn near unrecognizable. And don't give me any of that reverence-for-the-dead runaround. You're as jaded as they come."

"Perhaps that is true. But with all due respect, regardless of the case, Mr. Todd, none of this makes much sense. Why does a circus want a corpse? Even resurrectionists are going out of fashion with anatomists nowadays."

"While that may be true, you can save your breath, boy-o. There's nothing I can disclose that you won't dismiss as madness, and no amount of reassurance that will convince you of our good intentions. Well, there might be one thing." Ivory stood and strode backstage.

Outside, the circus was rising to meet the day's work. Hollers and conversation muddied the air.

The spiritualist reappeared with a fistful of sovereigns.

Four coins spilled into Atherton's hand.

"How's that for trust?"

Atherton's protests faltered at the small pile of wealth. His thanks fell to a shameful whisper, pausing longer still before pocketing the coins.

"You want some advice? Take this matter to your grave. Let it waste away in memory. That's all there is to do. Stay quiet, and our business will remain concluded."

Trepidation writhed in Atherton's stomach, thinking of what Mason would do if he caught wind of this. And when he met Ivory's eyes, he knew that that feeling was not his alone.

"Certainly, Mr. Todd. Certainly," Atherton said. "But if I am to forget this, I must ask you something. If you wanted the body yourself, why report it at all? She was by the city limits. Away from prying eyes. Alone. You could've kept your four pounds and had the case yourself."

Looking away from Atherton, Ivory fiddled with the fingers of his prosthesis, posing them to make more bizarre gestures. "I was honest from the moment we met. Our work with the dead binds us in ways you do not realize, or indeed, do not want to realize. You may choose to ignore it, but I do not."

Every time Ivory spoke like this, it felt like a black fog filled Atherton's mind. A fog of anger and distrust. All he could think about were the conversations he overheard between his grandfather and father as a child. The shouting matches. Grandpa would murmur stories to him at night that made his skin crawl, just the way Ivory's words did. The same ones his father scorned as ravings. The same ones he forbade him to speak about with Atherton. The same ones his father wouldn't suffer coming from his own son.

Visitors, Grandpa called them.

Atherton just stood there, flinching and massaging his hands.

"But you won't hear that, will you?" Ivory sighed, shaking his head. "Fine. I'll give you the answer you want. One can never be too careful. Perhaps she had relatives in high places, and they'd turn the city over, looking for her. Trust me, boy, when folks like us post up with tents, we get blamed for half the mess everyone else gets into."

Atherton lingered on that answer. "Right," he said with a halfhearted chuckle. "I should've thought of that."

"Go on. I can see it eating at you. That wasn't all you wanted to ask me."

Nodding, Atherton dug something out from his waistcoat pocket—a pendant of tarnished silver. "Would you tell me what this is? It's the same symbol on the flagstaff of your tent."

The gin and exhaustion fled Ivory. He took the emblem from Atherton's palm, turning it over. "So it is. Where did you come by it?"

"A decedent."

"*Decedent*," Ivory mocked playfully. "How polite. I'm not one of your clients, you know. So, a corpse. Whoever they were, they must have been a practicing Gehennic. A devout one, at that."

Atherton's brows furrowed. "That's not possible."

"Not probable, you mean. Maybe the time of burning witches is behind us, but people still frown on followers of ol' Blackcoat. Gehennics are partial to their privacy. I can speak to that, being one myself. You don't practice magic, do you?"

"No, sir."

"Good." Ivory flicked the emblem up like a coin. The metal rang in the air before landing back into Atherton's hands. "It's a sigil. Some Gehennics wear them at the time of passing, in the hopes of watching over their family for some time before they go beyond the veil."

"Does it work?"

"Work? You ask this as though you believe in such a thing. When you play with the beyond, the beyond plays with you. How's that for an answer? If that satisfies, I have shows to prepare for, Mr. Graves. It'd be best if you were on your way. I'm sure there's some poor fellow who's punched his last ticket." The spiritualist got up, walking toward the backstage.

"Mr. Todd," Atherton protested. "Yesterday, you told me that Betty was a thread. A thread of hundreds tied to me. Were you saying that to frighten me? A tactic to convince me to sell her to you?" When Ivory didn't reply, he added, "No. You meant it, didn't you?"

This seemed to test Ivory's patience. He drummed his foot on the stage, lifted his arms, and let them slap against his thighs as though Atherton had missed his chance. "I really must rest before my work this evening," he said with a forced gentleness. "Perhaps we can discuss this another time."

Atherton nodded in defeat.

"Good. Tonight, our men will be at your cemetery to exhume the body. They are professionals and will have repacked the earth before you can say 'interred.' Don't attempt to help them. It'll only draw attention."

"That's it, then? Put this all behind me; pretend none of it happened?"

"Precisely. Act your age and come enjoy the shows. Surely there's a lady you can bring along. Or, gentleman, of course. You'll find no judgment here. Circus folk have always enjoyed a more liberated sexuality. Ah, I see it in you! There is someone, isn't there?"

"There's no chance, sir. She'd never agree to it. Nor could I come tonight, even if she agreed. I have business at the mortuary that needs tending to."

"Tomorrow, then. A man who spends most of his waking life with the dead should never be afraid to live, Mr. Graves. Lest you become that kind of man who finds himself having arrived at old age, thinking his pessimism has safeguarded him from regrets, only to find it has poisoned even his happiest memories." Before Atherton could pipe up with another excuse, the spiritualist held up a finger. "Listen. Nobody likes a coward."

9

ATHERTON
MAY 10, 1886

"Coward. Bastard buys a rotted cadaver for a month's pay and calls me a coward. I have a word for him. Madman." Atherton scoffed and lit a cigarette. While Atherton waited outside the Queen's Gate, screams, giggles, and laughter emanated from the throng of bodies as it flowed toward the glowing maw of the Black Carnival. Amidst that crowd were nobles, smithies, and butchers, the varying classes unified in their desire to indulge in the forbidden, the scandalous, and the otherworldly.

Atherton's legs felt as though they were hinged on a single, faulty screw. Despite the chill in the evening breeze and spirited air, perspiration drenched his socks. Even the bouquet in his hands was wilting. But there was one merciful distraction from the thought of his company that evening. The clown was right—after nightfall, the circus was another entity entirely. Its radiant candescence could make the deaf hear music.

His eyes were first drawn to the tightropes suspended between tents; acrobats and tumblers moved about them as though the single cables were whole stages. Clubs, rings, and balls cascaded beneath the starless sky— the jugglers obscured by the towering tents. A lamppost with three heads burned gold, silver, and scarlet at the entrance, pulsing a slow heartbeat. It illuminated the giant, double-gated entrance swallowing people by the handful. Guarding it was none other than Boo, taking tickets and ushering them in. Even from this distance, Atherton recognized his hat. With each accepted ticket, a small burst of flames spewed inexplicably from Boo's hands, marking the entrance of every guest.

Atherton remembered the spiritualist, doubtlessly in the midst of a seance at that moment, and thought about Betty's grave in his cemetery, emptied the night before. And four. That number burned in his mind. Betty had been the fourth child in less than a month that he'd ushered into the earth.

"I'm curious. Do you keep the dead waiting this long when they require your attention?" A gentle squeeze on Atherton's arm pulled him from his thoughts.

Lilian's shoulder-length, curly, black hair bordered a wide smile with a subtle touch of rouge. Rimmed by dark, sooted lashes, her eyes arrested his. Tucked into a long, black skirt, her gray blouse with ruffled collar was accented by a cardinal bow. Beneath the glowing gaslight, her warm touch compelled Atherton's heart to stutter like the frantic flight of a dying moth.

"I must confess, I needed a moment to collect myself. What the dead wait for is beyond what I can do for what they leave behind," he said.

"And what of the living?"

"The living? I'm afraid that's outside my expertise. They're seldom my concern."

"You would do well to start practicing, then. Are those for me?" she asked, pointing at his bouquet of amaryllis. "I believe it's customary that I hold them. But here, I have something for you."

Lilian revealed a boutonniere of flowering nightshade. She brought it up to his lapel, having him hold it out for her to secure it, only for Atherton to draw back with a sharp gasp when the pin pricked his thumb instead.

"Oh! Goodness me." Withdrawing a handkerchief from her purse, she dabbed at the blood before pocketing it again.

"Our first night out and you've already drawn blood." He laughed.

"Well, you can't say I'm boring." She grinned, pinning the flowers to his vest. "I trust you'll find it in your heart to forgive me. Come, let's see if we can't forget the dead for an evening."

The pair had never enjoyed each other's company at such a late hour. All of Atherton's visits had been beneath the guise of polite gestures or even a professional expression of concern regarding her grieving process. But it had been nearly a year since Mr. Butler passed. The platonic excuses for requesting her company were dwindling. When she accepted the invitation he'd managed to murmur his way through. It had taken all his willpower not to whoop and holler through the city streets. He did that privately, at his mortuary.

Lilian took Atherton's arm in hers. She did this in total silence with a smirk, as if that action alone testified to their mutual abandonment of innocent pretence. He recoiled at first, and even swallowed a half-hearted protest. Cold, stiff, slimy—that was the kind of touch he was accustomed to.

The lights ahead swam and melded with the starry sky. Between his truncated responses to her small talk, he hoped to appear more composed than one of her orphans. As they neared the entrance gates, their exchange slowed.

Now hanging from the lanterns by his legs, Boo waited with an expectant gaze. The prongs of his fool's cap seemed to writhe of their own volition. The clown's lips now matched the dark paint stretching down his cheeks.

The undertaker stammered a greeting and produced his tickets. They emerged from his pocket like dust balls. Their faded lettering was beyond recognition, with the barest odor of that foul place from where they were first found.

Taking the tickets, a burst of cinders erupted from the clown's hands. The flames engulfed the paper in tiny, fiery jaws before spewing them back out, setting their faces alight in the intimacy of that odd exchange. With those bright ashes swirling toward the night sky, Boo said, "Welcome to the Black Carnival, Mr. Graves."

The couple wandered the grounds for a long while before exploring any of the tents. Along the paths, hanging lanterns cast faces in soft shades of amber and silver. An upbeat Romani melody roamed the air—a violin and accordion spilling out to a bombastic rhythm. The deeper they went, the more distant Atherton's troubles felt. In the glow of the carnival, the harsh edges of his memories dulled, any looming worries now shrinking to the size of a pin.

Before long, they purchased a showing to the Cascading Perils, a spacious tent where tiny, innumerable lights made the ceiling appear like a sky bespattered with stars. A ring of flames around a circular stage cast the performance troupe's silhouettes along the striped walls, surrounding the audience with shadowy titans. Three jugglers managed cascades of five clubs each, and three others with five orbs of glittering glass. Their patterns shifted, the objects taking flight in varying heights and arcs. Later, they selected a volunteer to stand beneath a pattern of seven swords managed between two jugglers, spinning in a hypnotic formation with a watch's precision.

Cinnamon and sugar coated Atherton's tongue as he bit into an apple fritter obtained from a cart before the show began.

"Have you ever felt guilt over a great relief?" Lilian asked.

Atherton wiped his fingers with his handkerchief before pocketing it again. "Evidently, the jugglers have not arrested your attention."

"They've done well enough. I confess, my mind wanders in and out at the most unlikely places."

That moment was sweeter to him than any confection. Murmuring low between the applause of the crowd, it seemed their words were shrouded in secrecy. "To answer your question," Atherton said, "I would first ask for what relief could there be a measure of equal guilt? Could you call such a thing relief at all?"

"Then I might ask you what is a husband who causes equal pain as he does companionship? Could you call such a person a partner?"

Atherton pretended to be distracted by the show to ponder his response. By then, torches being passed over a child performer had been added to the routine. Instead of balls, four disfigured human skulls bounced blithely between her two tiny hands. The other jugglers on stage knelt with hands held aloft toward her as she took the center.

"...bones purchased from St. George's medical college in London!" one of the ringmasters boasted to the crowd.

"You mean to say Mr. Butler's passing?" Atherton finally asked. "You grieved, Lilian—I remember that well."

A crowd member introduced a fifth skull into the child's act. After holding the pattern, she threw up all five objects, pirouetting before collecting them all. While the audience went to their feet with applause, Atherton and Lilian remained seated, heads bowed together.

"The loss of love is not the only cause of grief. We grieve for ourselves, don't we? The ghosts of our past selves, locked in those memories we failed to protect them from, now made to bear that torment forever. You understand, don't you, Atherton?"

Her fingers slid into his. She was close enough now that he could smell the cinnamon on her breath. The sweetness in his own mouth disintegrated to dust, and he swallowed, incapable of managing any thought besides that of pressing his lips against hers. "Certainly, I do."

"Another round for Simza the Skull Juggler!" the ringmaster roared.

Getting to his feet and joining the applause, Atherton peered through the hollering crowd to spot the child smiling gleefully with her armful of deathly visages, taking her bows.

❦

After Lilian had put her hand in his, Atherton made sure to keep it there as much as possible. They rejoined the sea of guests out in the grounds, now decorated with discarded handbills and popcorn bags.

"Where to next?" she asked. "I've heard their mirror house inspires sheer terror."

"Perhaps later. But this one here—I know one of the performers," he insisted, guiding her into the tent of the Flying Maffickers.

They'd arrived late to the performance. A Russian swing molded with an iron goat's head like a battering ram was positioned at the far corner of the tent, launching acrobats into the air toward a flying trapeze rig and netting. Drums and horns from the accompanying orchestra sounded as they took flight, imitating canon fire. They connected with catchers swinging from trapeze bars. Atherton pointed out Boo, still sporting his cap as he was pitched into the air, gliding like a sparrow in the silver spotlight. The clown tucked into a ball, flipping twice before his hands clapped with a cloud of chalk onto the wrists of a catcher.

The performance took on a more cautious pace when the show transitioned to an aerial fabric act. Choreographed dances—with scarlet silk used in the expression of blood—portrayed a gristly battle between thirteen artists. From what Atherton could see, Boo was the antagonist, his demise illustrated by his falling from the zenith of his apparatus, only to stop his descent abruptly just above the stage, rather like a hanging. His limp body swayed over the audience, eliciting a mixture of horrified gasps and applause from the spectators.

The imagery sent Atherton into memories of that night in the backwoods with the ghoul. His swaying feet and noose-gnarled neck. The despair in his milky eyes. The stolen tickets that brought him here.

He brought his hands together slowly, a hollow mimicry of the applause gaining momentum about him.

Boo came back to life and leapt to the ground, grinning broadly with a hand held aloft, summoning more praise.

A playful melody tinkling from the musicians heralded the end of the show, with the rest of the performers joining Boo on the stage. As they took their bows, a ringmaster opened the entrance of the tent. His mock hussar uniform was adorned with bones—animal jaws decorating his shoulders bobbed as he guided the audience out. Outside, the lights were a balm to the undertaker's memories. The performers mingled with the crowds before the next show.

Boo sat atop a stack of grates, enjoying a cigarette and eyeing the couple. The undertaker managed a nervous wave before averting his gaze.

"The Spirit Asylum with Ivory the Ghost Courter," Lilian read aloud. "I could do with something quieter."

Glancing in the direction she pointed, Atherton chuckled and shook his head. "Smoke and mirrors, Lilian. Spiritualists are con men, nothing more."

The courtyard where Atherton was just a day before had been barren. Now it hosted a ring of artists, including a stilt walker and unicyclist teetering over the guests, both dressed in elaborate plague doctor garments.

"I see I've touched upon something of a sore point."

"I'd be damned if some recluse with a scrying orb and a flair for theater understands the ever after any better than I do. It drove my grandfather mad, this sort of thing."

Despite his protests, Lilian pulled him toward Ivory's tent. "Don't you believe in ghosts?" she asked, trailing a finger down his hand.

Once more, he was trapped in a sensation he could hardly endure yet adored—confined in her black eyes. In their reflection, he saw the burst of a fire eater's draconic exhalation. A tumbler executing a back handspring on a tightrope.

He wondered if she could feel his hammering heart.

"Ghosts?" he whispered.

"Yes. The restless dead come to haunt us."

"Everybody is haunted by something, Lilian."

She took up both his hands, pulling him closer still.

"That wasn't the question," she said.

"The dead are in our dreams. Our memories. The ones we cherish or regret the most. That is where ghosts reside."

"Is that what you tell yourself?"

This time, when she inched closer, he felt her exhalations against his lips. "I thought you said we'd forget the dead for an evening."

"A white lie. So, will you brave the Asylum with me?" she asked, pulling away.

Atherton ground his teeth for not seizing that moment. "Brave? What are we braving? A charlatan's trick?"

"Well, now you've shown your cards. You're frightened, aren't you?"

"The dead are my daily business. This attraction is tedious at best to my sensibilities."

"Your sensibilities?" she mocked. "But how will you prove to me you're as brave as I think you are?"

"I don't need to prove anything."

Lilian arched an eyebrow.

Scowling, Atherton pushed through the tent flaps. The small stage was as he remembered it—only the table upon it was tidied, and seats were arranged in cascading tiers, rather like that of an operating theater at a medical college. With a packed house, they were left to stand on the sides among stifling cigar smoke and perfumes.

Before he saw him through the smoke, Atherton heard Ivory's voice filling the tent with a disciplined confidence. His words soothed him with their deep timbre and gravelly inflection.

"...assure you that nothing in this tent is safe. What you will witness here tonight may mark you indelibly. This is not so much a show as it is a public exhibition of a growing body of respected science..."

Ivory sported a neat waistcoat, shirt, and necktie as he addressed the audience. He paced around a table on the stage, spectacles glittering from silvery light exuding from glass orbs placed around a talking board. Unlike the other entertainers, his makeup was tame by comparison, with only slight contour and subtle, smoky eyeshadow on his eyelids.

"Oh, a talking board!" Lilian patted Atherton's arm excitedly.

Atherton could sense that his presence had been noticed. Ivory, in his addressing the crowd, paused and eyed him. He flashed the same smile he gave when the undertaker had visited his tent just days before. Atherton pretended not to notice as others turned to see where the spiritualist's attention had gone.

Sitting at the table was a young girl from the audience, a locket of hair in one of her outstretched palms. Black and red candles were afloat throughout the open air, and Atherton was tempted to outstretch his hand to feel for wires, but thought better.

"Mrs. Manfre," the spiritualist called with his hands on the shoulders of his guest, "my name is Ivory Todd. Your daughter is with us, and she comes with questions. If you would be so kind, move the planchette to indicate your presence."

Only seconds later, the wooden piece slithered across the board to *Yes*, arousing a wave of gasps.

Lilian's face lit with enthusiasm, and she joined the crowd in applause.

Ivory cut it short, holding up the prosthesis that replaced his left hand. "Let us not startle our most welcome guest," he said. "I'd ask you all for your continued silence. Now. What would you like to ask your mother, my dear?"

"Are you safe where you are?" the girl asked.

No.

At this, the audience forgot Ivory's admonishment, all but leaping from their seats to watch the board in stupefaction. The girl looked up to the spiritualist for guidance, who merely gestured to the table.

"Are you happy?" the girl stammered.

The planchette jittered, but remained on *No*.

Following another outburst, Ivory hollered, "Ladies and gentlemen, please, please!" Then his expression shifted, possessed by a smoldering bitterness. He took off his spectacles. "Are you so naive? Would you be so presumptuous as to think the passage between life and death is but some great catharsis? No. Heed our guest."

"Mother," the girl's voice trembled. "Where are you to go? Why have you not found your seat in heaven?"

Atherton clutched a nearby pole supporting the tent. His fingertips had gone cold. A low burning started in his lower abdomen—or rather, *against* it. It grew to a white flame. His vision blurred, Ivory's slow pacing appearing like the gentle hovering of a phantom. Atherton's breaths arrived haggard. The forms on the stage melted, coming apart and duplicating, until there were not two or three but nearly a dozen.

"Are you well?" Lilian whispered. "You've gone pale."

"I'm just fine." Atherton wiped the sweat from his upper lip.

"Exciting, isn't it?" she asked, squeezing his arm.

He gave a stiff nod.

There was a lengthy pause. Ivory drummed his fingers against his prosthesis.

"The spirit has left!" someone in the audience declared, only to be met by a *shhh!*

Then the planchette rattled and slid across the board, this time for the alphabet.

Moving over each character, a light trail of smoke, just visible, escaped upwards in the shape of its corresponding letter.

GEHENNA.

Equal parts horror and amusement filled the air in a booming uproar. The board flew from the table, sending the planchette into a gentleman who yelped, thrusting it aside as though it were a hot coal.

"Honored guests!" Ivory bellowed, "The connection has not been severed. It is merely your outburst that has upset her!"

"I need some air," Atherton said, moving to leave.

"But he's just said—"

"You needn't follow me."

Atherton fled the tent, gulping in the night air. He pulled a cigarette from his steel case and tucked it between his lips. His shaking fingers struggled with the match. Once the flame caught, he drew in deeply, the glow of smoldering tobacco arching the shadows of his cheekbones.

But the burning in his abdomen remained. It became unendurable.

He reached into his waistcoat pocket and dug out its contents to find the culprit. Between the sovereigns and shillings, he found it—the six-pointed pendant—the metal scalding beside the lukewarm coins. Having separated it from the funds, he flung it into the grass.

"Bloody thing," he murmured.

"Does it hurt?" a small voice piped up.

Atherton looked around, then down to see a child in clown paint staring up at him. Wearing a torn, striped tutu and ballet garb, she danced around him. Despite the innocence of her grin, her watchful yet hollow, dark eyes, and gaunt cheeks summoned the taste of iron in his mouth. She moved about as though the grass were as smooth as lacquered wood.

"You saw what happened?"

The child nodded. Her lips moved but issued no sound. As he focused on her, time itself seemed to coagulate. One moment, she was tugging on his trousers. The next, she was watching from a distance, only to return to his side.

Atherton clenched his eyes shut and shook his head.

Narrowing his attention, his gaze seemed to at last hold her in place. The innumerable faces and chaotic sounds of the mingling crowds blurred, turning to little more than a carousel of shadows and garbled voices.

"That piece of jewelry," he said, pointing to the grass, "burned me. What do you know about it?"

The child leaned forward, beckoning him closer. With her lips almost brushing his ear, a torrent of whispers came forth. The only words he made out were, "The flowers are cruel."

"Flowers?"

"Atherton, is everything all right?"

He stumbled backwards. There was no making sense of it.

The child had disappeared, and in her place stood Lilian with concern furrowing her delicate brows. The sequence of events collided in one patchwork recollection, feeling chopped and rearranged. Murmurs of things the girl had never said to him still seemed to coil about his head.

Blinking rapidly, he pushed past Lilian and searched the crowds. "How long have you been standing there?"

"Why, I've just come from the tent not a moment ago."

"That child. The clown ballerina. Where has she gone?"

"What child? Clown ballerina?" Lilian laughed, then put a hand against Atherton's forehead. "Heavens, you're burning up."

"Never mind that. Did you see her? Did you see the little girl?"

Lilian looked around. The audience had just finished flushing out of the Spirit Asylum. "I may have just missed her. Has she upset you? You should mind your trousers. I hear circuses like these have pickpockets."

Atherton patted down his pockets halfheartedly. "No, not at all, I just...has the show finished already?"

"It's been nearly a half-hour since you left."

"Half-hour?" Atherton huffed, running a hand through his now disheveled hair.

"Are you truly well? I shouldn't have pushed you. That was wrong of me."

He frowned, realizing he'd also somehow forgotten his cigarette, untouched and cold. "No. It must have been the crowd. All the excitement."

"Well, if it isn't the man who sold me a dog. Hello, Atherton Graves." Ivory emerged from his tent with a top hat and an expression of equal parts annoyance and amusement, still sporting that smile that appeared more wicked than the arch in the Devil's pronged tail. "I'd shake your hand, but the last time I did that, you robbed me blind."

"Sold you a dog? I've done nothing of the sort." He even squeaked with a laugh that was choked in his throat, expecting that Ivory was merely toying with him in front of his date.

"Let's drop the performance, Shakespeare. You've had your fun."

"You two know each other?" Lilian asked.

"Hardly," Atherton scoffed. "Mr. Todd here is terribly confused."

"Know each other? Regrettably so, I'm afraid. But me, confused? About this man before me, certainly not. I will admit it was entertaining, finding that you'd conned me faster than a dollymop on a bastard full up to the knocker. If it weren't over four pounds, I'd consider forgiveness. But please," he said with a laugh, "I'm not here to embarrass you in such refined company. Forgive me; Atherton's only spoken highly of you, miss. Not that I can vouch for him in turn, given he's revealed his true nature."

With a bemused expression, Lilian allowed her hand to be taken.

"*True* nature? Yet here you stand accusing me of a crime I've not the slightest clue of committing!" Atherton retorted.

"Now, now, let's keep our voices down. I'm not here to start a fight. Or a *row,* as you Englishmen call it. You may be a thief, but we can handle this like gentlemen, can't we? I'll keep this simple. I want my four pounds returned to me before the end of the night, or I'll turn you over to a man who will paint your insides black."

"Atherton, what's he on about? Is this true? Is that why you were so hesitant to go in?"

"What? Bleeding Moses, of course not!"

Ivory flashed another wolfish smile. "Go on, then. Tell her what you sold me."

After a long pause, Atherton relented. "Something I had no right in selling."

"Well, at least we can agree upon that." Ivory reached into his suit pocket, pulled out a small trinket, and flipped it like a coin. "Look familiar? Did you truly believe I wouldn't find it?"

Atherton caught it. It was identical to the sigil he'd found in Alice's throat, the very one he'd just tossed to the grass. Yet here was another. His eyes widened. "You found this on the...case?"

Ivory let out a booming cackle. "Unbelievable! First, you play the fool, and now this? You know, I found it charming at first. An unassuming lad such as yourself, and so young to boot. You knew full well what I wanted with your case and that *this* would render it utterly, thoroughly, and completely useless to me. But you showing your face after the fact, and before my stage! That was another insult entirely."

Lilian looked between the two men in stupefaction, mouth agape.

"Y-you've truly lost it," Atherton stammered. "If you found this in the case, and I am not the man you think I am, do you have any idea what that means? Where do you think I found the sigil I brought to you that morning? If it is not mine, then someone is behind this." Atherton bent to the grass, searching frantically before returning with the talisman he'd thrown. Bringing the two identical pieces together, he pushed them back into the spiritualist's hands. "These are not of my making, Mr. Todd."

The consternation and fury boiling behind Ivory's expression dissolved. He cleared his throat. "If what you are implying is true, then we must speak once more, privately."

"Why should we not discuss it now?"

"It appears I am not the only one who had a grievance against you."

10

ATHERTON
MAY 10, 1886

"Oi! Stiff-toucher!"

Atherton's stomach lurched. He recognized that voice. A momentary glance revealed a trio of men walking toward him intently, the silver crosses on their boots glinting. He grabbed Lilian's arm. "Let's wander this way, shall we? Wonderful show, Mr. Todd. It really has been a pleasure!"

"What in the Devil's name is going on?" Lilian dug her heels in and wrenched herself from his grasp. "I will not be pulled about like some marionette."

"The lady's right. Best face your demons, boy-o. Remember what I told you about cowards?"

Lilian sneered. "Atherton is no coward, and neither am I."

"I was pulling you away from men as foul as they come," Atherton hissed. But the opportunity for shameless flight had passed. "Oh, dammit! Why are they here? You ratted me out, didn't you? Unbelievable. I should never have trusted a bloody American."

Ivory summoned another laugh at the finger now being pointed at him. "I might've suspected you were a miserable cheat, but I don't turn coats, Mr. Graves."

"If I find you were lying to me..."

"Oh, save your breath. You're not impressing anyone, and I'm not your enemy here."

"You gib-faced twat! I know you can hear me! Who's the wagtail you've got with you?" Henry taunted.

"Those gentlemen are referring to us," Lilian realized aloud.

By now, passersby were slowing their pace in the courtyard. Even the entertainers in the center had stopped their acts; the tumblers atop the tightropes now sat with uncertain expressions. Nearby, a band of musicians continued with a frenzied melody, as though spurring on the altercation.

"My God," Lilian said, "is that him?"

"Mason bloody Cross." Atherton turned to regard the three men, now standing just an arm's distance away.

"You're feeling bricky now, aren't ya', Athie? That blower fixing you up nice?" Henry asked.

"You'd do well to spare my company your insults, Henry. Arthur. Mason." Atherton inclined his head. One hand slid into his back pocket, where his fingers touched around the handle of the straight razor Mason had given him. It wouldn't be the first time he carried a shaving implement for self-defense, though he never expected to use it against its benefactor. "I'm sure whatever rumor you've heard about me can be discounted."

Mason stopped several strides from the pair, a deadly gleam in his eyes. Somehow, the sight of him felt more colossal now than behind closed doors.

"Rumors. They're a funny beast, ain't they? Tough to tell what to parse and what to toss. You know, it's good to see you enjoying yourself. You always were so somber, Atherton. Just like your father." He looked about the courtyard, as though he'd just walked into somebody's home. "Speakin' of, he hadn't 'alf a mind 'bout what you'd done. Curious, that."

"Right. I suspect you bloodied my father up before you got here, is that it? And just what have I done, Mason?"

"Sharp as a whip, you are. You see, I didn't believe Atherton Graves, a businessman of true integrity, would slum both 'is father and the Disciples for a couple of sovereigns. But after the dice settle against us, we're all clowns ain't we? Now you've gone 'n made a fuckin' muff of meself *and* your father."

Atherton had always met with Mason sitting down. Now, standing in his shadow, it was enough to make staying upright a difficult task. Sweat rolled down his back. He swallowed, noticing the remnants of his father's dried blood on Mason's fists.

"Gentlemen, whatever business you may have can be dealt with after we've left," Lilian said.

"Nobody asked you, doxie," Arthur said.

"That's right. That ain't your prerogative, innit?" Henry chimed, to which his brother rolled his eyes.

"But it is most certainly mine," Ivory said, contentedly puffing on a cigarette. "This is a place of business. My business, to be precise. I have another show in ten minutes."

"Oh, but this *is* your business, Mr. Todd," Mason replied. "Business that you made mine the moment you purchased a case from this prig right here."

Lilian's grip tightened on Atherton's arm.

Ivory scoffed. "Pray tell, how could I have possibly known of this conflict of interest?"

"No. See, you'd not known any better. But our boy 'ere, did," Arthur said with a finger in his direction. "Athie 'ere had no intention of reporting the sale of that case. If he weren't to record the sale with his own father, why on God's honor would he inform us?"

With the crowd now forming a dense ring around them, Atherton felt as though he had slipped into one of his nightmares. He looked to Ivory for consolation, only to find that even his bold lies were quieted.

Mason paced forward. "Four pound. That's the rumor, leastways. If I were a bettin' man, I'd say a young bloke such as yourself would sport the whole lot for an evenin' such as this."

Though Atherton had begun to protest, it was cut short by a fist barreling into his stomach. He fell, wheezing, to his knees, the incriminating coins now spilling out of his waistcoat pockets.

"And there we 'ave it!" Mason declared.

Still choking, Atherton gasped, "I was going to tell you."

"The hell you were." Mason ground those words between his teeth. "Proverbs. '*A faithful man shall abound with blessings, but he that maketh 'aste to be rich shall not be innocent*'—and 'ave I not been gracious to you, to this city?" Now addressing the entire crowd, Mason threw his arms up and gestured as though preaching from a pulpit. "'Ere kneels before you lot a young man who's greed 'as blinded him to the good graces of the Disciples. Not only 'as he betrayed *you*, the very people he purports to serve, but now he's spat in the face of us. The men who protect 'im and 'is own!"

The lights and the crowd swam around Atherton. With Mason on a vengeful tirade, he wrestled with the idea that he might not survive whatever punishment he was about to incur. And with the onlookers just as fearful, he could think of nothing better than to light a cigarette and save his dignity, or at the very least, return to his feet.

"One body," he said.

"What's that?" Mason asked.

"One body. It was only one bloody body," Atherton took in a shaky breath.

"A man's loyalty is only as good as the lies he won't tell, Atherton. But it seems I've failed to remind you of our role in your operations. Mind you, I hate to do this in front of such glitterin' company," he gestured at Lilian, "and with a crowd watchin' at that. You pay us so magsmen don't come lurking at your parlor. If it weren't us, it'd be far worse men. And your business is no different. Corpses. Tobacco. Lush. They're all products." His voice ground like sandpaper against stone.

Atherton took a long drag, knowing full well he wouldn't get another. "That's right. They're products. And you're no better than those phantom thieves you claim to protect us from. You're just the same. A bloody scurf."

Mason hurled a punch.

The small freight train slammed into his cheek. Darkness spiraled out from the blow, so intense that he felt weightless, hovering in the carnival lights as gasps swept the crowd.

He became aware of a heaving throb at the bridge of his nose, with Mason now spitting more self-righteous quotations down at him. More sensations returned, such as the realization that he'd since landed face-first into the grass. Beside him was the payment Betty had fetched, glistening with his blood. Somewhere through the haze, he heard Lilian shout, "That's enough! Stop this!"

Dimly, he felt for the straight razor in his pocket. And, having crawled to his knees, he grabbed it while Mason was distracted by Lilian.

"Beggin' your pardon, miss. This ain't your concern. Go on, Athie. We've done this dance before, 'aven't we?" Mason spat onto the back of his head. "Show 'er you're all right."

Atherton's fingers shone red after he wiped beneath his nose. Blood dripped down upon the smoldering end of his cigarette, lying not far from him in the dirt, and extinguished it. Placing his fingers around it, he ground the tobacco between his fingers, tearing it apart.

"You put out my cigarette," he mumbled.

"What's that? I can't 'ear you from down there."

With an incoherent shout, Atherton unfolded the straight razor and shot up from his knees, sending the blade across Mason's cheek. The steel cut true. Blood flicked out in a glimmering arc, spattering nearby onlookers.

Atherton stood there, shivering with adrenaline. He'd dreamt of a moment like this for years, but even in those fantasies, he struggled to envision what he might do after.

Now, it was no different.

Arthur and Henry stepped back to take in the severity of the wound, the gathered crowd likewise stunned. A deathly hush fell over the ring, quiet enough to hear the rivulets falling from the gash on Mason's cheek. Beginning at his lower jaw and ending beneath his eye, the cut was broad and deep.

It was the most terrifying thing Atherton had ever seen, and one of his proudest accomplishments.

The two faced each other in an odd pause, both experiencing emotions neither had felt before. For Atherton, the euphoria of having inflicted a scar that Mason would never forget. For his counterpart, the surprise was that the boy finally had the stones to retaliate after so many years.

The mobster's ringed fist flew into Atherton's left socket, sending him falling into another sea of bright stars.

"Stop it!" Lilian screamed.

"Arthur, Henry," Mason called. He nodded toward Atherton, pushing away a thrashing Lilian with ease.

Fists dug into the earth, the undertaker retched out a wad of blood. His vision returned in time to see Arthur and Henry's boots marching forward.

As he contemplated what his final, conscious moments would consist of, he was surprised by just how numb his body had already become. Arthur gripped him by the roots of his hair, pulling him up for Henry. But before more blows came hammering down, he had only one thought.

Somebody murdered those children.

11

BOO
MAY 10, 1886

"Somebody should put a stop to this."
"May as well row with the Devil 'imself."
"...be over soon enough, won't it?"

The murmurs of the crowds drifted up to Boo. Crouched atop the high wires, he and the other performers watched while the onlookers grew restless.

"Ivory must've thought he was doing the poor bloke a favor. He'd only just signed his death certificate," another aerialist said. Wearing a black and crimson striped leotard, Florence was lean but sculpted, and shorter still than Boo. The sharp edges of her black hair bordered her face, shimmering with sweat. Lester had discovered her on a trip to Annecy, busking for change with a group of hand balancers and contortionists.

"Ivory, making a critical mistake? No, can't be him," Boo quipped.

Maybe it was the way Florence carried herself, or the pout in her hooked lips when she thought deeply, or even the fragrance she'd brought with her over the channel. Boo never attempted to explain it—his affection for her was intuitive, even compulsive.

"Only a matter of time before Lester steps in anyhow. If not her, Tommy," she said.

"Tommy won't, not without her say," Boo replied.

They were directly above Henry and Arthur, who were now trading kicks into Atherton's sides. The undertaker scrambled to his feet, only to be wrenched back by his hair and thrown into a flying knee.

The resulting *crack* was met with mismatched concern and amusement. There were hundreds watching now, some even placing bets on how long Atherton would last.

Lilian writhed in Mason's paws. "This is barbaric!" she shouted.

"They're going to put him in the earth right here," Boo said. "This is no row—it's an execution. I have to stop them."

"Excuse me, are you mad? Do you *know* that man? A local?"

"As a matter of fact, I do." A bell on Boo's hat chimed in accord, despite him sitting still and the windless air.

Bewilderment scrunched up Florence's face. She pinched the corners of her eyes together. "Is he your friend, then? Is that it?"

"It doesn't matter."

"Since when do you stick out your hide for strangers?"

Boo started to get to his feet, only for Florence to dig her nails into his arm deep enough that he winced and drew back. "Bloody hell!"

"You see that? *Him?* That will be us. The Disciples won't overlook this."

More bone-crunching blows came, punctuated by blood splattering across trampled grass.

"There is an agreement. A contract. Mason and his crew aren't allowed to scrap on our grounds," Boo hissed.

"To hell with the agreement. He isn't worth it!" she said with a shaky laugh.

"I would do the same for you."

"Well, *I* wouldn't, and I'd thank you for it! Our livelihoods aren't worth this *fils de pute*. There are hundreds of people here—there's a reason why not a single one's stepped in."

Bitterness curdled in Boo's throat. He rose up to the balls of his feet, preparing to jump. "I know that reason perfectly well."

"The Devil help you. Madman. *Fou.*"

A lifetime of hanging from fatal heights had taught him to measure his actions with the utmost care. Within the confines of the circus that so cultivated that discipline, anybody in his opposition would find more forgiving chances betting against death itself.

The prongs of his cap fluttered in the low wind.

Boo reached into a satchel strapped to his leg, finding a small pyrotechnic he used for impromptu performances. Lighting the smoke bomb with a match, he tossed it down into the center of the ring. Hissing, the bomb smoldered and gushed out emerald plumes.

"Sometimes I wonder why I bother with you. Do you know that?" Florence asked.

Boo didn't answer. Instead, he jumped off the tightrope, slamming Arthur's jaw with the full weight of his momentum, driven by his heel on the way down. With Arthur on the ground, he set his eyes on the younger brother. Picking up a pair of discarded, wooden juggling clubs, Boo swung them in hypnotic arcs as he stepped forward.

Henry released Atherton. Clumps of hair matted with blood were left behind in his fist. He turned to regard the clown. "You always were a nickey prick."

"You've done your work, Henry."

"I 'ave, eh? And you're the one to say we're finished, is that it?"

Henry threw heavy-handed punches that went wide, offsetting his balance as Boo darted between them. Biding his time, Boo claimed an opening, bashing the mobster's temple with a club and pairing it with an uppercut that sent him falling backwards.

Arthur scrambled to his feet, but Boo was quicker, flourishing his clubs before glancing them across his head in quick succession. Though the blows wobbled his knees, it was apparent Arthur had the grit of London's underworld in his veins—a thick substance brewed of hungry nights spent mixing misery with gin, and fights not all too dissimilar to this one, Boo wagered. Sweat and blood ran down his jaw.

"You don't know what you've done, Boo," he panted.

"You'd best worry for yourself, first."

Arthur spat a pair of molars into his hand and glared at the clown. "The price for this will be paid tenfold."

But, much to the crowd's delight, Arthur's attempts to make good on his words fell short. Boo baited out a desperate swing, only to duck and hammer another club into the back of Arthur's head, dropping him.

Just to be sure, the clown nudged the unconscious mobster with his toe.

All the while, Henry had collected himself among the roar of onlookers responding to the *thwack!* and *cerck!* of Boo's spinning clubs.

Through the fumes, he spotted a stark, painted smile leering at him.

Henry flicked open a switchblade.

In the fogged air, the circus lights cast their silhouettes into distorted shapes. Their attacks sprang like frenzied vipers—darting, lashing in the smog.

"Gigglemug prick. You'll be griddlin' by the end," Henry spat, but the taunt was as shaky as his legs. He glanced desperately toward Mason, watching the scrap with folded arms, an amused grin sprouting over the cigarette between his lips. The boy had survived nearly half the beating afforded to his older brother, mostly on account of the switchblade and a shallow cut he'd dealt the clown.

Boo sprang forward, striking the blade out of Henry's hand. Trading a punch on the chin, he drew one of his clubs back before swinging it forward. The bridge of Henry's nose took the full force. As he reeled backwards, another blow followed to his temple. He dropped to his knees with a strangled yelp. Savoring the luxury of an extra second, Boo wound up a kick and cast it to his chin.

Henry toppled beside Arthur's discarded teeth. The neat thud was lost to the cacophony of the crowd, already trying to coax another fight out of Mason. Lilian sprang free and knelt beside Atherton, pulling his weight up in an embrace. Slumped over her shoulders, his swollen eyes flickered with recognition up at Boo.

A chilling wind swept up the last tendrils of smoke.

The crowd quickly dispersed, already wandering to the gaudy shouts of barkers still ringing into the darkest hours of morning. A smirk played on Mason's lips as he offered a slow clap, a seething animosity cloaked in disinterest.

Blood dripped from Boo's clubs. All the while, regret squeezed his ribs with the gravity of what he'd just done. He dropped the props. In his peripherals, the weak movements of the life he'd just saved paled in comparison to the debt he'd created.

"Didn't know they trained the clowns to fight," Mason said. The wound on his cheek had since stained his collared shirt and gray suit a brilliant scarlet.

Boo had a cut of his own—shallow, at an awkward angle across his neck. He wiped at the blood and sweat on his face, smearing his painted lips and the stars drawn beneath his eyes. Venom dripped from his words. "No scraps on our grounds," he said.

Florence and another acrobat dropped from above to drag the unconscious Arthur and Henry toward the entrance gates.

"Can't imagine the lady up top will take a fancy to you meddlin' in a good dust-up not concernin' you," Mason said. "Thanks for the show, anyhow."

The two of them caught sight of Lester striding toward them in great, billowing layers. Thomas was beside her, an unmistakable giant towering over the throngs.

Mason winked at Boo, shoving his hands deep in his pockets as he strode away. "Oh, I do love this circus!"

❈

Nights at the carnival were rarely over after midnight. The majority of final performances went on until two in the morning, and concessions took down their signs and dimmed the lights just before three. As was custom, the entrance gates closed at midnight.

Tonight, the clown who perched atop the three-headed lantern between acts was nowhere to be found. In the Flying Maffickers tent, for a showing at one in the morning, two aerialists had been replaced at the last minute at Lester's behest.

Boo watched Florence's rich mahogany eyes as her delicate but rough hands threaded bandages over the cut on his neck. They were sitting beside a fire in a small encampment just beyond the circus limits.

Thirteen caravans encircled the space. Rain tarps mimicking the tents adorned the tops, with small ladders and stairs leading into the dimly lit coaches. The majority were empty, as most of the witches residing within were still performing.

The winds were growing colder.

Florence's voice nudged away the silence with a pronounced French accent. "It was right, even if it wasn't. I'll say that much."

A single bell of Boo's cap chimed.

Florence reached up and slid the hat from his head despite one of his hands moving to stop her. "One day you'll have to learn to part with this old thing. Gehenna knows it reeks to the heavens." An untidy mess of wavy, brunette hair fell to the sides of his face. Florence snipped off the excess bandage from her finished work and tossed it into the fire.

"I made a grave mistake," Boo said.

She took his cheeks in her hands and kissed him firmly. "You cannot weigh the truth in your actions by the uncertainty of their consequences."

For all the warmth her lips usually kindled in his chest, the spark sputtered, dying before it could catch. "I've damned us."

A figure emerged from Lester's carriage. Kayne Todd's hands were clasped together, her sharp features betraying only worry. "Lester is ready for you," she said, taking her leave as soon as the clown met her at the entrance.

Gas lamps with red glass cast the interior of the cramped dwelling in crimson hues. Lester's caravan was less of a living space and more of an office, piled high with papers, bills, and objects whose purpose was of some unmistakable yet distant importance.

A white cat called Simone was curled into a tight ball on the rug, her long ears twitching in a blissful sleep.

Oh, to be a familiar curled on a rug without the blood of vengeful mobsters on your hands, Boo thought.

On Lester's desk were a series of revolving ornaments, the most striking of which being an astronomical clock. Gold rings orbited a metallic globe, each one representing a celestial body. But Boo could never help but stare at what appeared to be Lester's most prized plaything: a glass globe housing a small angel.

Scarcely the size of a fist, the creature looked like a butterfly subsumed by a child's nightmare. Several pairs of wings cradled its abdomen—a single, milky eye which took to watching Boo.

Gehennics were not known for their moral purity, but even for Lester, her feud against that creature seemed terribly harsh.

"Oh good, you've had the sense to leave that damned hat out of this," she said. Her forced smile exuded more frustration than her voice as she watched him, her green eyes weary. The high collars of a black mantle framed her quiet fury.

Running a hand through her peppered hair, Lester gestured, "Why don't you take a seat."

"I would rather stand, thank you."

"Boo."

"I think I'll take a seat," he said, settling into a wooden chair that was older than him.

"Have one of these. You're going to need it." Lester pulled out a cigarette from a case and lit the other end once he'd propped it in his mouth. "You know, for how carefully you pick your words, sometimes it seems like your actions scarcely earn a moment's consideration."

Given that he'd once dumped a pail of elephant excrement on a man because he'd given him a sideways glance, Boo couldn't help but nod in agreement.

"But I won't let you by quietly. No long silences, no withheld conclusions. Nor will I stand up for you—I can't. I want to know every last notion that went through that head of yours when you decided to bring the wrath of the Disciples down on us—on your home, your family. On Florence, Tommy, Ivory—the lot of us. On me."

More than the betrayal of his countless colleagues, he felt that final word. For many in the circus, Lester was merely an eccentric if not strict proprietor who critiqued acts from every discipline. But to Boo, her glare was a needle through his heart, threaded with the ice of a mother's disappointment.

"At least *look* at me. You suspect I'm frightened, is that it? I assure you, I have every right to be. As do *all* of us after this stunt of yours. You pummelled those men within an inch of their lives. And if you misunderstand the weight of this, you're as much of a zounderkite as you pretend."

Boo stared into his cracked knuckles.

"Fine. You won't talk? I will. What appalling logic led you to this decision? It was Ivory who'd gone and made a mess of things, yet even he bit back his tongue, that windy-wallet. And don't you think I'll spare him the same lecture."

The image of Atherton choking out blood came back to him. Boo searched his hands for a response.

"Damnit, Boo. Answer me!"

"Give me one bloody moment!"

Lester's back went flush against her chair. She'd never heard Boo shout. Perhaps he himself hadn't.

"They broke their agreement," he finally said. "No scraps on our grounds."

"And so they did. But it was not your place to punish them, to make our relations with Mason and his men untenable."

"They've had their coin-pinching hands around us for far too long. But we've made a name for ourselves, haven't we? It's not like how it used to be —empty seats, quiet nights, performers twiddling their thumbs. We don't need their business anymore. Am I wrong? Can we not get on well enough without those...those bastards!"

Lester erupted in a spiteful cackle. "You've not severed our ties to the Disciples, if that was your aim. You've entrapped us."

Boo flinched. He drew in a long breath. "And what of my assumption?"

This time, it was Lester who prolonged the silence. "Yes. You are right —we haven't needed them for some time. But now look at us. They would string you up from the Tower of London to set an example, and that's just to begin with. Just by indulging in one fleeting act of violence, you've managed to darken the fate of those you had no right deciding for. Bravo."

He inhaled from the cigarette until the carriage walls spun. "Eight years ago, you found me in Bedlam. I was just a child. But you asked me to entrust myself to you. You envisioned a better life for me. Now I'm asking you to trust me—to trust us."

A nostalgic grin tugged on Lester's lips, leaving as soon as it appeared. "We are no better than those men. We never were. We hold candles to the Devil and stand in the shadows they cast. If we spill blood, we best be certain it won't haunt us. There's no God looking over these grounds, and make no bones about it—we would do well to make sure it stays that way."

Taking up the globe from her desk, Boo met the angel's soporific eye. "Not better than them," he said. "Just better off without them."

12

ATHERTON
MAY 11, 1886

A therton ground his teeth against the pain of the suturing needle piercing the skin on the side of his head. A pair of bloodied hands came into view, this time with scissors to snip the thread.

The doctor was clad in dark garments—waistcoat and trousers—trailing with unique, burgundy embellishments and frills that came from the unmistakable style of the circus's tailor. "You've held still well enough," she said, "but this part won't come so easily." She rolled up the sleeves of her blouse and splashed gin on her hands before rubbing them together. Then she applied the liquor to a cloth and pressed it firmly against Atherton's wound.

A violent jolt seized him as he stifled a scream.

"That should do you well, Mr. Graves," she said, unable to suppress her smirk. "And if I do say so myself, the needlework is bang up to the elephant."

The blunt and oddly comforting woman had introduced herself as Dr. Kayne Todd, who was as precise with her sutures as she was with her words. Her movements bordered on stiffness, and her gaze was just as precise. She appeared comfortable with gore on her hands. Every stitch seemed to have loosened her otherwise taut composure.

"Greatly appreciated," he managed.

"If it is any consolation, the gash you dealt Mr. Cross will require scores of stitches. He'll be wearing that scar for as long as he lives. They say you should dig two graves if you seek vengeance, but I say nothing satisfies like a true strike to an old enemy. Here."

Her words were as much consolation as a quilt on a man's deathbed. It made Atherton want to throw himself into the Thames. Mason was likely plotting his retaliation that very moment. She thrust the bottle of gin into his hands. Grateful for the offered reprieve, he took a heavy gulp, the harsh, stinging sweetness of juniper berries briefly distracting him from his throbbing skull.

"Though I am certain you needn't hear this," she continued, "a word to the wise: sleep with one eye open at night."

"Or not at all," he murmured.

"Indeed. Eternal rest will find us soon enough, huh?"

"May I speak directly?" Lilian asked.

"Seeing as how I've got your suitor's blood on my hands, I think it's only fitting," Kayne chuckled.

"I hadn't the faintest notion that circuses come equipped with infirmaries and a proper doctor to boot. And, well, a lady doctor at that!" Lilian couldn't help but exclaim excitedly.

The doctor smiled and gave her hand a gentle squeeze. "You're a sweetheart. Please, call me Kayne. But I'm afraid my reputation has made furthering my work quite the challenge. My experiments in surgical reconstruction were deemed too 'extreme' for the universities."

Lilian glanced at Atherton with her mouth agape. He, too, straightened his posture at that. "Surgery? As in, you're not only a doctor, but a surgeon?" he asked.

Kayne wound her finger around a strip of gauze with a pained grin. "Indeed. I've performed some amputations in my day."

Lilian appeared enthralled by her infamy. "You're extraordinary, Kayne," she said breathlessly. "You must be the first of your kind."

"Again, that's very kind of you. But I'm hardly the first. Though we are certainly rare. Our proprietor shares a vision of a world where women aren't shuffling around at home, waiting on their husbands' every beck and call."

Gesturing outside at the tents, Lilian quipped, "And that remains her most ambitious aspiration," to which they both laughed.

Feeling rather implicated, Atherton gave a weak laugh and pretended to be distracted by his hands.

"And on that note, you best be sure to be one of the good ones," Kayne said, lifting Atherton's chin with a finger, though her tone was not merely playful.

He blushed, happy to oblige her with a nod. Even still, he was eager to escape their scrutiny. "May I ask what occupies your time when you have no patients, Dr. Todd? I can't imagine this is a routine occurrence," Atherton said.

Several neatly made beds were laid out in the infirmary, all empty. A single lantern with blackened glass cast a meager glow over them.

"You're not wrong. Suffice it to say, the Black Carnival is not only exploring the edges of circus artistry. Besides, our performers are routinely injured. Physicians are good for that sort of thing. Better safe than sorry and all that." Packing her equipment into a small briefcase, she buckled it shut and stood by the tent flaps in expectation.

"We both owe you a great deal of gratitude in tending to him," Lilian said. "What shall we pay you?"

She held up a hand. "Nonsense. It's only sensible that we bear the cost of caring for your wounds after you incurred them on our grounds. I'm ashamed to say it's not the first time I've patched somebody who got tangled up in bad business with my husband."

Atherton's eyebrows hit the top of his head. "You mean to say you're married to Ivory?"

"Indeed. He's a good man who means well," Kayne sighed and quickly added, "mostly."

"Well, he knows his way around a stage. His charisma and presence! I couldn't believe the things I saw in there," Lilian scoffed. "I'm still trying to figure out how he did it."

"That's sweet of you, dear. As for you, Mr. Graves, my husband may still be mustering the courage to apologize, so I will do my part on his behalf, whatever it may be worth. Purchasing that...case from you was reckless at best and fatal at worst. He was aware of your ties to the Disciples—that should have been the end of it."

"Neither you nor your husband should apologize for Mason's savagery. It was as much my decision as his."

"Well then." Kayne gave a stiff nod. "At least one man is taking responsibility around here."

"Something else, doctor. Would you give my gratitude to Boo?"

"You know him?"

"We spoke at length not two days before. I suspect had we not, I would have, well, given up the ghost."

"Curious. I will do just that, Mr. Graves."

Her firm handshake gave Atherton's fingers the keen reminder that they'd just been stomped on not an hour before.

"My assistant, Mr. Barker, will escort you to the entrance gates. Until next time, if indeed there ever is one. One can only hope under better circumstances. Ms. Butler." Kayne inclined her head and strode off.

※

"What do you think she meant?" Lilian asked.

Once at the gates, they watched Mr. Barker make his way back toward the grounds, cigar smoke billowing all the while. The stench of him lingered—one Atherton knew all too well. His imposing height and frame seemed only fitting among the tents and performers. He would've been a regular titan in the city. Atherton thought of the ghoul he buried in his backwoods. How thin and malnourished he'd been in comparison. He shuddered to consider the amount of flesh this one consumed to retain his mass.

"Meant by what?"

"About them 'not only exploring the edges of circus artistry'?"

Atherton would have furrowed his brow were it not for the hot pain in his fresh stitches. Instead, he hummed and hoped this sufficed.

"Oh, I am awful, aren't I? Look at you. We must get you back to rest."

Through his swollen eyes encrusted with blood, he watched the dwindling displays of the carnival. Lanterns winked out of their own accord as concessions were packed away over laughter. Performers and attendants collected in small groups to talk over pipes and cigarettes.

"Atherton? Did you hear me?"

The undertaker wiped away a trickle of blood from his stitches. He cleared his throat and nodded. Arm in arm, they walked beyond the gates.

With the Butler Orphanage being at the edge of the city, Atherton had made sure to arrange a coach for Lilian. The driver hopped off to stretch his legs, and Atherton pressed a few coins in his palm. Lilian held up a hand. "We'll be only a minute longer."

Atherton knew it was time, though he was reluctant to see her off. That night had fractured a great many pretenses between them. Just like the shattering of a mirror, he couldn't help his hesitance in gathering up the pieces, let alone see what might be reflected when he did. He'd hoped to have revealed a few memories of his childhood, perhaps a secret he'd never shared before, but nearly being bludgeoned to death in front of her and ousted as a criminal was certainly its own kind of bonding experience.

"The spiritualist, Mr. Todd," Lilian began, "spoke of 'cases' the way I've heard you speak of them, Atherton. His wife, as well."

Atherton turned his back on the wind and lit a cigarette. Any excuse to avoid her eyes. *This is it, isn't it? She'll never speak to me again.* "Go on, then."

"Cadavers. Stiffs. That's what you sold to Mr. Todd, wasn't it? That's why the Disciples did what they did."

"It's true. I sold Mr. Todd one of them. A crime so odious it makes these wounds appear justified. And perhaps they are. Last night, I…" The words trembled from his lips. "Last night, a grave I filled with the irredeemable remains of a young girl was unearthed. Transported. The girl was destitute, a beggar in life. She had no friend nor kin, no companion in the end. You must believe me." Having steadied himself, he braved her inquisitive gaze. "Mr. Todd found her in the fields not far from here. His offer was extraordinary. More than greed, I was intrigued. But the true price was beyond my fathoming. My dignity, least of all."

"Dignity?" Her hands snaked up his chest and found his cheekbones. She cradled his bruised skin. "What have I told you about shame?"

Disgust, shock, even fear—he'd braced himself for all this. Instead, searching the deep shadows that night had cast along her face, he saw, of all things, a glint of amusement in her eyes.

"You reveal your sins to me like they are terrible secrets. But where would honesty be without a confession? Virtue without wickedness? The shadow of your shame is merely cast by a sense of morals, briefly stretched for a victimless crime. You stand as though prepared to face my repugnance. Yet all I feel now is curiosity—even a pleasant surprise. I do believe you've misunderstood me, Atherton. I am anything but a saint." Rising upon her toes, she kissed him on the cheek.

It was the gentlest pain he'd ever felt.

She drew away, the barest hint of blood tracing her lips. Before he could react, she slipped into the carriage. With a sharp crack of the reins, the horses took off along the packed earth.

Atherton stood there, chained by her words. Even in the chilling winds of the earliest hours of the morning, in the blazing remnants of a beating that promised only more torment, he had never felt less alone. Though perhaps he still felt a pinch of guilt for selling Betty's corpse, he had never been so grateful to find himself the victim of a stolen heart.

He took a final glance at the circus.

For however many times he might yet see it again, it would never be as it was tonight. And just as the lights above Ivory's tent glowed to life when he passed beneath them, as the undertaker put his hands in his pockets and began his walk home, the swirling flames in the three-headed lantern wilted, fizzling to darkness.

13

MASON
MAY 13, 1886

A coach stopped beside the neatly cobbled paths of Gloucester Road. The horse's heavy snorts issued steam into the chilled air. At that late hour, even to a man as callous as Mason Cross, it was unsettling to find he could not even see his own outstretched hand, such was the thickness of the fog blanketing the thoroughfare.

Having tossed a tip to his driver—"For the nippers and the rib, eh?"—he stood in the empty street, the clattering hooves fading among the hollers and odd rackets of London's underworld. Were it not his mind conjuring phantom silhouettes in the gloom, it would be those cries, the fetid air of excrement from the dismal boroughs just a walk's distance away. And were it not they, it would be the mark Atherton left on his cheek—raging scarlet, and with over a dozen sutures—that would serve to remind him of the squalor he'd spent most of his life crawling out of. The very same one he thought, until recently, had no surprises left for him.

Aglow like liquid cinders, gaslight shimmered in puddles throughout the street.

Stepping into his father's townhouse, Mason found the housekeeper snoring gently in an armchair not far from the entryway. In her lap, pages of *The Witch's Head* fluttered in the breeze from an open window.

The cramped foyer was a deception. The two-story home opened up into spacious quarters with floral paneling and leather furniture. But all of this was visible to Mason by memory alone. Darkness shrouded the halls, save for a candle dwindling on a nearby table.

"Oi. Bertha. This is no place for a kip," Mason said, nudging her.

She stirred. The recognition of his gravelly voice brought a grin to her face. "What kept you so long?"

"Unexpected complications. Come on, now. Up we get."

"Good heavens, what's happened to you?"

"An accident. Only an accident."

Of course, she knew better. She had pressed a cloth to the first bullet hole that tore through Mason and had nursed him after the Whitechapel peelers bashed his head in the first time he robbed a barber's shop. "I always feared this business would catch up to you. It's nearly taken your father. His condition worsens. It is not as it was before you left."

"His sickness 'as nothing to do with our business. Which you'll catch if you don't keep warm on account of me."

"God takes his retribution in every manner. I've only waited here so his state would not shock you when you arrive. A son should not have to bear his father's ails alone."

"What else are sons for, then?" Remembering the days when she would carry him on her shoulders, Mason offered an arm and guided her to her bedroom.

Even in the amber light of his bedchamber, Logan Cross looked every bit as pale as marble. The puffy rings beneath his eyes were etched with wrinkles, hanging heavy like his cheeks. Wispy locks of thinning, gray hair revealed his deeply receded hairline, swept to the side in damp streaks. A jar of distended, shining leeches rested beside the bed. Beside them was a Bible to match the rosary wrapped around his hand. His hands were broad and heavy like Mason's.

A sickly miasma choked the air. Placing another blanket over his father, Mason cracked a window and helped himself to a long pull from a decanter of whisky from his father's stores. Within a glass cabinet with dozens of bottles, the collection of scotch gleamed like topaz.

Perhaps it was his son's heavy sighs, or the smell of his best bottle being poured without permission, but Logan Cross awoke with a cough that echoed throughout the home. "I've only jus' started dyin' 'n you're already in my cellar."

"Just getting a jump on it, is all."

Logan grunted out a laugh. He massaged his hands, surveying them as if to see how long they'd grip onto what little time he had. "What kept you?"

"That's what Bertha asked. It's gotten the better of you, 'asn't it?"

Mason walked over to the bedside, the floorboards creaking beneath him. He took off his black wool coat and tossed it onto an armchair. Using a damp cloth from the nightstand, he mopped at the sweat beading on Logan's forehead. That same residue soaked the pillows and sheets. Mason's nose crinkled. He bit back a pained expression, but Logan must have caught his subtle wince before he turned back to the table with the decanter. "Never mind some old bastard dyin'," he barked. "Bloody hell, what happened to your face?"

Mason finished off the glass before pouring another. He could feel it in his bones—the numbing excitement of travel wearing off to give way to the deep ache of exhaustion. "The two of you's are like mother hens."

"Come here. In the light," Logan said, waving him closer. "Christ. Who done this?"

Logan struggled to upright himself as he let out several wet coughs. Mason heaped pillows behind him to help prop up his father. He removed and remoistened the sweat rag, then replaced it on Logan's head with a frown.

Logan groaned with relief.

"Back at New Sarum," Mason said. "The Graves."

"Allan finally found a pair of bollocks, aye?"

"It was the boy. His son. Atherton."

Logan paused. A fire stoked in his eyes. "That boy was always quiet as a ghost whenever I came to collect from 'is father. It was only three summers ago I last saw 'im. The work hardened the boy." He motioned for Mason's glass and polished off the whisky, asking for the rest of the details.

Even with a grandfather clock ticking well past midnight, Mason didn't fight him. He knew well enough that if his father wanted something, he'd get it, and if he didn't, his temper might burn him out faster than the fever. For a man who spent his life working with pickpockets and child beggars, building an empire of criminals, he worried about what would happen if he *didn't* think about the Disciples.

Mason spared no details. He talked until he felt like he was back at the circus. He could feel Ivory's cold stare after Atherton cut him. The tremors from the boisterous beasts in the menagerie. The steady patter of Boo's clubs, running red with the blood of Mason's lieutenants.

In the end, it had been Thomas who informed them of Ivory's dealings with Atherton. Smalltalk with Arthur that found its way to Mason—an innocent slip.

"I could've let the lad 'ave the four pound." Mason pinched the edges of his eyes and shook his head. "I should'a done it. It was just four bloody pound."

"Are you taking the piss? Horseshit. It never were about the four pound. Thomas Barker, hah! Now *there's* a pair of bollocks." Logan laughed until his wry cackle sputtered into a hacking rasp. He dabbed at the blood forming at the corners of his mouth, the handkerchief more burgundy than white. "Just count your stars it weren't 'im that got handsy."

"Barker comes from our world. He wouldn't."

"And that's a world we've sacrificed everything for. Aye? Don't let a gravedigger undermine what we've bled for. What we've built. Now, the circus—it's a misunderstanding. Lester will set 'em straight, sure enough. And she'll honor your patience. She's good like that. But ya' can't let them off, not clean-like. No." The loose skin beneath Logan's chin wagged as he shook his head with vigor.

"Fine. What about Atherton?"

"You kill 'im." The words came with no pleasure or malice. It was an errand at the bottom of a laundry list. "Had it been a private outburst, sure—you bleed 'im just enough to let 'im live. But he's gone an' shown the world the Disciples can be well and truly fucked with. Both Lester's lot *and* that city. If you feed a starved dog, it'll only come back an' take the whole hand. You've thrown gizzards to the whole pack."

Mason stood up, seized by the certainty of his father's words. Taking in the gravity of it agitated him, and he was pacing before long, itching for a smoke. The sickly air in the room felt thicker than blood, squeezing at his lungs.

"You make a show of it," Logan said, jabbing at him. "Let them know it won't stand. If some lad with a stick up 'is arse can do *that* to ya, what do you think the butchers will think the next time you come 'round to collect? The jewelers and the rest of the lot? Word spreads, Mason. Truth is, every day that you don't, some other poor bastard gets to thinkin' they can do well enough without us. Give 'em long enough, they'll muster the nerve to try."

Mason's hands were damp, wet from the same feeling that had stopped him from snapping Atherton's neck moments after he felt the blade drag through his cheek. What was it that stopped him? It wasn't shock. Nor fear.

"That boy 'ad the fear of God in 'is eyes and still he...he done it. This," Mason said, touching his wound. "Looked me in my eye after and just...he was ready. Ready to die. With a pretty dame on 'is arm too, eh?" He chuckled, but his voice had gone coarse, and his eyes red. "Fuckin' hell."

"Son, listen. Atherton was born in a shallow grave. Think of it—a boy so young with dead'uns for playmates. It's not natural nor godly." Logan paused to hack out a few more drops of blood. He grabbed the cup of water Mason fetched him and, with shaking hands, brought it to his lips. The air rattled through his throat when he finished drinking with a gasp.

"You can see it in 'im," Logan continued, thrusting the near-empty glass back into Mason's fist. "He's half-phantom already. Always with those eyes. Distant. Watchin' things that aren't there. You'd be doing the lad a damned favor."

Mason looked down at the glass. Spittle swirled with scarlet from his father's mouth.

"I've never killed a man I respected," Mason admitted.

"You'd be careful to do it well and clean, then," his father warned. "That's the blood that won't wash."

"No, no. There's another way, I'm sure of it."

"Another way? What other way? The other ways didn't pull us outta the stinkin' boroughs that would not bat an eye to see you drown in dog's piss. 'Ave your body washed up on the Thames like ravaged driftwood. Or 'ave your sons ground to their heels in the workhouse, 'an your daughters, made to be ladybirds, all of 'em, their bastards ready to start the bloody process again. But we've broken that cycle. We made something of the shit we'd been dealt. For folks like us, Mason, blood is salvation. 'An if it ain't ours, it's theirs."

Even after the decades that had worn Logan, his son couldn't help but notice their resemblance, etched into the lines of their faces. Yet there was an undeniable difference. He hadn't half the wrath his father expressed in his former years. It was rumored that the first life Logan took was during a highway robbery with a small gang when he was just sixteen. After collecting their trinkets, coin purses, and wallets, he demanded the victims strip down to their clothes so they, too, could be pawned off. When one man refused, Logan simply stated he'd kill him if that meant getting his waistcoat and trousers. The victim tried to call his bluff, saying the clothes wouldn't sell with bloodstains on them. Logan liked the forethought, so he had his associates hold the man up by his ankles so he could be bled upside-down.

Even after all the times Mason had asked about it, Logan never verified nor denied the details. Mason wasn't sure what was worse, that his father was capable of such a thing, or that he couldn't bring himself to admit what he'd done. He'd just say, "It were hard times, eh?"

While Mason's ambitions never extended to such extremes, he'd bloody his hands to find it somewhere within him. He'd do anything to maintain the Cross legacy, and be damned if a lone undertaker stood in his way.

14

ATHERTON
MAY 17, 1886

The mortuary was his sanctuary. So long as there were the dead, he could ignore his problems by tending to all and any besides his own.

The night before, the crack of a revolver had awoken the Bemerton District just after midnight. A man had taken his own life. Allan and Atherton had arrived at the Wilkes's residence not long after the constables, in traveling cloaks wet from rain. The wife and children had howled into the early hours of the morning until, finally, the Graves left with the body of Mr. Wilkes in their horse-drawn hearse.

The family was adamant about having his features restored for the burial, but even with forceps, Atherton struggled to manipulate the thread and needle through the entry wound. The back of Mr. Wilkes's head was irredeemable—a bucket of sopping rags attested to that.

Atherton hadn't returned to the circus since that night with Lilian. His father and mother had forbidden him, if indeed Atherton felt inclined to heed their orders, being nearly twenty years of age. But it had proven unnecessary. The memories crept into his body and coiled around his bones, made a home in his heart, and leeched all the while. Ivory's seance. His tirade. The child clown. Betty's matching emblem. And for every drop of occult paranoia in his veins was an equal, mortal fear for what wrath Mason would exact.

The little girl's voice was more distinct now than the moment he first heard it.

"The flowers are cruel," he muttered to himself. But no matter how many times he said it, he came no closer to divining a sensible meaning.

A drop of sweat fell from his forehead, sliding into the man's bullet hole.

Dusk set the clouded sky ablaze. It lent a gilded edge to the blood pooled in the table's furrows, reminding Atherton to work fast, lest he'd be stuck toiling by the glow of gas lamps all night.

Atherton's hands never shook when he worked. They did now.

"Have you finished?"

He heard what he thought was his sister's voice and felt her hand tug on the back of his trousers. Without turning his head, he replied, "No. Tell them I'll take supper late."

Again, Delma tugged. "When will you join us?"

"I won't be joining at all. That's the idea. Can't you see Mr. Wilkes and I are getting to know each other?"

"They're furious with you for selling the case."

"Told you about that, did they? Well, they should be. It was a damnable thing to do."

He felt a cold burst of air flutter through the hair on the back of his head.

One of Mr. Wilkes's arms slid off his chest and hung limply off the preparation table, sending a set of needle and thread to the ground in the process. It wasn't all too uncommon—bodies moved from time to time if they weren't situated well. It unnerved Atherton all the same.

Closing his eyes, he steadied himself with a deep breath. "Please don't test my patience. Why don't you go bother Mum instead?"

Kneeling, he bent to pick up the stray needle—an impossible task with the blood on his fingers. While he kept pinching, he couldn't see Delma from his peripheral vision as he expected.

That detail took a moment to settle in.

"You wouldn't have found it otherwise, would you?" the voice asked. "The necklace. That's why you're upset."

"How did you know about...?" His question crumbled to silence. Fingers frozen above the needle, the realization hit him.

He hadn't been speaking to Delma.

A trembling shock rolled up his spine. It spread to every inch of his body and turned his insides to a frosted slurry. He whipped his head about. There was nobody, save for the two other bodies in his care, both covered with sheets.

Atherton unfurled each, expecting to find his sister hiding there, as they often did as children. But it was only Mrs. Tanner and Mr. Mills on the tables. The embalming room was empty.

The mirror.

He'd forgotten to cover up the mirror as he always did when he worked.

Another wave of ice spread over him.

The next thought came from what felt like the edge of madness, yet he knew it was as true and real as the stitches in his head. *As soon as I look into that mirror, I'll face her. It. Someone or something that conjured those words. What shares this chamber with me now.*

His eyes wavered, unwilling to obey.

There it was, in his periphery—a silhouette, standing just behind him. She was covered in mud. Her clothes, as torn and weather-bitten as her flesh. That was when the smell arrived—that unmistakable, noxious gas of putrefying flesh. A stage of decomposition that had not yet possessed the bodies around him. What arrived next was a song, a rotting voice.

Atherton didn't dare move, nor flinch as a moist hand with slipping flesh and protruding bone grasped his wrist. He felt the bone of an index finger glide past his palm. The rest of her hand followed, too, now holding his.

> *Have you been to the water*
> *Have you been 'round the market*
> *We'd a-looked and drained the Thames*
> *But our bones ached, our little old legs*
> *Ran red looking for Minnie Pegs.*

"... Betty?"

A crash reverberated throughout the chamber. Atherton jumped and felt the flutter of skin and torn clothes slither past him. His white knuckles found the embalming table to keep himself from toppling over.

But the clamor had only been Allan, throwing the door wide.

"Why are you sweating? You don't look well," he said. His tone had been terse ever since that evening—he'd copped a black eye and a split lip from Mason's visit on the night of their quarrel.

Atherton chanced a full view of the mirror. Nothing.

"You startled me. I'm fine," he lied.

"Supper is ready."

"I'll be out in a half-hour. I'm occupied."

"It wasn't meant as a question. Some warm food would do you good. Wilkes won't run off on you."

The old joke fell flat on both of them.

The confused fear in his eyes wasn't the only factor contributing to Atherton's ghoulish appearance. It had been scarcely a week since Arthur and Henry rearranged the bones in his face. The results were messy blotches of olive and maroon skin.

"Father, I don't think you've fully grasped the severity of this predicament," Atherton said.

Allan was halfway through the door. He pulled back and slammed it shut behind him. "You wish to talk? Fine. I know damn well what crime you've committed. But I'm not certain you do. So why are you preaching to me about severity?"

"I've admitted my crime!"

"Then have some shame! Selling cadavers to a circus. By God! What kind of man have I raised? You should be on your knees thanking God that Mason didn't have half a mind to report you to the peelers."

"The peelers," Atherton scoffed. "This isn't about the law. Mason will have my head. Mine. Your son! Whether you've pride in me or not. It's worrying me sick, it is. I've half a mind to leave this bloody city and never give so much as a backward glance."

Atherton tried to fight the tears welling in his eyes, but the sight of them gave Allan pause. He removed his spectacles and wiped them with his handkerchief before placing them in his waistcoat pocket.

"You must listen to me, and hear me close. The Cross family and ours have a long history. When you were just a lad, Logan and I, well...suffice it to say you aren't the only one who's donned the coat of a resurrectionist for an evening. There was a time when our dealings were of mutual satisfaction. We could double a month's profits in a single evening."

The confession was harder to hear than it was to imagine. Atherton couldn't help but wonder how many bodies his father had sold.

"Your grandfather would have none of it, of course. He said it made the 'spirits' become more active," Allan scoffed. "He didn't give a damn about the authorities or the crime. No, it was about him and his 'visitors.' His priorities were always a bit eccentric."

Atherton dared to murmur, "Maybe he was right."

Allan grimaced. "Oh, please."

"Maybe grandfather didn't go mad like you say. Maybe we just weren't listening."

"I will not have you—" Allan started to fume.

"Maybe he saw and heard things you couldn't," Atherton interjected, his voice almost pleading. "Maybe the dead were trying to connect with him—tell him things."

"Enough," Allan said, his voice rising.

"Things of terrible importance. Things only the dead could possibly know. Things that could even save lives! If only you'd have listened to him!"

"Atherton, *stop it!*" Allan roared, slamming his fist on an empty embalming table.

Atherton's own balled fists trembled with sorrowful rage. He shook his head. No wonder grandfather had lost his wits.

At the sight of his distress, his father softened. "I'm sorry, Atherton." He placed a hand on his shoulder. "These sorts of discussions dig up things I'd rather leave buried."

"Evidently," Atherton replied stiffly, resolving to never speak of it with him again.

"As for the resurrectionist work, I'd long since left that behind me, for us, for the integrity of our business. Our *legitimate* business, Atherton. And now, Mason made his statement about the matter, and we've listened. You paid with your blood. It's done."

"I *cut* him. How many men do you think have done that and lived?"

"If he wanted you dead, you'd already be on one of our tables. If anything, that scar you dealt him earned his regard. Stubborn, vicious, callous, a conniving bastard—yes, Mason is all those things—but what he isn't is unprincipled. He might not have taken a liking to you standing up to him, but he respects you for it. Trust me in that."

A knot had been growing in Atherton's chest since the moment he struck Mason. He'd done everything in his power to ignore it. He buried himself in his work, convinced that at any moment Mason might gallop into New Sarum, clutching a bullet with his name on it. He wasn't sure what terrified him more—that thought or that his father would bet his son's life on a theory.

Either way, that pressure growing in his chest began to wane.

"All right," he said with a nod.

"Good. Then you won't keep us waiting. Your mother's cooked lamb."

Allan shut the door behind him before Atherton could reply, leaving him alone once again.

Of course, he was hardly alone.

The limb of the man whose wound he'd been tending to was still slumped over the edge of the preparation table.

Atherton stared at his reflection in the mirror, waiting for the girl to return. He had grown so sleepless that in the gloom, his bruises and bags made his eye sockets appear like deep, hollow pits.

He couldn't say how long he'd been looking, growing numb to the whispers at the edge of his mind.

Only that the dangling limb started to sway, as though waving at him. And when he felt a cool breath on his cheek, the hairs on the back of his neck didn't stand, for his body was growing accustomed to it.

Atherton set aside his stubbornness to eat with his family. But in the later hours of that evening, long after the rest of the Graves joined the dead in repose, he donned a cloak and slipped out into the rainy streets.

After midnight, New Sarum was typically quiet. But ever since Lester and her performers arrived, the city agreed to extend its curfew. They even kept the Queen's Gate open to let circus-goers pass to and fro after dusk. But the circus had long since shut the gates for its final evening in New Sarum. Among the thousands of guests shuffling back into the city, Atherton was the only one walking toward the luminous tents. Flutters filled his chest with a clammy concoction of dread and nostalgia.

When he arrived, he was met by a familiar sight—a towering man chewing a cigar at the corner of his lips. Wearing only suspenders, trousers, and a coat, his smooth chest glistened with rain. It was Kayne's assistant, muttering farewells to departing patrons.

"Oi. The gates are closed," Thomas said, before Atherton withdrew his hood. "Oh dear, oh dear. If it ain't the man who beat the Devil at 'is own game. I almost didn't recognize ya without your head all squashed-like. And lookin' like a right swell on the up, at that. How may I be of service, kid?"

With his thick build, wary eyes, and unwavering confidence, Atherton couldn't be sure, but it struck him that Thomas must have been one of the men who exhumed Betty's body.

"It's a pleasure to see you well, Mr. Barker. If I'd expected such a warm welcome, I might've returned sooner. Mr. Todd asked me to return before you were off."

"Naturally. The bastard who got you into this mess oughta have some words for you. It's the least he can do, aye?"

Thomas arranged to have somebody else guard the gates. For every step the ghoul took, Atherton needed two to match. Once more in the glow of the carnival lanterns, the costumes, bannerlines, music, and decadent aromas, New Sarum's dimly lit streets felt like a cruel, damp world.

"He didn't think you'd come, Ivory," Thomas said. "He's a good man, aye. He's only got a temper like a hound just crawled from Hell, is all. Wrath. That's 'is sin. And pride. He trusts 'imself too much, even when other lives hang in the balance."

With nearly all the guests cleared, the circus folk were congregating toward the cookhouse. The steam and smoke billowing from the cooking fires could put a crematorium's smokestack to shame. Atherton found himself searching the crowd for Boo.

"Do Ivory's decisions often play a role in the life or death of others?" Atherton ventured.

"I've said too much. Best forget it."

Even though he wanted to ask whether or not Betty became an entrée for Thomas, he held his tongue. "How is it, being Mrs. Todd's assistant?"

"Beats playing the crooked cross. Not that it's strictly honest work. Meaning no offense, mind you. The Devil knows you're the undertaker turned stiff-dealer."

"Oh no, no, I'm afraid you're mistaken," Atherton laughed. "It was only the once."

Thomas cackled. "Right! Hah! Whatever you say."

"I was speaking in earnest."

"Sure, sure. You know you've got some dash-fire, taking an anointin' from the man 'imself. I thought you would'a croaked. 'Course, you're as balmy as they come, giving Mason the chiv. Not that the lot of us 'ere aren't all daft in our own way."

When they arrived at the Spirit Asylum, Thomas looked as though he was about to let a stray dog run off into the middle of a busy street. Crouching down to meet his eyes evenly, he said, "You watch over yourself, now."

Atherton's stomach sank. It was written in his eyes. The ghoul thought he was talking to a dead man. "I will."

"Good. And, ah, y'know, if you ever find yourself in the Big Smoke anytime soon..." He trailed off, pointing to one of Atherton's coat pockets.

In it, Atherton found two crisp tickets to the circus. The black tickets boasted *LONDON* in bold, silver letters on the backside of *ADMIT ONE - THE BLACK CARNIVAL*, bordered with serial numbers.

"A lifetime of nippin' pockets is finally good for something," Thomas said with a wan grin.

With a final pat that nearly knocked him off his feet, the giant strode off.

Once more, Atherton stood with his heart in his throat before the Spirit Asylum, where the light in the gas lamps swirled about with no wick holding their flames in place.

15

ATHERTON

MAY 17, 1886

Atherton desired another moment to collect himself, only to hear Ivory say from inside, "It must be cold, standing in the rain out there. Come in."

But he wasn't cold. Though the wickless flames in the lanterns were far from him, their unearthly light warmed him from the inside. He parted the flaps and left their comforting aura behind.

Tobacco smoke trailed the spiritualist as he collapsed chairs around the stage. His waistcoat was unbuttoned, his necktie as untidy as the peppered hair about his cheeks. He must've been eavesdropping on the conversation outside his tent. They looked at each other over the silence drowned by an ocean of words that had built up inside both of them.

Ivory held up a hand before Atherton could stammer out the apology he'd rehearsed. "No," he said with a disdainful laugh. "I'll be damned if you come here with your head bowed to me in shame. Here." Letting the chair in his hands fall into the stamped grass, he dug into his trousers, producing four pounds.

But Atherton didn't reach out. Uncertainty hooded his eyes. "What is this?"

"It's yours. I picked it up after...after it happened."

He blinked at the coins without comprehension. Ivory's hand was trembling.

"Hell, I hardly blame you. The last time you did business with me..." Ivory shook his head. "Just take it. After everything, you may as well."

"Why? Why should I trust you?" Atherton asked without malice.

"I don't expect you to. But it was never about the coin to Mason. Men like him could piss out four pound in a single evening and not think twice about it. You think he'd stoop to pick up gilt in front of a crowd after a clown beat his men to Gehenna and told him to hitch it back to London? He'd sooner be caught licking shit, so just take it!" Ivory's shout was deafening in the enclosed space, met by the clattering of metal on wood when he cast aside the coins in blind rage.

Atherton flinched, but he knew that rage was not meant for him.

Ivory jabbed a finger toward the cookhouse, which emanated the din of the circus's cast and crew eating. "If it weren't for that fucking clown, you'd be dead by now! Do you understand that? And I just stood there. Petrified. 'Nobody likes a coward,' huh? A damnable thing for a hypocrite to say."

Before, it was a truth that hung loosely in his mind. Not his parents, not Lilian, nor anybody admitted it outright to Atherton. Even if he knew it in his heart of hearts, this made it real. Ivory's cracking voice, his trembling body, the regret—red and sleepless in his eyes. The alcohol that failed to wash it away. That night, death had laced its strings through his body and almost scurried away with another puppet, but at the last hour, a stranger came and snipped the only thread left to sew.

A tear slipped down Atherton's face. "We chance fate every time we step outside our door. Isn't that right? And if God exists, he is as cruel as his worst creations. For we starve and we cry, we writhe and rot, our pleasures and pains dictated by little else than a rolling of the dice. And it drives the world mad, it does. It creates men whose fates grow only darker, their hearts lost to places so black that no light would dare pierce it. So any pleasure might then be owed to the Devil, whose hands at least join ours in iniquity. Who celebrates our brief respite from such horrors. Isn't that right, Mr. Todd?"

Ivory looked at Atherton over that reflective expanse that he'd just invited in, where momentarily their souls were naked and bathed in the heavy silence that followed. It was interrupted only by a shallow sniffle and the dampened fall of Atherton's tear hitting the trampled grass.

"Yes," Ivory said, looking as if he was holding back his own. "That's right."

Atherton turned away in an attempt to hide the cracks in his composure, only getting broader. "So you have nothing to apologize for," he said with a shuddering breath. "My pain is not yours to carry."

Ivory closed the small distance between them, placing a hand on

Atherton's shoulder with a firm squeeze. "But we bear the responsibilities brought to our doorstep. And I invited you to mine." Unfurling a white handkerchief from his pocket, Ivory handed it to him. "At least you've survived my arrogance."

Atherton wiped at his face and nodded his thanks. He paced around the sideshow tent, surveying the remnants of Ivory's show littered about. Most of it was packed away into trunks on the stage. Venetian masks, scrying orbs, a talking board, worn porcelain dolls that looked lonely yet foreboding—all told stories neither had time for. A pile of taper candles—the ones he considered were held aloft by string—were half packed away into a duffel bag. He picked one of them up, finding no such strings.

"Barker thinks it's all for naught. He all but said it. Mason will return for me. What do you think?" Atherton asked.

"That Prometheus knows how men like Mason think better than any mobsman on London's high street. He's right, I'm afraid."

Atherton picked up a worn music box and unlatched the lid, revealing a carved, veiled woman with a Venetian mask in one hand. He cranked the device until melancholic notes leaked out. The wooden figurine jolted to life, putting the mask with a curling grin on and off. The tiny mirror on the underside of the lid had been obscured with black paint.

"My father thinks otherwise," Atherton replied, setting the box down. "He worked with Logan before Mason took over."

"Your father is naive. Maybe it runs in the family," he said with a wry grin. "Deep down, he knows keeping you safe means uprooting your life and sending you off to hide in perpetuity. He's not prepared to see you off. And if you went missing, well, Mason would only turn his anger on him."

"What choice do I have? There is no life for me outside New Sarum."

Ivory quirked an eyebrow. "Luckily for you, I didn't call you here merely to apologize." Ivory strode up to the stage and disappeared behind the curtain.

Atherton listened to a trunk being opened and closed, followed by what sounded like small, metal pieces rattling in a container.

When the spiritualist returned, Atherton was staring at the gleam of a British Bull Dog revolver in a case lined with velvet. Its short, filigreed gray snout and black handle looked back at him. Beside it was a case of ammunition, without so much as a fingerprint tarnishing their gleam.

He picked up one of the .44 caliber bullets.

Dangling by its straps from Ivory's prosthesis was a holster.

"A bulldog with six teeth," Atherton observed.

"Indeed. Small enough to conceal, but it's got a bite to match its bark.

As for the harness, you loop these over your shoulders," Ivory said, jostling the belts, "and the gun will be concealed at your back beneath your coat or suit. If Mason does indeed come to finish what I started—"

"What we started," he corrected.

"The Devil knows I wouldn't wish this task on my worst enemy, but it's fallen into your hands. A boy knows how to start quarrels, but a man ends them."

Atherton nodded and slipped out of his cloak and suit.

When Ivory was finished strapping it to Atherton's chest, he stood back as though appreciating him in a new pair of shoes. It was a tight embrace, a pleasant weight. The quiet assurance of a vicious ally ready to spray death.

"There are a few dozen rounds in that box," Ivory said. "Not enough practice to turn you into a marksman, but enough to get you acquainted. Go far out in the woods, some isolated place where the shots won't be heard."

"Mr. Todd?"

"I think it's just Ivory, now. Trading stiffs and plotting murder makes us more than acquaintances, don't you think?"

"These weren't the answers I came here for. Even if I needed them." The undertaker's countenance was heavy with exhaustion, a weariness more suited to somebody twice his age.

"You see them, don't you?" Ivory asked, though it wasn't meant as a question. He heaved a sigh. "The people whose bodies you tend to. They linger. In your dreams, your waking life. You hear their voices, feel their touch, as real as you and me."

Atherton doubted himself, even then, hearing the words aloud. "Some more than others," he admitted.

Ivory nodded. "Then it is not just a mutual enemy that bonds us. I knew it the moment I saw you, Atherton, perhaps even before we met."

"How?" His brows furrowed. Even after all he'd seen, this felt like a reach.

"You asked me why I bothered to call the constables when I found Betty. You were right. I suspected she had no living relatives who'd come looking for her. But upon seeing her, I felt something, like the needle of a compass directing me. The dead are not bound by the natural laws of the living. They have a way of tying the past to the present, perhaps even what has yet to occur. They connect us, Atherton. They brought us together, haven't they?"

"I've felt it myself," Atherton realized aloud. "The emblem you found in Betty's body. Where was it?"

"Her throat."

"Then it is as I feared. There was another child. A little girl, just weeks passed. Her name was Alice. I extracted the same emblem from precisely the same location."

"This disproves my original assumption. Whoever is using these symbols is doing so with a nefarious intent. You really don't know anything about it, do you?"

"Nothing more than you told me."

Ivory held up two fingers. "You have two things lurking in your city. One, a murderer. And two, a witch—not the good kind, either. In all probability, they are the same individual. Whoever they are, they walk the Gehennic path. Her practices, however, are more...radical. Evil, if you believe in such a thing."

"Am I in danger?"

"More than you already are, you mean? I doubt it. Unless somehow you were acquainted with them. But what would the odds of that be in a city of this size? No one was meant to find that body out here in the sticks. But one thing is for certain—that girl didn't die of natural causes. Whoever did this is practicing."

Ivory paced about, drumming a finger on his prosthesis. The tired stupor Atherton felt turned to morbid fascination. He looked to the spiritualist as though the culprit was merely lurking in his thoughts, and if only he'd keep speaking, they'd appear before them.

"Practicing? For what?"

"Who knows. A spell, perhaps a ritual. Preparations for something bigger."

"You perform the same magic, don't you? You didn't purchase that case just to feed Thomas or any other ghouls who work here. You harvest something from the bodies. Essences for your own spellcraft. That's what all this is, isn't it?"

Ivory turned stony. "Outsiders aren't privy to this information. We prefer to keep it that way."

"You said it yourself. We are more than acquaintances."

"And I have family back in the States. People I cherish, whom I write letters to frequently. They think I'm a charlatan who uses magnets and parlor tricks to turn coin at a circus. I don't make it a habit of correcting them."

"You're a Gehennic just like the person who murdered Betty. And Alice. Most of the performers here are, aren't they?"

"Only some. It's just like you said—we owe ourselves to the Devil. Folks like us are just more honest about it."

The music from the music box struggled out a final note.

Ivory took Atherton's cloak and offered it. The rain had worsened since he arrived. The relentless patter drummed on the canvas. Thunder bellowed, close enough to vibrate in their bones. "You have enough on your mind as it is. But should you find yourself in London in a few weeks' time, I will indulge your curiosity. Every question, and more you've yet to consider. If Lester Black knew what conversations had transpired here, I would be out of a job."

Taking up his cloak, Atherton unfurled it and buckled it about his neck. "I understand," he said, parting the tent flaps.

"You have my gratitude, Ivory Todd," he said, striding out into the rain. The downpour fell in thick, gray curtains, but he knew another kind of storm was coming, one nobody could prepare him for. And perhaps it was Ivory's unflinching recognition of ghosts that, for the first time, Atherton almost craved the presence of one, if only to accompany him on the trek back to the city.

16

ATHERTON

MAY 20, 1886

The external combustion engine of the steam car billowed a cloud of white vapor as Atherton adjusted the throttle to accelerate. The boiler replied with enthusiasm, rumbling while steam hissed from the engine and exhaust. Allan had paid well to have the automobile outfitted with a covered back portion large enough for a coffin. For picking up cadavers from neighboring towns, the steam car was unreliable at best, but for a bit of flair at a funeral, it was nothing short of spectacular.

Atherton killed the engine outside of Lilian's orphanage, much to the bewilderment of all seven children who came running outside long before he had even escaped the seat. Atherton folded his riding spectacles before hoisting one of the children up to show her the breaking lever and steering rod.

"How does it work?" Lola asked, getting comfortable in his lap.

"Why, with magic of course," he said. "Go on, give this horn here a squeeze."

Lola managed to wrap her fist around the horn, clenching it enough to cause a feeble honk. She continued with the project of blaring the warning signal as rapidly as possible.

"I suspected it was you behind this," Lilian called from the porch with folded arms. "Back from the dead so soon?"

"I try not to keep the bereaved waiting," he called back.

"James!" Lilian shouted. "Don't touch that part, sweetheart, you'll burn off your pretty little hands."

James squealed after having done precisely that, touching a piece of the exposed engine with his finger. He scrambled up the porch steps to his matron, clutching the mortal wound while whimpering fitfully.

Lilian sighed and picked up the inconsolable child. "Shall we take this inside, Mr. Graves?" she asked. "We were just fixing tea before you maimed my child."

With Lola and four others in tow, Atherton managed to pry the children's attention from the vehicle, rather crestfallen that it hadn't the same enchantment for Lilian. He snatched up the bouquet of amaryllis from the passenger seat, plucked that morning from his mother's garden. Then he headed into the building, where Lilian had already set to work mending James's finger.

"What's that smell?" James asked, scrunching up his face.

Lilian glanced at Atherton's miffed expression as she wound the bandage, and didn't attempt to hide her smirk. With lamb stew simmering and a loaf of bread baking just down the hall, this insult carried more weight than usual. "That's only Atherton, my dear."

"He stinks."

"He *always* stinks!" Lola agreed from across the parlor.

"It's worse than when Lola dragged home that dead eel," Matthew added. The eight-year-old's hands were occupied with the two halves of a wooden horse he attempted to mend with wood glue.

"Children, let's practice our finest manners around Mr. Graves."

"No, that's quite all right." Atherton chuckled. He snuck a sniff of his collar, only to find a bit of decomposed skin smeared on his sleeve. He rubbed the spot until it faded somewhat.

"He runs his father's funeral parlor, remember?" Lilian reminded Matthew.

"Mrs. Butler!" Morma, the housekeeper, called from the kitchen. Just old enough to be out of Lilian's care, she had been an orphan herself not a year before. "Might you give me a hand?"

"Just a moment." Lilian squeezed Atherton's shoulder before standing to leave.

"Do you love Mrs. Butler?" Lola asked as soon as she'd left the parlor. "You always bring her flowers."

"Well then!" He shot to his feet with a rush of heat to his face. Evidently, he was more comfortable setting the features of dead children than speaking to live ones. "You'll have to excuse me, Lola. I'm going to visit the water closet."

Of course, Atherton had no need for the water closet. He spent a few minutes fixing his necktie and sorting out the nest that was his hair after the joyride. When he'd finished, he hadn't made a single step outside before meeting Lola's expectant gaze.

"I'm sorry I said you stink," she said.

"Oh, that's kind of you. But you don't need to apologize. It's just the truth, isn't it?"

"I'm sorry," she said again.

"You are forgiven. Do you forgive me for smelling like a rotten sock?"

The child nodded with a giggle, fidgeting with the frayed ends of her dress. "Mrs. Butler told me you speak to ghosts," she said.

Atherton checked to be sure there were no other children in the hallway. Lips pursed in contemplation, he crouched to meet her at eye level. Having spent a fair amount of time with them, he was used to the children blurting out nonsense. It was another matter when it caused a chill to roll up his spine. He lowered his voice to a murmur. "Does that frighten you?"

"Only if it's true."

Atherton wiped a bit of drool sliding from the edge of her mouth with his sleeve. It was a reflex. All manner of things leaked out of the bodies he tended to. "When did Mrs. Butler tell you this?"

"She tells me stories at night."

"What kind of stories?"

"She says they help me sleep."

"Do they?"

Lola's lazy eye went deeper into the corner of its socket as she looked away. "She gives me the syrup 'fore bed."

"You know, sometimes I drink the syrup to help me sleep, too. Mothers use it all the time, to help quiet the imagination of particularly bright children who can't help but think all night."

Lola's eyes flicked back up. "You think I'm bright?" she asked.

"Of course I do," he said, putting a stray lock of auburn hair behind her ear. "I think you're the most brilliant young lady I've ever had the pleasure of meeting."

Lola didn't quite know how to react, so she just fell into his chest for an embrace. "Mr. Graves?"

"Yes?"

"What do the ghosts say to you?"

"Oh, but I don't speak to ghosts," he said, pulling away and placing his hands on her shoulders. "Mrs. Butler was only telling a bedtime story."

"She don't lie. She never lies. She told me 'erself."

He searched her eyes, caught between frightening the child and tainting her image of Lilian. "I'm sure she doesn't lie, but stories aren't lies. Stories are just that, stories. They say things in ways one otherwise never could. Does that make sense?"

It took some time, but Lola nodded.

Atherton's eyes fell upon a delicate, silver chain draped around the collar of Lola's dress. The jewelry at the end of it was tucked into her breast pocket. Following his gaze, the child took it out.

The room swam. Betty's mangled cheeks. Alice's cold, porcelain skin. He could almost feel that silhouette from the embalming room. That rancid odor returned, caught between the fabric of figment and reality.

There it was again, staring at him.

"Do you like it?" Lola asked.

"Well, sure," he stammered. "Where did you get this?" He traced the six points of the pendant with his finger, the cold metal licking his skin.

"From the market. I found it on the ground. Mrs. Butler said I ought not to, but I said I'd read every day for a week if she let me keep it."

"Oh," he managed, the knots in his stomach unwinding themselves. "And did you?"

"Yes," Lola said with a vindictive smirk. "I did."

"Children! Supper!" Morma called from the dining room.

The child squealed, tripping over her feet as she raced away. Atherton might've collapsed from the relief. He let his back slide against the wall of the hallway and sank to his haunches. A draft of fresh, spring air fluttered through an open window, caressing his hair, the cold sweat on his forehead, and whisking away the phantom smell that he assured himself was never there.

❦

By the time Lilian and Morma had finished washing up, Atherton and Matthew had made short work of a few broken toys in need of mending. Lola, Cassidy, and Vivie practiced handwriting at the dining table, its dishes and cutlery now replaced with books, candles, and tea beside a plate of shortbread. In a room across the hall, staccato notes played from an upright piano as Lilian helped Ella stumble through Beethoven's *Moonlight*

Sonata. Simon and James were engaging in warfare outside, firing imaginary cannons from the motor car.

Twilight swallowed their shadows, engulfed the countryside in its sable tones, the horizon bloody with clouds stretching to its darker edge.

"You like playing surgeon?" Atherton asked Matthew.

The boy was chewing at his lip, affixing the tiny head of a wooden soldier back onto its body. "I like it. Maybe one day I can fix myself," he said. The fingers of Matthew's right hand were fused together, leaving him with a single digit at the end of what was otherwise a stump.

"I saw a few people like you when I was at the circus with Mrs. Butler the other night. Nobody thought they needed fixing."

"Why's that?"

"Well, they had all sorts of talents. There was a man with no legs swallowing a sword *this* long. Three swords, actually."

"That's bollocks!"

"Matthew." Morma hummed from her reading chair.

"It wasn't real, I mean," Matthew corrected.

"Oh, but it was. There were fire breathers, magicians, and unicyclists. Deformities abounded at the circus, but they were wonders all the same. You hardly noticed. It made me think I needed more fixing than them."

"But you aren't like me," Matthew said.

"Maybe not on the outside, but some people need fixing in here." Atherton put a finger to his head. "D'you know what I mean?"

"S'pose. Will you be staying the evening?"

It was a question Atherton had meant to ask Lilian. Facing the real possibility that his days were numbered at New Sarum, he wanted as much time with her as could be afforded. He enjoyed the children, too. Despite their distaste for the aroma of his profession, the orphans didn't harbor the judgment that he bore curses or illnesses everywhere he walked. Such was the keen wisdom reserved for adults. "Maybe if you ask for me, Mrs. Butler will allow it."

Matthew bolted up and into the music room.

The boy returned with Lilian not long after. Ink stained her fingers from writing on the ledgers of Ella's sheet music. The look in her eyes mystified Atherton—romantic affection was no more familiar to him than sunlight was to nocturnal creatures.

"She said you could stay!" Matthew exclaimed.

"Morma, would you be so kind as to watch over the little ones a little later than usual? I think Mr. Graves has some important matters to discuss with me," Lilian said. "There's a bottle of sherry in my cabinet that you're welcome to."

Without looking up from her book, Morma said, "Sold. Run along then. We aren't going anywhere."

<hr />

Lilian's hand rested in Atherton's lap as they sped down the backroads behind the orphanage, the steam car sputtering as they bumped along.

"Quite a vocal contraption, isn't she?" Lilian asked.

"It grows on you," Atherton said, closing the throttle. With the chugging and hissing silenced, they could hear the gentle sounds of water lapping at Goremire Lake's gritty shores. Wind trembled the lake's otherwise placid surface—a sheen of gray clouds punctuated with reeds sprouting from its edges.

"Well, Mr. Graves, you've succeeded in bringing a widow out to the middle of nowhere. Have you brought your straight razor with you to finish the job?"

Atherton chuckled. "Only after you've seen the bats."

"The what?"

He pointed toward the wych elms bordering the lake, their boughs like black veins against the sky.

"I don't see them," Lilian said.

"Watch closely."

Twilight was the only time to catch the horseshoe bats flying between branches. They darted from the boughs, dipping and pirouetting. Here and there, a glimpse of one's full wingspan would break the spell of them appearing like nothing more than chunks of ash flitting about.

Atherton pointed again, and Lilian leaned forward to see their bodies bobbing through the grass, bending forward to drink from the lake.

"Flighty little bastards, aren't they?" she remarked.

"Yes. My mother used to bring me here when I was little."

"Strange, isn't it?"

"What is?"

"Moments like this make time feel so kind. Then you blink and there you are—bang. Years gone in an instant; suddenly, you're a different person. I bet you can shut your eyes and you're a boy all over again. I bet, sometimes, you look in the mirror and hardly recognize yourself."

"Lately, when I shut my eyes, I'm at the carnival again. Lying in your lap. That clown, looking down at me, wearing the blood of those men. Henry and Arthur."

"It suited him. Have you decided what you're to do about the Disciples? Will you leave?"

"I am taking...precautions. But leaving is out of the question."

Lilian hummed, caressing the nape of his neck. "Do you know what Mason will do when he comes back?"

"Don't you think it's about time I started wondering what *I* will do?" he snapped.

"Maybe it wasn't my place to ask."

He reached for his cigarette case and pulled out his matchbook. "No, no, it's not you," he mumbled, rubbing his eyes. "It's everything else. And you are my only reprieve from it. Forgive me."

But before he could place a cigarette in his mouth, Lilian took it from his fingers, leaning closer, until he had no choice but to face her.

"I think you brought me here expressly for a different purpose than sighting a few bats," Lilian said.

Atherton felt the heat of her thighs pressing against his own. One of her hands slid over his chest, the other into his.

A fire kindled, blazed, and rampaged through his ribs. He chanced her waist with his hand somehow, and was shocked that she allowed it to remain there. "And what would that purpose be exactly?" he asked.

"That night, just outside the spiritualist's tent, we were pressed together in a way not at all dissimilar to this."

"That's strange, I can hardly remember," he lied.

The blackness of her eyes seemed to devour his thoughts, giving none of hers away. "Well, do better," she said.

"Ah, right. Now I have it."

"Do you remember what you wanted to do in that moment? What singular thought left none other to be desired?"

"I do. And it's tormented me," he said, "more than most."

She ran the back of her hand along his cheek before cupping it, pulling him closer until her eyelashes brushed against his. "And did you think you were alone in that torment?"

"No. I knew it for certain."

In that fickle bliss was the promise of a greater pain, only making it taste sweeter. Atherton didn't care that his teeth knocked against hers as he pressed their lips together, or that his hands shook when he gripped her jaw. Neither Mason nor death could overshadow that rapture. He sank into her warmth—that sense of two colliding souls sharing a solitude surrounded by nightmares, the barest pocket of respite carved out of an ever-darkening, spiralling Hell. Her lips felt more plump and softer than all the thousands of times he'd fantasized about them. But what surprised him most was that they seemed to be paired perfectly, as though every curve had a matching ridge to sink into against his own, as though it would be blasphemy to taste anybody besides her.

The sky swam when they pulled apart.

That moment might as well have been his happiest. What else was there to do but try to recreate it? He hadn't taken a full breath before leaning back in, only for her to place a firm hand against his chest.

"I think you should stay the night," she said.

"But I've already spent time with the children, and it's nearly dark," he observed.

"No, my dear. I don't think you're hearing me. I think you should *stay* the night."

"Oh. But by that you mean to say..." he cleared his throat. "Oh."

※

Atherton splashed a thumb of whisky into a snifter, hoping to dull the tremor in his hands. The empty parlor fluttered with candlelight. In Morma's reading chair sat a scandalous novel about marital infidelity, a crow's feather sticking from its pages.

Venturing upstairs to where Lilian was putting the children to bed, Atherton stood beside the doorway of the bedroom shared by the four girls. The bedroom for the three boys was just down the hall.

A familiar melody drifted out from the girls' room.

> *Have you seen Minnie's scarecrow*
> *Have you been to the old brook*
> *We'd a-looked and shook the earth*
> *But our bones ached, our little old legs*
> *Ran red looking for Minnie Pegs*
> *Have you been to the water*
> *Have you been 'round the market*
> *We'd a-looked and drained the Thames*
> *But our bones ached, our little old legs...*

"Ran red looking for Minnie Pegs," he whispered to himself.

Crow-bitten legs swaying in the forest. An open throat, cold and yawning on a steel table. Maggots squirming against his palm.

He squeezed his eyes shut.

Lilian emerged from the bedroom. The aroma of doused candles followed as she eased the door shut behind her. "That should do it," she whispered with an eager smile. "Heavens, are you well? You look—"

"Nerves. Only nerves."

"There's nothing to be nervous about, I assure you," she said. Taking his hand, she led him up the old, creaking stairs to the third floor. Atherton had never seen beyond the hallway on the second story. As they went up the narrow staircase, his feet followed a line in the wood—an indentation in the center of the stairway—persisting through the doorway of Lilian's chamber.

The streak continued beneath the ornate rug covering her floor.

A vase housed the amaryllis that Atherton had brought that afternoon, sitting on her dressing table. Dark wood carved in floral wreaths cradled its mirror, marred from neglect. Lilian set about lighting candles, finishing with the candelabras beside her bed. The rusted metal was fashioned in the likeness of hands reaching out from the wall.

His eyes followed the curves of her hips beneath her dress and her arching spine as she went on her tiptoes to light the candles. Nakedness was nothing new to him. He'd seen, felt, punctured, sutured, and washed more naked bodies than could be counted.

Somehow, they failed to prepare him for this.

He was torn between throwing himself upon her or out the window. Should he undo his necktie? Unbutton his waistcoat?

He let out a short hum, simultaneously petrified and exhilarated by what was about to happen. "I'm afraid I don't know how all this works," he whispered with a bowed head.

"Oh, you sweet thing," she replied. "You don't have to."

She faced him, staring out of arm's reach. Candlelight haloed her head, casting a dark veil over her face. The look she gave him refashioned melancholy into something unfathomable, a puzzle he could never solve.

She stepped toward him. Each one accelerated his heartbeat. She took him in her arms when she was close enough—he made no mistake, knowing it could never have been the other way around.

"We stand at a crossroads," she told him, "between life and death, caught in the agony of prying joy out of seconds designed to destroy us. But there are moments like this one, where the barest sensation is all the difference between Heaven and Hell." Her eyes never leaving his, she undid the buttons of his waistcoat, his shirt, his necktie, just to slip a hand through the folds where she placed a palm over his heart. "Like this one," she said. "Like this one," she said again, kissing his neck. "Like this one," she repeated, taking his hands and bringing them to her lips.

Atherton rested his forehead against hers.

"You're crying," she whispered. "Why are you crying?"

"I don't know," he admitted.

"I call it love. What do you call it?"

"Grief."

Lilian traced a finger over his nose, lips, and finally his chin, nudging it up until he had no choice but to feel his inhibitions melt beneath her softening eyes. "You mourn for an evening that hasn't passed yet. For a love that is yet to be broken."

"I am damned to see things for what they will become, not as they are," he said as he wept, shattered that those words had left him. "I'm sorry. I'm so sorry," he said, turning away and wiping at the tears. "I hadn't intended for you to see me like—"

"Shhh," Lilian hushed, turning him back around. "You have nothing to be sorry for. Your sorrow is not unwelcome in my home. Are you sure you want this?"

Want this? Atherton repeated to himself. Lilian's love was a crackling hearth to all his winter nights, a symphony answering to the years of quiet solitude, a dream blooming from the fertile earth of all his writhing nightmares.

She took his hands in hers, guiding his fingers through the liberation of all the tedious laces and layers of cloth that stood between them, until they each stood naked in that flickering candlelight. Lilian's ravenous appetite was being revealed through a veil of placidness, growing thinner by the moment through her hungry eyes, her searching fingers, and at least through her delighted grin, which shed that mask entirely—an equal source of vindication and disquiet for Atherton.

"I could want for nothing more than to share this night with you," he finally answered.

"Then close your eyes."

He did.

"And what if I cannot bring myself to look away when I open them?" he asked, his cold hands nearly in pain against the blazing heat of her body, as she threaded her thigh between his and pressed herself against him.

"Then, even if just for one night, you will have to see the world the way I do."

"And how is that?"

"As only a theater."

17

MASON
JUNE 1, 1886

Eyes hooded beneath a bandit cap, Mason inhaled Whitechapel's putrid air, thick with the stench of families languishing in single rooms. Throngs of dirtied faces surrounded him, accompanied by the patter of barefoot children pushing barrel hoops with sticks.

With outstretched arms and a vulpine grin, Mason exclaimed, "It's a new day!"

It was, in fact, dusk. Brooding storm clouds robbed the dingy street of sunset, illuminated instead by the amber glow of a hazy, gaslight gloom.

Lighting a cigarette, he leaned back on his carriage. A silver *C* studded its doors. Inside, Henry and Arthur were deep into an argument about the quality of bordellos across the city. The parked carriage jostled as words devolved to insults and, rather predictably, blows.

"Spare a farthing, mister?" a voice piped from below.

Mason regarded the soot-ridden face of a child standing before him with a quirked eyebrow.

She leaned on a single crutch with a bandage over her left eye. Ragged holes pockmarked her trousers, the last threads of a single suspender clutching onto the threadbare fabric.

"Go on, then. Give us your show."

The child limped weakly in a circle before stumbling into a curtsy. "The workhouse won't 'ave me with me leg," she recited. "All's I need is a tuppenny for bread. 'Umbly, sir."

"A tuppenny, eh?" Mason bent down and wrenched off the bandage over her eye, revealing it to be perfectly healthy, to which they both widened in sheer panic. He kicked out the crutch from under her. The child stumbled, catching herself on her "bad" leg.

"Oi!" she called.

"I'll be damned. It's a miracle, innit? Leg's healed."

"It ain't! The pain is something awful, sir."

"Sure it is, love."

Reaching into his waistcoat pocket, Mason tossed a shilling up, catching it again before the child's dirtied fingers could. Grabbing her tattered shirt, he pulled her closer and jabbed a callused finger. "In my time, the kid wranglers would cut it off if you couldn't act it out proper. Next time, fall."

Mason chucked the shilling down the street. Even before the coin was bouncing down the torn cobblestone, the girl was off in a feverish dart, drawing other children to it like ducks for a scrap of bread.

"Bloody guttersnipes." He laughed.

The sound of hurried stomps came bounding from behind him. Done up in a herringbone waistcoat and pants, a young boy arrived panting with his hands on his knees. Silver crosses studded his shoes, the soles rubbed smooth. "Mr. Cross! I found 'em!"

"Took you long nuff, Leo," Mason said. "Give us the good news."

Heaving like a trout out of water, Leo held up a finger.

"Fuck's sake. This ain't a *matinée*, boy."

With sweat dripping through his black hair, Leo fumbled through papers stuffed into a messenger satchel. "Fleet Street, sir. Headed east toward St. Paul's Cathedral," he said, handing Mason a crumpled flyer. "They're making slow work of it, putting these up."

"Fleet Street? Christ, you ran far, 'aven't you?" Mason snatched up the herald and gave it a cursory glance. "Right. Anything else?"

"My friends saw them raising their tents just this morning," Leo said, hopping from one foot to the other nervously. "They must've just arrived yesterday evening."

"So they have." Then, calling behind him, "Bram! Ready the horses."

The coachman hollered back, setting down his newspaper and grabbing onto the reins.

Leo mopped at the sweat with the ends of his waistcoat. "I ran like the Devil was on me, sir. Just like you said."

"Of that I've no doubt." Mason hopped into the carriage, giving Arthur a hard shove to make room. "You heard the man, Bram. Fleet

Street, headed east." Shutting the carriage door, Mason tossed a sovereign up.

The adolescent caught the coin with a curse. Clamping his hands upon it, he looked to make sure nobody noticed before peeking between his palms, as though it might fly away. Before Leo could get on his knees to thank him, Mason held up a hand, "Spare me. Take the week, Leo. Fine work."

"Hell, with this I'll take the whole month!"

Mason clicked his tongue. "No, you won't."

"Right, sir. Just the week then."

"Good lad. And don't spend it in an alley. Bram!"

The coachman's whip cracked, a spark of life in a street brimming with plodding souls. Mason pulled shut the curtains, but not before crumpling the flyer and tossing it out. All about them were embittered expressions and hungry faces—denizens of Hell catching a whiff of angels passing through. It was the smell of fine tobacco, spiced cologne, gunpowder, tailored threads, and the smoldering of time ill spent—time enjoyed.

With the crowded streets of London being a ramshackle mess of commuting hordes in the early evening, the Black Carnival's performers were giving Mason a run for the sovereign he paid Leo. Not even Bram, whose shouts rang out louder than most, could disperse the crowds long enough to get the horses into a consistent trot.

Stretching all the way to St. Paul's Cathedral, Fleet Street was littered with flyers. Already, Lester's crew had disappeared among the sea of bodies navigating the thoroughfare. Every sideshow and tent had its own advertisement. Mason stepped out just to wrench off the portrait of a familiar face.

BOO: THE CLOWN WITH A JINXED CAP was advertised in bold letters, adorned with clubs and balls dancing about his head.

"I'll jinx 'is cap all right," Mason muttered beneath his breath, climbing inside the carriage with a slam.

"What'd you expect? Even those balmy tinkers won't make retribution easy." Henry shook his head.

Mason removed a glove and brought it hard across Henry's face. "No wonder you got your teeth kicked in by some mute clown," he said. "Next time, it's the fist."

Henry mumbled a weak apology.

Arthur snatched up the flyer. "The blasted coward he is. Next time I see him, I'll—"

"You'll do *what*? Earn yourself another pair of blinkers to match the crack in your jaw?" Henry interjected. It earned yet another blow—this time from his brother—knuckles landing square on the bridge of his bruised nose. Tears sprang to his eyes.

"Can't believe I work for you pricks," he muttered.

"Told you it'd be the fist. But your little brother's not wrong," Mason said to Arthur, who still had the faded indigo remnants of two black eyes. "Say what you will about Bip or Bop or whatever the fuck 'is name is, he knows how to fight."

"I told you he struck me. From! Above!" Arthur fumed. "It ain't right. If we'd 'ave seen that little piss mop coming..." Arthur just growled and shook his head, saying again, "It ain't right."

Mason scoffed, running his hands along his stubble. His knee drummed as his eyes scanned the crowds. "There's no 'right' in a scrap. You're just sour you lost. If I 'ave to endure another moment of you two whingin' about it, by God, I'll give you a mercy that clown couldn't."

After a pensive silence, Arthur nodded. "We won't let it happen again." Arthur jabbed a leg at his little brother, still nursing a thin stream of blood coming from his nose.

"Right. That's the end of it," Henry added.

※

With the sun well beneath the outline of London's crammed dwellings and shops, Bram had lit the lanterns at either end of the carriage. Then came calls from the coachman that set a keen grin on Mason's face. "Oi! Mr. Cross. They's just up ahead!"

The mobster thrust his head out from between the window curtains to see for himself. Never had the sight of juggling clubs dancing above crowds summoned such a vengeful fire in him, or perhaps anybody. "They're across the Courts of Justice. It's poetic, innit?" Mason dug into the pocket of his coat, sliding brass knuckles over his hand. Arthur and Henry withdrew billy clubs from beneath the upholstered seats.

Before Bram even had a chance to halt the horses, Mason kicked open the carriage door and leapt into the street, the long tails of his coat unfurling behind him. "Have it ready nearby, Bram," he called.

"Aye, sir."

Arthur and Henry followed suit, their carriage door knocking over a mother strolling with her children. She fell to the ground with a, "By God!"

"Apologies, miss," Henry tipped his hat and stepped over her. "Business of the Disciples."

For all the finery decorating his fingers and suit, Mason loosed himself upon the crowd gathered around the street show like the delinquent Whitechapel had raised him to be. "Right! Out the way! Oaf! Get a move on! Move!" he roared, shoving and swatting his way through. Learning from others who had been sent to the ground, the last row of Londoners cleared a path for the three Disciples.

The street show was outside a café, its surrounding walls plastered with advertisements.

There were four performers in total—three of them jugglers. A ticket seller in face paint stood nearby with a pouch for payment at his feet. Its velvet was brimming with coins. The transaction between him and a local halted promptly.

Having spotted the Disciples out of the corners of their eyes, the performers' triangle of cascading clubs came to a chaotic end. The props rained down, making a messy clatter of wood striking stone, the last sound before the dismayed silence that fell on the jugglers' faces.

When Mason set his eyes on them, he huffed with a petulant shake of his head. Not a freakish clown named Boo to be found. That's when he found a recognizable, petite, French acrobat spinning in a cyr wheel, her lean arms and legs spread out as it twirled on the wide pavement. She was moving too quickly to take keen note of the ominous air that had descended.

By the time she had, it was too late.

Mason pointed at the jugglers with a nod to Henry and Arthur, who went after them like starved Rottweilers.

"And you. You stay *right there!*" he bellowed at the ticket seller trying to make off with the sack of coins.

"Veno, sir," he said with a shaking voice, raising his arms up and planting on his knees.

"Veno? Your mum 'ad one too many when she named ya, eh? You already know mine, don't you, boy."

"Y-yes."

The brothers caught and dragged the jugglers back to their place beside the abandoned clubs, their vain attempts to slink through the crowd brought to a decisive end. Henry and Arthur hammered away at their heads, cracking whatever bones they threw up to protect their skulls.

Seeing the blood splash the pavement among the fray of coats and broken fingers, Florence stumbled out of her cyr wheel. She stepped backwards as far as she could, only for the wall of the café to halt her.

Customers at a nearby table fled. Fine china and teapots shattered beneath one of the performers being thrown upon a table.

"Come on!" Arthur taunted, but the unconscious juggler just slunk to the ground, groaning and clutching a broken arm. Mason towered over Florence, the sound of more shattering forearms cracking between curdling howls behind him. Henry threw his club back to bring down another blow. In doing so, blood flicked backwards, spattering neatly across Mason's face. "Not so nice being on the other end, is it?" he asked Florence.

"*Va te faire foutre,* you dog!"

Mason lunged forward, grasping a fistful of stripes in her blouse. His forearm trembled as he raised her up until her feet dangled above the pavement. "I remember you."

"Hard to forget this face, no?"

"You dragged my men through the mud like animals."

Florence hawked a thick wad of phlegm, spraying it over his face. "They enjoyed it, too. Virgins like it when pretty girls touch them."

Mason couldn't help but hiccup a laugh. "I would say you'd regret saying that, but all this was, well, preempted, you might say. This gives me no joy, *mon cheri*," he lied.

"You will rot, Mason Cro—"

The dull *clunk* of the mobster's brass knuckles colliding with Florence's skull turned her eyes upwards. Eyelids fluttering, her body turned limp as a doll, making it all the easier for him to toss her over his shoulder. He wiped at the saliva on his face with the back of his hand.

For a spell, that little pocket of Fleet Street was as quiet as a library, save for the shuffling of china pieces on the ground as Henry and Arthur observed their finished work, bleeding over the pavement. The peelers had since been called, but as was usual, they were dependably reluctant to intervene, having spotted the crosses adorning the mobsters' shoes.

Mason stepped toward the ticket seller, collecting the pouch at his feet with a satisfied grin. "Why, this almost weighs as much as this one."

"Her name's Florence."

"Charmed. Now, Vaino—"

"Veno, sir."

The mobster flashed a glare. Veno flinched, surprised to find his lower jaw still intact.

"Veno, then. You tell Lester Black we're square for Boo's little tantrum.

Well," he added, jostling Florence, "after she gets this one back. I can't speak to 'er being in the same condition, mind you. You tell Lester that your unbroken bones are a gesture of good faith. We're not monsters, just businessmen."

Turning toward the brothers, who were still giving half-hearted kicks into the maimed and battered troupe of jugglers, Mason called, "Ready, lads?"

The crowd, hundreds deep, parted for the mobsters bespattered with scarlet. Florence was the first to be thrown into the carriage that waited at the end of the street before the others hopped inside. And for all the countless onlookers concentrated around that café, looking on with little else than murmurs, for once, Fleet Street was remarkably clear of foot traffic.

It made Bram's job go on without a hitch, disappearing into the fog.

18

ATHERTON

JUNE 1, 1886

"The flowers are cruel."

Atherton bolted up in his bed with a galloping heart, cold sweat, and fabric clinging to him. Shadows flitted from the corner of his room, sweeping through the doorway. It eased shut with a click.

"Delma? Delma, is that you?"

No response came.

Moonlight broke through the clouds and shone through his window, falling on his chest now heaving with ragged breaths. A pocket watch on the nightstand ticked away the third hour of morning, those seconds impossibly loud. He swept aside curls of dark hair, reaching for the ladle resting in a water basin beside his bed.

Another hand found his first. Reaching from beneath the bed, gray, mottled fingers wrapped around his wrist.

Atherton leapt out of his skin, throwing himself backwards. He skittered to the edge of the bed frame and continued pressing himself against it, pushing his legs into the mattress, wishing it would fall backwards into an abyss, an unconscious void to cradle him.

It's just a nightmare.

But thinking it only made him realize how wrong that was. He waited, time moving only slower for it. A rancid smell engulfed the room, thicker and more corporeal the more he breathed. Somewhere between that grasping hand and the infinite ticking of his timepiece, his thirst dared him to lean over the bed once more. This time, he stared into the basin's water expectantly. His reflection shone back, eyes wide and searching. But no hand came.

He dunked the ladle in and gulped greedily.

"Only a nightmare," he said again, now splashing his face.

He struck a match and lit the gas lamp on his nightstand. Settling back into his bed, he felt something. It was cold. Or rather—as he came to the creeping, paralyzing realization—*she* was cold.

That same hand from before now slid over his arm, settling into his. A frigid, almost friendly intertwining of fingers. He could feel every crease and stiff wrinkle of her waterlogged skin where it touched his. Even her breath—how it curled about him with the weighted miasma of moldy crops. It was the first time he summoned the courage to look at one of his visitors fully. No mirrors. No sideways glances. No peeking out from beneath covers. His eyelid twitched, as though his sinews rebelled against the movement.

He took all of her in. Her desiccated feet, her tibias protruding like blades through the skin of her legs. The remnants of a night gown, revealing yet more flesh, pocked with bone. There was no glow, no translucent form like in the storybooks. She felt as tangible as anybody, yet rotted and still puppeteered by living motives. That was what unsettled him the most. The longer he stared at her, the more normal it all felt.

Alice's clouded eyes brimmed with a depthless yearning, searching his. Every so often, she'd look to the ceiling, behind him, or somewhere else as though distracted, only to refocus her attention. Her lips weren't blue like the day he'd carried her onto his embalming table. They had blackened, a colorless blight spreading throughout, revealing her cheekbones.

"Alice?" was all he could think to say.

"*Don't cry.*" She attempted a smile, but her taut skin only served to bare teeth shedding their gums.

Though a single tear slipped from his eye, he nodded. It was not from terror nor sorrow, though they certainly played their parts; the depthless twilight swirling in Atherton could consume a blade of lightning without catching fire.

"*Your father is wrong.*"

"About what?"

"*Everything.*"

Alice opened her mouth. Her bones creaked with the yawning of her jaw as she mimed reaching in and pulling out the emblem from her throat. But her fingers returned empty. "*Do you remember?*"

"Of course."

"*You still haven't found them.*"

"Found who?"

Alice's eyes shifted. That keen knowing dissolved, as though a kind of amnesia had rushed in. "*You took my doll, George. You took it. That wasn't fair.*"

Then he understood. The riddles. The speech stitched together from recollections muddied with time. *The dead don't just rot; they grow mad*, he realized.

"I'm not George."

"*...no. You aren't.*"

"You're here for a reason, aren't you? Do you remember what? Why?" he whispered.

"*Mother told me not to talk to strangers. I should have listened. But she seemed so kind.*"

"Your eyes were so blue, Alice. Blue like a frozen lake, the morning I carried you. When I met you. Do you remember?"

Alice reached up, tracing Atherton's face. "*You were so careful.*"

Rigid, russet bone protruded from the tips of her fingers. She was straining, struggling to speak, but produced nothing. Alice leaned nearer, her coarse hair brushing his skin as her lips touched the edge of his ear. The next words were so quiet, he was certain he heard them somewhere in the back of his mind.

"*The Crowley twins.*"

Then he felt the room heave, sway, lurch like a boat in a stormy sea. Something poured into his mouth and throat. He coughed and clutched at his neck. A thick, vaporous substance gushed out, spilling from his nostrils and mouth. Gasping for air, he stumbled out from his bed, grasping onto his dressing table. That bitter substance slithered back inside, filling his lungs and settling there.

When he turned toward his bed, Alice had gone. His bedroom was empty. But already he was moving, hands reaching for a nearby pair of trousers. He would not sleep any longer.

※

Rain lashed and made the earth a sodden quarrel with Atherton, and every stab of his shovel into the earth. He was grateful for the roaring downpour, masking his grunts and shouts as he dug with abandon. Lightning crackled overhead. It illuminated the etching *Clarence & Chester Crowley* on their tombstone, and cast their undertaker's shadow in the wild fray of his cloak whipping against the muddying winds.

When his shovel struck the coffin, he cast it aside and threw himself upon it. He clawed the last of the dirt away, soil caking into his fingernails. Atherton cursed as his hands, numb and slick, were bitten into by metal and wood as he fumbled with the coffin's latches. Then he heard the damp *clerghk* of their unlocking. Legs straddling the ditch on either side, he took in a final gulp of air before throwing the coffin lid wide.

A lifetime of practice failed him. The twins were laid beside each other, head to foot. Their rot had concentrated, a month's worth of accumulated gases with no means of escape. All at once, their putrefaction engulfed him in a spoiled embrace.

He retched—a reaction he prided himself on not succumbing to in years. "No one has to know," he assured himself as he heaved out the sick. Biting back yet more bile, he howled "I'm sorry!" to the disturbed twins.

Time had made clear outlines of their skeletons beneath their flesh.

Then he straddled the coffin, shaking his head.

I've gone mad, he thought, reaching into the first twin's mouth with a gloved hand. The stiffened muscles creaked as his fingers pried the jaw apart. Their half-lidded, sunken sockets seemed to scrutinize him. No matter how good his intentions, that sensation writhed around his heart like a serpent, constricting.

He struggled for minutes. Rain poured down his back, leaving no inch of him dry. It became apparent that he could not bring himself to choose between possibilities: the evidence for the murder of these twins or his abject madness.

In that instant, he could leave it, never to recognize a phantom or night terror as reality again, and ignore the whispers of the dead and all their disturbed ravings. He had enough on his mind without chasing ghosts, without reaching into the gates of Hell through the rotted mouths of the innocent.

Then he felt it. A sliver of metal.

Grasping its edge, he withdrew the emblem from the child's throat. Lightning thrashed overhead—just long enough to see it. Even marred by slipped skin and tawny blood, there wasn't a shade of doubt.

Atherton sank down, his head bowed.

"I'm not mad. I'm not mad," he said, but no matter how long he repeated it, nor how taut his hand grasped the rusting emblem, no surcease arrived. He was alone, without even the murmurs of wandering specters to accompany his muted sobs.

19

BOO
JUNE 2, 1886

Boo ran his hands along a set of aerial silks in the Flying Maffickers tent. He remembered how they had first felt to him. Slick, disobedient. When he had first arrived, the aerialists made it look second nature, as though the silks would lift him to the air, submit so readily to his will, and suspend gravity so long as he held on tight.

How wrong he'd been. Instead, it would take years of graceless conditioning, flailing, falling, grunting, crying, gritting. It was a wonder how graceful, seemingly effortless movements demanded such agony. There were ropes, aerial hoops, and trapezes hanging from the trussing like ornaments over a crib, glittering with the first rays of dawn.

It was time for breakfast at the circus, but Boo had been dodging the company of his colleagues every chance he got. Alone in the tent, he trained on each apparatus, his body contorting, spinning, climbing, and dropping masterfully on each one. Somewhere between them all, he was pulled away to a place of aimless thoughts and memory.

"What about tickets, hm? We can start with something small," Lester said.

An eleven-year-old Boo looked up from beneath the brim of his oversized fool's cap, too uncertain to give any indication of agreement at all.

"Here," she said, producing a ticket with a small puff of smoke.

The child took it into his hands, eyes wide. Now he was certain this was a dream.

"Now, hand it back."

He wanted nothing more than to keep it forever. Reluctantly, he placed it in her open palm. As soon as she grasped it, the ticket combusted in her fist. He grasped out for the firefly cinders as if he might put them together again, fearing he'd made a horrible mistake.

"Then I would say, 'Welcome to the Black Carnival.' Simple, yes? Now it's your turn," she said, producing another ticket, "I'll hand you the ticket, then you say it."

Few memories stood out more prominently than that quiet morning when he had walked through the gates for the first time a decade before. Craning his neck to look at the three-headed lamp swirling with dull, gray light, London's smokestacks fogged the sky behind him—the only world he knew. Cruel and cold, but familiar. Lester had been holding his hand as she showed him the circus grounds, yet all he wondered was when she would finally realize he had nothing to offer her and send him back to Bethlehem Asylum, where she'd found him.

His long days of training were plagued by memories of the hospital in the beginning. Sometimes, they still were. Though the circus was a new world, it teemed with all the shadows of an old one loath to release its fangs. The caustic cleanings, forced vomitings, and bleedings. Those choirs of moans from other confused, writhing souls trying to scratch themselves out of their own skin. He wouldn't let Lester near his head so long as she had a pair of scissors in her hand, so averse was he of being shaved as he had been so routinely. It would be a whole year before he let her take but an inch off, and even that ended in tears.

On the outside, he read an article by a doctor citing that Bedlam's conditions resembled a dog kennel. But even dogs get pets when they shiver and droop their ears. At Bedlam, they thought illnesses of the mind could be expelled through beatings. And for Boo with his persistent *melancholia* among a score of other maladies, that was a favored treatment.

When word had spread of what landed him in the hospital, the others withdrew their warmth around him. Beneath their pleasantries was a deep skepticism—even trepidation. And he could hardly blame them. The tragedy at Boo's residence when he was nine years old had sparked a frenzy in the press which reignited for months. Were it not for the squabble of lawyers and authorities clamoring to get a piece of the story, fate might've yet seen him dangle from a noose held by the law. There were nights at Bedlam when he'd wished it were so.

Then again, it was that same scrap of infamy which found itself in Lester's newspaper one morning, inspiring a keen intuition to investigate what brilliant madness might've curdled in the heart of a boy who had survived such a calamity.

THREE DEAD DISCOVERED IN HOME WITH LONE SURVIVING CHILD

No matter how many penny dreadfuls were written reimagining the events behind that gruesome scene, nor how many journalists cross-referenced the flawed details of Scotland Yard's investigators, none had gotten the story right.

After all, Boo was mute when the officers found him sitting in that home, bloodied and vacant with a thousand-yard stare. Even Bedlam's host of rather creative remedies never pried a word from his jaws. And though he'd slowly rediscovered his words over time, his muteness persisted around the nightmarish details of that day.

As far as Boo was concerned, some stories were better left to die with the person harboring them. Not that anyone would believe what truly happened, anyhow.

Boo dropped from the silks with a quiet grunt. His stomach protested for a warm meal.

His hands were damp with sweat, the way they used to get before performing. At least when the rigging needed doing, he had something to occupy his hands. Now he just lit another cigarette, as he had all night with the others, staring off into campfires, trying not to imagine what the Disciples were doing to Florence.

For once, Kayne's infirmary was full. Boo'd only mustered the courage to peek through the flaps to see the three jugglers lying inside. When Veno made it back with them, he knew he wouldn't see Florence limping out of the coach with the others. It was the look on his face.

Boo sifted through the muddy grass with bare feet as he walked toward the entrance gates, his hat jingling. He gripped the iron post of the three-headed lamp, rust dusting his palm as he caressed the swirling metal.

That was when he saw a black coach approaching from afar, its single horse kicking up soil and billowing steam as it trotted forward. The sunrise caught the silver letter *C* on its side.

His stomach lurched. The cigarette fell from his hand, hissing in the dew.

The coachman arrived with pitying eyes, and a foot kicked open the carriage door. Mason emerged from it with Florence in his arms, her head tucked into her own chest, eyes clenched shut. Bloodied bandages were wrapped about her wrists, clutched close to her breast as though to hide them. Her breaths were shallow. The color had drained from her soft complexion—even her lips were gray.

Mason dropped her like a sack at Boo's feet.

Mud splattered against their legs, a wet smack in the silence. There was something wrong—something missing with Florence's arms. But Boo couldn't bring himself to look—not yet. His whole body began to shake—a rage so foul that his breath stuttered through his bared teeth. All he could think about was grabbing at either end of that scar on Mason's cheek and tearing it open.

Then Mason threw a velvet pouch, the same one that Veno brought into the city. When Boo caught it, he didn't feel coins inside. Rather, something wet and fleshy.

Boo glanced behind him. The rest of the circus was in the cookhouse, and oblivious to what was happening. Mason's amused smirk grew as he noticed the tremors in Boo's hands. Florence's blood colored his suit.

Her movements were weak and sluggish as she crawled forward. One of her arms extended out, reaching for Boo. But there were no fingers there, only a wad of bandages, and no room for a hand beneath that clump of sodden linen. She stared up at him with a mixture of disdain and desperation through a half-lidded eye. The other was sealed, swollen, and encrusted with blood.

"I've 'eard tell the circus is in town," Mason said. "It never ceases to amaze me, you know. Like ants buildin' a hill. You lot disappear and then —" he snapped his fingers, "—up again in a few days' time."

"You'd be amazed what else we can do," Boo growled.

"Nah. I think I've seen the extent of it." Mason pointed at the pouch. "I noticed you 'aven't looked inside. You strike me as the curious type, what with your meddlin' in private affairs n' all."

"Spare me the sermon."

"Oh, that's what this is? Sermon, no. This is a true act of contrition on behalf of your fine company for *your* mistake. And you didn't even take the brunt! Not that you'd understand. You're the kind of man that pities 'imself every time he falls into the grave he's dug."

Grinding his teeth, he sank to his knees beside Florence.

"The things we say follow us around, don't they? 'No scraps on our grounds.' That's what you said, the night you battered my men. It was a rude awakening for me, that. But you know, when all's said n' done, I 'ave more of 'em. More men than I know to do with, if I'm bein' honest. It's auspicious, this. You and I, alone. I expected to leave 'er here and let you lot find 'er. But this suits us better, don't you think? God, look at you. All that fury 'n nowhere to go. It'll make you sick, eh? You want to hurt me, is that it?"

Boo bowed his head. If he chanced another look at the twisted self-righteousness painted on Mason's face, he wasn't sure he'd be able to contain himself.

A gust fluttered the mobster's overcoat. "Book of Mark: *'And if thy 'and offend thee, cut it off: it is better for thee to enter into life maimed, than 'aving two hands to go into hell, into the fire that never shall be quenched.'*"

Florence inched forward. Boo took her into his arms, cradling her against his chest. She was quivering, her silent weeping becoming whimpers. She sobbed Boo's name, each utterance clogged with more contempt than the last.

"Oh, I see how it is." Mason cackled. "You two were a pair, is that it? That'll put a wedge in things. Can't imagine she'll have the same job as before."

"What have you done to her?"

"Funny you should ask. An accident, wasn't it, Florence? You see, she found 'erself down in the East End. Steel factories and the like. We 'ad ourselves a tour. And, well, you can't be too careful around such machinery. I'm afraid Florence slipped, found 'er hands beneath one of those giant forge hammers the smithies use. You know, those great steam behemoths for beatin' metal."

Enraged tears slid down Boo's face, trailing black grease paint down his twitching lips. He looked up at Mason with London behind him, the smog and sharp arches framing his broad shoulders.

"Those machines are built to pound molten steel. *Boom. Boom. Boom,*" Mason said slowly, beating his fist into his palm. "You should've seen the mess it made of those delicate hands of hers. You could hear the *crunch*. But don't you worry. We took her to a sawbones. He stitched her up real pretty. It was the least we could do. So you give Lester my regards." Then, leaning close, his voice turned to gravel. "You're all paid up."

Oftentimes when Boo spoke, his voice came soft, as though his words weren't meant to be heard. But now they arrived unmistakably, a deep throttle in his throat that held Mason still, even after he'd turned to leave.

"No," he said.

"No, what? We're finished here."

"Don't," Florence whimpered.

Boo stood, walking forward with Florence in his arms. He submitted himself to Mason's cold glare, that apathetic glaze as he craned his neck just to meet them. "No. I don't just want to hurt you. I want to rip you open. I'll drag you to Gehenna myself, leash you up by your insides. You will pray, Mason Cross, like I was your savior, standing before you. Your last moments will be curious—the feeling of being split in two. You'll pray, and your God won't answer, but mark my words, the Devil will be there. I may be the kind of man who falls in his own grave, but trust this, I'll dig two next time."

Raising a pointed finger, Mason rested it on Boo's nose. The vein in his neck bulged with restraint. "That's the last chance you get—for Lester's sake. If it weren't for the respect I 'ave for that woman, I'd not stomach that. Welcome back to London." With a tip of his hat, Mason turned and got into his carriage.

Then the coachman cracked his whip with a holler, and the carriage left, leaving the two alone.

"Florence, I—"

"Don't. Don't apologize. You did this to me. You. You damned idiot. I can walk just fine on my own. I still have my legs." Florence writhed out of his arms and teetered, not making it a single step before collapsing in the mud. "They took everything from me. They've ruined me, because of you!" Banging her head against the earth, Florence's curdling wails echoed throughout the fields.

Against her protests, Boo hoisted her into his arms.

The rest of the circus came rushing from the cookhouse—a scramble of feet and anxious eyes. Hundreds of workers and performers thronged around Boo and Florence as they moved toward the infirmary. Faces he had grown up with—faces whose taut lips and disappointed expressions dripped with betrayal.

Nobody dared raise a word as that terrible understanding washed over them all. Florence's words proved quieter still. She lifted her head up, just enough so he could hear her.

"Keep your promise," she said. "No matter what Lester says. No matter how this ends. You kill him, Boo. That's how you make this right."

Darkened with London's smoke, the overcast skies harbored a storm black enough to make midday feel as quiet, as solemn, as lonesome as midnight. The crate Boo was sitting on near Florence's bedside in the infirmary creaked as his leg drummed ceaselessly.

Ivory arrived carrying a carnival lantern and hung it up in place of the oil lamp, its scintillating light casting a silver glow over them all. Boo watched the peculiar orb churning therein and felt the light washing over his skin, undoing the tight strings in his chest. He breathed a little better for it.

"Thank you, darling," Kayne said.

Ivory removed his bowler with a deep frown, looking at Florence's hollowed eyes in her sleep. "How is she?"

"She's stabilizing," Kayne replied, plucking out the ends of a stethoscope from her ears. "Her heartbeat is weak, but it's steady. The laudanum will ease the pain and help her rest. She's no fever, which is a miracle in its own right. Whoever stitched her up knew what they were doing."

Leaning against one of the tent's supports, Lester stood with her arms folded. "How long until she recovers?"

"Her body? Weeks, months, maybe. Mentally, well, that's another matter entirely. A lifetime may not be enough."

"Florence is strong. She'll find a way," Lester said, as if convincing herself. "How about your private research? Could you find…replacements?" Reaching for the velvet pouch, Lester glanced inside at the tatters of Florence's severed hands with a scowl. "Ugh. Animals."

"My experiments concerning transplant limbs are purely exploratory. Performed on dead flesh, no less."

"But you have done it?"

"Well, yes, but—" she stammered.

"But nothing. What is 'exploratory' can be made revolutionary. Ivory, just where do you think you're going? You are not excused."

The three of them shifted uncomfortably. Ivory stiffened, swallowing his protest. Lester rewound her wild, peppered hair around a tie, her face fraught with sleeplessness. "Explain yourself."

"With all due respect," Kayne continued, "surgical necromancy isn't exactly an accepted medical practice, and is the reason why my peers treat me like a leper. We are speaking of a practice combining occult rituals and earthly sciences. Even if I performed impeccably, the operation could take her life."

"See the work through. That is what we do here. We see the work through. Whatever you need, the coven is at your disposal," Lester nodded.

"That sounds like an order," Ivory remarked.

"It is, damnit! On account of you two." Rolling up a nearby newspaper, Lester swatted both Ivory and Boo over the head—not playfully. "Kayne, I want Thomas and his men digging up whatever cadavers they can find to further your research. Drop your other projects. I volunteer these two zounderkites, if they need more able bodies. As soon as you're confident, and if Florence is willing, you perform the operation."

"What you are talking about is the bleeding edge of my studies," Kayne said. "It would take a miracle and a half to restore her capabilities."

"In circus, *nothing* is impossible," Lester shot back. "I'll have no talk of pessimism in this regard. Florence lost her livelihood today—everything she's worked for. I don't care if we have to cut off the hooks of a seamstress—Florence's last flight on a trapeze will be on *her* terms. Not yours. Not mine. And certainly not Mason's. Have I made that clear?"

"Abundantly. I'll convene with my team." The long, crimson ribbons extending from Kayne's waistcoat trailed her as she stood to leave. Sighing, she said, "Not all of you can see her. She needs rest. Now, excuse me; I have other matters to attend to."

When Boo turned to see who she was addressing, his heart heaved. A crowd had gathered outside the infirmary, the closest being the other aerialists from the Flying Maffickers.

"As for all of you," Lester said, "this day will haunt Boo for the rest of his life. He will bear that burden. But the last thing I will have in the face of this is a broken family. Boo did not do this. This is the Disciples' work. If you want to point fingers, you'll do so at me. Is that understood? Boo may have started this war alone, but we'll be ending it together. It was my decision to do business with these bastards, not his. But he will answer for what he's done. This very evening, no less. Won't you?"

The clown squeezed the points of his hat until his knuckles paled. He chanced the expressions of everyone looking to him for an answer, not many of them anymore forgiving of Lester's defense. "I will," he said.

"I cannot promise," Lester continued, "that when we return, all will be well between us and our associates. It may indeed become far worse. You should all be prepared. Now, get a change of clothes and clean up your face. No makeup," she ordered, pointing at Boo. "Fetch Thomas after you're done. The three of us are going into the city."

"For what?" an aerialist asked.

Facing her circus, Lester replied, "To sever our ties with the Disciples."

20

ATHERTON
JUNE 2, 1886

The damned crowded him in his opium haze, the touch of bone and rotted skin cradling him. Atherton sank deeper into an intoxicated exhaustion, a womb of narcotic dreams. But even there, he wasn't safe. Recollections became visitors, closer than Lilian's kisses, than the wilted amaryllis at her dressing table, than the blood spilt in one heated moment now pooling, reaching out into every moment of his waking life.

The substance in Goremire Lake was up to his waist. It stained his skin, stretching in crimson veins throughout his clothes. His fingers knew the texture of it. Thicker than ink, and warm. Milky eyes gazed from beneath the surface. A child's hollow stare, ravenous for his attention.

The child reached up and pulled him under—a gentle tug, an invitation which soothed his fear. Beneath the surface, he inhaled the blood. The metal filled his mouth and diffused in his lungs. She pressed her forehead against his. Pieces of her skin flaked off, floating about them like pale petals. And momentarily, as they sank deeper into those depths, he had a distant hope that he might join her and never awaken.

"*The flowers are cruel.*"

Atherton's hand jerked to the pistol beneath his pillow. Heaving, he whipped it toward his locked door, finger on the trigger.

Only shadows waited there.

It had been nearly a month since Mason left for London. As his return to New Sarum neared, sleep became elusive. The waking world greeted him with deep aches. He sighed, resting his head against the muzzle of the revolver. After his work at the mortuary, he took early evening rides to the countryside, where he practiced his aim against tin cans and jars.

The sheets swathed him in cold sweat. He wrestled them off, reaching over to light the lamp on his nightstand. The match fizzled, catching the wick. As the light flared, it revealed that, once more, something had slipped into his home during those short hours of rest.

There she was—that child in the lake—now unmarred by the dream. He hardly flinched this time, but rather squinted his eyes curiously. The child stood by his nightstand, wearing that same yearning stare, her features obscured in the corner where the amber glow didn't quite reach. Her hair and clothes clung to her skin, water dripping from her chin.

A rhythmless *pat, pat, patter* on the floor.

She felt familiar, and yet, he failed to recognize her among the bodies in his care. Reeds, damp earth, and crow's feathers. That was the smell that filled his chamber.

"*You were too late.*"

The child gurgled a death rattle, spilling forth with murk and mud.

Atherton turned the knob on the gaslamp until the flame grew. Her face mostly brightened but was masked beneath her long, sopping hair. Then she faded until he was left staring at the empty corner. The space she'd occupied in his mind was now filled with only more unanswered questions, and from there spawned a loneliness that crawled over his chest and burrowed inside.

For once, he'd wished a visitor had lingered.

He stood for a while in front of the open window with a cup of tea, the winds cooling the sweat from his naked chest. On his dressing table was the boutonnière Lilian had given him. Dried petals were scattered about from the many times he'd run his hands over the memory. Beside it was an overturned bottle of laudanum. Finding it empty, he resolved to dress himself. Each movement was weighted by the knowledge that soon enough, he'd find himself crossing guns with Mason. There weren't enough tin cans in the world to prepare him for that moment.

The wailing, blustering wind made the early hours feel alive with secrets. Tree boughs slapped against the mortuary walls. Thudding, scraping, shivering.

With dawn only hours away, he fell back into reverie, back into the lake and its deep, crimson pools where fog lay heavy on its surface and suspended him there both weightless and heavy, pulling him further away until he, himself, felt rather like a ghost. Hour by hour, daybreak crept in faint strides upon the dense cloud coverage, with mist rolling through the streets of New Sarum.

※

That same mist reached about his legs as he stood just before the leaking fascia of the Butler House in the early afternoon. A bouquet of amaryllis hung from his hands. The house was holding its breath—no children stomping about, no shouts, curses, or ensuing chastisements from Morma. Having rapped on the door, all Atherton heard over the pattering rain was the tinkling of a piano.

Lilian appeared in the doorway, her fingers wringing together. As soon as he noticed the red around her eyes, she shut the door behind her, sliding into his arms.

"It's Lola," she said. "She's been missing for three days."

"Dear God. Missing? As in *missing*, missing?"

"Yes, as in *missing*, Atherton."

"What do you mean? What's happened?"

"I haven't the faintest idea. I tucked her in one evening, and the next morning, she'd vanished. She always had trouble sleeping. My God, I...I'm an awful mother."

"No, no, this isn't your fault. It cannot be."

"She could be anywhere." Biting her nails, Lilian looked out, glancing over the cityscape with frantic eyes. "I've already notified the constables—they haven't given me word since. And I'm petrified to leave the other children alone, even with Morma, for fear some foul, sinister person stole her away in the night."

"But who would do such a thing?" Even as the words fell from his lips, his mind was reeling with the cold faces of the other children. Alice, Betty, the Crowley twins.

And what would I tell her, then? That some crazed Gehennic has likely shuffled Lola off the mortal coil for a sick ritual? That her body will turn up with a pendant stuck in her throat? And what would the constables do, with only the word of an undertaker and not a scrap of evidence?

Worse still was feeling the tremors of a woman he previously thought unshakable. "No," he said, "the other girls would have stirred if somebody came in the night. Morma would have heard something. The house is ancient, Lilian. If field mice were to run across a plank of wood, the entire floor would creak."

"Perhaps you're right. Yet I can hardly sleep; the thought of it haunts me. Some monster coming to kidnap the others. I am consumed by fear, Atherton. For where she's gone. Where she might be. And what if she's..." Her voice faltered until it came out as a whisper. "...dead?"

"Don't say it. Don't even think it." Atherton rubbed her shoulders and ran a hand through her hair. "Lola has always been strong-willed. Chances are she's wandered off into the backwoods to sleep with the wolves for a few evenings. God knows they'd be terrified of her. No—she'll turn up. She will, with stories of forest nymphs and elves, no less. Soon enough, it'll be as though this never happened."

A grin flashed over Lilian's lips as tears wetted them. "Thank you. Would you stay for tea? Your company would be a welcome distraction for the children."

"Of course, certainly."

But she's right. That's precisely what happened, he thought as Lilian opened the door and left it ajar. *Some monster came to kidnap her, one way or another.*

To enter the orphanage would be to walk within yet another home plagued by the iniquitous force sweeping across the city. To do so without an anvil's weight sinking in his stomach would be to ignore the obvious—something only he understood. Atherton already knew what had become of Lola. He had seen her that very morning.

21

BOO
JUNE 2, 1886

London welcomed the rattling carriage into its smoky jaws. Thomas negotiated the bustling thoroughfares, snaking between the refuse, glamor, and strife of a city whose immortal soul gorged on anguish. The glow of gas lamps winked between the velvet curtains. Boo parted them more to watch people walking about the ashen air of the early evening. Even on days when he wasn't performing, he was seldom without makeup. Having dressed for the occasion of confronting Mason without a smudge of grease paint, he felt naked. He even combed his hair, but years of neglect made its ends protest in wild curls.

Lester watched him with as much scrutiny as Boo did the crowds. His makeup was not the mask she always thought it was. His unmarked face was an open book, though all its words were scattered.

"I won't tell you not to blame yourself for what happened to Florence," she said. "Throughout our lives, we will be forced to reconcile the consequences of decisions we considered well-intentioned. The damnable thing is that she will forgive you, eventually. I'm certain of that. The question remains if you ever will."

He fiddled with the buttons on his starched sleeves. The last time he'd worn anything befitting proper city wear was when they held a funeral pyre for a stray cat the circus had adopted, whose untimely demise involved a contortionist trying on stilts for the first time.

"Will you?" Boo asked.

"If I weighed people by what they have only ever done or failed to do, you would have been left to shuffle around in that asylum, perhaps for the rest of your days. And all the outcasts whom I have since brought to our family, our home, would be without one. I don't forgive. I hope."

Boo didn't particularly enjoy imagining how his life might've unfolded if Lester had never seen the news article which led her to visit him. Up until she'd arrived, his only friend was an elderly gentleman who, despite having the vocabulary of a single word, could play the piano with the ease of a composer.

A rolling river of livelihoods, dramas, and fragmented moments rolled by the window of the carriage. Being closer to it only made him feel more like an outsider, looking in on a game whose convoluted rules and unspoken taboos soured the entire enterprise. On stage, he was applauded by the same people who might've seen him in Bedlam all those years before, thinking his brightest prospects might be lighting lamp posts or sweeping the floor of a café, if rotting in a cot on opiates somehow ever became beneath him.

"I did the right thing," Boo said, "when nobody else would."

Lester pulled a timepiece from her coat pocket and wound it, her thoughtful gaze betraying an underlying resentment. "The right thing," she echoed with a sigh. "Sometimes right and wrong are but two injured hares splitting off at a crossroads, limping away from a fox. The instinct is to pick one, scoop it up into your arms, and save it. Or do you become a hunter yourself, and take out the fox? Well then, now you're really playing God. Who's to say the fox wasn't within his own right to start the chase, anyhow?"

"People are more complicated than foxes and hares."

"So they are," Lester replied. "The truth of the matter is, you did what was right by your own principles. You became a hunter, you played God, and if there's one thing we know about God, it's that he's got a lot to answer for. But yes, you did the right thing; I'll concede that. The trouble is, you did it in the wrong place."

Chewing his bottom lip, Boo looked out the window again. Murky light danced across his hazel eyes. "If I could go back, knowing what I know now, I doubt I'd have the strength to play it any differently."

Lester nodded slowly. "Then count yourself lucky you have a family who'd stand before an army of angels prepared to smite you down. Mason took his blood, as we well expected he would. We'll front him for any contraband yet unsold, make our amends, and be done with this mess. The Devil knows I started it. You're not the only one who bites off more than he can chew."

For the first time since the incident, Lester broke the iciness, reaching across to squeeze Boo's knee. He put his hand on top of hers, clenching back the guilt welling in his eyes.

The smell of the open sewers flooding into the carriage told him they were passing through Whitechapel. The carriage struggled against the cracked cobblestone between the stuffed tenements and alleyways cramped with waste.

Tales of rippers sprouted in the unlit passageways, made all too real by the shadows lurking within. Drunken squabbling and street vendors fending off beggar children filled the smog-fouled air. From the East End came the clamoring of industrial factories, where God's breath simmered in molten metal, his teeth biting at mortal hands as they hammered glowing steel.

Thomas whipped the horses to a faster pace, hollering curses at the people blocking their path. Leaving the district behind, they passed the Gehennic Chapel of Odium at the corner of Raven Row, its stone gargoyles watching with open jaws. The air in the Brompton District was cleaner—as clean as it could be, being just a stone's throw from boroughs where the air was choked with excrement.

Boo felt a hole open up somewhere in his stomach to pull in the rest of his insides when he heard Thomas *woah!* to halt the horses. Mason's manor was not unlike the circus tents he so preferred; they both endeavored to scratch the sky. Only, it was everything they were not—permanent, lavish, and free of horse manure. If Mason really did come from the streets like the rumors attested, Boo couldn't fathom why the man didn't stop while he was ahead, why he chased the lifestyle of the people who'd look down on him, if only for his sullied origins. Perhaps it was out of spite. Maybe he just wanted the privilege of laughing at the fate he'd cheated the Devil out of.

Though Boo had finally started earning wages from performing after years of training and stagehanding, he seldom spent a farthing of it. The cookhouse fed him well. His disciplines devoured his time. And by virtue, he often slept like a dreamless beast, as his body was always pleasantly tired. As for his earnings, the coins simply piled on in his caravan, like a shiny shrine to a deity he never worshipped. Sometimes, he'd surprise Florence with chocolates.

Thomas's boots crunched in the gravel of the Cross Manor as he walked over and opened the door. Interrupted from his musings, the clown swallowed his nerves and readied himself to leave, only for Lester's arm to bar the way.

"Remember, we are only talking," she said.

"Is that why you had me bring the barking iron?"

Lester's eyes flitted to Boo's Lefever shotgun. Holstered to his thigh, the sawed-off barrel of the weapon was readily concealed by his cloak. Silver filigree flourished in vines up the handle.

"That is merely a matter of assurance," she murmured and exited the carriage, bringing with her a black duffel bag.

"Cheer up, moucher," Thomas said with a hefty slap to Boo's back, "when I was a gonoph we had chats with bruisers like Mason all the time. They never went well, but we walked away alive. Well, I did, anyways."

"The soul of assurance, you are," Boo replied.

"Look at that, you take away his hat and the boy's confidence deflates," Thomas said.

"Trust me, I contemplated letting him bring the damned thing. You have the hands?"

Thomas grabbed the bag with Florence's hands from the seat of the coach. The bottom of the burlap sack was soaked burgundy. "If you feel sorry for yourselves, imagine how I feel holding dinner after I've skipped breakfast."

Lester led them up the polished stone steps of the mansion. Thin towers jutted out from the French roofs of the home, each one with a different saint watching over the courtyard with long, golden staves and crosses. She slammed the bronze knocker on the wide oak door, her raps cut short by the disparaging glare of a housemaid.

"I am Lester Black, proprietor of the Black Carnival, and these are my associates," she said before the woman could get a word in. "We are here to speak with Mason Cross. Is he present?"

"Why yes," she said, "I am afraid he is preoccupied for the evening. Did you have an appointment?" Her crow-footed eyes and careful restraint suggested she had a long career of greeting visitors with far better manners.

"No," Lester replied and pushed through. Thomas gave the door a final shove open and stepped into the sitting parlor with Boo trailing behind.

"Just take a look at those staircases," Thomas said, wiping his muddy shoes on the edge of one. "Is that marble?"

"I'm afraid I must ask you to leave at once!" the housekeeper said in a half-stifled shriek. "Mr. Cross is having a meeting of utmost importance in his chamber."

"In his chamber, you say?" Lester made for the stairs.

"We'll suit ourselves just fine from here. Thank you," Thomas chimed, with Boo quick to catch up behind them.

"Excuse you! You are most certainly not welcome here!" The housekeeper lifted the tails of her dress as she tramped after the three of them. "Never in my life have I been forced to endure such uncouth behavior, and by the looks of wayward vagabonds, no less!"

"We are not vagabonds, miss," Thomas said.

"Just interlopers," Boo clarified.

"And you!" The housekeeper jabbed a knobby finger toward Thomas, whose hungry eyes revealed he had a brief daydream of biting it off. "I knew exactly what you were the moment I saw you. Your kind is not welcome here! You belong outside these walls or not at all! You are expressly uninvited."

Without a solitary notion of where they were going, Lester led them through the ornate halls. Other staff arrived to add to the commotion, creating a trail of objections and affronted etiquette.

"I would like to hear your defense as to why I should not call for the authorities at once. This is unprecedented!" the housekeeper shouted.

"I am afraid we are here on urgent business that cannot wait," Lester said after trying several doors at random, all empty. "Rest assured, there is no need to involve the peelers. We mean you no..." Lester stopped speaking after she had turned the doorknob to the correct chamber. With the door thrust wide open, everybody present was given a clear view into Mason's "business meeting."

A prostitute kneeling at his feet yelped and fled with her discarded garments to the connected sleeping quarters. In the main study, Mason was seated at the edge of his desk with flushed cheeks and trousers around his ankles. He stammered, too stunned to say anything. A silver crucifix dangled against his sweaty, bare chest.

"Business meeting, aye." Thomas rubbed his chin thoughtfully. "I love those!"

Boo snorted so involuntarily that he covered his mouth and pretended no one had noticed, but the damage had already been done. Mason glowered while he pulled up his trousers and buttoned them, refusing to utter the variety of slurs undoubtedly brewing in his throat. The silence he chose instead made Boo anxious to grip the handle of his shotgun. If it weren't for Lester, he would've.

"Well..." Lester started to say, clasping her hands together, but her next words were interrupted by a cluster of actions that occurred so quickly, it reminded Boo of the first time he let go of a trapeze bar at the zenith of a swing.

The pounding heart. The sweaty palms. The momentary blackout, only to see Florence grinning down at him, hanging upside down in a catcher's pose from the opposing trapeze, grasping his wrists and giggling. He hadn't remembered to grab hers, but survival instinct is its own magic.

Mason loosed a torrent of curses—he knew that much. Then a drawer of his desk had been thrown open, and from it, a revolver appeared in his fist. Thomas was upon Mason that same instant, and were it not for the grasp on his wrist, the bullet that left the revolver's chamber would've blown a ruinous pit through Boo's left eye. He felt the air scream just a breath from his ear, and could hardly hear through the tormented fog horn that replaced his hearing.

Mason swung for Thomas, but the ghoul's hand was nearly twice the size and curled around his all too easily.

"He ain't worth it!" Thomas shouted. "He ain't fuckin' worth it!"

"Oh, tell me why I bloody shouldn't, Barker!"

Perhaps just as shocking as the relief of not having the back of his skull scattered behind him was the way Thomas managed to quell Mason's fury. The gangster huffed, holding on for a reply. Thomas let go of Mason's wrist first, leaving him to keep the revolver trained on Boo.

The clown flinched, wondering if his last thoughts would be concerning Thomas's gamble to appeal to the gangster's principles. Thomas always had a way with the Disciples, but he'd never wager his life on the ghoul's gift of the gab. He chanced a glance at Lester—her lips were tight, and her thoughts seemed to be screaming the same question.

Boo knew reaching for his firearm would be the last thing he ever did.

The ghoul let Mason and the rest of the room catch their breath. "He uh, he ain't worth the paint, aye?" he finally said. "Ain't worth the paint is all, eh, Mason? You're gonna bloody that pretty wall 'o yours with his brains 'n it'll be some time 'for the stain washes." And only then, after he relinquished his other hand around Mason's fist, did he chance a chuckle.

Mason looked between the three of them, nodding slowly as if the suggestion caused him great consternation. Then, (and this well and truly made Boo question if he was hallucinating and belonged back in Bedlam), Mason laughed. A laugh as broken as it was rich. The laugh of a man who hated how much he loved the taste of blood.

Thomas joined in with that booming cackle of his and clapped Mason on the shoulder.

"You've a bloody good point," Mason said, his spirits somehow lifted by the whole ordeal. He drew his dangling suspenders up and tucked them over his shoulders, at last settling down in his leather armchair and placing the revolver back in the drawer.

"Aye. I'm full of 'em," Thomas said. "Shall we?"

Mason nodded. When his gaze passed over Boo, it seemed that Mason had to douse a fleeting cinder of rage. Then the gangster gestured for the three of them to sit.

Boo took his seat, finding it difficult to ponder much else besides the fact that a bullet had been just centimetres away from blasting his happiest memories over some ornate wallpaper.

"Irene and the lot of you, you're all excused," Mason addressed his staff, who'd been frozen behind that spectacle the entire time. "Except you, Theodore—bring us four glasses."

The servants scattered like cockroaches from fire, a platter of caviar and cured meats clattering to the ground in the process. The one he called Theodore reappeared with the glasses, flitting to and from the chamber like a liveried gnat.

"Now, you've come 'ere on business," Mason said. He poured four glasses of gin, each double. "I won't ask you to excuse my behavior. Not that I need the pardon of Gehennics, leastways."

"The body wants what the body wants," Lester said, "though I will admit it was satisfying seeing a man of faith compromised by, well..."

"A wagtail," Thomas finished for her.

"The body wants what the body wants," Mason repeated and downed his glass. "Chastity was never my strong suit, but my sins will be forgiven. Not so sure of this one," he chuckled, wagging a finger at Boo. "Now, drink."

"We aren't here to drink," Lester said with a glance toward Thomas, who shrugged, having already upended his.

"Good, ain't it?" Mason asked. "Didn't know graveborns drank."

"This one does," Thomas said, setting down the empty tumbler.

Folding her hands, Lester cleared her throat. "Mason, we've come to clear the air."

"Oh, not to 'ave a bloody laugh, then? If it weren't for our 'istory I'd 'ave the three of you's in bags for interruptin' my...business meetin'. Maybe not 'im," Mason said with a nod to Thomas, "'cos that one's a fuckin' Goliath 'n he talks sweet. Ain't that right, Boo?" His words ground like charcoal over brick.

Boo just nodded, keeping his gaze lowered.

"Well, Mason, despite my performer's inability to contain his humor concerning the interruption, the respect for our history is mutual. Our, ah, collaboration has always been of mutual benefit."

Mason got up from his chair with a bitter chuckle and leaned over his desk, the wood creaking against his muscled frame. "As business should, Lester. We've known each other for, what, near on a decade now? My father's known you even better. Quiet, obedient, timely. If we're bein' honest, you've been 'bout as damn near close to my favorite. If it weren't for that, you'da been gutted by now. So what's this about?"

Lester grabbed the sopping bag from Thomas and tossed it into the mobster's lap. He hardly glanced inside before chucking it back. "Oh, come on now." He laughed. "What is this? You're off your rocker 'cause some bitch 'ad her daddles off? It's business!" Picking up a worn Bible from his desk, he gestured with it and quoted, "Matthew chapter five, verse thirty-eight: *'Ye 'ave 'eard that it 'ath been said, an eye for an eye and a tooth for a tooth.'* I'm a godly man. We're square for what your little lunatic did to my men. The score's settled. Is that it? You wanted to 'ear it from the horse?"

"You are missing the other half of that verse. But no, I wanted you to hear an apology from the clown himself, to leave no shadow of a doubt. Boo?"

Boo paused. Having to apologize to a man who nearly killed him for the mistake of laughter was a kind of torture he hadn't prepared to face that day. He bit down on his lip until he tasted blood. "I am deeply sorry," he said.

"That's a good lad. For what?"

Boo's scowl tightened. All he could see was Florence as she wailed in the mud, the way her blood spread out on his clothes. Taking a deep breath, he glanced at Lester. Her eyes betrayed a low panic, knowing full well his next sentence precipitated a reckoning neither of them had seen before.

"I am sorry that your men made fools of themselves on our grounds," Boo said finally.

"What was that?" Mason sputtered.

"They had no right pummelling one of our guests for a whole crowd to see, your personal affairs with the Graves family notwithstanding," Boo replied. "If he'd died, our reputation would've suffered. And what's more—"

"Boo, please," Lester interrupted.

"I enjoyed beating them," Boo continued. Every word was an indulgence. The more he spoke, the sweeter each syllable became. "It was easy.

It felt good. I may loathe myself for what you did to Florence, but I will never waste a moment regretting having put your dogs in their rightful place."

Even Thomas looked on edge, glancing uneasily at the three of them.

"Lester," Mason scoffed, "tell me this ratbag is making my day with the worst joke I ever heard."

"Lester doesn't speak for me," Boo said. "Nobody does."

"That much is clear. I want you to know, Lester, before I scatter 'is brains, that I gave 'im a chance. I warned him," Mason said, reaching back for the drawer of his desk.

This time, it was Boo's turn to act on instinct. Bolting to his feet, he swept aside his cloak and unholstered his shotgun. He leveled it at Mason before his hand even finished opening the drawer. "It appears I'm not getting through to you. Perhaps you'll understand this language better," he said.

"Boo!" Lester said through her teeth. "What the hell do you think you're doing?"

"No, no, it's a'right. He's just rattled, eh? Where'd you pick up this one? Some home for the lame?"

"Bedlam Asylum," Boo corrected and pulled back the hammer, "for psychosis and suspected double murder. I'm sorry, Lester, I can't stand here paying obeisance to some bludger who fancies himself a saint."

"Bloody 'ell," Thomas murmured. "Boo, you best think about what you're doing."

"I've thought about it," the clown said. Keeping the shotgun raised with one hand, he grabbed the duffel bag by Lester's feet and undid its buckles, never moving his eyes off his target. He reached in and, one by one, threw satchels of coin and wads of bank notes. Mason grabbed the bottle of gin before it could be knocked off, but the tumblers weren't spared. Wet shards scattered across the wood floor.

"This is what's owed for the contraband we'd been expected to peddle for you. The last farthing you'll see from us."

"We've covered the cost of unsold goods. You've got every coin out of it," Lester added, rising to her feet. "You made the mistake of thinking I regard those in my employ as expendable. They're not. You maimed one of my children, Mason. Boo merely bloodied your men. Florence may not share my blood, but she's family. Even so, I never intended for this meeting to go this way."

"Well, it 'as." Mason glared at her over the polished muzzle of the

Lefever. They were all tied in that terrible silence, bitterness thickening each word. "You really going to let a clown play your cards for you?"

"He's certainly a bag of surprises, but I trust him more than I've ever trusted you. There are no cards to play because the game is over. We came here to apologize and, well, we haven't precisely, but we're finished."

"That's a damn shame," Mason said, reaching for a case of cigarettes. Boo emphasized his eagerness to pull the trigger by advancing, allowing the gangster to grab one and light it with great caution. "'Ave it your way, then. I never wanted to see you burn."

"We won't," Lester said.

"Go," Mason growled.

With feet crunching glass as they moved for the door, the gangster's voice followed them. *"But the fearful, and unbelieving...the whoremongers, and sorcerers, and idolaters, and all liars, shall have their part in the lake which burneth with fire and brimstone."*

Though Thomas and Lester treated this Biblical if not ominous recitation as the most peaceful goodbye they'd get for the time being, Boo lingered in the doorway.

"You've got something more to say, eh? You tryn'a dig yourself deeper, mug?" Mason asked.

"Your book won't hide you," Boo said. "I see you for who you are, not what you say."

The gangster banged his fists on the desk and stood up. Before he could advance further, Boo slammed back the trigger.

His shotgun unleashed a torrent—a jaw of fire and metal that tore the air apart.

Those jaws bit at the edge of Mason's desk where his Bible lay. The leather bindings were burst through, sending a flurry of blackened, shot-bitten pages showering about the room.

Arms raised above his head, the gangster stood numbly in the shock of the blast, then patted his chest and stomach, checking to see if he'd been shot. But he hadn't. There was no blood in the room, save for the remnants of Florence's hands on the floor. There was only ink, charred words, and gunpowder smoke.

"Courtesy of the Black Carnival," Boo said before shutting the door behind him.

22

ATHERTON
JUNE 4, 1886

The Graves children were always fond of dirt. Delma's knees and dress were perpetually stained from crawling around in her mother's garden. Atherton found her there in the afternoon, whispering over her collection of stuffed dolls. Her expression twisted with each personality.

"And what drama do we have on display here?" he asked, crouching down.

"I found Rupert, so we're fixing him up again," she said, showing Atherton the severed head of the doll, one of his button eyes dangling from a pink thread.

"Goodness, you've been looking for him for ages. I remember him. He was my favorite, too. You know, I used to play with him when you were just a babe."

"Well, he's mine now. And he came back on 'is own. And I'm not a baby anymore," she said.

"No, no, you are not," he sighed. Atherton inspected the doll with a perplexed look before handing it back. His own childhood had been brutish and short. As soon as he was ten, toys were replaced with cadavers. "So, how are you fixing him?"

"With this," she said, grinning devilishly, producing a needle injector from its hiding spot beneath her dress.

"Hey! Did you take this from the embalming room?"

"Father said I could."

"You're lying, and that's mine!"

"I only need it just this once, Athie," she said. "Please, please, for Rupert."

"A'right. Fine, have it your way. Just make sure you clean it after you're done."

"Oh, what's it matter? The dead don't care."

"I care. Do you even know what that's for?"

"You close their mouths with it. Father showed me." Delma placed the head in the center of her six other dolls, assembled in a circle. "I'll fix him for good once we find his other parts," she said.

"Maybe it'd be better if we find you another Rupert. I don't even think the needle injector could bring him back. He's got an arm off."

"But I love Rupert. Besides, I won't be out here for long. Mother said she doesn't want me playing outside after morning," Delma mumbled.

"And for good reason, Del."

Delma lifted a cup of tea, nestled into the soil of a flower pot, to her lips. "Is it because Mr. Cross is coming? The one who hit you?"

"Yes. Precisely that."

"Mother told me to hide if he comes here. Will you hide?"

"I can't hide."

"Why not?"

"Hiding will only make matters worse."

"I don't want him to come." And after a pause, "I'm afraid. And I also don't want to be inside!" Delma threw down Rupert's head, which bounced a single, sad bounce. "Will he hit you again?"

"More than likely." He ran his hands through Delma's tangled, blonde hair. "But listen, I will never let that man hurt you. You have nothing to be afraid of. He's only here for me. Do you understand? You have no reason to fear. If he so much as tries to lay a hand on you, I'll...well, I'll make sure he doesn't."

Delma looked at him and asked, "Do you promise?"

Meeting his sister's doubtful, gray eyes, he nodded. "I promise."

Atherton spotted the peaks of two constables' hats bobbing above the garden's hedges. "Why don't you run on inside? Looks like the rozzers are here."

"But—"

"Inside," he said firmly.

Smothering her protests in grumbles, Delma snatched up Rupert before tucking herself behind the door to eavesdrop.

Wearing their navy blue uniforms, both officers were fidgety as they approached the young undertaker.

"Constable Bishop, Welsh." Atherton did little to hide the distaste in his voice. These would surely be the same men who would wave Mason Cross through the gates of New Sarum, knowing full well the consequences of doing so. "I'd imagine you gentlemen are here because some poor soul climbed the golden staircase. Shall I ready the horses and the wagon?"

"It'd be best if you have your father come along for this one," Constable Bishop said. He adjusted his cap to scratch his polished scalp before righting it again. The only hair left on his face came from his unkempt nostrils, undermining the otherwise steely look of his blue eyes.

"With all due respect, I have as much a hand in this business as my father. Regardless, he is preoccupied. You'll have to make do with me." Atherton neglected to clarify that he was, in fact, preoccupied with reading the morning papers.

The constables shared an uncertain look. Bishop composed himself with a bit more humility than his partner, whose uniform strained against his belly. Welsh also sported a moustache speckled with shortbread crumbs.

Welsh shrugged and said, "Let's hope you've got a pair of waders, then."

Atherton wasn't impressed. "Another floater? Gentlemen, please. You won't get one on me because somebody's drowned. I've dragged bodies out of mires. Remember that time..." he trailed off.

"Everything all right, sir?" Bishop asked.

A storm of chills had lit through Atherton's body. "Yes, perfectly fine. You may as well run on ahead while I gather my supplies. Give the family my regards and let them know I'll be there shortly."

"There's no next of kin as of yet. We have our suspicions, but we thought you might be able to confirm. And, meaning no offence—we haven't told you where she is, yet."

"She?"

"A child. Just a few years younger than your sister, I reckon," Welsh added.

"Where is she located?"

Atherton watched clouds chase one another across the rippling surface of Goremire Lake. He inhaled the fresh air and human decay, his wavy hair fluttering in the heavy winds. The comments and observations of the officers felt muffled, distant. Try though he might to catch their words, none of them seemed particularly interesting.

He was transfixed by the clouded eyes of the child that had visited him just days before, one of them looking off to the side. A lazy eye. He should have felt more standing at this crossroads, yet it felt predictable, like watching a losing game of chess unfold. Here she was, another token of death, yet much more than that. Proof of an undeniable connection, or a low madness with an uncanny intuition that he'd been trying to ignore.

Mud and algae were clumped in Lola's hair. After untangling her from the reeds and bringing her onto the gravelly shore, he knew her skin, fish-bitten and wrinkled, would tear at the slightest tug. A white floral dress clutched her frame.

"The flowers are cruel," Atherton murmured. He cleared the slick hair from her face. Mossy green hues stretched from her neck and up to her bloated, pallid cheeks. "What did you mean, Lola? I should have listened to you."

"What's that, lad?" Welsh asked.

"It's nothing," Atherton replied. "Just noting the decomposition. She's been in the lake for nearly two or three days, by my estimation." He ran his fingers along the mangled skin of her left leg. A bruise formed a ring around her ankle.

"Is it as we suspected? We're aware you have a relationship with Mrs. Butler and her orphans. We wanted a third opinion, to be certain."

Images of Lola thrashing in the still water flashed through his mind. Her screams bursting in bubbles from her mouth. The water racing in, swallowing the sound. "Yes. The child is Lola Summers, one of the orphans. But this is no accident, constables. She was drowned here, forcibly."

"And how in the blazes would you know that?" Welsh asked.

"The expressions of the dead tell stories," Atherton said. "Remnants of their final thoughts. Their emotions putrefy with the flesh—more disfigured with every day—but telling us what they felt all the same. Her face is not one of confusion or surprise. It is one of fear, betrayal. Pain."

"Anybody would panic, realizing they can't return to shore after going out for a swim in water deep as this," Bishop said. "It explains everything."

"Note the discoloration around her left ankle, here, where a rope likely tied her to some makeshift anchor to keep her below. The place where she was murdered was intended to house her body until it had sufficiently deteriorated. The water would vanish any telltale trace of a quarrel."

Then something glinted at him. The edge of a delicate, silver chain was peeking from the corners of her mouth. Atherton slid his fingers in, stirring mortified groans from the constables, until he gripped the necklace and drew it out.

Rising from her lips with a string of saliva was the talisman. A geometric symbol fashioned of tarnished silver, encompassed by a circle with six points breaking through its outermost ring. Turning around, he shook the pendant at them. "Do you not see? *This* is a Gehennic pendant. An occult symbol. This was no mere accident."

The officers held silent.

Finally, Constable Bishop sighed and said, "She's been missing for nearly a week, Mr. Graves. A child who can't swim, tangled up in some weed or other. It's not unheard of. As for the pendant, well, who are we to cast judgment? Or for 'ow Mrs. Butler raises 'er children, therefore. And with all due respect, you're no detective."

"You conduct your affairs with Mrs. Butler and care for the deceased, and we'll handle the crime, if indeed there is any to be found," Welsh finished.

Atherton shot up to his feet. "This child was murdered," he said through clenched teeth. "And her murderer, at large. This is not the first time a dead child has been found with one of these symbols on their person. A pattern has been emerging. I have a right to inform you, and you have a duty to find justice for her. Will you not?"

Bishop placed a brawny hand on Atherton's shoulder and squeezed. "This is rudimentary, Athie. I understand you're distressed. Don't you see what's happening?"

Atherton shoved the hand off with a disdainful scoff. "Oh, not this."

"Now, now, listen. Your relationship with the child, with Mrs. Butler, is clouding your judgment. That's all. I've worked with you for years, lad. You know better."

"The hell I do!"

"You've never been distraught over a case, not like this. But it's only natural. You're searching for an explanation, 'cause even murder's somehow better than a senseless tragedy. Perhaps let your father handle this one."

"Damn my father! And damn you two."

"Are you fit to tend to Ms. Summers or not?" Welsh asked pointedly. "I won't have you bandying about with some murderous conspiracy on your lips, stirring up the press, stricken mad with grief."

"Mad with grief? How dare you tell me how to conduct myself? What would you know about how I grieve? What would you know?"

Bishop's eyes fell with sadness on the girl. "Do your work, Atherton."

"As always, we'll be in touch, Mr. Graves," Welsh said before they both walked to their coach, leaving him alone with the child.

"This is not the first time, dammit!" Atherton shouted after them. "Do you hear me? And God strike me down where I stand if I'm lying; it will not be the last!"

But the constables merely kept trudging up the path leading back to the city.

As soon as their figures were specks in the distance, Atherton kicked gravel into the lake and screamed. He continued until mud caked his boots and his trousers, until he dropped to his knees, heaving ragged breaths. He tilted his head up to the sky, laden with charcoal clouds, his eyes red with dark crescents beneath them. Then he looked down at Lola, and her distorted face gazing at nothing in particular. The agony her visage created seared through all his calluses. He did not sob or shake as he wept. The tears simply fell down his muted expression, heavy and endless.

Before he knew what he was doing, he lay on his side next to her to watch the sky roll across her glassy eyes. A light rain drizzled their skin. He was not just looking at Lola. He was looking at every child that had taken a trip in his hearse that spring. Then every case before them. And all those he knew came next. Yes, even the living—a carousel of bodies stricken with the graceless anguish of being dragged past the gates of the great unknown, their masks twisting from the decay that would so quickly seize upon them.

And there he was among them, not quite an angel nor a devil of their earthly liberation. He began to wonder if he was as human as everybody else or some grotesque misfit with half his soul in another realm. Maybe he'd shaken death's hand one too many times, and it had blighted him. Perhaps that's why *they* were drawn to him—too much of him had already died.

Minutes or an hour later—he could not tell—he sat back up.

Not bothering with the gurney in the back of his wagon or a bedsheet, he slipped his arms beneath the child to lift her. Even soaking wet, Lola was light, her neck limp in the crook of his arm. Inside that delicate body were the memories they shared, locked away in flesh and bone and drowned by the lake.

"Forest nymphs and elves, right, Lola?" he asked as he laid her down in the wagon. After covering her with a bedsheet, Atherton sat beside her and dried his eyes, pausing to light a cigarette.

Deceased adults always felt like objects—there was nothing more inhuman than a human corpse. Children were different. Lola was different. Their bodies seemed to hold fragments of the soul. They smelled different, too. Adults harbored that foul decay of many decades. Children produced a different kind of stench in addition—a sickly, almost sweet aroma. Perhaps that was their innocence, dashed too soon.

"I'm sorry, Lola," he said.

Pocketing her necklace, Atherton clicked open his timepiece. It was a quarter past noon. He couldn't be certain when Mason would arrive, but Mollie had it on good word that it would be a day's time, maybe less. For all he knew, it would be that very evening.

Lola's resurfacing created another thread he hardly had time to pull. One thing was certain—whether departing on horseback or joining his dead in the earth, his final hours in New Sarum were numbered.

23

ATHERTON
JUNE 4, 1886

It was odd, approaching the Butler House with another bouquet of amaryllis, now in mourning. Lola's necklace was draped over one of his fingers.

He had never notified a family of a death before. By the time a case was in his care, their kin had long since been grieving. Even still, the idea of telling Lilian felt familiar. There were few conversations more comfortable for him than those passing on difficult truths.

When Lilian opened the door, her attempts at inviting him in were stopped short. He ceased replying, and his wan grin took on the deeper, underlying sadness that had been burrowed inside since the constables arrived at his doorstep that morning.

It was a slow realization. Surprise, confusion, and disbelief flashed across her face, clear as masquerade masks.

"No, no, that can't be. Not my Lola—she would never..." Lilian said.

"I know, I know," Atherton replied.

"Surely you are mistaken. It must be another child," she continued. "This is one of your jokes, isn't it? That terrible, bleak humor of yours."

Vivie appeared behind Lilian's legs and asked, "Is that Athie? I want to say hello!"

"Not now, dear. Take your brothers and sister into the music room." She ushered the child away and closed the door behind her.

"If only it were so," Atherton continued. "There could be no mistaking her. I'm sorry, Lilian." That was when he slid the necklace into her palm. "You recognize it, don't you?"

She fell into the folds of her dress, clutching the pendant until its six points bit into her skin. Until a light sheen of blood shone from her fist. Only then did she begin crying. Her body shook as she stifled her sobs into his chest.

When, where, how she was found—Atherton answered the questions she struggled to ask. They sat together in the tempestuous spring winds, in that deafening howling.

"I want to see her," she said finally.

"Under no circumstances," he replied. "You should not. You *must* not."

"I want to see my daughter," Lilian said. "I was—I am still—her mother. Do I not have a right to that at least?"

Atherton cupped her head in his hands. "You must listen to me. Whatever fond memories you have of her—no matter the love, the joy, no matter how bright they are—they will forever be blighted by the visage left behind. The lake has changed her. She is altered in a way no mother should have to see."

Lilian clenched her jaw, her fists bunched up in Atherton's sleeves. She took in a deep, shuddering breath. "You're right. I am not thinking clearly. I can accept that," she decided. "But promise me something. You must wear this." She pushed the bloodied amulet into his hands and closed his fingers around it. "She adored you. This would make her happy."

Atherton had spoken with mothers in shock before and had heard all manner of unimaginably bizarre requests. "Certainly," he said. "I will wear it. I promise."

"You look at me like I'm mad. You think I've gone mad, haven't you?"

"Of course not."

"Then promise me you'll wear it."

Atherton slipped the necklace over his head and tucked it behind his shirt. "I promise," he replied. "If you ever want it back, you'll know where it is."

Lilian sniffled and wiped at her nose, already tucking her emotions away. "You have that look in your eyes, the one that says you're needed elsewhere," she said. "You have to leave, I suspect, to prepare her remains. Don't you?"

"I could have my father tend to her, if you'd prefer I stay..."

"No, that's quite all right. It ought to be you. She would have preferred that."

Atherton felt a sudden reluctance to leave. He got the odd sense that, in that brief window while she was left alone, something between them would change irrevocably. "Are you certain?"

Cupping his cheek, she caressed him with her thumb. "This is not the first time death has visited my home, darling. Go on, then. Don't keep my girl waiting."

Though hesitant, Atherton nodded and complied, heading home to see to Lola's arrangements. When he finally returned to the orphanage, he discovered Lilian had left the housekeeper alone with the children.

"Heaven knows where she's gone off to," Morma said. "She left with little else than a word to mind the little ones. She could be anywhere."

But she couldn't be just anywhere.

Atherton found her standing in Goremire Lake in just her chemise and petticoats, the water wrapped around her waist. Her dress had been discarded in a heap at the shore. The wind played with her copper hair, frantic against a rigid body.

"You must be cold," Atherton said.

She kept her back toward him. "How long had she been here? Alone. Drifting. Did she suffer long? In her last moments, did she know only pain?"

The undertaker paused, finding a connection in the turmoil of their souls. Lilian was enduring the havoc death wreaks, while he hoped for the impossibility of dodging his own. He decided that some questions were better left without answers, and she didn't press him for them.

He removed his shoes, his socks, and bunched up his trousers to join her. The icy water stole his breath. Then he was holding her from behind, the warmth of her skin making his spine tingle. Mosquitos and other insects buzzed about them, specks glinting in what sparse sunlight scintillated through the clouds.

"Will you hold me when I am stiff like one of your cases?" Lilian turned to face him. "Will you bare your heart to me as you did when I was alive?"

"I can bare my heart to you now, as you are."

"Yet here we are," she replied, "made hostages by what takes us all, slave to its curious notions, and you as silent as the grave."

"Death is the great unraveler. What are words in the face of it?"

"And what about actions? Will you kiss me a final time to say goodbye, after I've gone cold?" She ran her fingers through his hair and found his cheeks.

As he looked into those burning, black coals, he was paralyzed. It was precisely the same sensation he'd felt when she first held him at the circus.

In her bedroom. She was looking into his eyes, but he couldn't quite see into hers.

"I would," he said, "and I would speak to you as I've never spoken to the dead before. As if blood still beat through you. As if you might reply."

"Oh, but you lie, don't you? You tell me this as if I haven't the faintest notion."

"Haven't the faintest notion of what?"

"Those nightmares you've spoken of before. You once called them hallucinations. But they aren't, are they? They are as tangible as this," she said, digging into his forearm. "As this," she said again, this time kissing him. "Not memories. But ghosts. The dead come to torment you."

He came away from her lips with little breath, grasping vainly for a reply.

"I resent you for keeping this from me."

"I—what?"

"You speak in your sleep, did you know that?" she asked, not waiting for an answer. "You speak novels. And you speak to the dead just as plainly as you address me now. Of this I am certain. You knew, didn't you? Perhaps Lola even visited you."

"Lilian, you're not thinking clearly."

"Don't you *dare* tell me I am mad! Tell me, was she murdered? It's not as the constables suspect. I heard it in your voice when you told me. But they won't lift a finger, will they?"

"Perhaps it's best we not discuss this now. Today, of all days."

She shook her head, angry tears sliding down her cheeks.

A broken smile cracked through. She laughed—a low, exhausted sound that crept into Atherton's veins, colder than the icy water.

"Don't take me for a fool. Today is the only day we have left," she said. "You know it as well as I. Tonight will cast both of us into oblivion. You, beyond Sarum's gates, and I into this Hell without you. That's what this is, isn't it? Your farewell."

"I never intended to leave you alone with this grief. How could I have known? You speak as though I orchestrated this. Mason's return with Lola's...Lilian, it is merely—"

"To blazes with grief," Lilian said. "I want you to tell me something." She clawed into the back of his hands, leaving bright, red trails. "Something true. You have already given me your heart—I don't ask for more of it. I want your trust. You want to console me? Tell me something, something you wouldn't dare whisper to yourself."

He searched for words in the rippling water. All the while, his timepiece ticked away in his pocket, as loud to him as Lilian's heartbeat thudding against him.

"All my life I have never been alone," he admitted. Already, he was trembling, but not from the cold. A part of him had waited for this moment all his life. "Shunned by the living, fostered by the dead. But the dead do not love like the living, for they forget themselves. I am without reprieve, without solitude, without grace. And I'm afraid. Terrified by the thought that no matter how far I run, I will never be free of this feeling, of these nocturnal visitors and their burdensome secrets. I fear I will be haunted all my life. That I was damned the moment I was born, and neither Heaven nor Hell will take me when I leave. But you, Lilian. You have been the envy of every shadow that has darkened my mind. A reprieve from terrors I cannot escape. You dared to love me, and were not repulsed when I gave it in turn. Even still, there is something, *something* about you that torments me."

With closed eyes, Lilian sighed with a grin. Her excitement faded. That desperate hold on his face softened into a cradle. "Thank you," she said. She wiped off the tears sliding down his cheeks. "I will miss you, Atherton Graves."

"You mean this is farewell?"

"You, of all people, should know that in every moment we say goodbye to something. But for now, this one is not on my terms. You have an appointment to keep, don't you?"

So he did. Atherton checked his timepiece and cursed the second hand as it marched the time away.

"You will come see me after tonight has settled, won't you?" Lilian asked.

"I will do everything in my power to make it so," he said, clicking his pocket watch shut.

He would have taken a hundred beatings from Mason's goons if that meant being able to spend another hour with Lilian, to feel his toes go numb while his hands caressed her stomach. After he'd pried himself away, the weight of the revolver against his back only felt more endearing.

Just as his toes touched the gravelly shore, Lilian called out, "You'll remember the flowers tonight, won't you?"

<hr />

Atherton's heels beat echoes throughout New Sarum Cathedral. A man with his head bent in prayer took the opportunity to chastise him with his best scowl; it wasn't half-bad. There were a few others scattered about the pews. His mother's silver-blonde hair gave her away. He shuffled his way over, the old wood creaking as he sat beside her.

"It's been some time since I've come to church," Atherton whispered. "Hell, I wish there was Mass. You know what they say in London about the Disciples? They don't kill anyone on Sunday. It'd be a laugh, wouldn't it? The priests pulling him off me right in the middle of the Eucharist."

Grace chuckled despite herself. "I'm glad you've a good humor about it. Your father and I are sorry about taking you away from Lilian. But blood and business come before love, especially at a time like this. How is she?"

"She is...grieving."

"She's gone mad from it, hasn't she? Poor thing."

"It broke my heart, Mum, leaving her like that."

"That's how it is, isn't it? Tragedy always comes knocking when we've enough on our plates as it is. But this isn't the end, Athie, not for you nor the two of you," his mother said. "God has watched our family long before you came along, and he's watched us since. The work we do is God's work. So long as you've done it, you've been in his hands. And you have to trust that. The virtue of your heart will carry you through this, as it's carried you through everything you've done for this city."

"But will God like it when He finds me fighting a man of faith who holds a candle to the Devil?"

"When has God ever forsaken you?"

"Oh, He's forsaken me plenty," Atherton spat.

"Is today the day you want to be picking bones with your maker?" his mother replied.

"He's been picking bones with me all my life. Now's a fitting time to start."

"God's plans are beyond our understanding. That's why they call it faith."

"Well, I won't take sides with somebody I don't understand. I may very well kill a man. And I know it may not come to it, but could I? Could I, if I had to? I've carried corpses before, Mum, but I've never made one."

"Oh, sweetheart. Who can be prepared for everything the world asks of them? The truth is, we rarely are. But can you stand up when those moments come? That's all that matters. To hell with being ready."

When Atherton closed his eyes, he could almost remember what it was like to be a child again. How afraid he felt the first time he saw a corpse. It was his grandfather. They kept him in the parlor and covered every mirror in the home with sheets. They made a lunch of it, inviting all the neighbors and family over to see him before the burial. He remembered what it felt like to smell Delma's fresh baby's hair, cradling her for the first time. And those endless summers, when the grass was warm and his laughter not embittered by cynicism.

The tolling cathedral bells shattered his reverie.

It was dusk. With every ring, he saw another cold face, another hollow expression begging for answers. With every ring, he felt his soul severed from what innocence he once knew. And with every ring, he felt the hoofs of Mason's horse beating toward New Sarum's gates.

The light in the church waned from the blooming twilight. It brought with it a suspicion too terrible to ignore, even if he couldn't bring himself to trust it. Atherton could feel it calling, pulling him up from his seat. His fingers found the pendant around his neck, his eyes distant.

"I must go," he said. "Forgive me."

His mother's protests pursued his rapid stride, all at once silenced by the heavy doors of the cathedral slamming behind him.

24

ATHERTON

JUNE 4, 1886

"The house feels emptier already. Funny, that," Lilian said with a sad grin, lighting the candelabras by her bed. "I used to joke that it was difficult keeping track of the lot; now I feel the number is too small. Six. Used to be eight before Morma came of age, started helping out."

"Come to think of it, where is Morma?" With a full tumbler in his hand, Atherton sat beside the open window, looking out at New Sarum's innumerable windows aglow beneath brooding clouds.

"I gave her the evening. She's staying the night at an inn in the city."

"And how are the children?"

"Fast sleep. It didn't require much. Crying has a way of tiring the body and the soul. There was no purpose in trying to hide it from them. Sheltering them from Lola's death would only make it that much harder, later. You haven't touched your whisky. The *Lagavulin*. It's your favorite, isn't it?"

"Spoiled by present circumstances, I'm afraid. Mollie has it on good word that the Disciples will be arriving tonight. They may already be here, for all I know."

Sitting down beside him, Lilian nudged the glass closer. "All the more reason to indulge, then."

"You say that as if I'm a dead man."

"I say that because you're trembling like a fawn's legs after popping out of her mother, and there's nothing like a slug of Islay fire to set you straight. Go on." Lilian waited for Atherton to upend the drink before tucking a cigarette between his lips. "How our vices tame us," she said, lighting it for him. "I see you've dressed for the occasion."

Taking off his suit to reveal the revolver tucked into the holster at his back, he said, "Appearances, and all that."

Lilian gasped, but only fascination gleamed in her eyes as she inspected the barrel. "My God, where did you come by that?"

"Do you remember that spiritualist at the circus? Ivory Todd. My guardian angel, as it were."

"More like the Devil in your corner. May I?"

Atherton was surprised by his own hesitation. Even still, he laid the revolver in her open palms. She lifted it up, its steel glittering in the candlelight. "Why, she's beautiful. Here you are."

Holstering it, Atherton said, "It just so happens I'm not Mason's only enemy. Mr. Todd made it sound as though I'd be doing him a favor."

"You mean you intend to use it…offensively."

"As soon as I find my moment, if there is one. Then again, perhaps my father is right. Perhaps nothing will come of this save another bruised face. A broken hand. But how daft would I have to be to take that on faith?"

Lilian's slender hand caressed his knuckles. He unclenched his fist, intertwining his fingers with hers. "The Devil has looked after you well enough."

"The Devil," he murmured. There it was again. That gnawing in his stomach. "You talk like them, you know that?"

"Like who?"

"The circus Ivory works for is run by a coven. Most of the performers are Gehennics—or so he tells me. Whenever God might come up in a conversation, they replace him with the Devil, just like you did, just now. I must confess I'd never spoken at length with a Gehennic before Ivory. I'm only curious. You never broached the subject with me."

Lilian's brows were furrowed, her black eyes deepened by the gloom. A corner of her mouth twitched. "Will you grab my wine off the dressing table? This conversation deserves it, don't you think?"

He was grateful to show his back to her, and walked to her dressing table at the other end of the room, to the half-finished wine glass smudged by her lips. Beside it was a letter, unaddressed, sealed with wax. He reached for the glass, only for his gaze to be commanded elsewhere.

It was a thin, silver chain dangling from a jewelry box. Just like the one he wore around his neck.

Lilian looked out at the city, elbows resting on the windowsill. "You are not the only one who feels outcast by the living, Atherton. What you said to me at the lake, well. It meant more to me than you ever might know. For most of my life, the orphans have been everything to me."

With the utmost caution, he pulled on the chain—slowly enough that it made no discernible sound.

"You know what separates adults from children? Children know they don't know better. But grown people. Adults," she scoffed, "all they think they have are answers. That's what I admire about you. You're not afraid to admit when the world terrifies you. Mystifies you. But you take it one step further, don't you? In your fear, you don't look to God for comfort. We're similar in that regard."

Atherton almost forgot to reply. He stared at another pendant in his palm. "A lifetime of tending to the dead will either beat the faith out of the pious or bolster it irrevocably," he managed.

With a glance, he made sure Lilian was still looking out the window. All the while, his hand found the handle of the drawer, edging it open. Blood pounded in his ears, just like when he sat over the grave of the Crowley twins. When Betty grasped his hand. When he found Lola.

"Gehennics don't worship. We don't pray. A man of faith will beseech God to intervene when life plays its hand against them. But a woman of the black—a witch, as we're called—we never bet on the Devil's hands. We just walk in his shadow."

Atherton thought his eyes betrayed him as he revealed the contents of that drawer. The floor shifted beneath him. Even as he beheld the small pile of pendants, he searched for another explanation. Any explanation. His heart kicked into a gallop.

In that wretched silence, he heard her turn. Felt her eyes boring into his back.

"There comes a time in most everyone's life when they feel abandoned. Left alone by God, the Devil, whatever you wish to call it. You said it yourself. You don't know if Heaven or Gehenna will take you. I suppose I decided for myself. But God cannot be so benevolent and the Devil so wicked, if indeed the two require the other."

"Lilian...why do you have these?" Grasping a fistful, Atherton let the pendants slip onto the dressing table. Silver and bronze clinking one by one in the silence. Seven of them, all identical.

She strode over to him. Her breath came hot on his neck. Her arm slithered over the belts on his holster, his back, and wrapped around his chest. "How long have you known?"

"I hadn't," he said in a coarse whisper.

"And yet, 'Something about you torments me.' Isn't that what you told me?"

Atherton squirmed from her grasp. His foot caught on the leg of the dressing table, knocking over the glass of wine. Burgundy shards erupted, shattered like his composure. His urge to draw his revolver was stopped merely by the fact that Lilian appeared unfazed.

"You're disturbed," she observed.

"Give me one good reason why I shouldn't be."

"Oh, how your gaze changes," she said. "You look at me as though I am a monster."

"You said it yourself. You feared a monster crept into your home and stole her away, but all the while it was you. You murdered those children. Alice. Betty. The Crowley twins. My God. Lola!"

"Remarkable," she scoffed. "You really do have a gift, don't you? How long have their spirits been attached to you? I intended for the sigils to be effective, but I never imagined this."

"Effective? What—no, no, this isn't happening. I'm dreaming. This is..." Then, for the first time, he saw Lilian clearly. For all the nights they spent together, this was the most vulnerable she'd ever been. She revealed a smile—malefic, broad, and playful, the one that had always lurked beneath the façade.

"Are your dreams always this morbid? Then again, one can only suspect they are."

"You wept in my arms for Lola's sake. At the lake. Tears as real as any grieving mother's. That was all an act?"

This, above all else, appeared to wound Lilian the most. She huffed. "An act? Has your opinion of me sunk so deeply at a moment's notice? I gave her a *good* death. And as happy a life as any child in this broken world could hope for. You dare think I was incapable of loving her?"

His throat tightened. Every word was an objection to the nightmare subsuming that moment. But it was futile. The dread was filling up the room and drowning his lungs, replacing every happy memory between them with the abject horror that had been hiding all along. "Of course! How *could* you? How?"

Stepping over the glass, Lilian placed her hands in his and stroked them. "Blood. Blood and words. They are magic, Atherton. Sheer magic."

"It's murder—the most vile sort. Please," he begged. "You see what you've done, don't you?"

"And more than you know. It was a *mercy*. You think 'begging Betty' wanted to live? Of all people, Atherton, I did not think you myopic."

"Myopic? Damn you. Get your hands off me."

"You will miss it, you know. My touch. Pretend all you like—it makes it no less real. Even now, you think you loathe me, but that thought is fleeting. It will rot quicker than autumn leaves. Our love is evergreen—this is only fodder for it. You will love me as you always have, for what I am, who I am, long after I've fed the soil. And you might quarrel mightily, but a word to the wise—you should never hate yourself for it."

There were no more tears left in Atherton. The pain had nowhere to escape, it clenched his insides and filled him with a frantic energy. "I will never loathe myself as I loathe you. I could never love somebody like you."

"You already have."

Stepping away from her, Atherton paced madly about the center of the room, running his hands through his hair. "How did you do it?"

"They call it *mother's friend*, if you must know. Laudanum. Another one of your vices. Enough makes their—"

"No!" he shouted, grasping her shoulders and shaking. "What did you do to me?"

Lilian's lips parted with a forced breath, as though his anger stoked another kind of fire in her. "Oh, delightful. Look at you. You're curious. You already know how."

It seized him.

"Ahh, there it is," she cooed.

"The flowers. The flowers are cruel," he realized aloud.

"Pardon?"

"The children. They've been telling me all this time, only I wouldn't listen. I was naive. The boutonniere. You gave it to me that night at the circus, y-you pricked me with it. Dabbed away the blood. And you used it. Is that what this is? Some kind of...*hex?* A spell? My God!"

"Again, astounding. No wonder that spiritualist took a shine to you. The children speak to you. You hear them as clearly as you hear me now."

"But that doesn't make sense! You've only had my blood since that night. But Betty—Betty and the others were long before then."

"I won't bore you with the mechanics of spellcraft theory, my love. Blood may be the most powerful conduit. But who's to say a stray hair doesn't do the trick?" She reached up to brush a lock of hair out of his eyes, only for her hand to be swatted away.

"Oh, don't narrow your eyes at me. You think I manipulated you. How easy that would be, wouldn't it? The dastardly temptress twirling about her young suitor. No. I may not have asked your permission for the ingredients, but your time—your affection—you gave freely. Are you not here, on perhaps your last night on Earth, to enjoy my company? The company of this 'monster.' Say what you will about me, I'm no thespian. My feelings for you are as true as they've ever been."

"You fret for how I see you, but not for what you've become. You murdered five children, Lilian. One of them was your own. You were her mother!"

"Don't you think it hurt me? Do you not think I wept as she thrashed in my hands? I loved Lola. Only I wouldn't let emotion undermine everything I've worked for."

"Worked for? Listen to yourself. You sound proud!"

"And you, captivated. You still let me near you. Your lips are just a fingernail's width from mine. You can feel my breath on them. And you know something, Atherton? You haven't pulled away."

Lilian continued digging into his skin. They grasped with that same yearning, the same one he indulged countless times before. She pressed her lips against him in feverish abandon.

They felt cold and unfamiliar. The wet beak of a stranger, a creature he no longer recognized. That's what he told himself, at least. But she was right. Tasting her rekindled a flicker of something that could be betrayed, but not so easily broken. A thunderous echo exuded throughout the house—raucous, booming bangs that shook the very floor they stood on. Mason had arrived.

"It appears our time's come to an end, my dear. I'd surmise that's your other appointment for the evening," she said.

Atherton pushed her off. With Mason in the city, there would be no constables available. No time to tell them about Lilian, even if he could reach them. His eyes searched frantically for answers, settling on her once again. For the briefest moment, she appeared to him as she always did—a placid woman with a curious gleam in her eye, that innocent grin curled with the slightest mischief.

"If I survive tonight, I will return here. But you must promise you will not hurt the other children. You must swear to me, Lilian. Swear it!"

Still, the pounding exuded throughout the house. But none of the children stirred. No doors opened, even as tableware and portraits along the wall rattled.

"If that's what it takes, I swear it," she said. "Anger suits you. Now imagine, if you will, how tedious a quarrel with a cutthroat like Mason Cross will feel after our engagement this evening." Fetching his suit and cigarette case from the windowsill, she took another out and offered it to him. "Steady yourself, my love. You will live to see darker days yet."

25

MASON
JUNE 4, 1886

Mason's fist grew numb from slamming against the door. A double-barrel shotgun hung at his side. "Atherton Graves, I do not conduct business with bloody cowards! I know you're in there!"

Just as he was about to continue abusing the wood, the lock clicked. The hinges groaned, revealing Atherton in the darkness, fists balled with an unrepentant gaze. Smoke trailed from the embers of his cigarette. Atherton gathered his cloak from a coat rack by the door and wrapped it about himself.

"Good evening, Mason." The undertaker looked the mobster up and down, seemingly unperturbed by the weapon. There was a deep dread in his eyes, a brokenness in his voice. It was not the first time a man stood before Mason, resigned to face his doom, but there was something unfamiliar about Atherton's demeanor. Perhaps a lifetime of being summoned by death made him all the more comfortable in the face of it.

"At last. The man of the hour." Mason inclined his head.

"My apologies for delaying you. I trust I wasn't terribly difficult to find."

Mason had anticipated having to haul Atherton by his lapels into the carriage. Yet the undertaker walked right past him and even greeted Bram, pausing to look up at the night sky.

"It's going to rain," he said.

Mason stood bemused on the porch steps before joining Atherton by the carriage. "So it is. Your little hideout gave me time to gather up your mother 'n father 'n that sister of yours. She's a handful."

"Oh, dull. So you intend to kill them as well. That's a pity. I hope you brought extra shells." He pointed to the shotgun.

Atherton's flippant remark needled Mason. He even felt insulted to find that Atherton did not understand the subtle principles behind his punishments. "Assurance. That's all this is. Ugh. 'Kill.' Nobody said that word. You did. *Oi!* You look at me when I'm bloody talkin' to you. It's all theatrics with you lot. Kill, kill, kill. And this," he hissed, pointing to the broad scar on his cheek. "Your pride damns you. You and that blasted circus. Now get in."

Mason held the door ajar, waiting for Atherton to situate himself before joining him. With a holler and a crack from Bram, the carriage rattled off. Mason kept the shotgun leveled at the undertaker as he absently stared out the window, watching the Butler House shrink behind them. *No point in bloodying the boy before anybody sees,* Mason thought, lowering the weapon. Taking off his bowler, he drummed his fingers on his knees. "Unfinished business, is it?"

"Of the sort you wouldn't believe. You, on the other hand—at least I can make sense of you."

Mason barked with laughter. "Women. Even on a night like this, some blower's got you torn up inside. She the one you brought to the circus?"

"Regrettably."

"Any woman 'er age is a force to be reckoned with. Not that she ain't fierce by any standard, mind you. S'pose you should be thanking me, takin' you away."

"Consider me obliged. I've seen enough murder to know that I can stomach it when there's reason behind it. Logic, no matter how ill-conceived. A wife poisoning her husband to inherit his estate. A friend, seeking vengeance. Murder for love, business..." he said with a nod to Mason. "I suspect you feel the same. But abject terror wrought upon the world for its own sake? You once asked me to discern the difference between fear and trust. But what if you can trust the person you love to commit the act you fear most? I once thought you were a madman, Mason. I was mistaken. You're as sane as any killer comes."

In the dim light offered only by jostling lanterns beside the windows, Mason squinted, scrutinizing the desperation hollowing Atherton's face. "Am I 'earin' this right? You mean that dame back there's a killer?" Mason jabbed his thumb behind them. "No. You're windin' me up. This is some ploy, innit?"

"I said you wouldn't believe it, didn't I?"

Mason ran his callused hands through his thick hair. He paused in the silence, uncertain what to make of it. Part of him was relieved, finding Atherton so numb. He would accept his punishment that much more easily. "Go on then, what was it?" he asked.

He opened his mouth a few times, but nothing came. There was pain written across his face, the kind that makes all other considerations immaterial. When his response arrived, it dripped like black oil from his lips.

"Children," was all he said.

The mobster's back went flush against his seat as he considered this. "Bloody 'ell," he cursed. He almost considered asking if Atherton had alerted the authorities, only to realize he was standing in his way. "I'm almost surprised it shakes you, given the world you toil in. Not all too different from my own, I s'pose. You're just always at...the end of it."

"If I didn't know better, I'd say that was a compliment."

"It was," Mason said, wincing.

"I am shaken. Of course I am," Atherton admitted. "But only because I didn't expect it of her. Or did I? Perhaps I was only lying to myself, hiding from the obvious."

"Nah," Mason said, shaking his head. "You can't blame yourself. The world makes fools of people who think they know it well. Their ignorance is loudest. Too loud for them to 'ear themselves. But you can't make sense of it all, no matter how 'ard you beat your skull in or writhe in those sleepless nights. You'll come to find people surprise you in the worst 'n best of ways. Fix that to your grave, and you'll never be wrong. But a man's not defined by 'is graces, or how right 'e is. It's how 'e loses. And God, I've lost more than most men. You're not the first man to scar me, and I'd be an 'alfwit to suspect you'd be the last.

"But mate," Mason said with a laugh, "you do 'ave a taste. You sharin' some murderess's company and the likes of me in the same evenin'. You must be in the wrong business."

"Evidently." Atherton's face betrayed no emotion as the carriage passed from the backwoods' dirt roads and onto the city's cobblestone. Gaslight slithered across him as the horses trotted on. Deep, mauve rings hung beneath his eyes, but his hands were steady as he lit another cigarette.

"What 'appens 'ere tonight ain't personal. You'd do well to remind yourself," Mason said.

"Likewise."

"Excuse me?"

The carriage lurched to a halt. Mason could hear a sizable crowd murmuring—the one he'd gathered not an hour before outside the White Horse. With the curtains shrouding Atherton's statuesque face in near total blackness, Mason got the eerie sense he was talking to a ghost.

"I never wanted it to come to this," Atherton said.

Something cold bloomed in Mason's stomach—a squirming, determined worm that wriggled its way up to his throat, making his heart beat that much quicker. It was a feeling he was no stranger to, yet for all the years it had been foreign to him, it felt that much more unusual, having to remind himself to push it back down.

Fear.

26

ATHERTON
JUNE 5, 1886

His hour had come. Atherton checked his timepiece. Midnight.

"Chin up," Mason said. "You take this on the chin, and we can put our differences behind us. All of it, eh? Let's bury it."

Atherton nodded.

As soon as he did, Mason kicked open the carriage door, but before Atherton could leave calmly, he was wrenched by his collar and pushed headfirst into the street.

On his hands and knees, he saw the crowd Mason had gathered, and felt the barrel of his shotgun at the back of his head. There were hundreds, if not a thousand, gathered—not a constable's uniform to be found among them. Delma, Grace, and Allan were on their knees by the gurgling fountain in the courtyard, their hands bound in their laps. Henry and Arthur stood behind them with a third gentleman Atherton couldn't name, billy clubs in hand.

One of the lenses on Allan's spectacles was webbed with cracks. Blood trickled from his temple, where knuckles had bitten bone. "Oh, thank God you're all right," he said to Atherton under his breath.

"Get beside them," Mason ordered. "Kneel!"

Mason wrenched Atherton up by his clothes and tossed him. "Well, well. Ain't this a charming reunion?" he said, swirling about to address the crowd. He laughed a deep, belly laugh, resting the barrel of his gun on his shoulder. "I've got to hand it to ya, Athie, you weren't ever one for hiding.

And look at these shining peaches," he added, pinching Grace's chin and tapping Delma's head.

For all the wealth and status the Disciples had beaten out of England, it never could polish away the origins of the Cross family. Mason might've dressed in fine suits and cloaks lined with furs, but he still stalked with the swagger of a pickpocket from Whitechapel. "So tell us—'ow are ya, Mr. Graves? And not you," he said with a growl to Atherton. "We'll get to you soon."

"Very well, Mason," Allan stuttered, wincing as the mobster circled him. "How's your father fairing?"

"Not well, not well at all, I'm afraid. Sick as a dog. He's got the ague. We may be in need of your expert services soon."

"Our prayers are with your father," Grace said.

"Much obliged, Mrs. Graves. Courteous as always. Now, I'm afraid I've some business with your boy 'ere."

"We are well aware, Mason, but is all this really necessary? Untie us, at—"

Allan was cut off, the air cast out of him by the hard kick Mason gave to his stomach, leaving him flattened on the ground. "I weren't finished, was I? You lot see this, don't you? Hell, most of you were there for it! This little mark gave me some 'ell, eh, boy? Seems you've got some friends in low places, don't you?"

Mason hauled Atherton by his collar and tie, lifting him up. Delma shrieked all the while. "Seems a clown at that carnival took a great liking to you. Goes by the name of Boo. That's your sole ally in this. A clown! If we're bein' honest, I was surprised you 'adn't run off with 'em. Do you 'ave any idea what this cost me?"

Spit hissed between Atherton's lips, the soles of his shoes barely scraping the ground. "Your pride, it seems."

Mason flashed a smile. They were close enough that he could smell the fish he'd had that morning. "Pride. That's precisely it." He heaved Atherton backward. The ground rushed to meet his back, and a white flash erupted in his side. A cracked rib. Despite his grinding teeth, a short scream burst out, tearing the silence apart.

Grace bent forward to help him.

"Don't! Touch! Him!" Mason bellowed. "I think it's about that time of evenin' we 'it the lush crib, eh? I'm calling a town meeting! That's right! All you watchin' from your windows, every last one of you can 'ear my voice yet unbothered, I want you out!" Mason's voice carried throughout the quiet streets. When nobody obliged him, he fired two rounds into the air.

"Out! Now! That's it. Come on, you cheeky bastards." Mason went to a few of the townspeople standing timidly in their doorways and hauled them out himself.

Arthur and Henry followed suit.

Somewhere between the pain in his rib and the night air, cold in his lungs, he felt the urge to reach for his revolver. But his instincts bayed at him. Everything would be wagered on that moment. He would stay his hand and bleed a little more, if that meant finding the right one.

The courtyard teemed with stirred citizens in night garments, clutching themselves against the cold. Mason took up a fistful of Atherton's hair and started dragging him.

Rushing to his feet, Allan shouted, "Damnit, at least do it with some dignity!"

Dropping Atherton's dead weight, Mason slapped the butt of his piece against Allan's cheek. The blow staggered him with the crunch of wood against bone. His spectacles flew, shattered and broken.

"Seems this town started to forget who runs things 'round 'ere!" Mason's shouts echoed.

"By honor bright, Mr. Cross," the butcher Mathison said, stepping forward, "we know full well. Please, don't hurt the Graves boy any more than he's already got."

"Arthur!" Mason said.

Arthur raised his billy club and approached the butcher, dashing him across the head. Mathison teetered into the fountain with a splash, blood pooling out into the bubbling water. "Any further objections?" he asked the crowd.

The stillness was interrupted only by Delma's wailing.

The smell of wet stone pervaded the air as storm clouds began spitting.

Mason picked up Atherton with the ease of a parent handling a toddler. He hauled him through the crowd, now shuffling about to make a path into the pub. "After you," he grunted, flinging the boy through its doors.

Heat blazed through his abdomen as Atherton struggled to his knees, a steady fire sparking with every moment.

"Mollie! Where's Mollie? There you are. Get this rabble a round," Mason ordered.

The barkeeper appeared from the backroom and started pouring beers for nobody in particular. The crowd bumbled in without so much as a murmur. When they were too nervous to drink, Mason berated them until they did.

"Now that we've settled in nice and close-like, let's be clear 'ere, eh?" Setting his shotgun down on the bar, he flared his coat and rested his hands on his belt. "I don't mean nothing untoward. And should you all behave, well, none of you lot 'ave to worry a shiny pence for your hides. Remember, we're 'ere to protect you. Problem is, the young corpse-bearer 'ad the mind to let you lot know he's above the code. A God-fearing code. Our code. Ain't that right, Athie?"

"T-that's right," Atherton said.

"And I know how word travels in these filthy fuckin' cities. Soon as he did me up pretty, you all knew 'bout it 'for the night was up. We're 'ere so none of you get any ideas, eh? Right then. Luther, the little one."

The man Atherton didn't recognize took hold of his little sister, whose cries and ceaseless tears all but incapacitated her. Luther was lanky, clean-shaven, with bony jaws.

"Delma, it's going to be all right," Atherton tried to soothe her as she was pulled ahead of him.

"You keep telling 'er that, lad. Bring her 'ere," Mason commanded.

Atherton's face lit up with rage as soon as Mason's paws found her shoulders. "Don't you fucking touch her!"

"Recognize this pretty piece, Athie?" Mason dug out a straight razor from his pocket. "A token of good faith, spurned," he said, flourishing the blade's sheen. "You left it in the dirt with my own blood on it."

"Damn you to Hell, Mason!" Henry's hands gripped Atherton's shoulders, pushing his knees down as soon as he made an attempt to stand.

Mason took the child's head in his hands, tenderly smoothing out the wet locks from her cheeks. "Proverbs. *'The fear of the Lord is the beginning of wisdom: and the knowledge of the Holy is understanding,'*" he recited. "Consider this your education, Atherton."

Atherton could feel Grace shaking beside him. Allan's blood decorated her white blouse while tears dripped from her chin to join it.

"Wait, wait, wait!" Allan shouted. "This is barbaric! Why are you punishing her for what we've done?"

"Arthur," Mason said quietly.

The baton came down quickly, landing with a hefty knock against Allan's skull. He wavered, slumping forward as though his bones had become gelatin. Luther held him firm, upending a nearby pint of beer over his head to keep him conscious.

"What your son did to me was barbaric, Allan. This is justice. An eye for an eye."

"Then take my eye!" Atherton replied.

"I would, lad," he said, almost with genuine sadness. "Trouble is, you can take a proper beatin'. You've proven that much. That will never lay you down 'alf as bad as you did me. But this will."

Pressing the razor against the bottom of Delma's jaw, he angled it upwards to leave a matching scar. Mason pressed down until her skin bowed around the blade. Blood flowed as the cut was drawn with dreadful slowness. Delma's thrashing was barely contained by the hand Mason had around the back of her head to steady her.

Through her unintelligible screams, Atherton could make out the words, "You promised!"

Having been stoked for too long, Atherton's wrath burst out.

He wrenched himself out of Henry's hands and threw his elbow into his groin. Screaming through the pain in his side, he crashed into Mason with total abandon. The two flew backwards, fracturing a table as soon as their weight slammed onto it.

Another crash ensued. This time, it was Mason's fist, not arriving with any of the patience it usually did. Atherton was flattened and alone on the ground, still reclaiming all his senses. Before he could ready himself for a second blow, and a third, the fourth arrived—each one heavier than the last. Mason was back on his feet, Atherton a limp, mishandled doll in his hands.

Thick, hot blood poured down Atherton's throat. He coughed and spat. Through a black and silver tide of stars, he saw that Delma had made it back into Grace's arms. The cut on her cheek was only the length of a needle.

For once, he was grateful Mason held him aloft. The walls of the pub spun like a carousel off its tracks. Slack in those brawny fists, with everyone watching in bated breath, it almost felt nostalgic. For a moment, he saw the softened man that he'd spoken to in the carriage—a lurking compassion.

Too quiet for anybody else to hear, Mason said, "Now you've forced my 'and."

"So I have," Atherton said with a bloodied smile. "You know, it feels like it did, years before." When he closed his eyes, he could almost drift off. It made the words come easier, feeling as though he'd already died, or perhaps lingered in another one of his nightmares. "Back when your father still ran things. We were just kids, eh, Mason? Do you remember that? Now look what you've gone and done."

He gulped down blood, laughing madly. He laughed because Mason hadn't discovered his revolver in the scuffle, because it was evident Henry and Arthur assumed their boss had already searched him, and somewhere in that undercity heart of his, it appeared Mason had grown too accustomed to someone else doing it for him.

"Damn you for makin' me do this. I've made something of myself. What've you done? Dug yourself a shallow grave for a fight you were damned to lose."

"I think you're digging yours," Atherton choked. "But I won't be the one to carry you."

"So be it. Henry, get the noose from the carriage!"

A meek wave of protests stirred, followed swiftly by Arthur and Luther's strikes and shouts to quiet them. When Henry returned with a spool of rope, its end was already fashioned into a noose.

"Going as planned, then?" Atherton quipped.

Mason took it, placing the knot around Atherton's neck.

Turning on his heels to address them all, Mason shouted, "This is what 'appens! This is what 'appens when you cross the bloody Disciples!"

Leashed up, drooling, and dripping scarlet, Atherton's legs wobbled beneath him. He let himself crash to his knees. All those countless, sleepless nights and weary, waking hours tormented by spirits culminated, anchoring Atherton to the depths of exhaustion as if a thousand dead bodies were tied to his ankles. Perhaps Henry and Arthur wouldn't bother tying his hands if he were already too maimed to stand.

"Think of your father, Mason," Allan protested. "Would he do this? Is this the legacy of the Cross family? Murdering an innocent man whose only sin is defending himself? Is this how you garner loyalty? This is madness!"

"What do you know about my father?" he roared back. "This is *my* business! My legacy! This isn't madness. This is what's owed. And your daughter's next if you can't bite your tongue. Take your son's life as my promise in that regard, and wash your sins in his blood." He handed the rope to Henry before taking up his shotgun and leveling it at the rest of the Graves.

Allan gripped Grace close, who tucked Delma into her chest.

"Don't look," she said.

"It's all right," Atherton assured weakly.

It took Henry several attempts before he managed to toss the rope around one of the ceiling beams. When he did, Arthur took it up beside him, prepared to pull.

Stumbling forwards, Atherton managed to stand below the rope.

"If you've any final words, Atherton—if you wish to reconcile with God, now's your chance," Mason said.

"Oh, I have things to reconcile," he snarled, "but nothing for you, and I've long since been forsaken by God. My bones are with them. With you, the whole lot of you! Take a long look at yourselves. You, Mrs. Welsh, I carried your daughter after the consumption took her. And you, Mr. Holmes, your son, the night you pissed yourself drunk after he'd gone and drowned himself." Atherton bared his teeth against the pounding in his head. "And you, Mr. and Mrs. Crowley, yes, I see you cowering back there. I buried your sons. Your sons, who suffered such strange and inexplicable deaths. And Alice Silvester's mother, though she is not here now. What I am about to say is for her, too. And you'd do well to tell her!"

Atherton wheezed, hair dangling about his battered, maddened expression. Blood seeped into his eyes, burning as he glared at them all.

Arthur and Henry looked to Mason, but he held up a hand. "Let 'im," he said.

"Your children were murdered. The Crowley twins, Alice, even that beggar we all walked over. That's right! Poisoned by a woman named Lilian Butler. And if it were not for these men, these criminals you serve so loyally, you would have your justice tonight. Before this moment, I didn't understand how somebody could be capable of something so foul, but now I see. *Now* I get it!" he seethed. "Now I understand how this world rears such monsters. None of us is innocent. Who else have I ushered to the earth? I'm cursed to remember them all, and more than I can count. Buried them, I did, with these blackened hands! Now I join your dead, abandoned by those I was damned to serve. I should expect no less from you all, rotten long before I could be summoned to curl my fingers around your corpses. You were right, Mason," he finished. "People will surprise you—in the worst of ways."

A muted horror seized them all.

Allan and Grace sat with their mouths agape.

"Well," Mason said. "You were bold to the end, Atherton Graves."

After Mason gave the nod, Arthur and Henry gripped the rope with pale knuckles. Pull by pull, they hoisted Atherton off the ground.

He felt the noose clench around his larynx, then a strong tug just under his jaw as it strained upwards, the rafters creaking as they drew closer. The higher he rose, the harder it became to breathe, and the more he saw Lilian's face. Her bloodshot eyes. Their depthless yearning. Then the city's innumerable dead flooded his vision, and with the breaths becoming harder to fight for, the clearer he saw them all, standing with their broken bodies among the living.

Arthur and Henry gritted their teeth through the strain, lifting him higher.

As time crawled along, he felt something else—a pale, milky vapor spilling from his mouth, rousing revulsed exclamations and astonished gasps. Arthur and Henry looked back at Mason for direction, who waved it away despite his own stupefaction. At the limits of the rope, they held firm. All that was left to do was wait.

Atherton's legs flailed against his will.

That was when he saw that ghoul, clearer still than the day he cut him down. He could feel the tickets he found in his pocket once more, soft in his palm. Feel Alice's cold fingers lace through his, lifting him up ever so slightly. Betty's foul, mire-ridden putridity filled his nose with every choked breath. The twins, each coiling around a leg to lessen the weight.

And Lola. *"Be cruel."*

He fought with each narrowing gasp to inhale that vapor back into his lungs—a gust of freezing air that revived a terrible clarity.

Then his body became still.

"You're nearing that staircase," Mason called up, pulling a cigarette from his case. "Any final revelations?"

"Yeah," Atherton strained. "A couple."

"Best be quick with it, then."

"Ivory sends his...regards."

Atherton reached behind him and unholstered his revolver, snapping the trigger back as soon as it was drawn and trained on his target. The violent recoil sent a shudder through his arm, a sharp pain where his shoulder failed to absorb it.

The air cracked. A burst of light. Smoke coiled from the hot barrel as the acrid stench of gunpowder fouled the air.

A clenched, choking laugh escaped from Atherton, still swaying from the kickback.

Mason stumbled backwards. He looked down in misunderstanding. The cigarette had been shot from his hand, and where the bullet had struck behind it, a red stain bloomed from his lower left abdomen.

The rest of the Graves seized upon the moment, hurrying behind the bar to Mollie, who outstretched her arms toward them.

After the realization settled in, Mason pointed his shotgun at Atherton and pulled the trigger. The lever clicked into that deadened silence. The two rounds he'd shot into the air earlier had left his chambers empty.

"You didn't bloody search 'im?" Mason roared.

"We thought you did!" Arthur shouted back, straining from the weight.

The brothers gripped the rope and glanced at each other in panic, left with the choice to sit like fish in a barrel or release the only certainty of finishing off Atherton.

Atherton fired another round toward Mason, sending him barreling for the pub's doors, followed shortly by a host of panicked patrons. The shot ricocheted off a coat of arms, shattering a nearby window. Only then did the screams start.

Turning the revolver toward his executioners, Atherton squeezed the trigger. The first bullet punctured Arthur's neck. Blood sprayed his sibling's face as the shot exited cleanly into Henry's chest. The rope whirled out of their hands, whizzed, and lashed wildly at the air. Atherton was hurtled into the remnants of the shattered table, crunching his ankle in the fall.

Luther charged him with a raised baton.

Atherton waited until he was close enough. Another fiendish round burst from the Bull Dog's muzzle, leaving powder burns on Luther's forehead. His body seized with a single, hideous jolt, falling upon Atherton in a ragged mess of brain matter. It was satisfying, knowing he wouldn't be the one to clean it up this time.

"Fucking hell," Atherton rasped, climbing to his feet despite his shaking legs.

Loosening his noose, he gave a firm tug on the rope and liberated it from the rafters.

Arthur and Henry were crawling for the doors, the pub heaving with hundreds of fleeing bodies.

"Are we having ourselves another row, lads?" Atherton screamed. He fired his fifth shot into Arthur's kneecap, whose howls defied the din of glasses and tankards clattering to the floor. Townspeople were still careening past them for the doors, not sticking around to find out if Atherton's rage would spill out onto them.

Henry whirled to face Atherton with a hand raised, the other pressed against the wound in his chest. "Please, we was only doin' as we were told! You know I 'ave nothing against you. Mason's the one you want!"

Arthur had since abandoned his brother, now crawling for the door but trampled by dozens fighting to leave.

"You know, honesty isn't a virtue when you're staring down iron," Atherton said. "But it was terribly kind of you."

"Kind of me, how?"

"Moving out of the way of these people," Atherton replied, firing his last shot.

The bullet pierced through Henry's chest, decorating the floor with blood, bone, and ripped cartilage.

A racket of crashing glass and screams blared about them. Through the ringing in his ears, Atherton pushed through the crowds. His clothes stained with bits of Luther's brain, the boy who had looked after the dead now stood among yet more bodies, his pitiless scowl speaking to no dissatisfaction in creating them.

Yet, they weren't finished.

Henry and Arthur clung to what time they had. Their curdling cries carried as Atherton made it into the street, just in time to see Mason's carriage barrelling through the Queen's Gates. With a growl, he pushed back through the crowds to find his family still crouched behind the bar.

"You did the right thing," Allan said with a trembling voice. "You did. Never doubt that. Was everything that you said true? The children? And where did you come by the revolver?"

"Now is not the time." Atherton took Delma into his arms, leaving bloodied fingerprints and kisses on her forehead. "You must go, all of you. Pack what you can, quickly, then make for Annesbury. Stay with Uncle Harvey. The Disciples don't know about him yet."

"Can you manage the horses?" Grace asked. "We'll pack while you ready them."

"Not we."

"What are you saying?" Allan asked.

"I can't go with you. Mason won't stop if I go with you."

"Darling, you're not thinking clearly. You've lost blood."

"She's right. We can hide you," Allan added.

"Damnit! Won't you two just listen to me for once in your lives? If not the Disciples, then it'll be the peelers. What will they brand this if not murder?"

"But you're innocent! You were defending yourself," Allan pushed. "They all saw it."

"Is that what Mason will tell them as soon as he reaches London?"

Delma cried harder into her brother's arms. He shut his eyes with his cheek against her head, trying to solidify that sensation in his mind forever. "You must flee without me. Do you think I want this any more than you?"

"Don't go! I don't want you to go!" Delma wailed.

"He's right. My God, he's right, Allan," Grace said.

"What of the gates?" Allan said. "They'll shut them before we've left."

"They'll be distracted. I will see to that. As long as you leave within the hour, they won't be thinking of the gates." He gave Delma back to his mother, already missing that feeling of holding her. "I can assure you."

"And where will you go?" Allan said.

"Somewhere safe," he replied.

Grace parted her son's hair, wiping the blood from his face. "We will leave Morgan—have her saddled and ready. She will ride far and fast. Will we hear from you?"

Somewhere amid the stampede of footsteps and falling glass, the pub had dwindled back to silence.

"I will write to you. Go. Go! I'll take care of this."

Delma held onto her brother's hand until she was pulled away, her fingers still reaching for him as Grace carted her off.

Atherton was alone with the two groaning men, the noose made to take his life, and a pub full of liquor. He took a bottle of gin first, wrenching off its cap and pouring it over the bar. Then he took two, smashing them against the walls. Before long, he took fistfuls and threw them, relishing every splintered shard, every eruption. He gritted through the sharp aches in his body, pulling on a bookcase full of priceless, aged whiskies until it toppled, the bottles sliding off in a deafening crescendo of screaming glass.

Slumped against a beam, a pale Arthur breathed raggedly with a hand over the wound in his neck. Though his eyes fluttered, he watched Atherton, who, unaware of himself, shouted as he demolished every last bottle.

"You won't do it," Henry said beside his brother. "You don't 'ave it in you." Air whistled from his lungs. The blood seeping from his chest swirled with the rivers of liquor. "You're a man of God."

Forehead shining with sweat, Atherton looked down at Henry. "No, I'm not. But you were."

"What are you doing?" Arthur stammered.

Using his noose, Atherton brought the two brothers together, binding them tightly. They had lost too much blood to do little more than flail weakly. Though his feet slipped as he strained, Atherton managed to haul them to the center of the pub, where, if the adrenaline allowed them to crawl to the door, by then it would be too late.

Calmly, Atherton walked to the doorway.

"The Devil take you!" Henry shouted after him.

Drawing out his matchbook, he struck one, watching its eager flame sizzle to life. He paused to consider all the dominoes that led him there—

a moment in which he hardly recognized himself. All the years spent cleaning up the mess of death's wanton devastation, it never occurred to him just how easy it would be to wield the scythe himself.

Atherton flung the match, shutting the door behind him and sprinting away.

It was as though the entire pub took in a deep inhalation—a rolling *whoosh*. First blue, translucent, almost imperceptible to the eye, it rolled over every surface.

Then it exhaled.

The alcohol in the air combusted in rich, roaring flames. Unfettered, they tore up the walls and, sparking what little sensation those two men had left, made certain they were awake in their final moments.

The courtyard was empty, a task made easy by the terror Atherton had inspired in the townspeople who feared his vengeance might spill over. Of course, that didn't stop them from looking. From behind cracked doors, between curtains, in the reassuring walls of their homes, they gazed on as their undertaker stood before the wicked pyre which consumed even the last of the men's final, howling screams.

How still he had become then, with his head bowed as though before an altar, the soot and cinders billowing above him in dark, terrible wings stretching into that glittering sky.

27

ATHERTON
JUNE 5, 1886

The ground shook beneath Morgan's thundering hooves. The pouch on his saddle was full of loose banknotes and clothes, thanks to Atherton's mother. In the distance, the city had gathered around the unquenchable fire consuming the White Horse. It was a solitary candle in the night, flickering with a deathly glow, casting shadows and smoke over all.

Atherton could not help but pull on the reins to admire it. That bright pillar of fire gleamed in his eyes, dancing and beautiful.

The city, its dead, and the center of the Disciples' meetings used to haunt him. Now ashes rained upon the city, and no amount of prayers could stop it. Just as the hundreds of pale faces kept his dreams company, from this night forward, that city would have fever dreams of that fire, those screams, and the great, black traveling cloak of the undertaker as he rode off into the night.

Allan, Grace, and Delma had made it through the Queen's Gate. Their carriage was a spot joining the blackened horizon.

He spurred his horse forward, but not for the gates.

The Butler House stood as dissevered from New Sarum as always, but even more so tonight, tucked away from the havoc. All its windows were unlit save for one. Lilian's.

Morma was sitting on the bottom steps of the porch, hands around her knees, with her head bent forward as Atherton reined Morgan in and leapt down.

"It's all right, Morma," he assured her, "nobody in town was killed. It was only Mason's men."

The housekeeper glanced up, but only briefly. "It'll be all right, darling—it'll be all right. You hush now. Hush. Shh, shh, it's all right," she said.

"Morma? Are you sleepwalking?" Atherton crouched down. "What's the matter?"

Her eyes were wide, staring blankly.

Atherton took her hands into his, finding them cold and wet. In the darkness, all he saw was a sheen, too thick to be tears. "What's happened?" He took her face in his hands. "Are you safe? Did Mason send his men here?"

"It'll be all right, won't it? How 'bout a bedtime story?"

Atherton took hold of her shoulders and shook her, and though their eyes met, there was no recognition. "Tell me what's happened. Are the children safe?"

"H-have you been to the water? Have you been 'r-round the market? We'd a-looked, we'd a-looked a-and drained the Thames ..."

Atherton climbed the porch steps. The door was already open, inviting him into the house's perfect darkness.

"Don't go in," Morma said behind him, the momentary cognizance in her tone freezing him in his tracks. "She's still inside."

Atherton swallowed and stepped inside. "Lilian! Lilian, what's happened?" he called out. Even without light, nothing appeared awry. Not a rug or step stool was misplaced. Had Mason turned back on second thought? Taken what he could before he left?

"Lilian!" he called out again. He paused in the foyer to listen for a response, but none came.

Then he felt something. A drop on his forehead. It slipped down his neck and through his spine. Another drip. Then another, sending spider legs crawling through every sinew.

He sparked a match.

The light from the faltering flame drew his gaze to the floor, to something he'd only seen out of the corner of his eye, but never questioned. It was a line etched into the wood, beginning at the foot of the staircase. Only now, it glistened, its edges brimming with the same substance that fell from the ceiling.

Atherton followed the line up the stairs. Long before he'd reached the top—no, as soon as he had entered the home—his expression betrayed the panic he felt. Fabricated from a dim hope he didn't believe in. But tonight, of all nights, he nearly tricked himself.

"Tonight will cast both of us into oblivion. You, beyond Sarum's gates, and I into Hell."

He stood at the top of the stairs near Lilian's bedroom. The door had been left ajar, with Morma's wet footprints a trail leading away. Candlelight spilled out, playing at the edges of the doorway. To him, the smell that arrived was mundane. It meant work. It meant quiet conversations with his father in the embalming room, stitching up wounds, fixing the expressions of the deceased.

To him, it was home.

Atherton's curiosity was always piqued when there was something "new" in his line of work. A disembowelment, perhaps, or a body left unattended for longer than usual. These experiences were tokens, standing out in an ocean of ordinary corpses.

He hated what he already knew: behind that door was something he did not want to see. It was the smell that warned him. Blood had always been familiar to him. It was heavy, metallic.

So why is it so overpowering? Why, he wondered, *is it the very air I breathe?*

His lips trembled—not just with sorrow, nor the flaming malice fighting against a cold despair. In fact, he wasn't certain there was a word to describe that feeling. He stood there, frozen, trying to place it, trying to prepare himself.

Through the sliver of the open door, he could make out a tiny hand. Smudged with red, it lay beside a pair of neatly tucked legs, as if the child were sitting cross-legged listening to a story. He pushed open the door, the old wood creaked with every yawning inch.

The dense candlelight made the seven bodies look like statues. Perfected, arranged, manipulated. They were in a circle, sitting neatly.

He made a single step forward before he retreated to a wall and slid down it. He sat with them, taking it in. Bile rose in his throat. He was as still as they were, staring at no specific detail in particular. He wasn't sure he could even if he tried.

Matthew, Simon, James, Cassidy, Ella, Vivie, and Lilian. Matching pendants glinted from their necks.

A candle had been placed in the laps of each of them. Spilt wax had solidified and molded around their little hands. They wore the same wound as Lilian, a wide stroke across each of their throats. Only her wrists were missing the slashes on theirs.

They were missing something she had, too. On all their faces was an unknowing, drugged sleep. On hers was a grin, wider and more jagged than all the cuts across their bodies.

The back of his trousers became warm and sticky from the small rivers seeping through the floorboards. Dimly, his eyes remembered that line which began at the bottom of the stairs. Before, what it led to was tucked beneath the rug. A crack, perhaps—that was what Atherton considered when he first saw it. But now the rug was missing, revealing the symbol beneath it.

Atherton took out the amulet that Lilian had asked him to wear. The geometric pattern was mirrored—a vast etching in the floor. Upon each point piercing the circle sat one of the children. In the center was Lilian, one of her eyes half-lidded, watching, as naked as she was that night she first invited him into that very same bedroom. There was something clutched in her hand beside the dagger that tore them all, and the candle in her lap. A letter. The same one he'd seen on her desk just hours before.

Atherton reached through the circle to grasp it. As soon as his fingers found its edges, he inhaled sharply. The letter had sliced him. He was reminded of the pinprick Lilian had given him that night at the carnival. That same spot on his thumb had opened up, this time from a razor blade glued to the corner of the letter.

A drop fell from his thumb and landed in the circle.

Light—soft and red—breathed up from the symbols beneath him. It spread like fire through the lines of the sigil with a low hum, illuminating the face of the witch and all her sacrifices. By that scintillating, scarlet glow, Atherton broke the waxen seal.

He unfolded the letter. As he read, the blood from his thumb continued to patter into the circle. With each drop, the sigil pulsed brighter.

Did you remember my flowers, darling? You must be wondering how this is possible, how somebody you loved so deeply could be capable of committing something so vile. I never believed in simplicity. Would you believe me if I told you I do, in fact, love you? Would you believe me if I told you I loved my children, though I ripped them from this world? Though you can undoubtedly deduce from their expression, I should tell you they left without pain. If it is of any consolation, I most certainly will not.

Mother's friend. That same tincture which got you

through so many restless nights with those unwanted visitors —I am afraid that is how all this has been done at all. You must understand, what passage awaits me in Gehenna is another journey with its own challenges, and though I required every drop of my beautiful children, I simply cannot afford them following me.

But you can.

You have kept the dead's company all your waking life. You kept Lola's, Betty's, the twins', and Alice's, did you not? You hid it well. It suited you. That boutonnière was as much an expression of my affection as it was a consideration of your aptitude in this ritual's efficacy.

Complexity is the heart of love, not faith. And you, my dear, are my favorite enigma.

Know this, Atherton Graves, that I am no monster. I have trusted you with the burden of these souls, and just as I have placed my faith in you to survive tonight, to find me here, to unshackle me from these spirits with the gift of your blood, I have faith in you to withstand their haunting. Perhaps there will come a day you even appreciate their company.

What greater expression of love is there than a belief in a partner's capabilities to sacrifice? Whether you believe it or not, I have loved you as deeply as anyone could. I will leave you with a final piece of wisdom from the years we never shared.

Though fear may haunt you, however difficult it may be, never let truth do the same, or it will consume you tenfold.

There is mercy in me yet. Lest your curiosity devour

you before you've begun your new life, find the grimoire at my desk. May it douse all your burning questions.

To our new beginnings.

With Love,
Lilian

Witchcraft, Gehennics, rituals—these were cultural fixtures that seldom entered Atherton's mind beyond a stray article in newspapers. There was no sense in questioning their reality now.

"You know," he sniffed, "I never do this. I always found it, well, disturbing when people spoke to their dead as though they were still living. But I, well..." The words clenched in his throat. It was unshakeable—the feeling that she was still listening. He forced the words out, no matter how difficult the tears made it.

"But I understand it now. I never lost somebody I loved before. And I hate you for it. Do you know that? Did you think of that when you were writing this? Damn you, for making me love you. For being the only woman who wasn't repulsed by me, who ever cradled me, who was the only damned *person* to listen to stories I wouldn't dare share with another lest I earn their mockery. Damn you for blighting the only hope for reprieve I ever had. And for leaving me with only more of *this*."

Atherton thrust the letter aside. Flames leapt from the candle in Lilian's lap, consuming the parchment in a single stroke. The six others followed suit. Scalding, bursting wax with infernal tongues. An unnatural gale blew through, then darkness. It left only the glow of the sigil, soaking their bodies in crimson light.

Without thinking, Atherton had thrown his hands up to shield his head from the sudden eruption. But what little adrenaline was left in his veins spluttered. There was no greater suffering he could endure than what Lilian had already inflicted. He relaxed his shoulders and let his hands fall back down to his sides. There was little else to do than fall on his knees. Even the wail pressing against his chest was quashed in the weight of that moment.

That was when he felt it—that thick, vaporous ectoplasm in his throat. He didn't resist the cool, dizzying substance this time. He inhaled until it disappeared, settling somewhere next to that scream he never let out.

Thin voices scratched at the insides of his ears. Then they were about his head, their whispers fluttering like insect wings. Their breath was on his neck, in his sleeves, spontaneous and muted.

An open window whose curtains fluttered in the breeze slammed shut, the mesh fabric settling. Following it with his eyes, Atherton spotted a pair of bare feet drumming behind it. He knew the others were about the room somewhere, watching him. From the corners of his vision, a pair of hands reached from beneath a dresser. Looking up, he discovered one of the girls pacing upside-down, her feet as obliged to the ceiling as his were to the floor. She walked from end to end, humming to herself.

The stream of mangled voices quieted long enough for him to make out, "*Will you stay awhile longer?*"

Atherton stood. Every movement felt heavy yet fluid, as though he were wading through the waters of a dream. Careful not to slip, he crossed the room to Lilian's writing desk, where the ink on her pen had dried beside its inkwell.

Matthew was sitting still on the second tier of the desk, staring blankly at a wall. It was only when he reached for the heavy, leather-bound grimoire that the boy's eyes shifted to follow his hands.

"*Are we playing surgeon again?*" he asked, the yawning cut on his neck moving as he spoke. The boy looked past Atherton to his own, lifeless body in the circle.

"Yes," Atherton replied to the apparition.

The boy traced the outline of the slash on his wrist, watching Atherton all the while. Blood spurted from the wound as though reignited by the realization. It dripped, suspending in the air before touching the wood, but making pattering sounds all the same. Then came the others joining in that sanguine downpour, and the room overflowed with what could only be described as the sound of rainfall.

It hushed just as quickly.

"*We can start with these,*" Matthew said.

Atherton flinched. A wrinkled, wet hand had slid into his.

He looked down to find the upper half of Lola wading on the floorboards, the wood and crimson rippling about her like the surface of the lake.

"*Thanks for carrying me, Atherton,*" she said.

He inhaled sharply, and a single tear slipped down his cheek. He was surprised he had any left. "Anytime, Lola," he managed.

The light in the sigil was fading, now. It seemed to fight for air like a fire, flickering and waning.

Once he made it to the doorway to leave, he felt the shudder of many small feet scampering to catch up to him. Glancing back before leaving, he thought he could make out a shadow, a silhouette of Lilian standing beside the bed wearing a contented grin, and a still, raised hand waving farewell.

Perhaps he would awaken as he did before, with dawn slipping through the windows onto the small of her back. As she stirred from his caressing her shoulders, he would tell her of this extraordinary nightmare. Lying together, they would stifle laughter, imagining the mad plots, the murders, the hideous deception. The children would tease him over breakfast, Lilian chastising them gently all the while.

But it was only wishful thinking, and darkness playing tricks on the eyes.

"Goodbye, Lilian."

He stormed through New Sarum's gates at a gallop. Shouts of "Murderer!" pursued him as he broke through a line of constables who were diving away from the horse threatening to trample them.

Rain thrashed the lone rider, his cloak a single, sable sail whipping in the rabid winds. Though the storm would eventually douse the raging conflagration in the White Horse, those flames still burned elsewhere.

A white wrath in Atherton's eyes.

28

KAYNE
JUNE 8, 1886

Nearly a week had gone by since Boo shot Mason's Bible to Hell. In the afternoons, playful banter and calls of *hep!* drifted from the Flying Maffickers' tent as the flying trapeze artists drilled routines. Over in the Cabaret of Curiosities, flashes and smoke punctuated sleight of hand and conjurations of magic. Performers bickered and laughed about choreography during rehearsals, aerialists took turns digging elbows and fingers into the knots in one another's shoulders and backs, and clowns discussed the comedic timing of a pratfall or revealing a gag in their pocket.

For others, their tireless effort would go unnoticed by guests. Without a sign and tucked away by the coven's caravan, Kayne Todd's tent had no name. The others called it "the Morgue."

Presently, Thomas and several other ghouls were unloading a large shipment from her carriage. Long and rectangular, the crate was heaved unceremoniously despite the corpse inside. Kayne wore a bloodied apron over her gray blouse, laced trousers, and knee-high boots, and she had tied a black leather mask beneath her ponytail.

After Thomas's crew pried off the nails, Kayne took a cursory glance, then gave a firm nod. Though technically a medical doctor, it'd been some years since Kayne worked formally in the profession. Even in a field where anatomists occasionally purchased stolen cadavers, her obsessive study of necromancy had long earned the reproach of her colleagues.

Kayne had no shame in pursuing her research beneath canopied tents at a traveling circus. With the hopes of her legacy and reputation dashed, progress was all she cared for. After Lester offered a space to continue her research in return for her and Ivory's expertise, how could she refuse?

She looked up to see her husband approach. With Ivory's performance schedule, the couple seldom saw each other, so he periodically visited her tent while she worked.

"Who's this one from, then?" he asked, tapping the delivery with a walking cane.

"Met him at a brothel in the East End. Herman something," Thomas grunted, muscling the weight. He transferred the shipment onto a church truck—a kind of trolley used for coffins—and wheeled it into the tent. "Holmes, I think it was."

Ivory gave Kayne a look that could wilt summer daisies and asked, "Mr. Holmes again, is it?"

"Yes, darling. Do you remember what we discussed back in New Sarum?" she retorted with a forced smile. "It was your idea to use ghostlight for the new carousel installation. And with Lester demanding I expedite Florence's operation, well, my hands are tied."

"Of course, my sweet plum duff, but remember what we settled on when doing dealings with murderers? That we would discuss it first?" Ivory flashed his own constrained smile.

Kayne dropped a few shillings into the ghoul's hand, but Thomas only looked uncomfortable to find another one of the couple's fights coming on. "You know, I should get back to other...things." Clearing his throat, he turned on his heels and fled.

Hundreds of bones hung throughout Kayne's tent in sets of forearms, skulls, and ribs. Wired together, they were etched with sigils similar to the one above Ivory's tent. Matching symbols were on the bottoms of lanterns, fire pits, the carousel, and all equipment in need of power throughout the carnival, fueled by nothing less than the spirits Ivory siphoned from the cadavers.

"I'll deal with this another time," Kayne sighed and walked off. Her husband's fascination with her research had always been endearing, until he started letting his apprehensions leak all over the place.

"Concerning the delivery or me?" her husband pursued, bonking his head on a hanging skull as he did.

"Both! I've been doing this for years, dear. Do I stroll into your show and tell you how to perform?"

Nearly a dozen of Kayne's apprentices were working over operating tables in the wide space. Some were dissecting, others harvesting parts for

Thomas and other ghouls the circus housed. One station dealt with "portioning" bones, as Kayne liked to call it.

"Now wait just a moment," Ivory huffed. "That's not fair. I merely fear for your safety, is all. Is that so appalling to you?"

A handful of masked apprentices glanced up from their gory prospects to share knowing glances with one another. Somewhere in the tent came the shudder-inducing *crunch* of a sternum being clipped loose.

Kayne stifled a groan and flipped through one of her research books at her desk, wishing it would somehow inform her how to melt her husband's worries. "Must we do this while I am working?"

"My love, you are always working. If not now, then when?"

"Have it your way, then." Kayne took off her mask and tossed it aside. "Holmes is like an escape artist. He has clean bills of sale to the University of Cambridge, among others. He works under their nose. If he's good enough for them, he's good enough for us."

"What's wrong with the resurrectionists we usually hire whenever we're in London?"

"Resurrectionists aren't often professionals, just scoundrels willing to steal stiffs for a quick dime. Every time we hire them, we risk them selling us out to Scotland Yard. Without the Disciples having our back, there's nobody to buffer us from the law. That includes Thomas and his crew. At least a man like Holmes has a mutual interest in subtlety."

"Granted. But I wouldn't exactly call it safe." Ivory scoffed. "At least the grave snatchers are only thieves. Holmes is dangerous. He's evil!"

"My darling, look where you are standing. We're hardly angels."

"And?"

Kayne pinched the corners of her eyes. "Holmes operates out of the States. His ties here are loose. He's only visiting England on business."

"Oh, don't give me that. He was here last time we were in London!"

"The man knows how to do business; what can I say? Just this morning, he said he intends to open a hotel in Chicago."

Ivory said, "And that's awfully industrious of him, but these cases are burning holes in our pockets. Whatever happened to Thomas doing the work himself? That's what he's paid to do!"

"Doing what, exactly? Risking his hide every time we need a fresh case? Is that what you mean? When we are prepared to take on that sacrifice once more, you'll be the first to know. Robbing graves isn't at all like playing with talking boards. Let's not forget which one of us is making the bigger sacrifice, here.

"Are you abandoning your namesake? Selling off your research so other physicians can take credit for *your* work, just so we can fill our coffers? Last I checked, you are not. But what would I know—I'm not in show business. I'm just a surgeon with a phantom discovery of separate blood types that may revolutionize blood transfusions. And who will get recognition for it? Whose legacy will be etched in history? Whoever is the highest bidder, I suppose!"

Ivory backpedaled, looking wounded. "But sweetheart, you know I never meant—"

"You've said quite enough for one morning, haven't you?"

The tinkling of a fool's cap drifted into the tent. Kayne was relieved by the distraction.

Boo appeared between the flaps with a letter in hand. Approaching the couple, he stopped to wiggle the toes of a man whose arteries were being carefully injected with coloring.

Kayne swatted his hand away. "What did I tell you about touching our cases?"

"Right. Sorry."

"I'll make this right," Ivory murmured. "I misspoke."

"Surely," she said under her breath, then to Boo, "Haven't I told you not to poke around here? Isn't there a trapeze that needs swinging from?"

"I've already trained that today. And as much as I love peeping in on a good dismembering, I'm here for Ivory," he replied, handing him the letter.

Ivory turned it over. "What's this?"

"A courier brought it to the gates."

"Who sent them?" Kayne asked.

"They claimed to be paid for their discretion."

"The seal on the letter is broken, Boo." Ivory flapped the envelope at him. "You read what's inside. Christ, is there no decorum in this place? So, what's this about?"

"A potential client. They wrote specifically for you, for a consultation. They said they saw your advert in the papers."

"Some desperate widow asking to speak to her late husband no doubt," he said with a shake of his head, looking over the writing.

"Not quite," Boo replied.

"It's signed 'Anonymous,' and they claim to be cursed. Hah! I don't have time for this. Anybody worth doing business with could at least give their name. They're asking to meet at a coffeehouse, this very afternoon, to boot. Imagine the entitlement."

"As you so lovingly pointed out, we could use the brass," Kayne said.

She took the letter from his hands and looked it over. "They seem sincere, at least."

"What could some fustilarian be willing to pay, anyhow?"

Kayne pushed the letter into her husband's chest and said, "You said you'd make this right. Consider this your apology," only to bat her eyes with a teasing grin.

"Damn you. The Hoxton, of all places," Ivory groaned, "I can already smell the rancid sweat of those malodorous philosophers and pseudo aristocrats. Well, what do you think?"

Boo folded his arms. "Since when do you care for my opinion?"

"You're right. I was being polite."

"For what it's worth, I think your wife is a rogue surgeon who knows her way around a scalpel. She's not someone I'd want to be on poor terms with," Boo pointed out.

Kayne re-tied her mask and nodded, relieved that fate would whisk away her husband for the afternoon.

"Well, there are certainly more effective ways to make an extra coin or two. This?" Ivory waved the letter around. "This is a joke in poor taste. If all my darling wife wants is a bit of effort on my end, I'll find something more lucrative to do in the meantime. Simple as that."

The clown tilted his head with a mocking frown. "Oh? You have other skills? Like what?"

29

IVORY
JUNE 8, 1886

Ivory grimaced at the Hoxton Coffeehouse's store sign dripping in the dismal rain. Steamy air fogged the windows. He could scarcely see inside. One table by the windows was occupied by a young gentleman, poring over a large book beside a teapot. He was wrapped in a traveling cloak, obscuring his face.

Ivory lit a cigarette and ventured inside. The anxious-looking lad in the corner met his eyes and gave a subtle nod. He recognized the young man's wavy, black hair. His nervous gray eyes rimmed with black bruises.

Ivory held a newspaper in hand, the advertisement stating his fee for a consultation. He would squeeze every farthing out of the boy if he tried to haggle.

"Ivory," Atherton said with a relieved breath, extending a hand. "Thank you for joining me. I hope you'll excuse the nature of my letter. It was the only way to ensure my safety." Despite the overcrowded, humid air in the cafe, he was dressed in a long coat.

"Safety?" Ivory whispered. "Are you mad?" Taking his seat, he glanced around to be sure nobody was watching them.

"I beg your pardon?"

"Mad. Stark, raving mad. You know, of the sort that would have you chained up in Bedlam."

"Believe me, I've considered it."

Ivory placed the front page of his newspaper onto the table, featuring a crude illustration of the person sitting before him. He tapped the headline.

TRAGEDY IN NEW SARUM: UNDERTAKER COMMITS ARSON, MURDERING THREE BEFORE FLEEING. SEVEN DISCOVERED DEAD IN NEARBY ORPHANAGE.

"This is you, is it not? You know, every time I see you, your face is bruised to a pulp. You're either the luckiest bastard I've met or an ill omen." He took a long drag, massaging his eyes. "It is a miracle you weren't marched to the gallows as soon as you stepped foot in the city. God, they might reinstitute the Tyburn Tree after they get their hands on you."

"It was only three," Atherton murmured.

"Three what?"

"I only killed three men."

"Oh. Oh, I see. You've only killed *three* men. Hey, hey, everybody," he hissed, "he only executed three. Well, that's just wonderful news. That really solves our problem."

"You were the one all teary-eyed when you put the gun in my hand. You all but asked me to carry it out. And I did. Well, to the best of my ability."

"Lower your voice." Covering his mouth, Ivory leaned forward. "I gave you the iron with the intention of taking care of Mason, not going on a rampage and making a goddamned parade of it. Christ. You failed, in any case. We have it on good word that Mason has since returned."

"Well, he is wounded. That should buy us some time. Biscuit?" Atherton asked, pushing a plate forward with vanilla and chocolate wafers.

Ivory bit into one despite his consternation, chasing it down with a sip of Atherton's tea. "Wounded—and enraged—that second part is important. Who did you dispose of, anyhow?"

"Henry and Arthur. Another man named Luther."

"Ah, yes, his two most trusted lieutenants who were his honorary blood. That won't make him see red."

A server appeared beside the table. "Something to drink of *your own*, sir?"

"I'm afraid not. I'll be leaving shortly. It's the air in this place. Would it kill the owner to crack a damn window?"

"Bloody Americans," the server grumbled as he strode away.

Ivory took a deep breath and smoothed out his suit. "Forgive me. I'm still trying to grasp this. You were aware that your face is plastered on the front page, and with ten murders to your name, you *still* came here."

"You told me to find you in London. Where else was I to go? I assumed Mason has someone watching the circus at all hours."

"Certainly. But your family's mortuary was a booming success, no? Enough to get you the hell away from England. You ought to be halfway across the channel by now."

"Running from the law isn't exactly a life," Atherton retorted. "I have no home now. And how should I…forget it." The young undertaker looked out the window with a bitter scowl.

This gave Ivory pause. Atherton had always been somber, but something was different, and it wasn't just the lives he'd claimed. "I'll be damned," Ivory said, now understanding, "two decades in this business and still I find myself surprised. The deaths at the orphanage. The witch. They were tied to you after all. It was that woman you brought to the circus that night, eh…" Ivory snapped his fingers, trying to remember her name.

"Lilian."

"Yes."

"Those children in the papers were her sacrifices. It was as you suspected, the makings of some ritual, and its curse cast upon me. Her orphans—they pursue me every waking hour. They are not like the others, Ivory. They lurk in every glance and crowd my thoughts with their own. There are too many. I must be rid of them. I can pay you well. Higher than your usual rate."

"The money is immaterial. My life is in peril just by meeting you here. If Mason found—"

"Don't make me beg. I would have fixed it myself, but not even death can rid me of this."

Ivory winced. "You shouldn't say such things. You're young. You have your whole life ahead of you."

"And wherever I go, death seems to follow."

"Right," Ivory said, helping himself to the last of Atherton's tea and a biscuit, "so we best make friends with it. Grab your book, Hamlet. We're continuing this elsewhere."

"Where are we going?"

"Where all desperate men turn. To barter with the Devil."

Ivory hailed a carriage to bear them past the East End, through the rolling smoke of St. Giles's slums. Their conversation was weighed by what seemed to be Atherton's every secret, and what few glimmers Ivory revealed of his past.

The longer Ivory listened, the more he felt he was speaking to a shadow of his younger self.

"Raven Row!" the coachmen hollered.

※

A choir of low hums welcomed the pair through the center aisle of the Chapel of Odium. Wooden pews rose in an octagonal shape, its cascading tiers forming around an altar beneath an airy, wooden ceiling. At the edges of the nave, doors lead to chambers winking with candles. Gloomy light filtered through crimson-stained windows, illuminating incense writhing toward the gothic buttresses.

Rising in sharp arches, the blackened walls were hewn with charred statues, their impish features hideously contorted. Seven flowing banners in gradients of scarlet enshrined the nave.

Odium was the centerpiece—one of Hell's seven princes.

Masquerade masks circled his head, with stony ribbons drifting about his frame.

Atherton's forehead was beaded with sweat. "The light here—it's red," he noted, lingering at the door.

"That's just the stained glass. Have you ever been to a Gehennic church?" Ivory asked.

The undertaker shook his head. "Is there nowhere else we might discuss this?"

"There is nothing to be afraid of. The damned must walk the path laid before them. Come." Ivory held out his hand.

"What are you implying?"

"You said so yourself. The dead have pursued you all your life. Did you believe this was no great indication? Did you not stop to wonder, perhaps, that what makes a spiritualist is not what he calls upon, but what instead calls upon him?"

Before Atherton could reply, a woman approached them in flowing, black garments. Her habit squeezed her body. Slits in the fabric revealed her thighs and hips, her collarbones protruding naked. A silver coif crowned her pale hair, its slender spikes enshrining her head in a metallic halo.

"Abbess Agatha," Ivory inclined his head, "your halls are graced with a celebrity. This is Atherton Graves. No doubt you've seen him in the papers."

"The Todds are always welcome in the House of the Morning Star,"

Agatha said, pulling him in for an embrace. Then, looking Atherton up and down, "As are those who cannot find solace elsewhere. Whatever fate awaits you, Mr. Graves, you may take refuge here until the authorities discover you."

"The men I killed made an attempt on my life," he replied. "I am innocent of the others."

Ivory nodded when Agatha looked at him for some confirmation.

Agatha's slender face was decorated with black, curving lines of soot beneath her eyes. She studied Atherton. "Then you are a welcome guest. Do not hesitate to seek our aid if Odium's chapel can be of any assistance."

"Actually," Ivory said, "I was hoping to glean your expertise. The other seven lives to Atherton's name were taken by a Gehennic, a witch using this sigil in a kind of ritual. Are you familiar?"

Agatha declined to take it into her own hands for closer inspection, as though whatever was upon it might rub off on her. "This sigil is historically used to direct the spirits of the dead, willingly or otherwise. But you already know this, Mr. Todd."

"Certainly. But I've never used it in this manner. With an abhorrent sacrifice of six children, leastways."

"If this was properly bound to Mr. Graves," Agatha continued, "the witch intended to use him as a scapegoat. A term used for those who bear the haunting of a ritual sacrifice. Murder victims often pursue their killers, in this life and the next. Six, you said?"

"And more before the fact."

Agatha grimaced. "That is no small burden, indeed. I'm truly sorry to hear it, for everyone's sake."

"Can it be undone?" Atherton asked.

"Actions cannot be undone," she replied, "only outdone."

"She also gave me this," he said, showing her the grimoire.

Once more, the abbess kept the object at arm's distance. "I would trust the veracity of the spells inside with my life."

Ivory took the book into his own hands, flipping between the pages. Flashes of heavy parchment scored with inky and burgundy stains. "What makes you so confident in this witch's ability?"

"Whoever created that book likely bound it with human skin, if her cruelty is of any indication. A forbidden practice. Of course, the witch in question is dead, as that is one step in this ritual, meaning your work is cut out for you, Mr. Todd."

"*My* work?" Ivory chuckled uneasily. "I am merely an entertainer. I don't deal with hauntings of this extent."

Atherton ran his hands over the leather with a deep frown.

"You may be surprised what humble efforts can produce in the face of a great calamity," Agatha said. "The duress brought on by this ritual has far more to do with the individual spirits and less with the magic itself. Meaning, Mr. Graves, you are in good hands. Fortunately, what you bear is not a curse. The bond you have inherited is called the Mark of Oblation."

"At least that doesn't sound terribly ominous at all," Atherton quipped.

"You jest, and yet to old-fashioned Gehennics, it is one of the highest honors a witch can bestow, particularly on a willing participant."

"I most certainly was *not* willing."

"Evidently, Mr. Graves, or else I trust you would not be here today. The ritual in question has been forbidden by the Gehennic Magistrate for over two centuries. It was a practice that scarcely survived the first decade of our founding. It is designed to give favor to a witch or magician desiring a high place in Gehenna. By all accounts, your witch has succeeded."

"*My* witch?" Atherton asked, and looked to Ivory for reassurance, who just raised his eyebrows and shook his head.

Agatha brought her hands together, pressing her fingertips to her pursed lips. "Mr. Graves, you must understand something. Blood is a powerful vector, seconded only by bone. The moment yours conjoined with hers, and with that of the lives she sacrificed, the two of you were bound in a way few souls seldom are. There are many ways to enter Gehenna voluntarily, but she chose this door. Considering you undoubtedly witnessed its aftermath, I do not have to tell you that her decision to involve you was not without great consideration. Do you know what the ritual she performed is called?"

"Her grimoire is written in what appears to be a kind of cypher," Atherton replied. "I cannot discern it."

"Another sign of a seasoned practitioner." Abbess Agatha's eyes were full of a thoughtful sorrow. "It is called *Matriarchatus Infernus Noctis ex Sanguis*. In layman's speak, the Matrimony of Blood."

30

ATHERTON
JUNE 8, 1886

London's alleys were plastered with advertisements displaying the outlandish intrigue of the Black Carnival. Discarded fliers whirled about the bustling thoroughfares; their promises were instant conversation pieces. A robust menagerie, daring aerial acrobats, magicians influenced by the Devil, a spiritualist who could commune with spirits.

Speculation around the carnival's unsavory connection to the Disciples was a spreading rumor among regulars. Since the notorious gang prided itself in dominating London's streets, many wondered if the circus was making a statement just by being in town at all.

With all their efforts to brand the city as their own, the circus was anticipating three times its normal revenue.

In Atherton's eyes, London was a different picture.

Lilian's orphans were permanent fixtures. He saw them in shop windows, between the legs of passersby. Their hands clutched skirts, windowsills, and sometimes even his own. No quiet moment was without their voices.

"Well, that was uplifting," Ivory said.

Atherton stared out of the coach window. He had given the driver the address of the inn he was staying at—a dingy room not much larger than their carriage.

"You should be beaming. You're a married man, after all," Ivory continued. "This calls for a celebration. Drinks?"

Atherton said nothing, instead smoldering his self-pity with long drags of tobacco.

"Married to a corpse. How fitting. In any case, I won't burden you with my presence any longer. As you've stated, it would be unwise to do business with a fugitive, and you've already done more than enough."

Ivory cleared his throat. "Perhaps I was too harsh."

The coachman hollered, announcing the arrival at the inn. He opened the door with an expectant, "Your destination, sir."

"We ask for but a minute more of your time, my good man," Ivory said.

"Now that we have arrived, I would prefer that you step out of the coach, *sir*," the driver insisted.

Ivory tucked a sixpence into the man's breast pocket. "Today is a special day. You've been hired to sit while I speak with my dear friend here."

The driver stared with depthless indifference until Ivory passed him another coin. Muttering something about Americans, he slammed the door.

"As I've stated before," Ivory said, "I have no interest in any sum you may be willing to pay for my services. I do, however, intend to help you. But there will be payment. If you'll agree to it, that is."

"Oh, and what's that? Want me to put another bullet in Mason?"

"Come work for me."

"Pardon?"

"Pay me with your work. Call it an apprenticeship, if you like. The truth is," he paused to light a cigarette, "I've grown tired of showmanship. The crowds, the seances. The long nights of entertaining the rubes are wearing on me. My bones aren't exactly what they used to be. I could be focusing on other work. Far more important work. That is, if I had the time to do so."

"You want me to perform on your stage? In your place?" Atherton asked. Doubtful that he could stand up without wobbling in his current state, this request was sounding less enchanting than Ivory hoped.

"In due time, of course."

"The closest I've ever come to charming a crowd is by presenting the clean-shaven body of their loved one. And even those people watched idly while I was strung up. Don't misinterpret me, Ivory. I am grateful, but I'm no performer." Just the thought of being in front of an expectant audience made his feet tingle and his palms grow moist.

"You know what your problem is? You think so little of what makes you different and extraordinary, and envy those whose lives are dull. You call yourself haunted, cursed. But to my eyes, this is a gift."

"A gift I would sooner be rid of."

Ivory clicked open his timepiece. "I will wait here for ten minutes. No more, no less. If you don't return here with your belongings by then, this carriage will roll beyond the outskirts of London without you, and this meeting will remain a curiosity. As for your situation, well, there may be others who might dare to help you, but the Devil knows my line of work is infested by charlatans.

"Should you decide to return, our acquaintance may prove to be a mutually beneficial partnership. And, who knows, that bane you're so desperate to be rid of may very well become a figment of the past." Ivory opened the carriage door. "The decision is yours."

Atherton studied the spiritualist's eyes. Through the smoke of his burning tobacco, for but a moment, they seemed to gleam.

"A minute has already passed, Mr. Graves."

JUNE 9, 1886

Once more, Atherton was standing before the Spirit Asylum with the grass around him rustling despite there being no wind. He watched the light in the lanterns dim as dawn bloomed across the sky, and felt his heart heave with the excitement, the foreboding, that the gray-and-black tents might, one day, be his home.

He was not allowed to consider this for long, as Lester Black herself stood beside him with an expectant expression, and gestured for him to enter.

"Time waits for no one, Mr. Graves," she said.

Atherton nodded. He followed the sound of an Edison phonograph croaking out a tune from the carnival's string quartet, and ducked his head through the tent flaps.

Spears of dawn followed behind him. This appeared to break Ivory, who was sitting at his desk on the stage, out of his trance. Steam curled up from a nearby mug of coffee. "I am not to be disturbed while I work," he said without looking behind him. He was turning over one of the carnival's lanterns in his hands, inspecting the light through several magnifying lenses on his spectacles.

"Are you going to say something, or just stand there like some—oh." Ivory turned, startled to find Lester standing with her eyebrows raised.

Atherton glanced about nervously, feeling rather like a stray cat that only one of them wanted. He arrived at the carnival as many had before him, with a single suitcase and a look on his face that asked what he'd gotten himself into.

"Shall we try this again?" Lester asked. "This young gentleman claims to have a business connection with you. He says you offered him an apprenticeship. Is this true?" Lester placed her hands on Atherton's shoulders, as though presenting him as an object for auction.

Through his goggles, the spiritualist's eyes appeared freakishly large. "Why, yes. I planned to tell you of my offer, but I was under the impression he'd refused, since he didn't return to the carriage."

"Evidently, he's changed his mind. Are you aware of his reputation?" Lester asked.

"Aware of his reputation," he snorted. "What do you take me for? Are *you* aware of his reputation?"

"I won't grace that petty tone with a reply. I trust you will conduct yourself with the utmost discretion while you are within our gates," she said. "We are taking an inordinate risk in keeping you here. It is good fortune for you that we have mutual enemies. Mr. Graves?"

"Of course, Mrs. Black. My apologies," Atherton said, only then realizing she was addressing him. "Consider me in your debt."

"You certainly are. And that's *Ms.* Black. Better still, Lester. You may as well leave your niceties at the gates. Now, if you intend to walk about the grounds, see yourself to the clown alley. You'll find our costume artists there. Can't have your mug in plain view without makeup. As for you, I'd prefer it if your tent wasn't in shambles the day prior to opening. Sort this mess, or I will have you sorted. See me after Atherton here is settled in; you have yet to convince me of his value here."

Lifting up his goggles, Ivory asked, "Such a warm welcome to our new associate here. I'm surprised he's not blushing. Is that all, master?"

"No. You will take the utmost care of our outlaw. We don't want him ending up like the last one."

"The last one?" Atherton echoed.

"It was a pleasure meeting you, Mr. Graves," she said, excusing herself from the tent.

"She was only making a joke, wasn't she?" Atherton asked.

"Oh, of course. That's our Lester!" Ivory said, waving it away unconvincingly.

"Is she always like that?"

"She is seldom fond of newcomers brought in outside her supervision. As far as introductions go, this one was comparatively pleasant."

"Consider me flattered." Atherton placed his suitcase on one of the folding chairs facing the stage, his gaze lingering on it for a long while. Somehow, it seemed this gesture made his arrival feel real.

"Yes, yes, anywhere will do," Ivory said distantly. "We'll arrange a place to house you later. So, what changed your mind?"

"Well, I hadn't much of a choice, did I? How else would I stir from this nightmare?"

"Some nightmares are merely dreams in disguise. Trust that, together, we may yet find some purpose in yours. Come, join me on the stage. I trust you've found little sleep since our last meeting. How is your condition?"

"Unchanged," Atherton said, hopping onto the platform.

"I'll be the judge of that."

The spiritualist began prodding him with a series of instruments. From his pocket, he produced a small, silver contraption—a kind of compass that whirled before pointing at Atherton. Dials in the device purred and clicked, measuring the air.

Ivory peeled back Atherton's eyelids, opened his mouth, and peered into the back of his throat. He reached in, swiping his tonsils with a metallic swab.

This evoked a rather unflattering retch, and Atherton asked, "What in the blazes are you on about?"

Ivory showed him the slimy, gray residue he collected. "Ectoplasm. You're riddled with it."

"Is that a bad thing?" Atherton asked.

"Not in our business. Here, have a look." Ivory rummaged for a hand mirror somewhere in the mess of his desk. "Observe. What do you see?"

"I see myself."

"Look into your eyes. Look deeply."

After staring for some time, Atherton shook his head with a frown. "I see only myself."

"The living perceive with waking eyes. The dead observe through dreams and memories. But we share the same world—the same plane. Now, don't sharpen your senses, Atherton. Dilute them."

"With what?"

"Of all your recollections which stand beyond the pale, which ones do you remember most? What feeling did they evoke?"

"Fear," Atherton admitted. "Terror."

"Wonderful! That's the ticket." Ivory clapped his hands against Atherton's shoulders, holding them firm. "Tell me, why is it that most ghost stories begin in the dark?"

"Even the most innocent forms or silhouettes seem insidious when one hardly knows what they are looking at. The mind plays tricks on itself."

"That is the old saying, isn't it? But you know better, don't you? Society passes off phantoms as conjurations of a vivid imagination. Skeptics propose that paranoia is the culprit behind ghost sightings, but it is only so far from the truth. It is the lure."

In great haste, Ivory sealed up any light coming from the tent flaps before returning to twist a knob on the lantern nearby. He dimmed it until they could scarcely see each other.

"Now close your eyes, and think on the night of the ritual. Of the murder." Taking a folding chair, Ivory pushed him into it. "Focus," he said. "Take me back to those first moments."

"What are you having me do?"

"Why, we are summoning the dead, my friend."

"Is this the only way?"

"The past speaks in riddles, a coiling of truth around fiction. The mind cannot make heads or tails of ghosts and memories. Only through here," he said, tapping Atherton's head, "can you invite them into the room. Now, tell me about that night."

With his eyes closed, only the ticking of Ivory's contraption filled the darkness.

"I am walking," Atherton began, "up a staircase. There is only one source of light. Candles, coming from the bedroom. All the while I can hear the housekeeper murmuring to herself. She's gone mad. That's when I start to smell it. It is unlike anything I've ever felt before."

"And what is that smell?"

"Blood."

"Good. Continue."

"I want to see what's inside, yet I am petrified by the thought. The door is cracked. I see a hand. It belongs to a child. So I reach out to open the door fully."

"What did you feel in that very moment?"

The dials of Ivory's instrument began reaching their limit. They clicked furiously, the only sound besides their voices and the muffled calls of the circus humming about its preparations outside.

"I can feel them," he said.

"You felt them—the children—before you entered the room?"

"No. I can feel them now." Atherton swallowed. "I push open the door and I see them—I see them all—but I can't truly *see*. There is too much to take in. That's when I feel my legs give out beneath me. I sit with them as if I am one of them. For the longest time, all I can do is stare. That moment feels endless, as if I might never move again, and rather remain as they are. Even now, I am there with them, with *her*. And I can feel the blood in the floorboards seeping into my clothes, on my hands. There is a letter—a letter in her hands. I pick it up but there is something wrong, something *done* to it, and that's when…"

Chest heaving, Atherton gripped the chair tighter.

A small grin stretched on Ivory's face as the undertaker began coughing. A wan light seeped between his eyelids, and he doubled over, the substance catching in his throat.

"Now look," Ivory interrupted, holding up the mirror.

Atherton gazed into the smudged mirror. A silver substance swirled in his irises.

"There it is," Ivory said. "It's beautiful, isn't it?"

"It is," Atherton breathed. His eyes possessed a subtle glow.

Then something else called out to his vision. The first, leaking vapors of ectoplasm falling from his lips. The brief wonder in his expression quailed, overcome by panic. He clutched onto Ivory's arm. "I can't breathe," he choked.

"You can," he replied. "Just let it out."

Gagging, he fell from the chair, clutching the stage.

Ivory left, throwing about objects until he found an empty lantern somewhere in the backstage of his tent. He returned with its window opened.

The heavy, gray silt of the ectoplasm was floating about his face. Atherton heaved, his fingernails collecting splinters as he clawed into the stage.

"That's it," Ivory encouraged. "You're nearly there. Now collect it, gently."

He reached up, grasping at his face until the substance wrapped around his shaking fingers. With a final series of coughs, the last of the vapor spilled from his lips. Cradling it in his hands, Atherton gulped in air.

Then he sat, staring at it uncomprehendingly.

It wove between his fingers, gently writhing.

"That's one less worry of yours," Ivory remarked, ruffling the boy's hair. "Quickly now, get it in before it scurries back."

THE BLACK CARNIVAL

Atherton ushered the substance into the lantern. As soon as it was inside, Ivory clamped the window shut and turned a tiny latch to lock it. Another satisfying *snap* exuded from inside, and the ectoplasm bloomed, shedding its dull, gray body for bright silvers and golds that flowed over themselves and filled the stage with wondrous luster.

"And there you have it," Ivory said. "Ghostlight."

Bemused, Atherton looked between the lantern in Ivory's hands to the one on his desk. Both exuded that same, inexplicable light that decorated the circus by the scores. For the first time since he left New Sarum, he laughed. "But that means...all of them?" he asked.

Flashing a toothy smile, Ivory replied, "All of them."

"You collect spirits to illuminate the circus. Like fireflies. God, there must be hundreds of them. The rumors are true, then. The circus is haunted."

"Oh yes. Terribly, I'm afraid." Ivory laughed. "That's hardly the half of it."

31

ATHERTON
JUNE 10, 1886

That night was the first Atherton could remember having slept without the aid of laudanum. After Ivory showed him to a cot in a spare carriage, parked beside the other caravans, he collapsed in it before sunset. The pillows were musty and worn from travel. The blankets—patched and softened with age—smelled of long nights beside campfires. But he wrapped himself in it all, in the strange comfort of being farther away from home than he'd ever been, in the budding hope that his troubles would somehow not follow him there.

Before Ivory left him, he'd insisted on hanging one of the carnival's lanterns above his berth. Atherton thought little of it until he found his body craving the glass bottle of laudanum he'd left in New Sarum. The lantern's glow caressed the pain of withdrawal from his bones, replacing it with a warm hum. For once, his heart beat without fear. Quiet rapture pulsed through him and filled up that nest, making it impossible to fight the heaviness pulling him into deep repose.

His mind had always raced in the silence of the mortuary. Now the circus's discordant melodies drowned all thoughts. The Romani music, so fantastically lamenting and celebrating, the high, eerie warbling of the singers evoking a world beyond dreams, the ringmasters announcing acts in the big top—all lulled him into eventual, exhausted sleep. His vision blurred to darkness, and so did the lantern's light, as though its watch over him had finished.

Atherton stirred to songbird chirrups in the early dawn. A pleasant nip bit at the edges of his patchwork cocoon. A plate of mashed potatoes, boiled carrots, and a small, stout meat pie—now cold—had been placed on the upholstered coach seat beside a corked bottle of water. *Dinner* read a note by the battered, tin plate. Without a second thought, Atherton bolted down the meal and washed it down, only then finding a fork tucked into a neatly folded napkin.

He also found himself utterly stark naked.

Clutching a blanket around his waist, he crept outside.

It was as though the circus had never catered to a single soul. The food stalls were neatly closed. No props, apparatuses, or equipment littered the grounds. There was not a soul to be found wandering the dewy, trampled grass between the innumerable tents. His clothes, washed and still damp from the morning fog, hung from the carriage's awnings. He slipped into them.

The circus was arranged differently than at New Sarum. The misty maze of black, white, and red stripes was somehow more intimidating, now that he was obligated to understand its intricacies. The big top was his north star, its six points fluttering with scarlet flags.

He crept through the wide, triple-ring stage. A trapeze net hung over the center stage, taut and awaiting. Venturing beneath the stands, he found the backstage. Clown alley. Vanity tables and costume racks lined the narrow space. Just as he thought it was as empty as the rest of the circus, he heard the sound of rustling fabric.

"H-hello?" he called.

"G'morning," a croaky voice answered. Then, after Atherton turned every which way, "Up here."

A woman peered at him over the frame of a bed constructed on two old trapezes, suspended from the rigging high in the ceiling. Sleep had made a mess of her brunette curls. She was several years older than Atherton—that was certain—but her smudged makeup made it impossible to discern. A faded, pointed black heart at the center of her lips stretched as she smiled down at him.

"You must be our new ghost courter," she said. "Lester told me to expect you." A charming, rugged Slavic accent tugged on her words.

"She asked that I come here before I roam the grounds publicly."

The clown crawled out from her bed, reaching for the rope hanging from its frame. She eased herself down, her biceps bulging through a white undershirt. "You were right to come. I am Miriana. For some, Minnie. The pleasure is mine, despite the hour. I'll forgive you—this once. Most of us sleep the morning away."

Atherton stifled a surprised gasp. Her frilled skirt trailed as she climbed down, but no legs followed from its gray and white stripes. "Atherton Graves, and likewise. Forgive me; I meant no inconvenience."

"Shocking, I know," she sighed. "You've never had a mortified limb, have you? I don't recommend it. Kayne said it was ergot. Bad batch of rye bread. Can you believe that? She lopped them off herself."

At the bottom of her rope, the clown settled into a contraption beneath her bed. It was constructed of four unicycle frames welded to a padded chair. The two wheels in the front moved independently, steered by wooden handles that Minnie maneuvered as she swiveled to meet his eyes.

She cranked a red handle.

Her seat rose with a few tugs of the lever, its mechanism clunking until she met his eyes evenly.

"The others call me 'spider.' Not the most flattering, but it's grown on me. Crafty, isn't it?" Minnie tapped the device. "Ivory devised it for me. He's an arrogant bastard, but, then again, most geniuses are. He says he's working on a motor for it, soon as he finishes that damned ticket booth."

"I'm terribly sorry; I had no idea."

"Oh, save it. We're all broken somehow. You couldn't beat me in a footrace, anyway. I'm faster on wheels than you are on legs."

Atherton raised an eyebrow. "Is that a challenge? I might just take you up on it."

Minnie's full lips cracked into a smile. Black and red diamonds hung from faded lines beneath her rich amber eyes. Her voice fell to a thoughtful murmur. "It's been ages since we took on a new member. A man with blood on his hands, no less. Have a seat."

Obliging her at the nearest vanity table, Atherton found his countenance in the mirror. He was due for a shave. Indigo and black bruises pockmarked his face.

A slender, feminine figure appeared behind him. A cadaverous hand with bright, blue veins fell on his shoulder, and his heart lurched with a tired thump. He turned away from the reflection.

Minnie pulled on another lever. The mechanism shuddered, her seat sinking down to its base with a jolt.

"That's always fun. You look nervous," she said.

"I've never worn makeup before. A clown's, leastways."

"Have you seen our clowns? They aren't your normal fare. I don't relish turning our cast into a cliché. All our performers wear makeup. Nothing to be nervous for." She reached for a cup of brushes, a tin of black greasepaint, and a small basin with murky water. "Just small accents, Mr. Graves. We don't hide who we are. We beautify it. After I'm finished here, nobody will look twice at you."

Minnie wiped at his face with a cloth dipped in clean water. "It's a funny thing. As soon as you stand out of the crowd, that's the moment folks assume they know everything about you. At precisely the same moment, they fail to see anything."

After applying a layer of foundation, she drew the first line of cool, wet greasepaint beneath his lips.

"And what do you see, Minnie?"

"Whoever you are, Atherton Graves, you kill to protect your own." Pinching his chin between forefinger and thumb, she made him meet her eyes. "The real question is: would you do that for us?"

By the late morning, all the strung lights and fixtures had come alive on their own accord. Atherton scoured the grounds in hopes of finding the clown to whom he owed his life. If Boo seemed like a tall tale as a guest, he was even more so within the circus itself.

Atherton went to the Cascading Perils first.

"It's rubbish, innit?" Marvin folded his arms, letting his cascade of seven knives fall to the ground, each one landing point-first into the grass. Atherton darted to avoid one. "He hasn't put the time in, simple as that. Yet he juggles as if he's been doin' it all 'is life. Five, six, even seven. It's that bloody cap of his. He cut a deal with some magician way back 'for he came here. The Devil knows what he gave in return. His soul, likely."

Behind him, a knife thrower, Ruth, hummed her agreement as she flicked stilettos. Even her partner—strapped into a spinning wheel as blades landed between her arms and legs—nodded in affirmation.

"Well, I have some words for him," Atherton said, wincing as the blades thudded closer to flesh. "Where might I find him?"

"Last I saw him, he was in the den with Tristana," Ruth said, pinning her partner's trousers to the wheel with another throw.

"The den?" he asked.

"You really are green, ain't you?" Marvin laughed.

❦

A lifetime of inhaling the stench of decomposition couldn't prepare him for the air in the menagerie. While perusing the creatures inside Blasphemous Beasts, Atherton found Tristana, a beast handler.

Muddied riding boots hugged her thighs, scarred like the rest of her body. She rivaled Thomas's height.

"Make no bones about it," she said, slopping gloop into a feeding trough for Bartholomew—a boar so wide and tall it warranted a cage half the size of most tents. "Boo's a demoniac. Not that anybody believes me, anyhow."

"A what?" Atherton asked, pinching his nose against whatever breakfast was being served to the beast.

"Look. Any witch worth her salt has handled a few demons, kid, and that man shares a body with one. It's in the hat, and he never takes the damn thing off. Aye! Bethie!" she called to the giant sleeping in her cage. "I'd clear out of 'ere if I was you." Tristana strapped on a leather mask. "Her morning breath is something fierce."

"Ruth said I'd find him here," Atherton said, holding back a gag as the beast yawned awake.

"Never trust blade twirlers," she said, "I'd check your pockets, if I were you. The jugglers like to play dipper when the crowds are out. Nimble fingers. Worse than the freaks, even. That's where I saw him last, mind you."

At the carnival's freak show, The Blessed, Atherton found Zada, a one-eyed tarot reader. She manned a stall with a sign stating, *The Divining Cyclops!*

"Boo's a specter, aye. The specter of t'all," she said.

"Of what?" Atherton asked.

"This place," she said, shuffling a tarot deck. She flourished the cards as she spoke, twirling them about with hypnotic precision, making them disappear and manifest with a flick of her fingers. "He's everywhere, see? There one moment, gone the next. An' he always knowin' what's the going-ons. If you wipe your backside in the grounds, sure as sin, he knows 'bout it."

"What makes Boo so special? He's just a performer, after all," Atherton said.

"You shouldn't speak of things you ain't knowin' nuffin' of," Zada snapped. "They say he was born in Gehenna 'n Lester plucked 'im right out. You two ain't so different 'nyhow."

"What do you mean?" Atherton asked.

"You 'aven't heard, eh?" The woman's face lit up, her single eye fluttering while a devilish grin stretched across her face, revealing more missing teeth than not. "Boo was brought to Bedlam like an orphan, see. But he weren't always that way, eh? The bobbies, they found 'im in 'is own home, alone, after neighbors made a complaint about a wretched smell. Well, he weren't alone, strictly speaking." The cyclops brought a card up and drew it along her throat. "They say he cut 'em a smile each. His parents. Poor things. 'N all he had was that bloody hat on 'im when the peelers showed. Shiverin' in their blood. Scared stiff he was. Just a lad. And 'is poor sister, her parents 'ad gone mad with grief. They'd drug her out of t'grave after she'd died, kept 'er in the house like a mantelpiece. That's what'd gone 'n took away Boo's words. Aye. He don't speak much, 'less he likes you. But mind you, I wouldn't take it lightly. It ain't the simplest thing, eh, talkin' to seers."

"Boo does readings, too?" Atherton asked.

Zada shook her head. "You're missin' the point. The Devil put 'is eye in that poor boy, for what he put 'im through. That's what I think. That's why he wears the cap, eh? It tells 'im things what haven't happened yet."

In a single stroke, the fortune teller unfurled six cards onto the table. "Now, how's about a reading, eh?" Turning one over, she revealed the Hanged Man.

"Maybe another time," he stammered. "I heard from the den that I'd find Boo here."

"Tristana told you that, eh? That old didikko thinks she's a laugh. Boo's a freak in 'is own right, but he don't hang around 'ere much. He takes to the magicians an awful lot, though. Likes to watch 'em before his shows. You might ask Vira over at Curiosities. And tell 'er she owes me a half crown."

"For what?" Atherton asked.

"She'll tell ya." Zeda winked.

Atherton parted the violet banners into the Cabaret of Curiosities. Geometric sigils were stitched in boggling sequences along each one. The air was rife with incense and vanishing powder—combustible substances set alight to distract the eyes.

"Boo? If you've a mind to thank him, I'd spare your breath," Vira said from her stage. A plume of black smoke erupted from her feet. The next moment, she was standing in front of Atherton, curls of vapor trailing from her black-and-red striped capelet.

Her large, brown eyes bored into his. "Don't look so spooked, lad—it's only mirrors. That's what the audience says, at least."

"Why am I wasting my time?" Atherton asked.

The magician folded her arms. Her dark skin had a silver edge from the ghostlight inside. With an inquisitive look, she edged closer to him, too close for Atherton's comfort. "He don't talk much, least of all to new folks. They say—"

"I've heard the stories," Atherton interrupted. "I just need to know where I can find him."

"Oh, look who knows so much already." Vira sat down and crossed her legs, though there was no chair beneath her. She produced a nail file and went to work on her thumb.

Atherton ventured a hand into the space beneath Vira's backside, feeling nothing.

"I hear Ivory's got you in shackles to his talking boards," she said. "If you ever want to learn real magic," she said, brandishing a gun, "you can always work for me. Fine piece of iron, this."

Atherton's eyes widened. He patted down his chest, finding his holster empty. Just as he reached for it, it had vanished from her hands.

"Looking for that?" Vira asked, pointing toward him.

Reaching into his holster, he found the revolver returned. "What in God's name?"

"The Devil's name," she corrected. "God doesn't snoop around here much. Oh, and don't forget these," she said, dumping the six rounds from the chamber into his hands.

"Before I go, Zada told me to tell you that you owe her a half crown."

"So I do," Vira smirked, tossing him a coin. "Be a good lad and run it for me."

"If you don't mind me asking, what did you bet on?"

"You coming back. In any case, you might try the morgue. Last I saw him, he was helping Thomas and his crew with a shipment."

"You—we have a morgue?"

"You're an undertaker, aren't you? You'll be right at home."

And he was, though he hadn't missed the smell, which was precisely how he found the place. Bordered by the caravans he'd slept beside, the unlabeled tent was barricaded by empty crates and large, wooden parcels, as well as gurneys and other equipment he knew too well.

"Hey, pip! You're not allowed in there!" Thomas called too late, as Atherton had already let himself in.

Kayne looked up from the spread of textbooks and illustrations on her desk.

Taking in the sight of a dozen cadavers being worked over by her apprentices, Atherton stiffened, emitting a rather surprised, "Oh." As he padded forward to greet her, a hanging skull knocked against his.

"Just what do you think you're up to?" Thomas asked, clamping down on his shoulder.

"Well, I—"

"Mr. Graves is a most welcome guest," Kayne insisted, pushing his hand off.

"The boy's only just arrived," Thomas protested.

"Don't you have work to attend to?"

"My work is guarding this place!"

"Then take a break!"

As Thomas skulked off muttering about death workers, Atherton braved the manic excitement alight in Kayne's eyes.

"How are you settling in? It's all a bit overwhelming, isn't it? Have you considered joining my anatomists? Spiritualism isn't an exact science, you know. But here, we demystify the innermost workings of human physiology itself."

"Yes, h-how exciting."

"Come, come. You are just in time to witness an unprecedented experiment. Observe the machinations of death defied before your very eyes. Here you are—these will help. Ladies!" Kayne snapped her fingers and handed Atherton a pair of welding goggles.

His eyes were drawn to a wooden table at the far end of the tent. The cadaver resting on it was a young man. A bracelet of stitches on both wrists marked hand transplants, the mottled, gray hue of the fingers mismatching the evenly gray complexion of his body.

Two apprentices moved to either side of the table. There were over a dozen straps by his arms, legs, and chest. One belted the gentleman in, while the other apprentice began cranking a lever that hoisted the table up until the whole construct was upright.

"Are you afraid of him escaping?" Atherton asked with a chuckle, putting on the goggles.

Kayne put on her own set. "We have learned from experience, I'm afraid."

Though he laughed, her confused expression suggested she wasn't joking.

Two great, bulbous electric conductors with copper arcs running along their steel frames were behind the operating table, hooked up to a galvanic reactor twice as large. With great care, the apprentices went about placing rods inside incisions throughout his body.

"We are doing what Galvani himself only dreamt of," Kayne explained. "An intertwining of Gehennic theory and galvanic practice. Observe."

Upon closer inspection, Atherton saw occult symbols etched into the table. They aligned with his hands, feet, and torso. Rather like a crown, the most complex sigil enshrined his head.

Connected to the arc reactor were two vials of foggy, glimmering substance.

"What's inside those?" Atherton asked.

"Why, that will be your speciality, my dear. Ghostlight."

Taking a vial of blood from a nearby stand of equipment, an apprentice uncorked it and poured. The fluid flowed until every gouge in the wood brimmed with it.

Then Kayne shouted, "Ready!"

Her apprentice placed her hand on a lever connected to the reactor and nodded.

"Lux!" Kayne commanded.

Throwing the lever down, the machine crackled, buzzed, and erupted with arcs of electricity. It ran down its conductors, filling the room with scalding light. The hairs on Atherton's arms sprang up, and his teeth jittered, or perhaps the ground shook. Ghostlight lashed from the machine like wild tentacles before finding the man's face, pouring into every orifice. Through the unrelenting blasts, he caught sight of the tame, scarlet glow coming to life from the symbols beneath the man's corpse.

The body began to lift against its restraints. Then came the convulsions, the man's hands gripping the table as a groan escaped his lips, the sound like a death rattle being electrified to a crisp.

"My God!" Atherton exclaimed.

"No, my dear, He has nothing to do with this!" Kayne shouted over the zapping, then, "That's enough, ladies!"

The reactors' loud hums dwindled after it was switched off.

The body slumped back into its frame, groaning and writhing beneath the straps.

"What have you done to him?" Atherton asked.

"What Galvani failed to do," she said, whipping her goggles off. "Reanimation. And, judging by his movements, a successful hand transplant."

"Is he conscious? Can he feel pain?"

"Well, we're not monsters, of course. We pump them with opium before every procedure."

"Them? How many times have you done this?"

"Eighty-four, counting today," Kayne said.

"You mean to say that they live, truly?"

"Not for long." Kayne sighed. "Our most successful subject lasted several minutes. And it appears this one won't come close. A crying shame. But we learn something with every attempt. It may simply be a matter of proportions. Ghostlight, electricity, sigils. Perhaps the blood levels were too high, too low, or the reactor too hot, or even the body too old. The freshest subjects seem to fare best."

Even as she said that, the cadaver's movements began to falter. Like a puppet whose strings were snipped, his body and limbs slumped one after the other. Finally, the ectoplasm oozed out of his mouth—limp, watery, and bubbling at his lips.

"Even still, nothing goes to waste," she continued. "His bones will be harvested to keep the lanterns burning, the carousels spinning. Every spirit needs a body to call home. They don't seem to care whose bones they belong to, or where. Some of our wagons' engines have even been modified to run on it. Unlike petroleum, the soul takes a while to burn out."

"You've commodified death itself."

"A most ample resource, often wasted on tradition," she said.

Kayne removed her mask, revealing a striking beauty tempered by the callousness of her craft. She regarded Atherton with knowing eyes and placed a hand on his arm. "It was prudent for you to see this sooner rather than later. Some of the others can hardly stomach it, but I knew you would be appreciative."

Atherton hadn't decided what he thought, partly because the likely conclusion was that he was back in New Sarum, unconscious and in some kind of eternal, deathly dream from the rope choking him. Yet the notion struck him as oddly reassuring. Were he to ever suffer some untimely fate, perhaps Kayne's research would have developed enough by then to bring him back.

Like crows, the apprentices descended on the corpse, jotting down notes on clipboards.

"You know the cardinal rule, don't you?" Kayne asked.

"Enlighten me."

"What you see here, stays here."

32

BOO

JUNE 11, 1886

Blades of dawn sliced through mist in the wide entryway of the Flying Maffickers tent. Climbing a pair of crimson aerial silks, Boo wrapped the tensile fabric about his body, creating a wrap to sit in. It laced through his thighs, around his hips, and behind the pit of his knee. He let his body sink into the tension, sighing as the stripes above him spun.

Boo enjoyed training without the other aerialists lately. Though they did their best to hide it, he knew their resentment had been brewing ever since Florence was kidnapped.

A shadow was cast as somebody stepped inside the tent. Peeking over the silks, Boo spotted a familiar face. A grin spread on his lips.

Thin, black triangles were drawn beneath Atherton's eyes, with scarlet curls accenting the corners. Parallel lines fell from his bottom lip to his chin. He was dressed in a simple collared shirt, with a black necktie tucked into his waistcoat. A thin, silver chain linked a button to one of his pockets. The undertaker climbed onto the stage, running his hand along a trapeze.

Boo jostled his apparatus, causing the rigging to tinkle.

A smirk tugged at the corner of Atherton's mouth, and he craned his neck to see Boo swaying six or so yards above the ground.

The clown danced his fingers in a wave.

"I've looked everywhere for you," Atherton said. "I went into every tent, asked every performer. I must've stood here a dozen times, expecting to find you precisely where you are now. I even attended the shows here last night, yet you were in none."

Boo unwound the wrap about his hips and inverted himself, wrapping them in a different knot. With the tail of the fabric in his hands, he extended his legs in a straddle formation and let his weight drop, his body and legs spinning as he plummeted, creating a windmill effect. Just before his body met the stage, he halted his fall by hooking a leg onto the silk, the rigging protesting with a quiver and a clang as it absorbed the shock.

"Impressive," Atherton remarked.

Boo hopped to his feet and removed his fool's cap. "You'll have to forgive me for my absence. I was in the city, taking time for myself. But I trust it was all too familiar to you, chasing ghosts."

"Just so."

"It suits you—the greasepaint."

"A small price to pay for anonymity. Would you like one?" Atherton extended a cigarette from a silver case.

Boo nodded, running it beneath his nose. The smoky, Virginian aroma was unmistakable. *So Thomas shared his stash with him. He's getting on well with the others.*

They sat at the edge of the stage, tobacco plumes curling in thick tendrils as they faced the empty rows of seats.

"Thomas told me everything that happened back in New Sarum, the night you arrived," Boo said. "Of course, I wanted to hear it from you. I stopped by the caravan. Thought we could share supper. But you were out like a ton of bricks."

Another grin spread on Atherton's face. "So it was you. You were the one who left the plate and the note. Ivory took credit for it, you know."

Boo laughed, a low chitter like a hyena. "Of course he did."

They fell into a lengthy silence, thick with the comfort of companions who'd known each other for years.

"Believe it or not, it was Thomas who started all this," Boo said. "An accident. Smalltalk between him and Arthur during one of their routine visits. It got back to Mason that you'd sold the stiff to Ivory, and, well, here we are."

The undertaker nodded slowly, taking it in with a long drag. "The others don't know, do they? And you don't intend to tell them."

Boo scoffed, scrunching up his face. "Why would I? Every tragedy needs a scapegoat. Thomas is a good man. What am I? A permanent shadow of this place. I'll be performing in it long after my colleagues have left for simpler lives. My soul belongs here. We can't fix the past, only try and halt its repeating."

The undertaker's fingers threaded around the chain from his waistcoat pocket. "I never did thank you properly for saving my life."

"I might say anybody would've done the same, but..." Boo tilted his head with a click of his tongue. "Fear can turn good people into bastards precisely when their virtue is needed. I respect them all, everyone who lives here. S'pose the only difference is I feared the kind of man that would make me, letting Henry and Arthur do you in like that. Sometimes you do the wrong thing for the right reasons. But you already know about that. I read the papers."

Boo met Atherton's gray eyes. He could almost see the silhouettes of the men burning in them. The blood splattered on his clothes. Then he noticed the undertaker's outstretched hand, clenching something.

"This is for you."

Boo opened his hand. An amulet fell into his palm. A metallic frame in the shape of a motley diamond housed tiny panes of glass. It pulsed gently with the same, silvery glow of the carnival's ghostlight lanterns.

"Ivory helped me make it. He said it won't burn for long. Said the spirit was too young to last, but—"

"It's brilliant." Boo clipped the chain around his neck, admiring it with a broad grin. "You must be making fast progress with him. You know why we use ghostlight, don't you?"

Atherton shrugged. "Ivory said it saves coin on oil. Lights up the carnival from afar, draws in the guests."

"That's only half the story. The light has a curious effect on the living. It soothes them. Helps the mind wander, as though in a dream, so they yearn to return. Seldom does a guest only visit us once."

The undertaker stared at the pendant, as though he understood perfectly yet still couldn't bring himself to believe. "It's ironic, isn't it? All my life, disquieted spirits have disturbed my sleep, my waking hours—"

"—and now you summon them to draw in the very same people that would be petrified to know you've done it," Boo finished for him. "Fancy that. Who's inside this one?"

"A little girl named Lola. This incredible ball of joy, she was always..." The words broke in his throat. "Well, maybe another time, eh? You know, I can't pretend a small token could begin to repay what you did for me that night. Perhaps this is the beginning of my attempts."

Boo tucked the pendant beneath his shirt. "You don't owe me anything. Everybody deserves to find their place in the world. Where they fit in. Where they can trust their efforts mean something. Some people know where it is, but struggle to get there. Some people become lost along the way, convinced their dreams are somehow beyond them. Never underestimate the bitterness of somebody who loathes what the world has turned them into.

"If you wish to repay me, you'll find your place. Maybe it's doing what you've always done. Maybe it's here with us. Whatever it is, hold yourself to it. Damn what anybody else expects. Promise me that, won't you?"

Boo took a shuddering breath, fiddling his thumbs. He never spoke at such length with anyone. The words soured in his mouth. Then he saw the look on Atherton's face. The maze of recollections he traversed, and that sourness began to sweeten.

"The last time I made a promise, I killed three men, just to honor my failure to keep it," Atherton told him. "My sister looked me in the eye like I could dictate the world. I promised Mason wouldn't lay a finger on her. And I let him."

"One day, she'll appreciate what you did."

"Even still, the last time a promise was made to *me*, it was kept with a reckoning so foul it may have opened a door to Gehenna at my feet. That woman said she wouldn't hurt the children. She swore to me. But I was blind. Of course, she'd already given them..." Atherton shook his head and pinched off the last ashes of his cigarette. "I only realized after. You don't have the faintest idea what I'm talking about, do you?"

"Perhaps in time you'll find it in yourself to tell me." Boo almost placed a hand on Atherton's shoulder, only to lower it awkwardly back to the stage. "I have my own promise to keep. Mason."

"How do you intend to do it?"

"Well, you're the expert, aren't you?"

"Do you have a bit of rope and a few hundred bottles of liquor, because that's my recipe."

"Is that what it takes?"

The two tittered.

"Earnestly," Atherton said, "is there nobody who'd help you?"

"Lester's made us all swear to keep the peace," Boo said.

Striking another cigarette, Atherton said, "You know, I have made no such oaths. Curious, that."

Boo grinned back at him. "Curious, indeed."

33

ATHERTON
JUNE 13, 1886

The seats in the Spirit Asylum were empty as Ivory drilled his new apprentice. In the evenings, Atherton watched from behind the stage curtains as Ivory performed his routines like a finely wound clock. In the mornings and afternoons, he worked. Work that made his bones ache in a way the mortuary never had.

Six candles hovered unsteadily over a talking board. Sweat dripped from Atherton's forehead onto the table, the drop of liquid reflecting the wavering flames. He clenched his eyes shut, his palms flat on either side of the board. Whispers flooded his thoughts like the dresses of innumerable dancers whipping past him. His mind was elsewhere, straining between the veil separating the living and the dead.

Fingers drumming on his chin, Ivory paced around the table. "The candles are sinking," he sang.

Wax dripped onto the faded lettering on the board. A planchette moved over numbers and characters at random.

"You've recovered the candles. Good. Spell your name," Ivory ordered.

A groan crawled out of Atherton's throat as the planchette jittered toward the letter *A*. The vein on his forehead bulged.

The planchette flung from the table, hitting a bannerline above the stage.

"Steady. You're losing control. Now, counterclockwise with the candles," Ivory said.

Atherton huffed. Chasing children hopped up on sugar and black tea with lead weights on his heels would have been easier. A knob of pain drummed between his furrowed brows. Gasps hissed between his teeth.

Ivory regarded his timepiece. "Stay with it. It's only been twenty seconds."

"I'm...trying."

One of the candles tipped, spilling wax onto Atherton's hand. The pain spasmed across his skin. He flinched, retracting the arm. A terrible screech like a train's thrown brakes reeled through his mind.

In a spray of liquid fat, the candles dropped all at once, splattering him for the fifth time that afternoon. Encrusted with the wax, Atherton opened his eyes, finding Ivory's displeased expression. Their clothes fluttered—a gust from the phantasmic departure.

Ivory sighed. He snapped his pocket watch shut. "Hardly thirty seconds. Great. You've lost them again. You've lost the wraiths! Look, there they go! Farewell!" He gestured to nowhere in particular. "Not good enough. Not good enough at all. Once more."

Atherton erupted from his chair, flinging it behind him. "Oh, bollocks! Not good enough? I'm making candles *fly* for the Devil's sake!" He spat out a wad of filmy ectoplasm.

Uprighting the candles for another session, Ivory gave him a withering look. "The candles are merely the atmosphere in this act. You can scarcely keep them hovering without soiling your trousers. How will you address the guests while performing a seance, let alone keeping your damned eyes open?"

Atherton regarded his now splattered waistcoat with a disgusted grimace.

"I advised you to wear something you wouldn't mind dirtying," Ivory pointed out. "Yet another piece of advice you've disregarded."

Stammering, Atherton ran his hands through his wild hair. "It wasn't a week ago that I would have told you you'd be raving mad to believe in such things! Now I'm levitating objects like some wizard in a fairytale. Would it kill you to lend a little affirmation?"

"For the last time, *you* are not levitating the objects. You are manipulating the spirits at play here. Did you want me to do a happy dance for you? Natural talent can only carry you so far without discipline."

"Oh, shut up. I've made progress, haven't I?"

"Yes, you've progressed—backwards. If you want to play smoke and mirrors with the magicians over at the cabaret, be my guest!"

"Don't be petty. I need a break." Atherton plucked a cigarette out from his case and tucked it between his lips.

Ivory yanked it and thrust it across the stage.

"Oi!"

"You can smoke when you've earned it. Keep the candles aloft for a single godforsaken minute, and then—*only then*—can you have your smoke."

"How will I do that if I cannot relax?" Atherton seethed.

Ivory took a long, deep breath with closed eyes. He splayed his hands out, pardoning the entire drama. His voice came out evenly. "Let's run this back, shall we? To attract spirits into this space, you must seek out a place in your mind—preferably a memory. The more grief and despair in it, the better. But you aren't using Lilian's bedchamber for your summoning locus anymore, are you?"

"I told you I will not return there any longer. Asking me to meditate on the most depraved experience I've ever had the misfortune of enduring is out of the question."

"Well," Ivory scoffed. "You are miles away from where you were yesterday. You must reconsider."

"I will not. It's too painful."

"Painful. But that is precisely the point, Atherton. The spirits are like moths to grief. Do you not realize what you have? Lilian gave you a golden ticket to the most powerful locus any spiritualist could ever dream of. Hell, I'm jealous of you!"

"Damn your locus. Lilian gave me a gutful of death!"

Ivory flinched, his ears ringing. The shout all but rattled the talking board. "I apologize. Fine. That memory is still raw."

"Damn right it is."

"So then, where has your locus been these last sessions? Where do you go in your mind?"

"The pub, sometimes." Atherton uncorked a bottle of water and guzzled it. "Christ, I'm burning up."

"That'd be the ectoplasm. Your body treats it like an illness." The spiritualist shook his head. "No. The pub is too chaotic. You were enraged in that moment, not grief-stricken."

"I use the mortuary as well."

"Have you listened to a single word I said? That is where you worked. A place of monotony and tedium. Ugh, no. That will not do."

"You don't know what it's like. Day in, day out, carrying everything from putrefied bones to bodies just hours old. The mortuary is the breeding ground of grief. But what do I know? I only—oh." Atherton cleared his throat and smoothed out his wax-stained waistcoat. "Good afternoon, Lester. Forgive me; I didn't see you standing there."

"Yes, forgive him. He was just in the middle of lecturing me, the instructor." Ivory let his hands slap against his sides in exasperation.

Lester gathered up the ends of her skirt, settling into a front row seat with an unusually buoyant grin. "Good afternoon, in any case, gentlemen. Goodness, this tent always feels so crowded." Lester massaged her arms, rubbing out the goose pimples. "Don't mind me. I've only come to observe your new apprentice at work. How is the training coming along?"

The two looked at each other. Ivory clapped his hands together, stammering a string of unfinished syllables that never made it to a coherent word.

"Splendid," Atherton blurted.

"Dismal," Ivory confirmed simultaneously.

Lester's eyebrows nearly made it to the back of her head. She took off her wide-brimmed black hat with a snicker. "That good, then? Well, I trust at least something has come of it. A little demonstration, perhaps?" She spread out her hands. "If you're willing, that is. Pretend as though I'm not here, if that helps."

Of course, Lester wasn't asking.

Atherton checked to see if the nervous sweat rolling down his back had matching stains in his armpits as well. Of course he did. Since he'd arrived, Lester was in a foul mood more often than not. Her veil of cordiality was perilously thin.

Swallowing, Atherton realized what was required to gain her approval. He collected the chair from the ground, sitting in it once more. With a struck match, he lit each candle on the talking board.

Ivory placed the planchette in the center and, stooping to pick up the music box on the stage, wound it until the music started and its wooden figurine swayed. Its sorrowful melody tinkled out into the tent.

Atherton took several long breaths, preparing himself for the dive.

Then, he plunged beneath the surface.

The tent melted away above him, becoming less tangible as he sank deeper.

He was ascending the stairs in the orphanage again. Instead of air, there was blood—an entire sky and sea of it. The light from Lilian's bedchamber emanated through the cracked door. It opened of its own accord, beckoning him in.

The silhouettes of her and the children were thinner than wax paper. He hummed their lullaby in his head, striding with the lightness of a diver on the ocean floor, stopping at the center of the sigil etched into the wood. He cast their silhouettes aside with a sweep of his arm, placeholders swept off to leave vacant spaces.

Like sharks to chum, spectres flooded in from the open windows and hallway. They were unfamiliar faces of the damned, though some he faintly recognized. They took up the six candles that would have been resting in the laps of the children.

Atherton reached out, tapping each of them on the hand.

He heard Ivory's avid encouragement somewhere far beyond the depths.

Like a conductor, Atherton signaled with his hands. The ghosts twirled around him, candles in hand, eyes locked on his, lapping up every ounce of his attention. They were what Ivory called the quiet dead—obedient husks of the departed searching for affirmation of their fading mark among the living.

The candles rose in perfect unison above the board. They revolved with mounting speed, cascading up and down, coming together within a hair's width before spreading out again. It was a ballet, a glittering dance.

Letters from the talking board rose up before Atherton, jumbled and out of order. He reached out for the planchette. It felt as though sandbags were tied to his limbs, growing heavier by the minute. Another phantom's hand—blackened and shriveled—slid over his. Together, they reached out with the planchette, finding the sequence.

In the tent, dark smoke curled up from the characters as the planchette hovered over them. All the while, Atherton's hands on the table were perfectly still.

WELCOME LESTER

Ivory's excited guffaw rippled in a distant muffle.

A subtle smirk played on Atherton's lips.

Then another silhouette joined the circle. Unlike the others, her features were distinct. She traipsed through, ignoring the spectral crowd. Before Atherton could sense her fully, he felt her hands cradling his face, neither cold nor wet but burning pleasantly. A distended gash on her neck mirrored her broad smile. Her black eyes, as shimmering as the last night he saw them, found him with that unwavering adoration, that malignant glint she'd hidden for so long.

"*I knew you would return, my love.*"

It was ink, not blood, which poured from her hideous wound. A steady, shimmering torrent, heaving with the mournful longing in the final letter she had written to him, and all those words that had been left unsaid—if only because time disallowed it. It spilled onto his lap—a freezing rain of unrepentant affection. She leaned closer, lifting his chin with a single finger, and pressed her stained lips against his.

Atherton awakened from the trance with a startled gasp.

The candles fell from the air.

The summoning collapsed with a *crack*—a clap of powdery air above the board. Atherton was propelled backwards, the back legs of the chair grinding into the stage as it skidded across, still holding his weight.

He stumbled off, catching himself on the wet pasta that had become of his legs.

"Yes!" Ivory hissed, clapping his hand against his prosthetic. "Stupendous! That is what I wanted to see! Yes!" Then, he cleared his throat and righted his spectacles. "Well, that's what we'd been working on, anyways. Our worst run, really."

Atherton couldn't tell what gave the spiritualist more pleasure, his success or the stupefied look of Lester gobbling humble pie.

Lester approached the stage, tapping her umbrella on the ground with a bemused expression. "I'll come out and say it," she said, pointing the umbrella at Atherton. "I didn't expect much to come of you accepting our good graces. You wandered in like a limping stray—too wounded and sad-looking to turn away. Ivory was insubordinate, inviting you without my permission. I anticipated giving you the boot as soon as we left London. It is rare that I am proven wrong on such matters. Nevertheless, young man, I have never been more thrilled to be categorically mistaken. You belong here. I promise you this: your talents will not go squandered, peddled like some freak-fare as they would in other sideshows. Of course, that leaves us with only one question. Will you work with us?"

Taking off her white glove, Lester extended her hand.

Ivory loosed a piercing holler, jabbing his fist into the air.

"Settle down, old boy," Lester snipped.

Her eyes were sparkling in the dim light—pearls Atherton had managed to pry out of a fanged oyster. Profound enough to stifle the terror Lilian had instilled in him just moments ago. A sizzling courage swelled in its place.

"Yes. W-why, yes, of course," Atherton said, thrusting his hand into hers.

"Ahah! Good man!" Ivory exclaimed.

"Welcome to the Black Carnival, Atherton Graves. Our new ghost courter. Bravo!" The proprietor's grip was unyielding. She shook his hand triumphantly, as though closing the sale of a lifetime. "Now, let's talk business. For the time being, your pay is food and board. Whatever coin you make outside these gates is yours to keep. After London, a pound for every two weeks. Ten shows per week. We can progress from there. How's that sound?"

"Actually," Ivory jutted in, "my client and I will consider those terms and get back to you with a fresh quote."

"No, you won't," Lester said with a murderous laugh.

"Your offer sounds brilliant as it stands," Atherton confirmed.

"I thought it would," she said. Clasping her hands together, she giggled excitedly. "Oh, my two ghost courters. How handsome. You'll pack the house! See me after today's training, Atherton." Tipping her hat, she sauntered out of the tent.

As soon as the tent flaps closed behind her, Atherton's legs gave out beneath him.

"Steady there," Ivory said, gathering him up and placing him in the chair. "Easy now, easy, whoa." Before he could say anything, Ivory popped a cigarette into Atherton's mouth, followed with a prompt light and a wolfish grin. "Now, about that break."

34

LESTER
JUNE 13, 1886

The circus proprietor tossed up a piece of popcorn from a red-and-white striped paper bag, catching it on her tongue. The salted caramel coating the crisp edge had been reduced with whisky. The peaty smokiness bloomed as it melted in her mouth, coercing a groan as she closed her eyes to savor it.

"I always tell myself I'll indulge in only one of these bags a week. I lie every time," she confided in Atherton.

"Our bulwark against sin can only withstand so much."

"Would you like one?"

"After the breaded lobster, candied orange rinds, and peppered frog legs, I think a single kernel would risk popping a button on my vest. I must confess my palette isn't accustomed to such richness. My mother was more the potatoes and cabbage type."

"Oh, you're no fun. A bottom-feeder like lobster hardly constitutes a rarefied palette. They all but give them away at the markets. We make a killing on them. Oh, look!"

Atop a circular, wooden platform outside the Flying Maffickers, Boo balanced on a tall unicycle that was twice the length of the acrobat, idling back and forth as he juggled five clubs. If the unicycle wasn't already towering, the platform itself required a ladder to ascend to.

"Remarkable, isn't he?" she asked.

Atherton hummed in agreement, trying to understand the complexities of what Boo was managing. How every club managed to find its hand, how they cut through the continuous pattern within a few centimeters of one another. The unicycle wheel swayed back and forth while he pumped the pedals forward and backward, always just within a forearm's length of the edge of the platform.

"It's not in his contract to do these sets before the aerial show, you know," Lester remarked. "But oh, he does it anyway. Every damn night."

"A true freak of nature," Atherton agreed.

"A jack of all, and master still. The other performers were always suspicious of him—even jealous—long before his little skirmish with Mason's thugs, the Devil rest their souls," she said, tossing the bag into a bin beside a cooking stand, billowing spiced smoke from roasting almonds. "How ironic, that you would kill off the very men Boo sought to protect you from."

"Life's full of funny little surprises."

"You might think I'm trite, but it feels like yesterday when I visited him in Bedlam. Even in that hovel, he was making toys with odds and ends, balancing on his hands, doing cartwheels in the yard to keep himself busy. Circus was in his bones, whether he knew it or not. Between you and I, I think he'd rather streak naked through the streets before spending his time doing anything else."

Collecting four of the clubs, Boo hurtled the fifth one high, giving him time to vault from the unicycle in a backflip, collecting that final club from the air after his feet planted evenly. Applause erupted from the ring of onlookers. He held it aloft, his black lipstick stretching broadly as he beamed.

"It's no small thing, him taking a shine to you. Even if he's nearly more trouble than he's worth," she added with a laugh.

"It's not natural, is it? To an untrained eye, what he's doing is nothing short of sorcery."

"No more unnatural than your affinity with the dead. But that's the ticket, my dear. After all, what is magic besides something you can hardly comprehend that makes your heart sing?" Steering him away, Lester led him toward another act in the courtyard, now flush with the stragglers who left Boo's act.

Ruth, a knife thrower, flicked three blades into a scarecrow pinned with rubber balloons. The ones on its head, torso, and left hand popped simultaneously with sprays of red paint. She tucked another blade between her toes, executing a back handspring that flung the knife into the balloon on its right hand.

The closest onlookers shrieked gleefully as they were dotted with the scarecrow's blood.

Atherton joined the applause with an astonished exhale.

"I can hardly remember the last time I had a young man on my arm," Lester confessed. "You're no acrobat, but you've got dash-fire in your own right. There must have been hordes of women pining for you back home. Surely somebody besides your family will miss you."

Lester stole a look at the undertaker, a head shorter than her. Shadows waltzed over them from acrobats tumbling on the high wires above. His eyes fluttered at every spectacle with that newcomer's bewilderment. Behind every display were years of pained practice.

The night sky was a gray canvas of clouds, brooding like Atherton's eyes.

It was only then she realized what she'd said. "Goodness, they must not have cooked out the alcohol from this batch. I wasn't thinking."

"No, no. That's quite all right." He offered a reassuring grin, fragile as a worn thread. "I'm afraid my romantic entanglements often end in misfortune."

"You are green, yet. You know, it's my job to critique every act. That final, terrific eruption from your seance wasn't planned, was it? You looked surprised. Scared, even."

"No," Atherton admitted. "It was a stroke of beginner's luck."

"You're honest. That's good. I can work with honesty. So tell me, do you feel you are in danger?"

His thoughtful expression contorted into surprise. "You felt it. Her."

"A witch sees more than she lets on. I've sensed a fair share of disquieting entities in Ivory's tent, but I'll admit, wherever that woman's soul resides, she's left fragments in you that will prove difficult to exorcise. No matter if you dispense with the spirits she's bequeathed to you."

Lester spotted animosity stoking itself in her newest recruit.

"Lilian wasn't a woman," Atherton said. "Wasn't *human,* least of all. The English language is ill-equipped to describe such a person."

"No, my dear, she was as human as they come. That's the trouble. We give devils a run for their money and put angels to shame. Let's not forget, you're the arsonist with three murders to his name." She placed a hand on his shoulder and squeezed. "One can only hope she hasn't tarnished your perception of witches. We did wash your clothes, after all," she added with a wink.

"A'right, ladies and gents! My name is Ruth, and I have the honor of being your executioner this evenin'!" the knife thrower hollered. Boasting a top hat over luscious, platinum locks, the entertainer bobbed as she collected knives from the scarecrow. Her burgundy and gray striped leotard glittered in the ghostlight, with matching armbands and ruffles around her thigh trim. A corset with crimson filigree was tied tight around her hips with black lace. "Only joking. 'Course, it wasn't a joke to the bloke last week. Behold. The Wheel of Affliction!"

"Oh, this is the best bit," Lester whispered, tugging him closer until they stood at the innermost ring. The musky mildew and sweat from London's alleys enveloped them from the audience.

Ruth unfurled the tapestry covering a sizable wheel set with leather restraints. She set it into motion with a spin. Leonardo da Vinci's *Vitruvian Man*—carved into the dark wood—whirled into motion. The engraving was untouched, while every inch around it was steel-bitten and gnarled. Over Ruth's corset was a wide, leather belt strapped with dozens of knives varying in size, catching the ghostlight from lanterns hanging overhead as she strutted. Blades twirled restlessly in each of her hands.

"Do I have a volunteer?" she asked.

With a cough, Lester shoved Atherton forward. He stumbled into the open space, eyes wider than a child's caught with a hand in the biscuit jar. He waved sheepishly to the throng.

"Ah, a member of our own cast, then? Get on up here, Mr.—erhm." Ruth looked to Lester for direction.

"T-Todd," Atherton decided. "Yes. My name is Lucian Todd."

"Mr. Todd! Of course, the son of our infamous ghost courter."

Murmurs spread through the crowd, followed by half-hearted applause.

"I didn't know he had a son," somebody said.

"Indeed, put your hands together for our brave volunteer! It's only fitting, risking our own hides to assure our most venerable guests. Now, in the straps you get—yes, just like that. Splendid." Belting Atherton into the restraints, Ruth asked, "Comfortable?"

"They're a little tight."

"Good!" Giving the wheel a shove, Ruth stepped backwards, tossing a pair of knives between her hands. All the while, Atherton's body spun into a blur of black and white threads. "Of course, we only practice the utmost safety within these—ope!" Ruth feigned a misstep, flicking a blade between Atherton's legs as she 'stumbled' to the ground. "My apologies, ladies and gentlemen, I might've had a few too—oh! There goes another!" A second steely tooth sank through the air. It wobbled to the left of Atherton's temple, trapping a single tuft of hair.

Guffaws erupted with vigorous applause, even lecherous whistling, as Ruth moved almost sensually as she flourished her knives.

"Maybe if I just..." Two more blades whizzed, steel singing in their flight. Then a third, fourth, fifth, and half a dozen more studded the wheel with vicious thuds, Ruth vaulting, darting, striking poses with each.

The wheel creeping to a lazy halt, Ruth took a bow. Her belt was empty.

Atherton's chest heaved with panicked breaths.

Only then did they see it. Blades studded the spaces between each of his fingers.

Taking off her hat, Ruth offered it to each member of the crowd. Coins tinkled in. Bulls and banknotes fell from the more affluent hands, with some insisting that they'd be next. All the while, an upside-down Atherton glared at Lester, covering her mouth as she snickered impishly.

"I nearly forgot he'd need a moniker," a voice came from behind her.

"Bloody hell!" Lester gasped with a hand over her heart.

It was Ivory, grinning broadly with hands folded behind his back. "It's an easy enough story to sell," he said, "not that Kayne and I ever considered conceiving children in such a place."

"This is a fine environment to raise a nipper!" she insisted, smacking him on the arm playfully. "He's rather like you, you know, in his own way. He has that temper that turns at the drop of a hat. What else could allow a young man to set a pub alight with three men still inside?"

"Please, as if I ever...!" Hearing his own voice nearing a shout, Ivory cut himself short. "Point taken. So, we have that in common."

Meanwhile, Atherton protested loudly, reminding Ruth he was still confined. She pretended not to hear. Coins were still pouring their way into her hat.

Lester hummed with an arched eyebrow. "Dare I say it, he admires you."

Ivory blew a raspberry. "Hardly. The first time we met, he called me a charlatan."

"Well, who could take you seriously with that accent, anyways?"

"Considering your unusually spirited mood this evening, I'll pretend as though I didn't hear that, *love*."

"What do you make of his performance this afternoon? You saw her, just as I did."

"As corrupt and relentless as they come," he agreed. "He doesn't know he's all the better for it, speaking strictly in terms of his act. A spirit as robust as Lilian's will only serve to bolster his connection to whatever petty entities waltz into his locus. He could gather armies. You would hardly believe the details of what he told me about that night. He'll take that memory to his grave, fresher than the moment it found him. His potential is...intimidating."

Lester held out her hand. A light rain had started. She let tiny specks form on her finger. "Good."

After Atherton was released from the restraints, Ruth gave him a prompt smack on his backside that sent him shouldering his way through the crowd with flushed cheeks.

"Thanks for that, yeah. That was brilliant; I enjoyed every moment. Let's do it again," Atherton said to Lester. "Remind me to give Ruth a wide berth. She's barking mad—I mean it."

"Oh, be nice," she said with a pinch on his cheek. "She grows on you. You were terrific."

Putting an arm around Atherton, Ivory said, "I'm afraid I'll have to steal your company. My assistant and I have to earn your salary."

"*Merde*, my friends."

Lester whipped open her umbrella as dense sheets broke out of the temperamental sky.

The courtyard throngs sought refuge in ticket booth eaves, purchasing shelter in the dozens of acts rolling on in the main tents. She stood alone, long after Ruth had packed up her knives and placed a tarp over the Wheel of Affliction, after Boo had stowed his equipment back in the clown alley, after the acrobats on the high wires scattered for a well-earned cigarette by the caravans.

Listening to the rain, the muffled clamor from the tents lining the walkways, she sighed with closed eyes. For the briefest moment, she nearly forgot about Mason.

Then she did something that surprised even her.

With a head bowed to the ground, she prayed.

"Just one more week, then we'll be gone," she murmured to whatever god or devil was listening. "One week. That's all I ask."

35

ATHERTON

JUNE 19, 1886

It was the most profitable week in the circus's history, and the happiest of Atherton's life. The evenings were so packed that they opened the gates in the early afternoons, altering acts to cater to the rising demands of young families. The decomposing visages of the orphans in his mind were steadily replaced by the delighted expressions of children arriving from every borough in London. With the last of Lilian's orphans proving agreeable to being rehomed in the lanterns, Atherton passed off his inability to force their hand as exhaustion.

In truth, he was reluctant to say goodbye so quickly.

His sessions with Ivory lengthened—whole hours elapsed in the blink of an eye. The spectres that gravitated to his locus became familiar partners in a dance. Every weft and weave of their movements expressed an equally graceful display upon the stage.

Candles were only the beginning. Together, they manipulated glass orbs, clothing—even chairs and curtains. Before, Atherton's knees would wobble when he watched Ivory from backstage. A different tremor soon arrived—an eagerness to perform.

His hands, accustomed to the weight of cadavers, instead were used to lift his own body after the Spirit Asylum's acts were concluded, when Boo inevitably convinced him to join in his training regimen. During the day, he went where Lester pointed.

He washed down Tristana's boar Bartholomew, brushed horses in the menagerie, polished the magicians' mirrors, and learned to help out with rigging for the aerialists. Though menial chores to seasoned workers, to him, such tasks divined the abundant mysteries harbored by the carnival. In the clown alley, he helped Minnie with stitching together small tears in costumes.

Between these duties, it seemed every discipline had a few artists all too eager to show him the basics. He was flung onto mats through his first backflips, hoisted onto stilts, coerced into climbing to the top of an aerial rope, and of course, Boo all but shoved him off the board of the flying trapeze rig. The first time he took off with the chalked bar in his hands, he hung petrified from the trapeze long after the swinging stopped, reluctant to trust the wide net beneath him. When his grip inevitably forced his hand, the troupe clapped and hollered.

"Well, at least we know your dead hang isn't half bad," Boo noted.

Atherton was not particularly brilliant at any of the skills besides ghost courting, but they all assured him that was normal—each discipline required a short lifetime to master.

A pleasant ache throbbed in his body each morning. By the evening, he sank to depths of sleep he previously thought only infants enjoyed. In his dreams, he wandered into the loneliest corners of the circus, where the rich paranoia of nightmares deepened the reveries cradling him.

Atherton grew fond, too, of a nightly ritual: the cookhouse. Each evening, hundreds of famished workers and entertainers congregated to feast. Cheap ingredients from local markets were prepared with a zeal that turned humble plates into dishes fit for aristocrats. They indulged over laughter, shouting, and music just as boisterous as when guests packed the circus by the thousands.

One night, Florence emerged from Kayne's infirmary to dine with the rest. Boo and Atherton sat beside each other, each tucking greedily into shepherd's pie. As she approached, the conversation around their section dimmed.

Boo stood up from his seat in surprise, a bit of green pea stuck to the corner of his mouth.

Sitting across from them, both Ivory and Kayne scrutinized the meeting over the steady burning of tobacco. Were it not for all the hundreds of others dining beneath that long canopy shielding them from the downpour, the barest sound of cutlery tinkling against plates would be heard in that silence.

"Make room," was all Florence said, nodding toward Atherton.

He complied, and the aerialist plopped down beside him with a sigh.

Uncertainly, Boo took his seat beside her.

"Are you finished with that?" she asked, eyeing Boo's dinner.

"Well—"

Not missing a beat, Florence placed her stubs on either side of the plate and bent her head down, taking a mouthful. When her face came up, she chewed and swallowed heartily. "So," she began, dabbing at her cheeks with Boo's shirt, "who's this mug?"

"Atherton Graves," Ivory said, "or, if any locals ask, Lucian Todd. Your newest associate. He's already familiar with you."

"A pleasure," Atherton managed. "I've heard good things."

A bemused scoff escaped Florence. She turned to regard him with wild eyes. "No. You mean *this* Graves, the one in the papers? You're telling me this boy burnt those men to a crisp?"

"Gave Mason hell, too," Kayne added.

"Well, you missed the important one, then," Florence replied. She bent her head down again, taking another mouthful. "Still impressive, I suppose. Welcome. So, doctor, how is the research coming?"

"Ah, promising. Very promising," Kayne replied. "A couple dozen more runs on the cadavers should see us through. After that, well, it's merely a matter of your courage, my dear."

"Good. I'm looking forward to slapping this *pitre* with a fresh set of hands," she said with a nudge in Boo's side.

"I'll join you. I think about it every day," Ivory murmured, only to receive a less shallow elbow from Kayne.

Somewhere at the center of the gathering came the loud chinking of a spoon against glass. It was Lester, raising up a shot of gin as she cleared her throat. "A moment, if you will, everyone! Everyone!" she shouted, louder still.

The din ebbed.

"I'd like to take a moment to formally introduce you all to our newest member. Of course, you all knew him from the papers long before he joined us. That's right—we have a murderer in our midst. But he is not just any murderer. The blood that stains his hands belonged to the men who harassed us. Who reaped our profits. Who bludgeoned several of our jugglers. Who took Florence's hands. Before, we needed their business, but tonight is one night in a long series that has proven we are better off without them. So his vengeance is our vengeance. His burden, ours to share. Everyone, please welcome Atherton Graves, who will be entertaining as a spiritualist with Ivory in the Spirit Asylum."

Lester gestured over at Atherton, with applause arising at the sweep of her hand. When she upended the shot, the rest of the circus found their glasses and polished them off. Boo slapped a bottle of gin into Atherton's hand, motioning for him to do the same until he took a pull.

"Now that most of us are nearly full up to the knocker, I think it's only fitting I share some sobering news," she continued. "Yes, these have been our most profitable shows. And yes, you all have cause to celebrate and rest before we make the next jump. The Devil knows you've earned it. But nothing can ever be so simple, can it? The truth is that Mason Cross is a rabid dog. Once his fangs are in, he never lets go. Tomorrow night marks our final evening in London, and he bloody knows it as well as we all do. Heed my words. He will return for one last, final act of spite. Be on your guard. If you see anything suspicious, don't hesitate to report it to Thomas or me. Take shelter, if you need. End shows early, if you must. Beyond that, do what you do best—what you have always done. Give this stinking city a night to remember. Good night."

"I don't understand," an aerialist murmured, sitting to Boo's right. "If you know he's coming, why don't we run?" Amelia's large, blue eyes darted about the others at the table. "We could leave a day sooner than advertised. Am I wrong?"

"Oh, absolutely," Ivory said, puffing on a cigar, saying nothing else.

"Darling, please," Kayne chastised.

"Is he always like this?" Atherton asked.

"*Yes*," came a unified reply from everyone listening.

"If we run, Mason will only pursue us," Atherton explained. "He'd send mercenaries across the Channel if that's what it took."

"Nowhere's safe," Boo agreed. "A circus isn't exactly hard to find. Moreover, we can't blacklist this city. It's too profitable."

Atherton and Boo locked eyes. With a nod, they got up from their seats to follow Lester.

"Excuse us," Atherton said.

The rain had ceased. A full moon crept through the clouds, casting a silver sheen on Boo's button nose as they trailed Lester, her cloak billowing behind her long strides.

"We should just do it ourselves and be done with it," Boo whispered. "This is not a good idea. Worst case scenario, we fail and nobody finds out. Best case, we kill him and the whole thing's done with."

"I only just arrived," Atherton replied. "If Lester found out, she'd have me on my arse before you can say the word 'arse,' and that would be that. I can't afford to lose this. I have nothing else."

With a petulant growl, the clown relented. "Fine."

"Fine."

"I'll tell you I told you so," he added.

It was only in the ring of the coven's caravan that they made their presence known.

The circus proprietor stopped with a weary sigh, lifting her head up to the stars glinting through a break in the clouds. "You two are not half as quiet as you think. The answer is no," she said flatly.

"But you haven't heard our plan," Boo pushed.

"You two should be celebrating, not plotting murder."

"Lester, you know this is right. You said it yourself, he *will* seek vengeance," Boo said.

The circus proprietor turned around, but when she approached, she targeted Atherton. "Are you so hungry for death? Have you not had your fill? Perhaps not," she thought aloud, the words arriving heavy and slow. "You court tragedy. That's your sin, isn't it? You don't know who you are without it. It itches something you don't know how to scratch otherwise."

Atherton shook his head, his balled fists betraying him. "This isn't about me. I would sooner have Mason's blood on my hands than that of those who sheltered me from him."

"Then you do not fully understand the gratitude you owe us, if you would so quickly throw that gift away."

Atherton gnawed on his bottom lip. Braving Lester's gaze was like squinting into the sun.

"We will be discreet," Boo continued. "In and out. One bullet. That's all it would take."

"We're not through," she said, ignoring Boo. She placed a hand on Atherton's shoulder, pulling him closer. "Taking a life is a sacred act, not a solution. Henry, Arthur, Luther. You killed those men to survive. And by some miracle of the Devil's spaded tail, you made it out alive. This is different. This will scorch the heart out of you."

"And what little of it remains, at that," he returned. "I would sacrifice it without a second thought."

"You are as green as summer grass, Atherton. You do not know the profound loathing that writhes in you. It will consume you more than the flames you made to lick the flesh of those men clean. You're already haunted by your past. Don't let it damn your future."

"My heart is blackened from the rot I carried all my life," he returned. "I know how to carry this weight. Lester, I understand I can only begin to repay you for what—"

"You can begin now by listening to me. You may have made an ally of death, but Boo hasn't. Boo's hands are clean, and I would see to it they remain that way. I will not have him follow your shadow."

"I am not a child anymore," Boo replied. "This was my idea."

"A damnably foolish one! The same kind that got us into this mess in the first place." Taking a shuddering breath, Lester ran her hands down her frilled dress and composed herself. "Let us imagine, shall we, hm? *If* by some unfathomably slim chance, I let you go, how would you enter his estate? Do you not think he is guarded day and night after what happened in New Sarum? And if you somehow slipped by his men, if you did away with him, how would you return without being discovered?"

"In circus, nothing is impossible," Boo recited. "We could be done with it in an hour's time."

"I will not lose you!"

Her shouts shook both of them.

She placed her hands on Boo's shoulders and caressed his cheek, smoothing out the wild, copper locks bordering his face. Tears shimmered at the edge of her eyes, refusing to fall. "Blood be damned, you are my son. I won't lose you to this."

"Think of Florence." Boo's voice quivered.

"If you go through with this, if I hear one more word about it, I will throw you both from these gates personally. That is a promise. Have I made myself clear?"

"Yes," Boo and Atherton answered weakly.

"Get some rest, both of you. Good night."

Boo shook his head as Lester walked away.

The pair meandered away from the cookhouse and toward the Flying Maffickers. Atherton clicked open his cigarette case and fished two out, handing him one.

"Go ahead. Tell me," Atherton sighed, taking a deep drag and lighting his friend's.

Embers burned in the clown's eyes as he let the smoke expand from his mouth and inhaled through his nose. "I damn well told you so."

❦ 36 ❦

BOO
JUNE 20, 1886

The evening wilted with a creeping pace. Time in the Flying Maffickers often blurred from one act to the next. Now, Boo felt every ache, pulse, and pant for breath. He climbed his silks before an audience of hundreds, focusing on his hands while he ascended higher still. The sticky rosin he'd rubbed into his palms aided his grip as he inverted.

It was the final show for that night. With Boo in the center, five other aerialists were dancing in the air on either side of him—Ophelia, Clarence, Amelia, Stella, and Violet. Swinging between and over them were trapeze artists, their flights punctuated by the clasp of chalked hands—powdery bursts in the amber and silver spotlights haloing their silhouettes.

Boo deviated from the rehearsed movements, hooking a leg around the silks to hang upside-down, gathering his strength before the finale. The others followed his lead, improvising with clever knots that allowed them to rest in ornamental poses. Tiny, innumerable lanterns burning ghostlight rimmed the stage—a death sentence away. One slip of the hand and they would hurtle. Splat. A standard aerial routine was often five or six minutes at most, but Lester pushed her acrobats to perform for upwards of fifteen.

A keen eye could catch the sweat dripping from their foreheads.

In the orchestra pit, cellos voiced a low, mournful tune, accented by the chirring violins spurring on the tension. Dressed in black paramilitary garb, the trapeze artists' costumes were outfitted with small pyrotechnics rigged to plume like gunfire as they flew above the aerialists. The trapeze rig was placed behind the trussing for the aerial silks, layered cleverly in the background, but high enough to yield a full view.

Ophelia climbed to the zenith of her silk first, wrapping it about her in preparation for a drop. A trapeze artist executed a double backflip in flight above her, arms extended for his partner. The pyrotechnic strapped to his chest sizzled and cracked with a spray of flashing sparks. As though hit by a bullet, Ophelia released her grip and tumbled down, her crimson silk unfurling wildly until she halted, swaying limply at the bottom.

Just beside Boo, Clarence followed suit. His "executioner" leapt off the board. *Sssclerk* and pop! Clarence's full weight hurtled until the rigging sprang with a clamorous protest—a heaving jolt stopping him just inches before the stage.

Applause crackled between each movement with hollers, whistles, and popcorn kernels being thrown about.

Boo's drop was the finale.

To his left, Stella and Violet followed their rehearsed movements without a hitch, timing them to the bright, golden streaks raining down from the flyers above. Drums boomed out from the orchestra with a thunderous, mounting cadence. Boo's heartbeat strummed a similar tempo in his chest. The closest to him, Amelia, climbed to the top of her silk, wrapped in an intricate design that would allow her to tumble safely to the bottom.

Still hanging upside-down, Boo looked out across the crowd. He thought about the next city they'd visit. He wondered how Atherton would fare with the long days of travel, how he'd tolerate the ticks and leeches on their skin when they washed themselves in whatever lakes they could find.

Time tugged on his bones, slower still. His heart quivered, skipping a beat. Through the smoldering spotlight, he made out a long, tubular shape protruding from the uppermost row of seats. He lifted a hand to shield his eyes.

A pole? Flagstaff?

Boo heard the trapeze catcher's queue—a single *hep!* to alert his partner that it was time to take flight from the board. His eyes widened.

A rifle.

It would be two full swings before the flyer performed his layout—Amelia's queue to drop. By then, it would be too late. Boo untangled himself from his wraps, gripping the silks with one hand and reaching out toward Amelia with the other.

"Let go!" he shouted. "Now!"

Amelia's serene expression fractured into perplexity. She turned her head to where Boo pointed. Another crack in the air sounded before the pyrotechnic.

It came from the audience.

A single, bright discharge of light followed by an unmistakable trail of smoke. A warm substance splattered across Boo. White chunks scattered from behind Amelia's head, followed by wet, meaty slaps upon the stage. Her body tipped backwards with a ragged lurch, tumbling down the fabric. A doll tangled in string.

Boo's screams were lost in the crowd's curdling cries. The throngs surged from their seats, some tackling the gunman while others made a mad scramble for the exit.

Other shots rang out. Too many to count.

Boo wrapped his leg around the silk and let go. He growled, the fabric searing his hands as he hurtled freely. Bullets whizzed by, cutting the air around him. He leapt to the stage, running toward Amelia. Stagehands pulled the curtains shut, but the barrage was ceaseless. Spears of light scintillating with dust broke through the bullet holes.

He picked up Amelia. The fabric was drenched, her blood already running down his arms. He refused to believe what he'd seen, what he saw now. Uncomprehending murmurs fell through his lips.

"Run!"

"Run, Boo!"

The cries from the other aerialists taking shelter in the wings were distant. Boo looked into Amelia's eyes, but only one stared back. A gaping hole had replaced the other.

More bullets peppered the curtains. Cradling her body, he bent his head into her chest, the shattered remnants of her skull shifting against his fingers. He howled, a protracted scream that rent his throat raw, a scream that drowned even the gunfire.

That was when the sky rained fire.

37

ATHERTON
JUNE 20, 1886

"Agh! Fuck!"

Atherton cursed, balling himself tighter into the cover of the upturned table on the stage of the Spirit Asylum. Blood oozed through the fingers he'd clamped down on his thigh. Ivory was crouched behind him, ducking as more bullets flew overhead.

The audience streamed out of the tent, howling and trampling over one another, as the ground shook.

Somewhere beyond the Spirit Asylum, searing arms of flame reached to the stars, an explosion so bright that light danced through the tent flaps.

"Are you hit?" Ivory asked.

"Yes, I am fucking hit! Are you blind?" Atherton shouted.

"Don't insult me while we're being shot at!"

A hole in the table erupted with splinters beside Atherton's head. "Fuck! They're getting closer!"

Ivory's spectacles were webbed with cracks, his prosthetic fingers now jagged splinters. "Give me the gun!" he shouted.

Atherton reached into his holster and tossed the revolver at Ivory.

As soon as the next pair of shots rang out, the spiritualist stood up and pointed toward the disarray of seats, firing three times.

Two strangled yelps groaned out, followed by a heavy thud.

Another rumble shook the stage. Ivory stumbled, keeping the gun firmly pointed. He righted his spectacles out of sheer habit. "Hands up, or by God I will put you down like a dog!" he shouted. "I see you!"

"My hands are raised!" returned a muffled voice.

Atherton peeked above his cover to see two hands raised above the backseats, a revolver dangling from the Disciple's bloodied palm.

The guests had flushed out, save for a woman lying limply over the stage.

"Miss, it's not safe," Atherton stammered, reaching toward her. Then he saw the pool of blood stretched over the talking board, reaching toward him. "Oh."

"Drop the iron and come out, and there will be no harm done to you! I swear it!" Ivory demanded.

A man sporting a bowler unsteadily rose from behind his cover. Gunpowder smudged his face, his wide eyes glittering in the low light. The gun clattered at his feet, settling beside the upturned seats, candles, umbrellas, and other articles abandoned in the chaos.

"Come out fully!" Ivory ordered.

He limped into the aisle between the seats. Dark stains expanded from the bullet hole in his leg, trailing down the bottom of his trousers.

"And the other one in here!" Ivory continued. "I know you're hiding in that back right corner!"

"He's a'ready dead," the man said. "You got 'im."

"Good. Where is your boss? Where is Mason Cross?"

"He's not 'ere. I swear, sir. H-he's only sent us in 'is place. I was only following orders. Please, sir. I've family!"

"You should have thought of that before you tried to play God!"

Once more, the ground quivered from yet another explosion. That low, eerie wail of fire ripping the air grew closer.

"What are those explosions we are hearing? What have you done?"

"Bombs, sir. Dynamite sticks, with petrol vials 'round the walls of the tents."

"How many?"

"At least a dozen, sir. Please, sir, I was only—"

"Shut up! Why are we still standing here, then?"

"Mr. Cross said he wanted the boy alive. That one, there," he added with a trembling finger pointing at Atherton. "Said to spare 'im. Couldn't rig this one to blow then, could we?"

"Who else is here with you? Answer me!"

"N-nobody, sir."

"If you're lying to me, by God, you will regret it!" Ivory emphasized, jabbing the air with his revolver.

"I swear it! I swear! It was just us!" The Disciple moaned. His knees were trembling. A dark, yellow trickle seeped around the soles of his shoes.

A final gunshot cracked the air open.

The Disciple's head snapped backward. Blood and bone smacked the canvas wall with a sopping slap. Distant gunfire snapped in distorted pops throughout the grounds, with screams tearing the gaps between, growing more distant by the moment.

Ivory waited in that eerie racket, steadying his breaths as his eyes flitted around the seats. When there was no movement, he knelt beside Atherton.

"How bad is it?"

Atherton swallowed, preparing himself. He released his hand from the wound.

"It's just a graze. They've only grazed you," Ivory said through a sigh, rubbing the back of the boy's neck, slick with sweat. The undertaker fell forward into his arms, embracing him.

"You're a'right. You're a'right," Ivory hushed.

Adrenaline shivered its way through Atherton's bones. "It's all my fault," he said. "Mine. I've brought this upon them."

"No, this isn't your doing."

"You lot will suffer for my bloodshed. Mason will build a mountain of your bodies to find me. I have to turn myself into his men, don't I? It's all that's left to be done," he said, getting to his feet. "Give me the iron." Atherton reached for the revolver, fighting Ivory when he didn't relent. "I'll kill them. I'll kill as many as I can while I do. Give it to me!"

White heat flashed across Atherton's face. He stumbled back from the blow, touching the reddened flesh of his cheek.

"Damn your self-pity," Ivory shouted. "If you surrender yourself to Mason, then you squander all we have done. Do you not hear it? Listen! Those are the screams of those who would sooner die in defiance than allow *you* to subject yourself to such tyranny. I was wrong. This *is* your doing. Yours and mine. So collect yourself and face it."

Atherton wiped at the snot and grime on his face, nodding.

"Good man. Now, take what weapons you can find on their bodies."

Ivory moved to the other body in the tent while Atherton strode to the Disciple in the aisle. He retrieved the man's snub-nose revolver and ran his hand through the soiled pockets, finding loose coin and spare bullets. The weapon was quaint, tiny. This wasn't at all like New Sarum, when he had weeks to prepare. His shaking fingers fumbled with the sticky bullets as he reloaded the chamber.

Ivory stood over him, the other Disciple's gun tucked into the back of his trousers. "It's already beginning to quiet," he noted.

Black smoke crept in through the entryway, filling the air with the acrid fumes of burning canvas and grass. Bold, amber light shimmered over Ivory's spectacles as he stole a glance through the tent flaps.

Placing his hands on Atherton's shoulders, he said, "Now listen closely. If you so much as see a man with iron in his hands, you take aim and pull the trigger. Trust yourself."

"I will," he swallowed.

"Repeat what I said."

"I-if I so much as see another man with iron in his hands, I will end him where he stands."

A tender grin pulled on Ivory's lips. "You're the cold-blooded outlaw from New Sarum with three men to his name, aren't you?"

"Yes."

"The boy who stood up to Mason Cross when nobody else would, and gave him a scar to remember it by. Yes?"

"Yes."

"The boy who slept in death's crib since he was just a babe. Isn't that right?"

Atherton took a deep breath. They would have to brave the courtyard soon, or the smoke would consume them. He nodded. "That's right."

"But you're no more a boy than I am," Ivory realized aloud. "And not just a man. No, the world has bent itself over backwards to reduce you to dust, and still you stood against it. It made you something else. Something more. You have no cause to tremble, Atherton. A person who walks in death's shadow does not bow to the fears of the living."

Ivory twirled his revolver, extending the handle to Atherton. "She belongs to you. She knew blood in your hands before mine. I'll use the one I found on that poor bastard."

Taking it, Atherton swallowed the dread in his throat.

"We'll make for the caravans. Lester and the others will be thinking the same." Ivory used the barrel of his gun to part the tent flaps, glancing about. "There's only smoke. Can't see a blasted thing."

"Shouldn't we leave from the back?"

"That's too obvious," he said, "if there's anybody guarding it, they'll be expecting us. Come on, then. Stay close."

Ivory parted the entrance and stepped through, sweeping his weapon across the courtyard.

It looked as though a fiery behemoth had trampled the circus. Pieces of canvas from the towering tents fell in flaming sheets, smoke pluming over lapping arcs of fire. The bodies of guests and Disciples decorated the ground. Costumed performers were beside them, unmoving, their striped leggings and shirts curled with burnt, crisped edges. Patches of seared flesh peeked through. Most striking was their hair.

Like human torches, still ablaze.

Atherton hardly recognized their blackened faces. It was Ivory whose gaze lingered over each one, clenching his jaw in bitter rage.

Through the umber haze, silhouettes sprinted toward the exit—the last of the guests who'd managed to struggle free from the tents.

"It appears they've done their work," Ivory said, pacing forward. "The others must have fought off the rest."

Atherton strode backward with his back against Ivory, surveying the disorder. Ghostlight lanterns littered the ground. Those that bathed in the unendurable flames fractured, popping with brief, spectral wails. The spirits raced out, dissolving among the smoke.

"They knew they had to scatter quickly," Ivory thought aloud, walking quicker now. "The fire brigade will arrive soon, and even the Disciples couldn't be caught orchestrating a massacre. Come on, then. Quickly now. The others must suspect we're dead. We'll disappoint them, huh?" he added with a low chuckle. "Boo is going to—"

A stupefied groan grunted through his teeth. Ivory stumbled backwards. Atherton turned, heels digging in the mud beneath the weight of Ivory falling into his arms.

Somewhere before them was a *pop*—almost quiet in the guttural, hissing flames, the erupting lanterns, the heat enveloping them on all sides.

The gunman was as discreet as the small caliber weapon in his hands.

A gust of wind cleared the fumes enshrouding him, just long enough for Atherton to make out his peculiar features—not peculiar by any normal standards, but because he was half the size of a man. Dressed in a herringbone vest and trousers, he held the smoking gun.

Atherton raised his revolver, squinting in disbelief.

It was just a child. Leo. Mason's messenger boy.

His finger trembled on the trigger. "Ivory, what do I do?" he stammered. "Ivory!"

"I got one!" the boy squealed. "And you! Stay there, Mr. Graves!"

Ivory grew heavier, sinking into Atherton's arms.

When Atherton fell to his knees, that's when he felt it: the warm substance spilling onto his chest, his legs, and soaking his socks.

Ivory coughed and wheezed. A spatter of blood splashed across Atherton's dazed expression. He heard a low whistle and gurgle through Ivory's shirt from where the bullet pierced a lung.

"D-don't," he managed, pulling down the revolver.

An imposing figure came bounding from behind Leo.

Streaks of blackened smoke curled around Thomas's bare chest. He wrenched the gun out of the child's hand, laying him into the grass with a single, dull strike to his temple.

Never did the ghoul appear so small to Atherton, standing over Leo, watching helplessly as he made sense of Ivory in his arms, his jaw dropping when his eyes found the bullet hole. If time had crawled in those moments, it redoubled its efforts, racing like a jackrabbit fleeing a predator.

Atherton dropped the revolver and pressed his hand into Ivory's wound. It poured through his fingers, wetting every crevice of his nails and hands.

"It'll be all right. We'll get Kayne and she'll—fetch Kayne!" he screamed at Thomas.

Throwing the child over his shoulder, the ghoul sprinted off into the passage leading from the courtyard toward the caravan.

"It's a'right," Ivory coughed, straining to survey his wound. Seeing it, he let his head fall into the crook of Atherton's arms with a bitter chuckle. "You're the expert...but I think this is the end of my rope."

"No, no, it's not," Atherton stammered. "You don't mean that."

The smoldering heat and fumes wrapped their ashen arms around them. The flames from the menagerie and the Flying Maffickers rose higher still. Their monstrous walls fell, their steel rigging and support poles falling down like a house of cards.

"We have to get you out of here," Atherton said, struggling to hoist Ivory's weight. But as he tried, he felt hot rivers leaving Ivory with greater haste.

Ivory protested with an agonized groan. "No. Here. Here is just fine."

"*Here?* What do you mean? I can't let you," Atherton said. But his body didn't mirror his words. He fell back to his knees, clutching Ivory closer. Tears slipped from his eyes, pattering their chests.

"A whole life spent working for death, and you still don't know when it's standing right in front of you." Ivory reached up, using his thumb to wipe Atherton's tears, mussing his face with more blood. He kept his hand there, cupping his cheek.

"It's not. I won't let it. I won't."

"That's not your choice."

Atherton's chin quivered. His voice came hoarse and broken. "You can't leave me like this. You're the only one who understands what it's like."

Ivory fought to keep his eyes open, choking through his words. "That's not true. You were never alone. Even when you thought only the dead cared for you. I t-tried to tell you when we first met. Remember?"

Atherton couldn't hold it back. His chest heaved with a choking sob.

"You know that now, don't you?"

"Stop talking like you're already gone."

"Give Kayne and the others my love. You'll look after her in my place, won't you? She takes her coffee with two spoonfuls of sugar when we have it." Blood teemed through his lips.

Atherton's chest tightened. He bit another sob, holding him tighter still. He couldn't lie to him. Not now. "I will. I promise. Sugar with her coffee, got it."

Patting his cheek, he said, "G-good. You'll make a fine performer. Boo will look after you."

Ivory fumbled for his spectacles. He took them off to look up. Between the circus's sooty exhalations, pockets of stars gleamed through.

"Don't..." His voice came in whispers. Atherton bent forward just to make them out over the crackling blazes. "Don't let this haunt you."

He knew instantly.

The moment he lifted his head, he saw it. That look he'd seen in thousands of faces. The emptiness—a hollow caricature of everything the person was or ever could be—solidified in a heartbeat, leaving behind only this.

Corpses always snapped him to composure, to an air of professionalism and cordiality. Not now.

He was standing on a set of train tracks, watching the lights grow nearer, larger. Then it hit—blistering steam, a metallic behemoth's iron teeth colliding against him. But he was just a phantom on those tracks, standing still as that colossal force rushed through him, over and over.

Atherton rocked back and forth with the body in his arms. The flames grew around him, lapping closer. The smoke filled his lungs, caking his throat as he wailed. His tears gathered the ash on his cheeks, dripping black on Ivory's scarlet shirt.

Whether it was unconsciousness or madness, or hours or minutes elapsing, he could not say. Somewhere in that swirling darkness, he felt somebody prying his hands from Ivory. Somewhere, he felt himself fighting to hold on, cursing and kicking at the limbs reaching for him.

How many hands reached out to him? It seemed there were thousands. An army of dead grabbing at his body. Finally, he was lifted up. A perfume of salted caramel, sweat, and chalk clung to the clown's striped leotard.

"Breathe," Boo told him. "Just breathe."

Following behind them, Thomas cradled Ivory limply in his arms. Kayne walked beside, never looking away from her husband's face.

That was the last of what he remembered the night the circus burned brightest. That, and a familiar feeling he thought he'd left behind in New Sarum. It was a vain hope. A wish that the next time he woke, the past would be little else than a nightmare.

38

LESTER
JUNE 27, 1886

"All nightmares come to an end."

Those were the first words Lester spoke to her remaining performers. Thirteen had perished the night Mason's men attacked. In the following days, several others would succumb to their wounds. Lester realized she couldn't promise anyone, even then, that this was the end of Mason's vengeance. Dozens of workers and stagehands quit—some in despair, but mostly out of fear. Hands in their pockets, they left the gates behind, searching for another life in the city, or perhaps just to be swallowed by it.

"In circus, nothing is impossible. But even we cannot escape the confines of mortality. In fact, our work is an ode to it," she said. They'd all gathered around a bonfire, their ashy faces and still eyes lost in the flames. "You can try your chances elsewhere, but out there, it is no different. It may be disease. Violence. A misstep on a scaffold. A broken heart. We have our own dangers, here. The beasts in the menagerie. A poorly executed flip. High wire acts."

After the fire brigade fought off the flames, they carted off the materials that couldn't be salvaged. The equipment that melted in the heat. The bodies that had been trapped in the wreckage.

"The difference is, we're a family. The largest you'll ever find. We look out for one another. When the going's good and when the Devil decides, like last night, to play favorites."

Scotland Yard had rolled in soon after, lingering well past dawn, interviewing survivors and inspecting bodies. Lester didn't lie. As soon as the Disciples were mentioned, it evaporated any scrutiny that would have fallen on the circus, and simultaneously, any hope that Mason or his men would be brought to justice.

"Not a farthing was stolen from our coffers," she told them. "They came for blood, and they got it."

The press called it *CATASTROPHE AT THE CIRCUS*, suspecting a robbery gone terribly wrong, implicating nobody.

Before the following afternoon, Lester had already taken stock of what was lost. Telegrams, letters, and funds were transferred to the appropriate factories. The tents, the equipment, rigging, and all else that was lost were already being replaced.

It would be waiting for them in the next city.

"Coin can buy you just about anything in this blasted world, except for people. You can't replace that. Anybody who wishes to leave now does so with my blessing and a warning: the world won't treat you as kindly as we have. If you wish to continue with us, we'll leave in just a week's time. We'll move on."

And they did. They loaded a train with only a quarter of their usual shipping containers, assembled a caravan half as long, and left with London shrinking away behind them. The jump wasn't the gaudy celebration it often was. There was no music. No laughter as the horses bore them away from the blackened fields.

"As for our transgressors, we'll be pursued by them no more. Of that, you have my word. And so we will set off as we always have, from darkness to bring the people stars."

ATHERTON
July 2, 1886

"You think this'll work?" Boo asked.

Atherton's expression betrayed nothing as he parted the smoke-stained curtains from the window of a derelict hotel room in the East End. *The Spade*. Its glass was fogged from the six bodies huddled together.

He eyed the building at the corner of the street. *Leverton & Sons Funeral Parlor & Crematory*. Silty, gray smoke plumed from their retort smokestacks, joining the fumes fouling the sky from neighboring factories.

Rain seeped down in thick streams down the panes, a kaleidoscope of glinting umber from the street lamps three stories below, fending off the deepening twilight. Atherton cracked the window. Smoke rushed through the opening. A puddle grew at the edge of the windowsill, spilling over.

The covers on the two queen beds were almost undisturbed. Sleep was the last thing on any of their minds—few in the circus had gotten much of it since that night.

"It'll be over by the time he realizes what's happened," Atherton replied. "I can assure you of that."

"Can't say it's any worse than our first plan," Thomas added from behind them. "'Ell of a lot more loose strings, far as I'm concerned. But it's crafty, I'll give ya that."

The ghoul looked like an oversized figurine in a dollhouse. Leaning against the farthest wall, he ran an oily cloth along the barrel of a full-sized Lefever shotgun, clenching an unlit cigar between his teeth.

Sitting on the floor with a gnarled deck of cards, Stella and Ruth were flipping through their tenth round of blackjack, betting on loose change they didn't care for. Ruth's belt and two thigh holsters were beside her, the steely edge of her throwing knives gleaming after she'd driven them all mad, sharpening each one over a whetstone.

Boo looked to them for a response, receiving only shrugs.

"Just tell me where to go. I'll follow," Stella said.

"And you?" Boo asked.

Kayne rose from her bed and joined them by the window. The chain of Ivory's pocket watch was wrapped about her wrist, the piece hanging from her fingers. Her hand lingered on the back of Atherton's arm. "Far as I see it," she said, "I don't care how it gets done, so long as it does. Are you sure of this?"

"I'll die trying," Atherton replied.

"Sorry to disappoint you, ar' kid, but none of us are dyin'," Thomas said. "We'll 'ave to knock some poor blokes out just to start things off proper, however. They'll be wearing black eyes by the time they wake. Blokes that 'ave nothing to do with this, mind you."

"Sure. A little fractured skull never hurt anybody," Ruth said.

"No," Kayne said. "Nobody innocent is getting hurt. Ivory wouldn't have wanted that. We bribe them. Violence talks; coin is quiet. I'll front it."

Thomas frowned. "'Ave it your way, then."

They looked strange to Atherton, wearing city clothes. The muted colors. The blouses, coats, cufflinks, and neatly fitted trousers. Thomas, for once, wore a collared shirt and waistcoat, the threads straining against his shoulders and biceps.

Dousing his cigarette in an overflowing ashtray, Atherton sat on one bed with his back against the wall. His eyelids fluttered shut all too easily. But like all the times he closed his eyes since that night, all he saw was Ivory.

His wet, strangled gasps. His bloodied grin.

Don't let this haunt you.

As Atherton nodded off, he smelled Kayne's unmistakable aroma as she settled in beside him—a lavender and anise perfume that failed to mask the lingering ammonia on her clothes, which only made him feel more at home. She unfurled a bedcover over their legs.

Hisses sputtered as Boo doused the candles. He and the others curled into the opposite bed. Thomas made a nest of blankets and a pillow on the floor.

Atherton sank somewhere between nightmares and dreams, a collection of terrors tamed by time alone. Homesickness squeezed his ribs. But for the first time, it wasn't for the mortuary.

It was the circus.

At least tonight, some of it was with him.

He awoke as first light broke, shivering in cold sweat. The East End was already wide awake, clamoring away. Dark silhouettes crowded the streets between the rolling carriages, the hollers, and stamping feet across puddled cobblestone.

Kayne's head was slouched against his shoulder, her brows furrowed, lips murmuring in protest. He eased a pillow beneath her head and tucked the blanket around her. Slinking out of the bed, he reached for his waistcoat and tie hanging from the frame.

In the bed across from them, Boo, Ruth, and Stella were coiled together like a litter of wild animals. Atherton supposed that a lifetime of traveling in caravans had taught them that body heat dulled the bite of wintry nights. In summer, it was likely only habit.

He found Thomas fully dressed, looking out the window.

"'Bout an hour out, I reckon," he whispered, passing him a cigarette. "We should wake the others."

Looping his necktie around his collar, Atherton said, "Ivory told me you're from Mason's world. The betting rings. Gentleman thieves and the like. You think he'll be expecting this?" He lit the tobacco, taking in the smoke through his nostrils. A pleasant buzz started at his fingertips, sizzling through his body.

Thomas shook his head with a scoff. "After what they did, and with the rest of us 'alfway across the Channel by now, no. If he had lookouts, they've been thrown, aye? I'd say he's in for a surprise. That poor prick won't know what hit 'im. I can hardly believe we're here, myself. Besides, it's not just his world anymore."

"What do you mean?"

"Take a look at yourself, kid. This is your world, too. Aye, it is."

Atherton took another drag, letting the smoky tendrils stream slowly from his lips.

"Think of it," Thomas continued, his eyes sweeping across the bodies sifting through the street. "Back when Ivory offered to buy that stiff off ye, you could'a refused. You didn't. You played the crooked cross. You wanted to beat Mason at his own game, even if it were just a few bloody pounds. Back when 'e wanted to make a lesson of ya, you could'a stayed your blade. You didn't. You wanted to show 'im that blood don't pay easy, and that men like 'im bleed like the rest of us. And oh, he didn't like bein' reminded of that, kid. No, he did not." He let out a low laugh. "And back when he came to deal your last, you could'a folded. Let ya wee sister bear your shame for you. And all would'a been settled, wouldn't it? It would'a been a wretched life, a bleak life, the kind of life a man looks back on n' regrets in his last. But a peaceful one all the same, aye."

"I was tired," Atherton admitted. "Tired of being beaten. Tired of running from the person it was turning me into. Sometimes, it feels good to fight, even when you know you'll lose."

"See, that's the problem with people like us. Peace is easy. Shame is easy. Aye, it is. But we'd give an arm n' a leg 'fore we settled for that kinda life. And by the Devil, we may just give 'em yet. There's summat hungry in our bones. We'll suffer tenfold if that means gettin' just a tenth of the freedom, goin' our own way. That's why Ivory wore a smile breathin' his last, eh? You see ar' kid, it didn't matter what took 'im. He was just happy. Happy he 'ad nothin' to regret, and a bold friend to hold 'im then, in the end. And as far as I'm concerned, that's as good as any of us can hope for."

Atherton's eyes grew hot. He wiped at the corners, giving the ghoul a pat on his arm. "Thanks, Tommy."

The Scottish giant smiled back, returning with one of those slaps on the back that could collapse a horse. "You bet."

Across the street at the funeral parlor, a hearse drawn by two horses was led out from its alleyway before being parked in front of the shopfront. The driver hopped off, striding into the parlor.

"I don't recall you ever giving me a speech all nice and sincere-like," Ruth said, stretching her arms with a yawn.

"Piss off," Thomas advised. "Get dressed, the lot of ya. It's time to move."

39

BOO

JULY 2, 1886

They dispersed through the street to avoid suspicion. Thomas stuck out no matter where he went, so he placed himself opposite the funeral parlor to distract any prying eyes. Boo, Stella, and Ruth lingered nearby, pretending to have nothing better to do than kick around smalltalk and loose stones while the sky bled brighter.

Obscured by the cowl of his cloak, Atherton knocked on the funeral parlor's door with Kayne beside him. Boo assumed he'd be prepared to charm whoever answered with some glib pun about business being dead or the clients being untalkative.

A young brunette with her hair tucked into a round cap with a short, leather lip and matching black funeral attire opened the door. After a few remarks from Atherton, she threw her head back, laughing loud enough to attract the attention of passersby. She opened the door wider, beckoning the two of them inside.

Boo shook his head. "Undertakers," he muttered to Stella and Ruth.

They hummed in understanding.

There was a brief hour of brilliant, gilded light breaking through the skyline over the boroughs of the East End. It set the fog ablaze with a bronze sheen, making the dew on the wet rooftops and stone arches shimmer. It soaked into the dark fabric of Boo's cloak, which he'd clutched against the morning chill biting at his cheeks and nose. It made him forget, briefly, that one of his hands was curled around the sawed-off Lefever shotgun holstered at his thigh.

Huddled together, the three watched ships glide through the Thames, throwing loose bits of stone from the street into the river. Not a half-hour later, a whistle turned them back toward the funeral parlor.

Atherton and Kayne emerged, now sporting the same caps as the undertaker who'd greeted them at the door. Climbing onto the driver's seat of the hearse readied outside, Atherton took the reins, giving a subtle nod to Thomas. Kayne opened the double doors at the back of the hearse, revealing its black leather interior. A polished white coffin with gold handles lay inside with a bouquet resting on a gilded crucifix.

Stella, Ruth, Boo, and Thomas funneled in, crouching on either side of the coffin.

Throwing a final set of glances, Kayne joined them inside, pulling the doors shut.

Atherton gave a resounding crack of the whips, rolling them into the thoroughfare at a trot. Thomas peeked through a curtained window, prepared to shout directions.

Taking out a cigarette, Boo struck a match, only for Kayne to swat it away. "Not in here. If Mason smells anything off, all this will have been for nothing," she said.

"Yeah. Not in here, Boo," Ruth added.

"Yeah. Who do you think you are?" Stella echoed, pocketing her own pack.

"I heard her the first time!" he said, throwing his hands up. "Just nervous, is all."

"We all are," Kayne said. "Assassination isn't exactly routine."

"What did he say to them in there, anyway?" Ruth asked.

"Apparently, our new spiritualist has the gift of the gab. He could charm the scales off a siren, that one. Just about flattered that poor girl to death," Kayne grinned. "Ivory would've—"

The carriage lurched to a sudden halt, banging the coffin against the wall. The five of them cursed, throwing their hands down to steady it.

"Sorry!" Atherton hollered.

"I said *left* at Wilkes Street!" Thomas shouted back.

"Your left or my left?"

"We're facing the same direction! I thought you said you knew how to do this!"

Mumbling curses about London's cramped roads, Atherton gave another sharp flick of the reins.

"We'll be lucky if we make it there without running over some poor bloke," Stella remarked.

"In any case," Kayne continued, "Atherton gave one of the directors the impression that he was a member of Mason's family, and he'd like to transport Logan's body personally. Said it would be 'a heartfelt surprise on a tragic day.' He also mentioned that he was a member of the British Institution of Undertakers, whatever that is, though that bit was likely in earnest. We paid them a modest sum on behalf of the Cross family and, well, here we are."

"Killing a man on the day of his father's funeral. Now that's ironic," Ruth said, unlatching the coffin and peering inside. Pearly satin lined the insides, with a matching pillow. "A bed for a king, huh?"

Inspecting his shotgun for the umpteenth time, Boo added, "Sure is. It's a shame there aren't two."

40

ATHERTON

JULY 2, 1886

Once they were a handful of streets away from the Cross Manor, Kayne joined Atherton at the driver's seat. He was tucked into the high collars of his coat, his cloak wrapped about him, cap pulled heavy over his brow. His knuckles had gone pale, clutching the reins.

"Everything will go as planned," she assured, rubbing his arm. "Just be certain to park the hearse with its back facing him. They'll handle the rest."

Atherton gave a stiff nod.

"Look at me," she said. "In circus, nothing is impossible."

"Yeah," Atherton gave a shaky laugh. "But we're not at the circus now, are we?"

"You carry it with you. You carry *him* with you. Always. That's the point. All that we do at the Carnival is beyond comprehension. Alone, it would truly be a fantasy. Alone, we would be outcasts with dismal prospects, but together, the impossible is made easily possible."

"Thanks, Kayne."

Even with the tremors in his legs and hands, he tried to savor those last moments of peace. Atherton steered the horses for their final turn down Brompton Lane.

Towering, tidy buildings with ornate terraces overlooked the polished walkways with sycamore trees lining the evenly laid cobblestone streets. The air was quiet and crisp with the sycamores' spicy, fresh scent, not fouled by refuse tossed in the gutters like in the neighboring districts. As though for the very occasion of Logan's funeral, the skies were filled with bright, sumptuous clouds. Sun broke on their backs between their chalky, curling edges.

Tucked away at the end of the lane was Cross Manor.

The saints guarding it in stony reverence taunted him with their gilded scepters. A crowd of several dozen was gathered at the bottom of the steps leading into the manor, observers of Logan's wake spilling out of its door. Dressed in their finest for the procession, children played by the fountain, splashing their hands in the water.

Atherton spotted Mason patting another gentleman on the shoulder and laughing, his collected yet imposing demeanor somehow more frightening than he remembered. They drew close enough to make out the silver and gold rings decorating his fingers and the crosses studding his boots.

There were other Disciples scattered throughout the crowd. Atherton reminded himself that every ruby and emerald on Mason's hands was purchased with threats or murder—one way or another.

"You should know what Ivory said to me that night," Atherton said with a hint of panic, "if this doesn't go well."

"Shush. You'll tell me after. You can't continue my husband's legacy if you're dead, now, can you?"

"After what I've seen, I'm not sure what's impossible anymore."

"Precisely. That's the spirit."

"Easy now," Thomas said from inside. "Turn her in nice and gentle-like. Give us a clear view. You won't be alone up there much longer."

"My husband chose you for a reason. I like to think that choice was not made in vain," Kayne pushed, squeezing his hand. "Besides, you belong here, remember? We're just here to transport a body. How many times have you done that?"

"Enough for a dozen lifetimes."

"So act like it."

She's right.

Confidence budded in his chest.

His bones harbored the ache of thousands of tragedies—all their grief, held at a distance. His fingers knew the touch of earth pried open to consume innocence, of warmth fading from those carried miles upon miles. His lips tasted the shadows that lingered in those long, twilight hours. His blood propelled an infernal bond that would make angels weep —an unwitting love for a monster.

You will live to see darker days yet.

Atherton steered the carriage until the back of the hearse faced the manor. He pulled down his cap with a firm tug and unbuttoned the strap over the handle of his revolver.

"Nearly a 'alf an 'our past schedule, Mr. Leverton. All the same, thank you for coming," Mason said with his arms splayed out wide, beckoning them in.

Atherton dismounted the carriage, fiddling with the straps on the horses with his head bowed and his back to him. "Sorry to disappoint you, Mr. Cross. We were delayed. Where is your father located?"

"He's in the sitting room, laid out nice and peaceful-like. Say, you're not Chester, the lad I spoke to back at the parlor. I thought he'd be the one 'ere."

"Chester's, ah, come down with something awful, Mr. Cross. I'm the other son," Atherton lied, keeping his face obscured. He couldn't afford to only wound him, not this time.

"Well, it's no difference to me," Mason said, stepping closer. "You tell your father I won't hold it against 'im. What's a 'alf 'our on a day like today, anyhow? Not like the dead 'ave appointments to keep." He barked with laughter.

Atherton grinned. "Well said, Mr. Cross. Always good to find humor in such circumstances."

"Obliged. To be honest, I thought Leverton only had one son. But I only do business with men I know," he said, tilting his head to try and get a good look at him.

"I'm just the transporter, sir," he said, turning away from his scrutiny. "Today is about you and your father. How's about you show me where he is?"

"Let's not be 'asty. Don't be a stranger. Come now. What's your name, boy?" Mason was towering over him now, leaving him with no choice but to shuffle backwards and ready himself for the only outcome remaining.

Atherton undid the clasp around his cloak, letting it slide to his feet. He took off his cap and reached into the holster at his side.

Then he looked up.

"Graves."

He drank in Mason's expression—the blazing scar running down his cheek, the dumbfounded shock that made it twitch.

A cluster of clouds blotted out the sun. It cast the congregation in shadow and deepened the furrows of loathing etched into the undertaker's glower.

"I'm the one you couldn't bury," he said.

Atherton gripped his revolver firmly, pulling the hammer back with a meaningful click. The mobster's figure obscured their interaction from the gathering behind him, oblivious to the threat.

Mason's weight shifted as he lifted his hands slowly. His expression was a picture of the one he had the night of Atherton's hanging, only now the distance between them had been severed. "Now, now. You and I can still sort this out," he said. "What you did to Henry, to Arthur, I've no qualms with. They were good men. Well, not precisely. But you did what you 'ad to. I respect that."

As much as Atherton wanted to cull every excuse, savor his honeyed groveling, he knew a dead man when he saw one. The sands in Mason's hourglass were down to their last grains. To stand in the way of what must happen would be in defiance of the force he'd served his entire life.

The bullets halted the next words brewing behind Mason's lips, stopping his slow advance with a shudder. He dropped to a knee. Two shots had burst through him, sending a shockwave of stupefaction through the bubbling congregation.

A murder of crows scattered madly from a nearby tree.

Atherton lifted his chin, looking down on him with an etched scowl.

"You shot me. You fuckin' shot me, Athie," Mason said.

"You've forced my hand," he recited, lips shaking. "That's what you bloody told me."

The man was reduced to a dazed oblivion, brushing his fingers against the bullet holes in his abdomen. All that could be heard was the wild beating of crows' wings against the air.

Then the hearse burst open.

One of the Disciples by the fountain already had a pistol trained on Atherton, waiting for a clear shot. The hearse's doors were thrown wide. Boo greeted the Disciples with a blast of buckshot. With a spray of blood, the gunman fell into the water, Boo's stout Lefever collapsing him like cannon fire.

Boo hopped from the hearse through the sulphurous cloud, raising the shotgun to another Disciple and squeezing the trigger again. The second target collapsed just as quickly. Splitting the barrel, Boo tossed out the spent rounds and reloaded two more, snapping it back into place. Between the blasts was the slick, slapping sound of blood raining on gravel and strained groans.

One of the Disciples charged Boo with only a billy club, only to be sidestepped and studded with a trio of knives flitting from Ruth's fingers.

The knife-thrower unsheathed more from her belt, sending them out in one precise, lethal motion.

Thomas launched from the hearse to a firing position on his knees, pumping the air with his shotgun at the handful of Disciples fumbling for their weapons. The crowd broke into rampant flight, rushing for the manor steps with trailing screams. The remaining Disciples stayed their ground, dropping quicker than targets at a carnival game.

Crouched from the driver's seat with a pistol, Kayne added to the barrage. In her eyes was that chilling physician's detachment. The Disciples returned fire, but only desperately. Some managed to find cover by the fountain, before that, too, was ripped apart by bullets.

All the while, Mason half-stumbled, half-crawled toward the manor, leaving a bloody trail of drips and smears behind him. Atherton followed patiently, kicking him when he wasn't fast enough. The air teemed with gunpowder smoke, knives, and whistling lead.

A stray bullet pierced through Atherton's coattails.

"It was just business!" Mason protested as he clambered up the manor steps. "I never wanted to kill you, Atherton. *They* deserved what they got."

"You can only take so much from a man until he's not one any longer. And I am one of them."

"No, no you aren't," Mason cackled, spitting out blood, scrambling backwards with a raised hand. "Those soulless 'eathens. Those dirty tinkers. They've no virtue. No code. No 'onor. They break bread with the Devil and call it a life. But you're more than that, Atherton. Admit it—I made you the man you are now."

"You strung me up like a dog and smiled while I choked!"

"You left me no choice!"

"Get inside!" Atherton roared, jabbing the gun toward the door. "I want you to die with your dead just as I have lived with them."

Gritting his teeth, Mason relented, tripping his way into the foyer.

Atherton stole a glance behind him. The courtyard was a massacre of Mason's men—a little more than a dozen—their torn bodies unmoving. The fountain gurgled red. Stella and Ruth stepped around the bodies, inspecting each one. Standing by the hearse, Thomas soothed the horses.

Boo bounded up the steps behind him. Without his greasepaint, his expression was indecipherable, save for the blood dotting his face, dripping with murderous resolve. Kayne was beside him.

Atherton stepped inside the manor.

Mason had discovered some composure standing beside his father's body. Logan was laid out on a bed with fresh sheets. Their suits matched.

Mason left a crimson handprint on his father's cheek, speaking quietly to him.

The blood from his stomach was pooling onto the polished, wooden floors. Atherton watched the rosy hue fade from Mason's lips. He regarded the crowd, now gathered on the staircase leading to the second floor.

"Get in the chambers," Atherton ordered. "Lock the doors, lest you reap the same reckoning this man is owed. If you so much as crack a window to alert the authorities, this home will be in ashes before you can leave it."

At that, the bereaved gathering scattered.

Boo and Atherton stepped into the quiet parlor. Atherton holstered his revolver, leaving Boo to raise his shotgun. Behind them, Kayne folded her hands behind her back, waiting expectantly.

Hacking up blood in a fit of moist coughs, Mason settled into an armchair by his father. An Eastman Interchangeable View camera was set up on a tripod, trained at Logan's cadaverous expression—manipulated with hidden wires and makeup to look as healthy as he was before the consumption.

With dripping fingers, Mason retrieved a cigarette from his case and placed it between his wet lips.

Taking a matchbook from his waistcoat pocket, Atherton struck one and raised the flame to it.

Mason nodded gratefully, taking a long drag and exhaling with a sigh.

"People will surprise you, in the worst and best of ways," Atherton said.

"That's the beauty of it," Mason replied. He gave another one of his vulpine grins, blood lining his teeth. "You surprise yourself, too. Look at the man you've become. Not a day's gone by since that night in New Sarum, I don't marvel at that shadow of a boy you left behind."

Boo clicked back the hammer on his shotgun. "We don't have much time, Atherton. The peelers will have heard the shots. You really want to hear the dying words of this fork-tongued bastard?"

Kayne put a hand on the barrel of the gun. "Let him," she said.

"And you," he said, nodding weakly at Kayne, "What've I taken from you?"

"My husband."

"Hell. Figures. My condolences." Mason spat out a wad of blood. "It was written, *'To me belongeth vengeance and recompense; their foot shall slide in due time: for the day of their calamity is at 'and, and the things that shall come upon them make 'aste.'*"

"Damn right," Boo growled. "I told you I would rip you open."

"Hah!" Mason sputtered, laughing and grunting against the pain. "Always knew that bit was for me. Didn't think it'd ever fit you, Athie. Yet 'ere we are. God, look at you. You're as cold as them corpses you carried all your life. You a'ready buried your heart. Somewhere deep. Deep beneath the earth. 'Idden from the sun, it is. That's why we're the same. Ain't that right?" It took all of him just to heave those words between staggered breaths. "You became what you feared, 'cause that's 'ow you survive it."

"We're not the same. You ordered the death of a man by the hand of a child."

"I never bloody ordered Leo to do it," Mason snarled. "I forbade 'im. The boy went of 'is own accord. But you'd only despise me more if I'd pulled the trigger meself. What've I to gain from lyin' now, eh? Now, as seraphim descend to collect my tainted soul. No," Mason said, "you're lyin' to yourself. That man next to you. That clown, twitchin' on that trigger. All 'e craves is vengeance. It's simple. But by God, you 'arbor something darker n' more loathsome than the Devil 'imself. I know what murderers look like, plain as day. You're something else, Atherton Graves. Not demon nor 'uman nor ghost, but some blasted thing 'tween it all. I don't envy you. Not even now as I am." Mason gasped, gritting and clawing to get the words out. "S-stood before St. Peter, I'd not beg to switch places. And I'm sorry, Boo, I can't give you the satisfaction. 'Cause I won't pray to you. My soul's my own business. I won't let it be yours."

"Blood will suffice," Boo said.

Atherton flinched at the thunderous boom from Boo's shotgun. A few muffled shrieks exuded from the guests upstairs.

It did just as he promised it would.

Mason and the armchair were flung backwards.

By the time the chair teetered over its shattered leg and the smoke cleared, Mason Cross was in two pieces, his insides spattered throughout the parlor floors, walls, and the ceiling. It was a surprise even to Atherton, who thought he'd seen it all. He pitied whoever would have the task of transporting him.

He waited for something to change in him. A weight on his shoulders to lift. His grief to dissipate. Watching Mason's eyes flutter their last, his recognition of the mortal world dimming before that same dark angel who stood before Henry and Arthur, Atherton recognized what feeling crept through his veins and wove webs in his ribs. And he realized, like he did with all those lost souls still clinging to his bones, that it would be a lifetime before it left.

"Well done," was all Kayne said, as she strode for the door.

Boo grimaced and rested the smoldering barrel on his shoulder. "I think we got what we came for," he said, giving Atherton a gentle touch on the back before following Kayne's heels.

But Atherton couldn't help but linger in the parlor, standing alone with the bodies, and all the memories soaking into the floorboards.

41

ATHERTON
AUGUST 16, 1886

A train billowing steam and smoke swept across the English countryside on the Great Western Railway, bearing with it the six fugitives responsible for the massacre in the Brompton District.

For the first handful of days, that event captured every spot of ink the presses could muster. Witness testimonies from Logan's funeral swore they spotted the arsonist that haunted the papers not a month before, orchestrating the slaughter himself. As weeks wore on, speculation about the Cross family, their tenuous standings in high society, and the notion of Atherton Graves's ties to their fall were relegated to the second and third pages. Any comments retrieved from Scotland Yard regarding their inability to capture the culprits were dodgy, and even dismissive of a gang known as "the Disciples."

Only a month later, updates on the investigation were lucky to get a thumbprint's worth of writing. Even still, journalists became obsessed with getting the story straight or twisting it however seemed fitting. One popular theory was that the circus fires a week before the Brompton killings were Graves's way of making himself known to London.

After the Cross Manor massacre, they suspected the killer was hiding out in the city. It was only a question of when he'd strike again. When the press steadily let the story slip through their fingers, penny dreadfuls resurrected it, feeding into the public's ravenous imagination. The city lapped up fictitious tales depicting an overblown vestige of what remained. A renegade undertaker turned arsonist. A cannibalistic ghoul from New Sarum capable of infanticide. A vigilante unhindered by morals, executing justice upon a gang whose existence was denied by authorities. Or, simply, a maddened killer.

Despite their variations, all interpretations brought with them a similar motif: Atherton Graves was a phantom. Uncatchable. For all they knew, he was stalking Whitechapel's alleys that very moment, preparing to outdo himself with another spree.

He was not.

He was, however, carrying a steaming mug of coffee on the train that was now two cities west of New Sarum, heading for Plymouth, where a ship would be waiting to take them across the Channel.

Atherton knocked and slid open the compartment door to Kayne's cabin.

The doctor was stirred from her musings, alone, watching the lush landscape in all its summer glory, emerald hues fading to twilight. One of her fingers bookmarked a page in *Frankenstein* by Mary Shelley.

"You won't believe it. They had imported coffee," Atherton said. "Times really are changing. I can't stand the stuff, myself."

"Goodness, you didn't have to go through the trouble," she said, taking the cup. She closed her eyes, inhaling the aroma. "Oh, did they have any—"

"Black, with two spoonfuls of sugar," Atherton said.

Kayne tilted her head with an amused scoff. "How did you know?"

"You wouldn't ask a spiritualist to reveal his tricks, would you?"

"After being married to one for eight years, I wrongfully assumed I knew them all."

Giving a bow of his head, Atherton excused himself, sliding the compartment door open.

"Oh, Atherton. A moment?"

Stepping back inside, he eased the door shut and took a seat in front of her.

"You don't regret it, do you?" she asked.

He paused. That was the same question he'd wrestled with every waking moment since that day. "I would trade a dozen Masons for Ivory. Pull that trigger a thousand times. But it's worse than that, isn't it? Mason destroyed countless lives before we put an end to him, and still, his violence will ripple long after he's turned to dust. In light of that, no, I don't regret it. But I will sleep no better for having that knowledge. My profession is, or was, to care for the dead, not to create them."

Kayne took a sip. Her eyes wandered back to the window. "What we did won't bring Ivory back."

"I know."

"You mustn't call upon him, no matter how much you wish to. No matter how many times I ask you. I suspect I will. I may even beg. But you mustn't. Instead, you will remind me of this conversation each time. No matter how tired a habit it becomes. I know how time withers the sanity of the dead. How it rots their memories. I couldn't bear it, to see him like that."

There were no tears in her eyes—only hard, furrowed lines as she explained herself.

"It may be difficult to hear this, but I'm afraid I've already tried," he admitted.

"What?"

"For many nights, while we were biding our time in London, I made attempts to reach him."

"And you failed?"

"No," Atherton said. "My skills may be rudimentary, but your husband taught me well. Wherever Ivory is, he's made no attempts to linger. I suppose he left this piece for me to discover myself, a theory I'm well aware he already entertained. One that feels clearer to me by the day.

"I believe we've had it backwards. It is the living who haunt the dead, not the other way around. And, so long as we feel our business is unfinished with them, they are called back to us, tied in imperceptible threads to our very souls. And without a sigil to bind him, I suspect that Ivory's spirit was free the moment word spread of his passing. After all, from what I could see, nobody at the circus held a grievance against him. Even you admitted that a farewell in the form of a seance would torture you. He knew that. The both of you did."

Kayne nodded slowly, her lips pursed. "And what of your intentions?"

"I only meant to practice reaching out for him, for you. In case you ever asked. I didn't wish to see him like that, either. Ghosts are just that—fragments. Mangled remnants of who we were, trying to make sense of what we couldn't understand in life."

Kayne took Atherton's hand in hers and squeezed tenderly. Wetness glistened in her eyes. "Thank you for your honesty. I think I could use some time to myself, now, if you'd be so kind."

Standing up, Atherton smoothed out his waistcoat and tie. "Naturally. If you need me, I'm just a few cabins down."

Sliding shut the door to his own cabin, Atherton let out a deep sigh and tore off his false moustache and nose. "These bloody things itch terribly."

"Just wait 'till you can grow one yourself," Boo teased.

"Ha-ha. I'm howling with laughter. Stop—my sides hurt."

"Can't imagine that conversation was terribly uplifting," Boo said. The clown was sprawled out on his side of the couchette. He folded up the newspaper he'd been reading, tossing it aside.

"No, not terribly," he admitted.

Boo cracked the window and lit a fresh cigarette using the smoldering end of his own, passing it to Atherton. His coppery hair fluttered against the night air.

"You know, if I have to read one more article about you, I think I'll be sick," Boo said.

"Just retch outside the window, then. You've been gorging yourself on the same few papers since we left."

"And it's as delightful as it is infuriating, seeing them bungle the story every time. They never give me a debut, not even in those sickly penny dreadfuls. I shot six of the bastards myself."

"Let's work on our quiet voice when speaking about murder. If you're so bothered, send in a letter with your opinion. I'm sure they'll print it."

"You like being famous. Just admit it."

"Infamous," Atherton corrected. "That is a very important distinction. You think I enjoy wearing disguises everywhere we go?"

"Bah. It's all the same. They raise you up as a hero just to tear you down as a villain."

"I think it's just the second bit. But, as soon as you're feeling up for plotting a spree, my door is open to you. I'll get you sorted. Not that anyone will believe your name is 'Boo' anyways. You know, you never did tell me your actual name."

"That is my *actual* name, prick. It's short. Easy to remember. Nobody forgets it. *B-O-O*," he spelled it out. "Boo. See?"

Atherton massaged his temples. "You're chattier than a landlocked sailor on his fifth pint. I can't believe I volunteered to bunk with you."

"Go ahead. Go into Tommy's cabin. Endure his rancorous breath. See how long you last. Go on," he said, wagging a finger toward the door. "No? Right. Thought so."

"You're mad."

"That's right." Grasping the handles on the sides of his booth, Boo pulled out the convertible sleeping berth and tossed himself upon it. Lying down with his arms folded behind his head, he closed his eyes and sighed with a broad, contented smile. The light in the lantern pendant about Boo's neck was waning like the light outside. At that very moment, Atherton caught it dimming before it winked out forever, the little soul inside used up—extinguished.

Boo didn't notice.

Atherton just took a seat across from him. "What's got you so happy?" he asked.

"Isn't it obvious? We're going where stars gleam even during the day. Where all that can be imagined is somehow made real. Where people taste flight and balance on the edge of impossibilities. Where oddities are venerated artists, and death itself is disobeyed before a sea of applause. We're going where people like you and I belong, Atherton Graves. We're going back to the circus. And soon it'll be autumn, when the carnival lanterns burn brightest."

Atherton stared out the window at the sinking sun, his thoughts wistful and still subdued by a lurking melancholy and all those shadows who'd made a sepulchre of his body. "Do you think we'll ever be able to leave it behind? Everything that happened, I mean?" Atherton asked.

"I sincerely doubt it. But we can learn," Boo said, "to live with it."

ACKNOWLEDGMENTS

The first thing I came to understand through the circus community is that nothing is accomplished alone. Even seemingly solitary achievements stand on the shoulders of ghostly giants. And if you could, somehow, walk an entirely isolated journey, in circus it's always wiser and to the artist's benefit to lean on their peers and those who've come before them. It not only makes the art better, it brings people together.

With this in mind, I am sure this list will fail to name all the countless people who pulled me along, one way or another. The names appear in no order of significance; you are all so loved and appreciated.

Firstly, my family and brothers have always encouraged me to walk my own path, and never once suggested I stray. Astrid Tobrand, whose art is both on the cover and between the pages, was monumental; we spent countless hours discussing the story, and shared the joyous grief of the final sentence being written. Without her, so many steps of this journey would have been walked alone.

Paulette Kennedy, a talented author and friend who was always an email away to answer a question or shed light on any doubts I had. My circus duo and partner Achillea, for leaping off trapeze boards, performing, and weathering the storm of being a full-time performer with me. Ash and Igor of Circus Something, who opened up their home and stages to Grim Theatre and supported me in pursuing only my highest ideals. Rose Bonomo, because you make me ugly laugh way too much, and showed me what it meant to connect with the audience.

To the circus communities of Portland—JaJa Circus, Nightflight Aerial, and Superhero Fitness—through which I trained, met so many extraordinary artists, and ultimately was emboldened to continue my path. To my fellow performers and training friends. Gregory Bartning, whose photography and friendship never ceases to make me feel seen and cherished. My Patreon and online communities, who've supported and followed my work since its infancy. My publishing house, Quill & Crow, and their exceptional crew, namely Cassandra, Lisa, and Alma, who treated my vision with the utmost care. Thank you for such a wonderful debut experience.

To the global community of circus artists, who remind me on a daily basis to reach higher, train harder, and create more. Without circus, and all the remarkable people I've met through it, this story would not be what it is today.

- Harlequin Grim

ABOUT THE AUTHOR

Mortuary worker turned full-time circus artist, Harlequin Grim leads a dual life as an entertainer and writer. He co-founded The Grim Theatre, a troupe dedicated to creating dark yet whimsical stories through literary, illustrative, and performing arts. The Black Carnival is his debut novel.

THANK YOU FOR READING

Thank you for reading *The Black Carnival*. We deeply appreciate our readers, and are grateful for everyone who takes the time to leave us a review. If you're interested, please visit our website to find review links. Your reviews help small presses and indie authors thrive, and we appreciate your support.

More Historical Fiction from Quill & Crow
The Secrets of Blackthorn House, Marie McWilliams
All the Parts of the Soul, Catherine Fearns
The Bone Drenched Woods, L.V. Russell

INDEX A
GLOSSARY OF TERMS

To help readers navigate the late 19th-century world of *The Black Carnival*, the following glossary has been provided for archaic idioms, slang, and phrases often used during the time period.

Bang up to the elephant: perfect, complete, unapproachable
Blower: a prostitute
Bludger: someone who lives off of others, a thief
Brass: money
Bricky: brave
Bruisers: thieves who use primarily violence and intimidation
Bull: money
Chavy: a child
Collie shangles: a fight or row, typically used to describe dogs
Daddles: hands
Dead-oh: extremely drunk
Dead-uns: dead bodies
Dollymop: a prostitute
Doxie: a promiscuous woman
Dust-up: a fight
Flams: lies
Gigglemug: a habitually smiling face (in reference to Boo's makeup—he rarely smiles unless he is performing)
Griddling: begging or pleading

INDEX A

Gulpy: nervous
Guttersnipes: thieving beggars
Kip: a nap
Ladybirds: prostitutes
Lush: alcohol
Lush crib: a bar or pub
Magsmen: criminals, thieves
Mizzle: to steal
Moucher: a vagrant, a gentleman of the road
Muff: an incompetent person
Mutcher: a thief who steals from drunks or otherwise intoxicated people
Nickey: simple-minded
Nippers: children
Playing the crooked cross: to betray, swindle, or cheat
Prig: a thief
Rattled: disturbed
Rib (the): a person's wife
Rozzers: the police
Rubes: someone uneducated or uncultured
Sawbones: a surgeon
Scurf: a gang leader or thief
Slum: to cheat
Snakesman: someone deceitful or treacherous
Windy-wallet: a talkative person partial to exaggeration or boasting
Zounderkite: an idiot who often makes clumsy or awkward mistakes

INDEX B
TRIGGER INDEX

Alcohol/Drug Use
Blood/Gore
Dead Children (graphic)
Death (graphic)
Gang Violence
Murder of children
Suicide (ritualistic)
Violence toward women

www.ingramcontent.com/pod-product-compliance
Lightning Source LLC
LaVergne TN
LVHW091939120925
820586LV00003B/7